BILLIONAIRE, BOSS... BRIDEGROOM?

BY

KATE HARDY

First Published in Great Britain 2016
By Mills & Boon, an imprint of HarperCollins*Publishers*
1 London Bridge Street, London, SE1 9GF

ISBN: 978-0-263-91969-1

23-0316

Our policy is to use papers that are natural, renewable and recyclable products and made from wood grown in sustainable forests.The logging and manufacturing processes conform to the legal environmental regulations of the country of origin.

Printed and bound in Spain
by CPI, Barcelona

Kate Hardy always loved books and could read before she went to school. She discovered Mills & Boon books when she was twelve and decided this was what she wanted to do. When she isn't writing, Kate enjoys reading, cinema, ballroom dancing and the gym. You can contact her via her website, www.katehardy.com.

For Charlotte Mursell and Sheila Hodgson—
with love and thanks for letting me have
so much fun with this story x

CHAPTER ONE

I'm coming to get you, Bella texted swiftly. *Hold on.*

For once, it looked as if she was going to be the rescuer instead of the rescuee. With her new job to boost her confidence, she thought she might just be able to handle it. For once she would be the sister who was calm, collected and totally together instead of the flaky, ditzy one who always made a mess of things and needed to be bailed out of a sticky situation.

She glanced around and saw a black cab waiting at the kerbside. Relieved, she rushed up to it and jumped in.

'Can you take me to the Bramerton Hotel in Kensington, please?' she asked the cabbie.

There was a dry cough from beside her, and she whipped her head round to discover that there was already a passenger sitting in the back seat.

She'd been so focused on getting to Grace that she hadn't even noticed the other passenger when she'd climbed into the taxi.

'I'm so sorry,' she said. 'I didn't mean to be rude. Look, I realise that you were here first, and technically I ought to leave right now and let you get on with your journey, but I really do need to get to the Bramerton as quickly as possible. Would you mind finding another taxi and...and...?' She waved a desperate hand at him. 'Look, I'll pay for your cab.' It'd mean extending her overdraft yet again, but what were a few more pounds if it meant that she could return the favour for once and help Grace? Besides, she was about to start a new job. Next month, her cash-flow situation would be a bit better.

'Actually, I'm heading towards Kensington myself,' he said. 'I'll drop you off at the Bramerton.'

Relief flooded through Bella. She'd found the modern equivalent of a knight on a white charger: a man in a black cab. She wouldn't have to let her sister down. 'Thank you. Thank you so much.' She gave in to the impulse, leaned forward and kissed him soundly on the cheek. 'You have no idea how much I appreciate this.'

'What's so urgent?' he asked as the taxi drove off.

'It's a family thing,' she said. It wasn't her place to tell anyone about her sister's situation, let alone tell a complete stranger.

'Uh-huh.' He paused. 'Did I see you just come out of Insurgo Records?'

She looked at him, surprised. The man looked like a businessman on his way home from a late meeting, and he was hardly the target market for an independent record label—even though Insurgo's artists were a real mixture, from folk singer-songwriters to punk and indie bands, with a few oddities thrown in. 'Yes,' she said.

'Are you one of their acts?'

In her black jeans and matching plain T-shirt, teamed with a shiny platinum-blonde bob, Bella knew that she probably looked as much like an indie musician as she did a graphic designer. 'No,' she said.

But the man had been kind enough to let her share his taxi, so she didn't want to be rude to him. Besides, making small talk might distract her enough to stop her worrying about whatever had sent her normally cool and capable big sister into meltdown. She smiled at him. 'Actually, I'm a graphic designer, and I'm starting work at Insurgo next week.'

'Are you, now?'

Something about the way he drawled the words made alarm bells ring in the back of her head. But he was a total stranger. She was making something out of nothing. 'Yes, and I'm really looking forward to it,' she said with a bright smile. 'I'll be designing website graphics, album covers and band merch. Actually, I'm still trying to get my head round the fact that I've just been offered my dream job.' In an ideal world she would've preferred to have Insurgo as a client rather than as her employer, but working for someone full-time again meant that she'd have a regular income for a while—and right now she needed a regular income rather more than she needed her freedom.

'You don't know who I am, do you?' he asked.

'Other than a stranger who's been kind enough to let me share his taxi? No,' she admitted.

'Allow me to introduce myself,' he said, leaning forward out of the shadows and holding out his hand.

Bella caught her breath. He was gorgeous. Dark hair that was brushed back from his face, cornflower-blue eyes, and the kind of jawline that would've made him a hit in any perfume ad. She really had to resist the urge to reach out and trail her fingertips down his clean-shaven cheek. And that mouth. Almost pouting, the sexiest mouth she'd seen in a while.

Almost in a daze, she shook his hand, noting how firm his handshake was. And she studiously ignored the fact that her palm was tingling; after the way Kirk had let her down, she was officially off men. Even if this one was very easy on the eye and was wearing a beautifully cut designer suit, what looked like a handmade white shirt, a silk tie and highly polished Italian shoes.

No involvement.

Full stop.

Because she was never going to let anyone make her feel as foolish and useless as Kirk had made her feel, ever again.

'Hugh Moncrieff,' he said, and he waited for the penny to drop.

It took five seconds.

'Hugh Moncrieff—as in *Insurgo's* Hugh Moncrieff?' Bella asked in horror.

'That would be me,' he said. And he looked as if he was enjoying her reaction.

He was her new boss? 'But—you can't be.' Even though it would explain why he'd asked her if she was one of the artists; he must've thought that his second-in-command had signed her up in his absence.

'Why not?'

'Because you—you—' She gestured to his suit. 'You don't look like an indie record label owner. You look like a stockbroker.'

'The bank always likes the company's MD to wear a suit,' he said mildly. 'If I'd turned up to the meeting in ripped jeans and an avant-garde T-shirt, with funky hair, they'd have seen me as less of a professional and more of a risk.'

The bank? That nasty feeling got a lot worse. If he'd been to the bank for a meeting, all dressed up, at this time on a Friday evening, did that mean the company was in trouble and her job would be over before it had even started?

Her fears must've shown on her face, because he said, 'It's our annual review, and I went for a drink with a business contact afterwards. Don't look so worried. So you're my new graphic designer?'

'Bella Faraday,' she said. 'And I'm very good at what I do.'

'I expect you are, or Tarquin wouldn't have hired you,' he said dryly.

'So what are you doing in a taxi, when you own a record label? Why don't you have your own car, or a limo or something to drive you around?' The question was out before she could stop herself and she groaned inwardly. Way to go, Bella, she thought. Just grill your new boss, two minutes after you insulted him by saying he didn't look like the owner of an indie record label. Carry on like this and you'll be picking up your cards on Monday morning instead of starting your job.

So much for never letting herself feel foolish again. Right now she felt like a prize idiot.

'That's an easy one.' He smiled. 'My car happens to be in the local garage, having something fixed. I'd rather put my money into the business than waste it by hiring a flashy limo to do little more than wait around for me all day. Hence the taxi.'

Bella could feel the colour swishing through her cheeks. 'I'm sorry. It's not my place to question you. Look, um, please ask the cabbie to pull over and drop me off, and I'll get out of your way and find myself another taxi.'

'You said it was urgent—a family thing.'

'It is.'

'Then let me get you to the hotel. Tarquin obviously

overran with the interviews and made you late in the first place, so it's Insurgo's fault.'

'No, it's not,' she said. It wasn't anyone's fault. But right at that moment she was more worried about Grace than about making a good impression on her new boss, so she'd accept the offer. 'But thank you for the lift. I really appreciate this.'

'No problem.'

She texted Grace swiftly.

In taxi now. Wait for me in Reception.

Finally the taxi driver pulled up outside the Bramerton Hotel.

'Thank you again, Mr Moncrieff,' she said politely. 'How much do I owe you for the cab fare?'

'Nothing. You're practically on my way,' he said.

'Thank you. Really. And I'll work late every night next week to make up for it,' she said, and left the taxi before she could say anything else stupid.

When she walked into the reception area, Grace was waiting there, white-faced and silent. And there was no sign of Howard. Why wasn't Grace's fiancé waiting with her? Had something happened to Howard? No, of course not, or Grace would've said something in her texts. Not just that single word: Help, followed by rejecting Bella's call and sending a second text: Can't talk now. And now Bella was seriously worried. What on earth had happened?

But Grace had been right about one thing. They couldn't talk about it here. Not with Howard's parents' golden wedding anniversary going on in one of the function rooms. Whatever it was, Bella had her sister's back. And they were leaving. Now.

'Come on. Let's get out of here,' Bella said softly, put her arm round Grace and led her out of the hotel.

Back in the street, she looked around for a taxi.

Then she realised that the taxi that had dropped her off was still waiting at the kerb, exactly where she'd left it. And Hugh Moncrieff was still there too, though he'd moved seats so that his back was to the cabbie. He wound the window down and beckoned them over. 'Can I give you a lift somewhere?'

'But—' she began.

'Everything's clearly not OK,' he said softly, looking at Grace, 'so I'll drop you and…your sister, I presume?' At her nod, he continued, 'I'll drop you where you need to go. What's the address?'

Bella definitely didn't want to leave Grace alone tonight, and her own flat wasn't big enough for two. Biting her lip, she gave him Grace's address. 'Thank you so much,' she said. 'We both really appreciate this. Especially as you didn't have to wait.'

'No problem.'

She helped Grace into the car. Grace still hadn't said a word. Worried, Bella took her hand and squeezed it; but Grace didn't return the pressure. And this time nobody seemed disposed to make any small talk. With every second, Bella felt more and more awkward.

Then, just as the taxi turned into Grace's road, Grace threw up. All over Hugh's posh Italian shoes and suit trousers.

'I'm so sorry,' she mumbled.

She looked almost as mortified as Bella felt—and Bella had no idea what to say. What could you say when your sister threw up over your new boss? Apart from an equally apologetic, 'I'm so sorry.'

Hugh brushed it aside. 'These things happen. Do you need help getting her indoors?'

'Thank you, but no—I think you've done more than enough to help us, this evening.' Bella took a deep breath. 'Look, I'll pay for valeting the taxi and I'll pick up the bill for dry-cleaning your suit and replacing your shoes.'

'We'll sort it out later,' he said. 'Are you sure you can manage?'

'I'm sure,' Bella fibbed. At least she had Grace's spare door key, so actually getting into the flat wouldn't be a problem. 'And thank you. And sorry. And—'

'Just get your sister safely inside,' Hugh cut in. 'We'll sort out everything later.'

'Thank you. And I'm sorry,' Bella whispered again, and helped Grace out of the taxi.

This really wasn't how Hugh had expected to spend a Friday evening. Or how he'd expected to meet the newest member of his team.

The poor woman had looked horrified when her sister threw up everywhere.

Did Bella often rescue her sister like that? he wondered. Funny, the other woman had been dressed so soberly, in a navy linen dress and sensible shoes. Looking at them together, most people would've guessed that the younger woman was the one who partied too hard and would be most likely to throw up in the back of a taxi and need looking after.

Or maybe Bella's sister hadn't been drunk. Maybe

she'd been ill. But then surely Bella would've said that her sister was ill, or even called an ambulance?

But it was none of his business. He should just take a step back and ignore it.

'I'm sorry about all that,' he said to the driver. 'If you can drop me home, I'll pay for the cost of valeting the taxi and lost fares.' He gave the driver the address.

Though he still couldn't get Bella Faraday out of his head. Especially the moment when she'd kissed his cheek; it had felt as if he'd been galvanised. And then, when she'd shaken his hand, every nerve-end had been aware of the feel of her skin against his.

Hugh was definitely attracted to her. More attracted than he'd been towards anyone in a very long time.

But.

After the whole fiasco with Jessie, he'd learned his lesson well. Hugh would never, ever mix work and pleasure again. As Tarquin had just hired Bella as their new graphic artist, it meant that she came firmly under the category of work. So he'd have to just ignore the pull of attraction in future and treat her just the same as he did every single one of his colleagues—by keeping her at a professional distance.

Even if she did have the sexiest mouth and sparkliest eyes he'd ever seen.

No involvement.

No risks.

This time, he'd stick to the rules.

'I'm so sorry I was sick everywhere,' Grace said once they were sitting down inside her flat.

Bella frowned. 'Didn't you eat anything to line your

stomach before you started knocking back whatever it was that made you throw up?'

'Champagne. No,' Grace said miserably. 'My stomach was tied in too many knots to eat.'

And Grace hardly ever drank. It wasn't a good combination. Not to mention really worrying—what had been so bad that Grace had had to get drunk? She took a deep breath. First things first. She needed to get Grace sober. 'Right. First of all you're having water—lots and lots of water,' Bella said. Then she looked through Grace's cupboards. Please let there be something that she could actually cook. Or, failing that, cereal to soak up all that champagne.

Then she spied the box of porridge oats. Perfect. Even she could follow the instructions on the box and make porridge in the microwave.

While the porridge was cooking, she took a banana from Grace's fruit bowl and chopped it up. She added it to the finished cereal and put the bowl in front of Grace, who immediately pushed it away.

'I can't.'

'Eat it,' Bella said firmly. 'Your electrolytes are all over the place and bananas are great for sorting that out, and oats will help because they're bland carbs which will raise your blood sugar without upsetting your stomach.'

'How do you know all this stuff?' Grace asked, looking bemused.

Bella smiled. 'Remember I dated a doctor a couple of years back? He gave me the lowdown on the best food to eat for a hangover.'

'I'm sorry,' Grace said again. 'Was the taxi driver very angry?'

'Don't worry,' Bella said airily. 'My boss is sorting it.'

Grace did a double-take. 'Your *boss*?'

'Uh-huh.' Bella flashed her sister a grin. 'Guess what? I got the job.'

'I—oh, my God. Are you telling me that I just threw up over your boss before you even started the job?' Grace asked, looking horrified as Bella's words sank in. 'Oh, no. I'll talk to him and explain, so he doesn't sack you or—'

'Gracie, it's fine,' Bella cut in.

'It's not fine at all! I've messed things up for you. Look. I'll pay for the dry-cleaning.'

Bella smiled. 'I already told him I'd do that, and I said I'd pay for valeting the taxi as well.'

'My mess, my bill,' Grace said. 'I'll pay.'

'Gracie, just shut up and eat your porridge. I don't want to hear another word from you, young lady, until that bowl is empty.'

'You sound like Mum,' Grace muttered.

'Good,' Bella retorted. Usually Grace was the one who sounded like their mother and Bella was the one hanging her head in shame.

She made Grace eat every scrap and drink two more glasses of water before she resumed her interrogation. 'Right. Now tell me—what happened?'

'I can't marry Howard.'

It was the last thing Bella had been expecting. Her older sister had been engaged for the last four years. OK, so Howard was a bit on the boring side, and his parents were nightmares—Bella had dubbed them Mr Toad and Mrs Concrete Hair with good reason—but if Grace loved him then Bella was prepared to be as sweet as she could to them. 'What? Why not? Don't you love him any more?' And then a nasty thought struck her. 'Is there someone else?'

'Of course there isn't anyone else.' Grace shook her head. 'I wouldn't do that to him.'

'Not deliberately, no, but you can't help who you fall in love with,' Bella said. She'd fallen for Mr Wrong enough times, and Kirk had shattered her trust for good. She'd never trust another man with her heart again, no matter how attractive he was. It had taken her six months to rebuild her life—and she was still angry with herself for being so naïve and trusting. Why hadn't she been able to see that he was stringing her along?

'I love Howard, but I'm not in love with him,' Grace said. 'There's a difference.'

'I know.' Bella squeezed her hand. 'And it's a big difference. A deal-breaking difference.'

'He's never made me feel breathless and dizzy, as if he'd swept me off my feet.'

Not surprising: Howard was cautious and sensible. Which wasn't a bad thing, Bella thought, but the occasional bit of spontaneity wouldn't have hurt. And it might have made her sister's world complete—which clearly hadn't happened. On paper, Grace and Howard were the perfect match—both sensible and cautious—but there was a little thing called chemistry. Without that, life would be miserable. 'You can't spend the rest of your life with someone who doesn't make your world light up.'

Grace bit her lip. 'I think you're about the only person who'd understand that. Mum's going to be so disappointed in me.'

'No, she's not, and neither is Dad—they both want you to be happy, and if marrying Howard wouldn't make you happy then you definitely shouldn't marry him,' Bella said firmly.

'I'm not sure if he was in love with me, either,' Grace said.

'Of course he was—you're gorgeous and you're clever and you're nice. What's not to love?' Bella demanded, cross on her sister's behalf.

'I think we both loved each other,' Grace said softly, 'but not *enough*. I mean, we've been engaged for ever—who stays engaged for four years in this day and age?'

'A couple who's saving up the deposit for a house?' Bella suggested.

'Apart from the fact that we already have enough money for that between us, you know what I mean—if we'd really wanted to be together, we'd have got married years ago rather than waiting. We don't even live together,' Grace pointed out.

'Mainly because Cynthia of the Eagle Eyes and Concrete Hair wouldn't let her little boy shack up with someone,' Bella said. 'Is that why you got drunk tonight?'

'No. That was the cartoon you drew for me,' Grace said. 'Fifty Shades of Beige.'

Bella winced. 'Sorry. I meant it as a joke, to make you laugh and relax a bit. I knew you weren't looking forward to the golden wedding party.'

'But it was so accurate, Bel,' Grace said. 'I was the only woman there not dressed in beige.'

Bella couldn't help laughing. 'Ouch. I didn't think it'd be quite that bad.'

'Oh, it was,' Grace said feelingly. 'I really didn't belong there. I drank three glasses of champagne straight down to give me courage and I didn't even feel them, Bel.'

Which was really un-Grace-like. She always stopped

after one glass. Sensible, reliable Grace who looked after everyone else and was usually the one mopping up, not the one throwing up.

'I was just numb. And that's when I realised,' Grace said, 'that I was walking into a life I didn't actually want. In fifty years' time, I don't want to be sensible Grace Sutton, whose heart has never once skipped a beat, and whose mother-in-law directed the whole of her marriage.'

'If anyone could live until well past the age of a hundred, marbles intact and with an iron fist, it'd be Mrs Concrete Hair,' Bella said feelingly. 'You've done the right thing, Gracie. It's much better to call a halt now than to wait until after you married Howard and then have all the mess of a divorce to go through.'

'Really?' Grace didn't look convinced. She looked guilty and miserable and worried.

'Really,' Bella said firmly, 'and Mum and Dad will back you, too.'

'I just feel that I've let everyone down—all the work that's gone into arranging the wedding.' Grace swallowed. 'Not to mention the money.'

'But you haven't let anyone down,' Bella said. 'Well, except you should have told me all this a *lot* sooner, because I'm your sister and of course I'm going to support you. I hate to think that you've been miserable all these months when I could've listened to you and made you feel better. You're doing the right thing, Gracie. And cancelling the wedding won't be that hard.' This was slightly surreal; it felt almost as if she and Grace had swapped places and it was her turn to be the sensible, super-organised one instead of the one who needed rescuing. 'Just give me a list of the names and contact details of the people you've invited and your suppliers, and I'll ring them all and explain the wedding's off.'

'I can't make you do that!' Grace protested.

'You're not making me do it. I'm offering. That's what sisters are for.' She took a deep breath. 'Have you told Howard?' Was that why her no-longer-future brother-in-law had been so conspicuously absent?

'No. I'm going to do that tomorrow.'

A nasty thought struck Bella. 'Does he actually know you've left the party?'

Grace nodded and winced. 'I told him I had a migraine and was going home.'

'And he didn't even offer to take you home? That's atrocious!'

'How could he leave? It's his parents' golden wedding anniversary party.'

'OK, so he probably had to stay there with the Gruesome Twosome,' Bella allowed, 'but he still should've made sure you were all right first and at least arranged a taxi to take you home.'

'I'm sure he would've done, but I told him you were coming to collect me,' Grace explained.

'Hmm,' Bella said, though she wasn't mollified. What on earth was wrong with the man? Howard had been Grace's fiancé for four years and he hadn't even made sure that she got home safely when she'd told him she felt ill—whereas Hugh Moncrieff, a man Bella had met only a few minutes ago, had not only come to the rescue, he'd offered to help them indoors. So her new boss had a good heart as well as a gorgeous face.

Not that she should be thinking about that right now. Or ever, for that matter. Even if she wasn't officially off men, her boss was completely off limits. She needed this job, to get her finances back on an even keel. 'So what are you going to tell Howard tomorrow?' she asked.

'The truth—that I can't marry him.' Grace closed her eyes for a moment. 'And that means I'll lose my job and my home, too, Bel. No way can I go back to work at Sutton's, not when I've just split up with the boss's son—and in the circumstances I can hardly ask them to give me a reference to work anywhere else. Plus I've already given my landlord notice on my flat. I know he's already found my replacement and signed a contract, so I can't ask him just to ignore my notice and renew my lease.' She blew out a breath. 'I've really burned my bridges, Bel—and who knows how long it'll take me to find another flat?'

'You don't have to. Come and stay with me,' Bella said immediately.

Grace hugged her. 'I love you, sweetheart, and thank you for the offer, but your flat's barely big enough for one person. You don't have room for me to stay. I'll ask round my friends—one of them will put me up until I can find somewhere—and I'll sign on with a temp agency. If I explain the situation, I'm sure they'll understand about the problem with references and help me to find a way round it.'

This sounded more like her level-headed older sister, Bella thought. Planning. Being sensible. The oats were clearly soaking up what remained of the champagne. 'It'll all work out, Gracie. You know what Mum always says: when one door closes, another opens.'

'I know,' Grace said.

'I was going to take you out for sushi and champagne tomorrow, to celebrate my job—because I wouldn't have got it without you—but we can take a rain check on that, because I'm guessing you won't want to see champagne again for months.'

'Definitely not.' Grace winced. 'And you might've lost the job, because of me.'

'Of course I haven't. I'll talk my boss round,' Bella said, sounding slightly more confident than she actually felt. 'Go and have a shower, clean your teeth, get in your PJs, and then we're going to snuggle under a throw on your sofa and watch a re-run of *Friends*.'

'I love you, Bel,' Grace said. 'You're the best sister I could ever ask for.'

Even though they were total opposites, Bella thought. And, weirdly, tonight, it felt more as if she was Grace and Grace was her.

'You came straight to rescue me without asking any questions,' Grace said.

'Of course I did! You've done it often enough for me,' Bella said. 'And you're the best sister I could ever ask for, too, and I love you to bits—even when I don't understand you. Now go and get yourself sorted out. I'm going to raid your fridge because I'm starving, and I'm sleeping on your sofa tonight. Tomorrow, you can talk to Howard and we'll make that list and work through it together. And then things will start to look better. You'll see.' She hugged her sister. 'Nothing fazes a Faraday girl, right?'

'Right,' Grace said. 'Nothing fazes a Faraday girl.'

CHAPTER TWO

ON MONDAY MORNING, Bella left her flat at what felt like the crack of dawn. For the last couple of years, she'd been able to set her own working hours—meaning that she could sleep in until ten a.m. and work until late, which suited her body clock better—but she knew that she needed to make a good impression on her first day at Insurgo. Particularly given what had happened at her first meeting with the boss. She couldn't afford to put a single foot wrong from now on, not if she wanted to keep her job and get her finances back on track.

And getting up early would take her mind off what had been a truly lousy weekend. Seeing Grace—the person she'd always looked up to as a tower of strength, someone who knew exactly what to do to sort out any given situation—fall apart had shocked Bella deeply. Right now Grace was in the almost same position that Bella had been in six months ago: recovering from a wrecked relationship, worrying about her job and her home and her finances, and feeling as if the sun would never rise again.

OK, so Grace had been the dumper rather than the dumpee, in this case, and she hadn't lost her best friend and the contents of her bank account as well as her partner; but it was still going to be a huge change in Grace's life. Even though it had definitely been the right decision.

Privately, Bella thought her sister had had a lucky escape. Howard was a nice enough guy, but he was completely under his mother's thumb. Marrying him would've basically meant having the rest of her life run by Cynthia of the Eagle Eyes and Concrete Hair, the most cold and judgemental woman that Bella had ever met. And finding another job might just mean that Grace's new employer would appreciate her and give her the promotion she deserved. At Sutton's, Grace had been totally taken for granted. They'd expected her to work way more than her fair share of hours, under the guise of being 'almost family', but they hadn't actually given her any of the privileges of being 'almost family'.

Howard had barely raised a single argument when Grace had gone to see him on the Saturday morning and called off the wedding. So he clearly hadn't loved Grace enough to fight for her. And Bella thought her sister deserved a lot better than a man who was nice enough but didn't have a backbone and would never stand up for her.

Today was a new chapter in both their lives. And hopefully this one would be better for both of them.

Bella paused outside the Insurgo Records building. The basement was a recording studio and practice rooms that local bands could book as well as being used by the Insurgo artists; the ground floor and mezzanine comprised a seriously upmarket café—the sort that offered coffee made in a way that looked more as if it was some kind of laboratory experiment than a hot drink, but apparently brought out the floral notes in the coffee; and the top two floors were the record label's actual offices.

'All righty. Welcome to your new life,' she told herself, and went inside.

She was the first member of staff to arrive in the office after Tarquin, Hugh's second-in-command—to her relief, Hugh didn't seem to be there yet—and Tarquin handed her a design brief, a portable CD player and a pair of headphones. 'Welcome to Insurgo, Bella,' he said with a smile. 'We're doing a limited edition of coloured vinyl for Lacey's third single. She's one of our singer-songwriters. I've given you a rundown here of our target market, her career history, and the PR schedule. What I need you to do is have a listen to the album—the song we're releasing is the fourth track on the CD—and come up with some ideas for the vinyl cover and a promo T-shirt, based on what you hear. Or if you have ideas for other promo items, bring them along. If you'd like to have a second listen in one of the studios rather than working on headphones, just yell and I'll sort it out. And then maybe we can talk about it, later this afternoon?'

'That sounds fine,' Bella said, smiling back. She was being thrown in at the deep end, but she'd always thrived on that. And this was her chance to shine and prove they'd made the right decision in hiring her.

'This is your desk, over here,' he said, and ushered her over to a desk by the window with a drawing board and a computer. 'As soon as Shelley—our admin guru—comes in, we'll get you set up with a password and username. The meeting room's on the floor above, along with Hugh's office, the staff kitchen and the toilets. I'm over there in the corner, and I'll get everyone else to come over and introduce themselves as they come in.'

'That's great,' Bella said, trying to damp down the sudden flood of nervousness. She was good with people.

She knew she'd find her place in the pack and quickly work out how to get the best from the people she worked with. She always did. But these first few hours in a new role were always crucial.

'Is there anything else you need before you start?' he asked.

Yes, but she couldn't exactly explain why she needed to see the boss without making things awkward. But she'd just thought of the perfect excuse to go up to the next floor. Hopefully Hugh wasn't in yet, so she could leave the neatly wrapped parcel in her bag on his desk. Or, if he was at his desk, hopefully he'd be alone and she could snatch two minutes to apologise to him in person while the kettle boiled. She smiled. 'How about I make us both a coffee?'

'Excellent idea. Thank you.' Tarquin smiled back. 'Mine's black, no sugar. I'm afraid it's pretty basic stuff in the staff kitchen—tea, instant coffee and hot chocolate—but help yourself to whatever you want. If you'd rather have something fancier, you do get a staff discount downstairs at the café.'

'That's good to know. And instant does me just fine. At this time of the morning, any coffee works,' Bella said with a smile.

To her relief, she discovered that Hugh's office was empty. So she wouldn't have to confront him quite yet, then. There was a pile of post set neatly in the middle of his immaculate desk; she left the package and accompanying card on top of it. Then she boiled the kettle and made herself and Tarquin a mug of coffee before heading downstairs to her desk and making a start on the design briefs. And please, please, let Hugh Moncrieff accept her apology.

* * *

Hugh wasn't in the best of moods when he drove his car into the tiny car park behind the record label offices. His shoes had just about recovered from their ordeal on Friday night, and his dry cleaner had said that there would be no problem with his suit. But he hadn't been able to get Bella Faraday out of his head.

Worse still had been the slew of texts and emails and answering machine messages over the weekend from his mother, his brothers and their partners, all reminding him that his brother Nigel's engagement party was coming up and they couldn't wait to see him. Which meant that Hugh was in for another bout of familial nagging. Why was he still messing about with his record label? When was he going to treat it as the hobby it ought to be and get himself a proper job?

He knew what the subtext meant: he was the baby of the family, so they'd let him have his dream and do his degree in music instead of economics. Now he was thirty, they all thought it was about time he gave up his financially risky business and joined the long-established family stockbroking firm instead. Which was why Bella's comment about him looking like a stockbroker had really touched a raw nerve on Friday night.

He happened to like his life in London, thank you very much. He loved what he did at Insurgo—finding promising new talent and polishing their rough material just enough to make them commercially viable without taking away the creative spark that had caught his ear in the first place. Insurgo had made a name for itself as an independent label producing quality sound, from rock through to singer-songwriters, with a sprinkling of oddities who wouldn't fit anywhere else. Hugh was proud of what he did. He didn't want to give it up and be a stockbroker like his older brothers Julian, Nigel and Alistair.

But the question that drove him really crazy was when his family asked when he intended to find a nice girl and settle down. That wasn't going to happen any time soon. Jessie had cured him of that particular pipe dream. He knew his family meant well, but couldn't they see that they were still prodding a bruise?

His business, his heart and his music had all taken a battering. And finding a new, suitable girlfriend wasn't going to repair any of the damage. Sheer hard work and some quiet support from his best friends had rescued his business, but nowadays his heart was permanently off limits. And the music that had once flowed from his fingers and filled his head had gone for good. He didn't write songs any more. He just produced them—and he kept a professional distance from his artists.

He ran through a few excuses in his head. None of them worked. Even being in a full body cast wouldn't get him a free pass. He was just going to have to turn up, smile sweetly at everyone, and metaphorically stick his fingers in his ears and say 'la-la-la' every time his career or his love life was mentioned. Which he knew from experience would be about every seven minutes, on average.

He collected a double espresso from the café on the ground floor—on a morning like this one, a mug of the instant stuff in the staff kitchen just wasn't going to cut it—and stomped up to his office, completely bypassing the team. What he needed right now was music. Loud enough to drown out the world and drown out his thoughts. A few minutes with headphones on, and he might be human enough again to face his team without biting their heads off even more than he normally would on a Monday morning.

And then he stopped dead.

On top of the post he'd been expecting to see, there was a neatly wrapped parcel and a thick cream envelope. It wasn't his birthday, and the parcel didn't look like a promo item. It was the wrong shape for a CD or vinyl, and in any case most unsigned artists pitching to him tended to email him with a link to a digital file on the internet.

Intrigued, he untied the ribbon and unwrapped the shiny paper from the parcel to discover a box of seriously good chocolates.

Whoever had sent them had excellent taste. But who were they from and why?

He opened the envelope. Inside was a hand-drawn card: a line-drawing of a mournful-looking rabbit with a speech bubble saying 'Sorry'. Despite his bad mood, he felt the corner of his mouth twitch. Whoever had sent this was saying they knew he wasn't a happy bunny—and Hugh had a very soft spot for terrible puns.

He opened the card to find out who'd sent it, and a wad of banknotes fell out.

What?

Why on earth would someone be giving him cash?

He scanned the inside swiftly. The writing was beautifully neat and regular, slightly angular and spiky—the sort you'd see on hand-drawn labels in an art gallery or upmarket bookshop.

Dear Mr Moncrieff

Thank you for rescuing us on Friday night and I'm very sorry for the inconvenience we caused you.

I hope the enclosed will cover the cost of valeting the taxi, dry-cleaning your suit and replacing your shoes. Please let me know if there's still a shortfall and I will make it up.
Yours sincerely
Bella Faraday

He blinked. She'd said something on Friday evening about reimbursing him, but he really hadn't been expecting this. Since the parcel and the card had been hand-delivered, that meant that their new graphic designer must already be at her desk. Most of his team didn't show their faces in the office until nearly ten, so she was super-early on her first day.

And, although he appreciated the gesture, it really wasn't necessary. His shoes had survived and the rest of it hadn't cost that much. He really ought to return the money.

He picked up his phone and dialled his second-in-command's extension. 'Can you send Ms Faraday up?'

'Good morning to you, Tarquin, my friend,' Tarquin said dryly. 'How are you? Did you have a nice weekend? What's new with you?'

Hugh sighed. 'Don't give me a hard time, Tarq.'

'Get out of the wrong side of bed, did we? Tsk. Must be Monday morning.'

Hugh knew he shouldn't take out his mood on his best friend and business partner. Particularly as Tarquin dealt with all the stuff Hugh didn't enjoy, and with extremely good grace, so Hugh could concentrate on the overall strategy of the label and actually producing the music. 'I'm sorry. All right. Good morning, Tarquin. How are you? Did you have a nice weekend?'

'That's better. Good, and yes, thank you. I'll send her up. And be nice, sweet-cheeks—apart from the fact that it's her first day, not everyone's as vile as you are on Monday mornings.'

'Yeah, yeah,' Hugh said, but he was smiling as he put the phone down again.

Bella was leaning back in her chair, eyes closed, listening to the music. Lacey, the singer, had a really haunting voice, and the song was underpinned by an acoustic guitar and a cello. The whole thing was gorgeous, and it made Bella think of mountains, deep Scottish lochs, forests and fairies. Maybe she could design something with mist, and perhaps a pine forest, and…

She yelped as she felt the tap on her shoulder; reacting swiftly, she sat bolt upright, opened her eyes and pulled off the headphones.

Tarquin was standing next to her, his face full of remorse. 'Sorry, Bella. I didn't mean to give you a heart attack.'

Bella's heart was galloping away. 'You did give me a bit of a fright,' she said. 'I was listening to the CD—it's really good.'

'Yeah, we think so, too.' He smiled. 'Lacey's a bit of a character. She always performs barefoot.'

'Like a fairy.' The words were out before Bella could stop them. 'Sorry. Ignore me. Did you want something?'

'Yes. Hugh just called down. Can you go up to his office?'

Uh-oh. This must mean that Hugh had seen her parcel and her card. And she had absolutely no idea what his reaction was going to be. 'Um, sure,' she said.

'Don't look so worried. The boss knows it's your first

day, so he probably just wants to say hello and welcome you to Insurgo,' Tarquin said kindly.

Bella wasn't so sure. If that was the case, why hadn't Hugh come down to the open-plan office? She had a nasty feeling that she wasn't going to be hearing a welcome speech but a 'goodbye and never darken our doorstep again' speech. Clearly the parcel she'd left on her new boss's desk hadn't been anywhere near enough of an apology.

Her fears must have shown on her face because Tarquin said, 'His bark's worse than his bite. He just isn't a Monday morning person, that's all. Whatever he says, don't take it to heart, OK? Everyone else in the office will tell you the same—and if he does say something horrible to you, he'll come and apologise to you in the afternoon when he's human again. It's just how he is.'

'Right,' Bella said, forcing a smile she didn't feel. 'I'll, um, be back in a minute, then?' She switched off the music, scribbled the word 'mist' on a pad to remind herself what she'd been thinking about, and then headed for Hugh's office, her stomach churning. Hesitantly, she rapped on the closed door.

'Come in,' he said, sounding brusque.

Tarquin obviously hadn't been joking when he'd said that the boss wasn't a Monday morning person.

And then her jaw almost dropped when she walked in. The last time she'd seen Hugh Moncrieff, he'd been clean-shaven and wearing a formal suit. Today, he was wearing black jeans and a black T-shirt with the Insurgo Records logo on it, and his dark hair looked as if he'd dragged his fingers through it instead of combing it. Teamed with the shadow of stubble on his face, it made him look as if he'd just got out of bed. He should've looked scruffy and faintly disgusting. But the whole package made him seem younger and much more approachable—not to mention sexy as hell—and her mouth went dry. Oh, help. She really had to remember that he was the boss, not just another one of the team. That made him totally off limits. And, besides, she didn't want to risk her heart again. Which gave her a double reason not to act on the desire flickering through her—even if he was the most gorgeous man she'd ever met.

He indicated the box of chocolates sitting on his desk. 'Why?'

Hugh was clearly a man of few words when it came to work. Or maybe it was his Monday morning-itis. 'Why the gift? Or why chocolates?' she asked.

'Both.'

'The gift is to say thank you, because you went way beyond the call of duty on Friday night. They're chocolates, because I can hardly buy a man flowers,' she said. 'Did I give you enough money to cover everything, or do I still owe you?'

He handed her the envelope, which felt thick enough to contain most—if not all—of the money she'd enclosed with the card. 'My shoes survived, and the taxi and dry-cleaning bill weren't much,' he said.

She knew that wasn't true. The taxi firm would've charged him for valeting the cab and for lost earnings while the cab was out of action, being cleaned. 'I'd rather you kept it,' she said, putting the envelope back on his desk. 'To cover the inconvenience.'

'No need,' he said firmly. 'Is your sister OK? She looked terrible.'

Bella was grateful he hadn't mentioned the 'incident'. 'Grace barely even drinks, normally,' she said, not wanting him to think badly of her sister. 'Friday was totally out of character for her. She's the sensible and together one who sorts everything out; I'm the flaky and unreli—' She stopped mid-word, realising what she was about to blurt out. 'Not when it comes to my job, obviously. I'm very together where my work is concerned,' she added swiftly.

'But in your personal life you're flaky and unreliable?' he asked.

'Not unreliable, even—just the one who opens her mouth without thinking things through,' she said ruefully. 'As you've just heard.'

'But you rescued your sister when she needed your help,' he said softly. 'That definitely counts in your favour. Is she OK?'

'She will be,' Bella said. 'I've never known her to drink three glasses of champagne in a row, let alone on an empty stomach. I think that's why… Well. What happened, happened,' she finished, squirming slightly.

'Thank you for the chocolates. They're appreciated,' he said. 'And you have good taste.'

'I have good taste in a lot of things.' And then, when she saw the momentary flicker in those amazing blue eyes, she wished the words unsaid. 'I wasn't flirting with you,' she added quickly.

His expression said, *much*. 'Take the money,' he said. 'I don't need it. Use it to take your sister out to dinner or something.'

'Just no champagne, right?'

This time, he smiled. 'Right. Welcome to Insurgo, Ms Faraday.'

'Thank you, Mr Moncrieff.' Formality was good. It put distance between them. And it would stop her getting crazy ideas about a man with a mouth that promised sin and eyes that promised pleasure. Ideas she most definitely couldn't let herself act upon.

'Are you settling in all right?' he asked.

'Yes. Tarquin's given me my first brief and I'm working on it now. The limited edition single.' She paused. 'He said it was coloured vinyl. I have to admit, I don't know that much about how records are physically made. Can the vinyl be any colour you like?'

'Yes.'

'So you could do clear vinyl with little wisps of mist running through it?'

He looked surprised. 'Yes. Would that tie in with your design?'

'It's what the music makes me think of. Obviously it's just an idea at this stage,' she said swiftly, not wanting to put him off. 'I'll do some rough mock-ups of three or four ideas, and then I'm discussing them with Tarquin this afternoon.'

'Good. I look forward to seeing what you come up with.'

She blinked, surprised. 'You're going to be in the meeting as well?'

'Not that one,' he said. 'But when you and Tarquin have agreed which one to work on, then you come and convince me.'

'Challenge accepted.' The words were out before she could stop them. Oh, for pity's sake. This wasn't about a challenge. This was about...about...

Why had her brain suddenly turned to soup?

He smiled, then, and it felt as if the room had lit up. Which was even more worrying. She didn't want to start feeling like this about anyone, especially not her new boss.

'I think I'm going to enjoy working with you, Bella Faraday.'

There was a faint trace of huskiness in his voice that sent a thrill right through her. This was bad. She could actually imagine him saying other things to her in that gorgeous voice. Things that would turn her into a complete puddle of hormones.

No.

This was *work*. She was really going to have to keep reminding herself that her relationship with Hugh Moncrieff was strictly business. Maybe she'd ask her friend Nalini to put a temporary henna tattoo on her hand saying 'work'—written in Hindi script, so Bella would know exactly what it meant but anyone else would think it was just a pretty design. The last thing she needed was for anyone to guess how attracted she was to her new boss.

'Good,' she said. 'I'll get back to it, then.' She gave him what she hoped was a cool, capable smile, and forced herself to walk coolly and calmly out of his office. One foot in front of the other. One step at a time. She could run once that door was closed behind her.

She'd just reached the doorway when he said softly, 'Bella. I think you've forgotten something.'

Oh, help. She had to suppress the surge of lust. 'What's that?' Oh, great. And her voice *would* have to be squeaky. She took a deep breath and turned to face him.

He waved the envelope at her.

'Keep it.'

He coughed. 'As your boss, I'm pulling rank.'

If she was stubborn over this, she could lose her job.

If she took the money back, she'd be in his debt.

Caught between a rock and a hard place. Or maybe

there was a way out. 'Then I'll donate it to charity,' she said. 'I'm sure you can suggest a suitable one.'

'Bella, this isn't a war,' he said softly, and she felt horrible.

'Sorry. It's just... I don't want to be in your debt. And I don't mean just you—I mean in *anyone's* debt,' she clarified.

'The dry-cleaning bill wasn't much, and the taxi firm is one I use a lot so they were pretty accommodating. And,' he added, 'I'm not exactly a church mouse.'

'Church mouse?' she asked, not following. Then she remembered the proverbial phrase. 'Oh. Of course.'

'Take the money,' he said softly, 'and it's all forgotten. As far as I'm concerned—and everyone else at Insurgo, for that matter—today's the first day we've met. And I'm notorious in the office for not being a Monday morning person. Nobody usually talks to me until lunchtime on Mondays because I'm so horrible.'

That made her feel better. 'Thank you,' she said, and took the envelope.

'Have a nice day,' he said, and that smile made her feel warm all over.

'You, too,' she said. But this time she lost her cool and fled before she could drop herself in it any more.

CHAPTER THREE

EVEN THE IDEA was crazy.

Asking Bella was completely out of the question. She was practically a stranger; and she worked for him. Two huge reasons why Hugh knew that he should put this whole thing out of his mind.

Hugh paced up and down his living room. The problem was, now the idea was in his head, it had taken root. And he knew why. He could tell himself that asking Bella to play the role of his unsuitable new girlfriend was simply because she was vivacious enough to make it convincing. It was true enough. But he knew that the real reason was a little more complicated than that. Spending the weekend together in Oxford would give them a chance to get to know each other better. See where things took them.

Crazy. Stupid. Insane.

He knew better than to mix work and pleasure. Last time he'd done it, the whole thing had gone so badly wrong that he'd nearly lost Insurgo—letting down his business partner and the people who depended on them for their jobs. Only the fact that Roland, his other best friend, had bought into the business as a sleeping partner had saved him from having to shut the business down.

He'd worked stupid hours and he'd managed to stabilise everything, but he would never take that kind of risk again.

Strictly speaking, he knew this wasn't quite that kind of risk. Bella wasn't Jessie. She was part of the team, not one of his artists. She'd signed a contract with him rather than making a verbal agreement she could back out of because it would be her word against his. Getting to know Bella wasn't going to put Insurgo at risk.

But it still made him antsy. Since Jessie, he'd promised himself he wouldn't trust anyone with the battered remains of his heart. He'd keep an emotional distance. So why couldn't he get Bella Faraday out of his head? Why did he keep remembering that frisson of awareness when she'd kissed his cheek in the taxi? Why did her smile make him feel as if the room lit up?

And, more importantly, what was he going to do about it?

By Thursday morning, Bella felt as if she'd been working at Insurgo for ever. The rest of the team turned out to be total sweethearts, and they all shared a love of music, cinema and art. Everyone pitched in with ideas and suggestions, and nobody minded if theirs was passed over for a better one. And she absolutely loved working there.

The previous afternoon, they'd had a discussion in the office about which song fitted them, so that evening she'd made little name-cards for everyone's desk with a quick caricature of them and the title of 'their' song in place of their name.

It seemed mean to leave Hugh out just because he was upstairs rather than in the open-plan office with everyone else, so she made a card for him as well. 'I Don't Like Mondays' fitted him to a T, she thought.

That morning, as the rest of the team filtered in to the office and saw the name-cards on their desks, there was much hilarity.

Then Hugh walked into the office—clearly not in a good mood, again—and Bella rather wished she hadn't done a name-card for him after all.

'Ms Faraday—a word?' It was more of a command than a question, and his expression was completely impassive.

'Yes, Mr Moncrieff,' she said, and followed him meekly up to his office.

Even though he didn't say a word to her on the way up, she had a pretty good idea what this was about. He hadn't been amused at all by his name-card.

'I'm sorry,' she said as soon as he closed the door. 'We were messing about yesterday—' Then she stopped as she realised how incriminating her words were. 'Over lunch, that is,' she said swiftly, hoping that she'd saved the situation. She didn't want to get her new colleagues into trouble. 'We were talking about the song title that could be used instead of your name to describe you, and I drew the cards last night at home. It was just a bit of fun and I didn't mean anything by it.'

'You picked an appropriate one for me,' he said.

Though every single day seemed to be Monday, where his mood was concerned. He really wasn't a morning person. She winced. 'Sorry. Are you very cross with me?'

'No—and, just for the record, I don't mind a bit of messing about in the office. It helps creativity, and I know everyone on the team puts the hours in. As long as the job gets done on time and within budget, I don't actually care *how* it's done.'

'Then why did you want to see me?' Bella asked, now completely mystified. If he wasn't about to haul her over the coals for unprofessional behaviour, then what?

'Your hair.'

She frowned. 'What's wrong with it?'

'You were blonde, yesterday. Platinum blonde.'

'Ye-es.' She still didn't follow.

'And today your hair's red.'

A tiny bit brighter red than she'd intended, because she'd been so busy making the name-cards the previous evening that she'd left the dye in for a few minutes longer than she should've done, but she liked it. 'Yes.' Where was he going with this? 'Is there a problem with my hair colour?' she asked carefully.

'No, not at all.'

She really didn't understand. 'Then why did you call me into your office?'

'Do you have a boyfriend?'

Apart from the fact that you weren't supposed to answer a question with a question, what did that have to do with anything? She frowned. 'You're not supposed to ask me things like that. My relationship status has nothing to do with my job.'

'I know. I'm not asking you as your employer.'

She caught her breath. Did that mean he was asking her out?

No, of course not. That was totally ridiculous. Just because she had a secret crush on him, it didn't mean that her feelings were in any way returned. And in any case her boss was the last man she'd ever date. It would cause way too many problems, and she really couldn't afford to give up her new job. There was no guarantee that the receivers dealing with her former client would give her any of the money owing to her, because she'd be way down the pecking order in the list of creditors. And, with Kirk having cleaned out their joint bank account so she no longer had any savings to her name, she was stuck. 'Why do you want to know?' she asked, trying hard to sound polite rather than aggressive.

'Because I need you to do something for me, and I need to know whether I'm going to have to have a conversation with an overprotective boyfriend first.'

She was still none the wiser. 'Now you've really got me worried.'

He raked a hand through his hair. 'Bella, don't be difficult.'

That was rich, coming from him, she thought. Hugh Moncrieff was the walking definition of difficult. He was also the walking definition of sexy, but she had to keep a lid on that thought.

'Can you just answer the question?' he asked. 'Are you single or not?'

'I'm absolutely single,' she said crisply, 'and I intend to stay that way.' Just so it'd be totally clear that she wasn't trying to flirt with him—or anything else.

'Good.' He gave her a sweet, sweet smile. One that made a lot of warning bells ring in her head. 'Bella, remember when I helped you out last Friday night?'

The warning bells got louder. 'Ye-es.'

'Good.' He paused. 'I need a favour.'

So much for him saying that they'd forget what had happened. Clearly there were strings attached, after all. How *disappointing*. 'What sort of favour?' she asked carefully.

'I need you to be my date for a family event.'

That was the last thing she'd expected. Had she misheard? 'To be what?' she asked.

'My date for a family event,' he repeated.

That was what she thought he'd said. The words 'date' and 'Hugh Moncrieff' were a dangerous combination. 'Why?'

'A more pertinent question, in the circumstances, is "when?",' he said dryly.

OK. She'd play it his way. 'When?' she asked sweetly.

'Next weekend.'

What? 'As in tomorrow or as in next Friday?'

'As in a week on Saturday,' he clarified.

Talk about lack of notice. Did he think that she didn't have a social life? 'Where?'

'Oxfordshire.'

'Right.' She stared at him. 'So let me get this straight. You want me to go to a family do with you in Oxfordshire and pretend to be your girlfriend.'

'Yes.'

She folded her arms. 'Now I think "why" might be pertinent. And I think I deserve a proper answer.'

'If you want to know the truth, it's because you,' he said, 'will annoy my family.'

She looked at him through narrowed eyes. 'That's not very nice—to me or to them.' And it made her feel as if he was using her. Just like Kirk had. Even though Hugh was being upfront about it rather than pretending he loved her, the way Kirk had, it still stung.

'Given that you told me you were flaky and unreliable in your personal life, I think that's a fair assessment.'

He had a point. Just. 'It's still not very nice,' she said.

'I didn't expect you to go all Mary Poppins on me,' he drawled.

She resisted the urge to slap him or to say something rude. Just. 'That's because you don't know me very well. What do you want to achieve?'

He frowned. 'I don't know what you mean.'

'You said you want to annoy your family. What do you really want to happen?'

When he still looked blank, she sighed. 'Look, you're at point A and you clearly want to be at point B. What do you need to do to get from A to B, and is having a fake girlfriend really the most effective way to do it?'

He raised his eyebrows. 'That's a bit sensible.'

'Coming from me, you mean?' She rolled her eyes. 'It doesn't come from me, actually. It's the way my sister looks at things.'

'Your sister Grace? As in the woman who downed three glasses of champagne on an empty stomach…?' he said, with mischievous emphasis.

She put her hands on her hips and glared at him. 'Don't you dare be rude about my sister,' she warned. 'I already told you: that was really unlike her. It was due to special circumstances—and don't bother asking what they were, because I'm not going to tell you. It's none of your business.'

'Absolutely,' he said, disarming her. 'Actually, I like the way you stand up for your sister. And you have a point.'

'So why you do want to annoy your family?' she asked.

'This,' he said, 'is even more confidential than anything commercial I talk to you about.'

'That's *obvious*,' she said, rolling her eyes at him.

'You're my boss, so anything you say to me in this room stays in this room unless you say otherwise.'

'Thank you,' he said. 'Since you ask, the reason is because I'm sick and tired of them nagging me to settle down. So if I turn up to my brother's engagement party with someone who looks completely unsuitable, maybe they'll shut up and get off my case.'

She digested this slowly. He was saying she was unsuitable because of her hair? 'So basically you're asking me to play the kooky wild child. You want me to turn up with a mad hair colour, wearing ridiculous shoes and a skirt that's more like a belt?'

'What you wear is entirely up to you,' he said. Then he looked thoughtful. 'But, as you mentioned it first, yes, I think you probably have the chutzpah to carry off that kind of outfit.'

She still couldn't quite work out if he was insulting her or praising her. Instead, she asked the other thing that was puzzling her. Well, apart from the fact that he was single. Even though he tended to be grumpy in the mornings in the office, she knew he had a good heart. He'd rescued her and Grace when they'd needed help, even though at the time they'd been complete strangers—and at the time it hadn't felt as if there were any strings. Plus he had beautiful eyes and an even more beautiful mouth. The kind that made you want to find out what it felt like to be kissed by it.

She shook herself. That was something she shouldn't be thinking about. 'So why does your family want you to settle down?'

When he didn't answer, she pointed out, 'If you ask me to design something for you, then I need a brief to know what your target market is and what you want the design to achieve. I need to understand *why* before I can design something to suit. This is the same sort of thing. If I don't understand why you want me to play someone unsuitable, I'm not going to be able to deliver the goods, am I?'

'So you'll do it?'

'I didn't say that. I still reserve the right to say no.' If saying no was actually an option. Would her job depend on this? 'But if you tell me why and I agree with your reasoning, then I might consider it.' She spread her hands. 'Anything you tell me is confidential. But I would also like to point out that I do have a social life, actually, and I did have plans for the weekend.'

'I'm sorry.' He raked a hand through his hair, suddenly looking vulnerable. Which was almost enough to make her agree to help him, regardless of his motives.

Weird.

Hugh Moncrieff was old enough and tough enough to look after himself. You didn't get to be the successful owner of an independent record label if you were a pushover. He didn't need looking after by anyone. But that expression in his eyes had touched a chord with her. It reminded her of the look in Grace's eyes when she'd confessed that she didn't fit in with Howard's family and didn't think she ever could. That she'd felt trapped and miserable.

Was that how Hugh felt about his own family?

And why did she suddenly want to rescue him, when she was usually the one who had to be rescued?

'Of course you have a social life,' he said. 'And I don't expect you to say "how high" every time I ask you to jump.'

'Good,' she said. 'I'm glad that's clear.'

He gave her a wry smile. 'And I know I'm out of order, asking you to play a part.'

'It does make me feel a bit used,' she admitted.

'I don't mean it quite like that. I need help to deal with a tricky situation.'

'Just like I did—and you helped me, so it makes sense that I should return the favour.' Put like that, she thought, his request was much more reasonable.

'If it's possible for you to change your plans for the weekend and you do agree to help me by being my date, just be yourself. That'll do nicely.'

'Because I'm unsuitable?' she asked. Just when she'd started to feel OK about it, he'd made her feel bad again. Stupid. 'That's a bit insulting.'

'That isn't actually what I meant. You're confident,' he said. 'You're direct. You don't play games.'

'But you're asking me to play a game. Well, play a part,' she corrected herself. 'Which is pretty much the same thing.'

'I guess. I don't mean to insult you, Bella. I apologise.'

'Apology accepted.' She paused. 'So why do you need a date?'

He sighed. 'I'm the youngest of four boys. The other three are all stockbrokers in the firm started by my great-grandfather. My family would very much like me to toe the line and follow suit.'

She winced. 'Ouch. That's what I called you on Friday. I said you looked like a stockbroker.'

'I'm not one, and I never want to be one,' he said softly. 'Don't get me wrong. I'm not saying that it's a bad career—just that it's not right for me. My brothers love what they do, and that's fine. I'd support them to the hilt, but

I don't want to join them.' He gave her another of those wry smiles. 'That's why the label has its name.'

'Got you. Insurgo's Latin for "to rebel".' She wrinkled her nose. 'And, no, I didn't go to the sort of school that taught Latin. I looked it up on the internet. The only Latin I know is "*lorem ipsum*"—the stuff used as filler text in a design rough, and that's not really proper Latin.'

He smiled back. 'Actually, "*lorem ipsum*" is a mash-up of Cicero's *De finibus bonorum et malorum*.'

'Trust *you* to know that.' The words came out before she could stop them.

He laughed. 'I'm afraid I did go to the kind of school that taught Latin.' He dragged his hand through his hair. 'I love what I do, Bella. I like hearing artists play me raw songs—and then a different arrangement flowers in my head, and I can see exactly what they need to do to make it a hit without losing their original voice. I've never wanted to do anything else but produce music that I love—music that makes the world a better place. But my family worries about me, because the music business isn't exactly stable. Insurgo's doing well—well enough for some much bigger labels to have offered to buy me out, though I've always refused because I'm not going to sell out my artists like that—but I'm still at the mercy of the markets. We've managed to weather a few storms, but all it takes is one wrong decision that loses the business a lot of money, or for a couple of my biggest customers to go bankrupt and not pay me, and we could go under.'

'Tell me about it,' she said feelingly.

'I knew you'd get that bit. You've been there,' he said.

So either Tarquin had told him that she'd once had her own business, or he'd read her résumé. Or maybe both.

'Small businesses fail all the time,' she said, 'and I kept mine going for two years. If my best client hadn't gone bankrupt, owing me the equivalent of three months' salary, I'd still be a freelance designer now. But when one door closes another opens—and now I have a job I like here.'

'I take it back about being Mary Poppins,' he said. 'You're Pollyanna.'

'I'm just me,' she told him firmly, 'not a stereotype. But, yes, I believe in looking for the good in life.' She whistled the chorus from 'Always Look on the Bright Side of Life' and smiled.

'It's a good philosophy,' he said.

'You're right—you're perfectly capable of being a stockbroker, but it'd make you miserable. You're doing what you love,' she said. 'And there's nothing wrong with that. Why doesn't your family see that?'

He sighed. 'They have this little box ready for me. I'm supposed to fit in with a sensible job, a sensible wife, and two point four children or whatever it's meant to be nowadays. A *pied-à-terre* in London for me during the week, and an ancient pile in the countryside for the family, where the kids can grow up until we send them to boarding school.'

Was he describing what his own childhood had been like? 'I guess I'm lucky,' she said. 'All my parents and my sister want is for me to be happy and fulfilled.'

'Are you?' he asked.

She nodded. 'Are *you*?'

'Yes.' But she noticed that he didn't meet her eye. So did that mean he wasn't? And what, she wondered, was missing from his life?

Not that there was any point in asking. She was pretty

sure he'd stonewall her. Getting the information so far had been like pulling teeth.

'OK. So you want me to pretend to be your girlfriend, to show your family that you have no intention of meeting any of the criteria to fit that little box they've made for you. You already have a job they don't approve of, so what you need is an outrageous girlfriend to horrify them even more. That will be the icing on the cake, if you'll excuse me mixing my metaphors,' she said, hoping that she'd summed up the situation without missing anything.

'That's pretty much it.' He paused. 'So will you do it?'

'It's one way to get from A to B,' she said. 'But I think a much better one would be to sit down with your family and talk to them. Make them see how much you love Insurgo. Show them your passion for it. Play them the raw stuff, and then the final version with all the changes you suggested, so they can hear exactly what you do. Then they'll understand and be happy just to let you do it.'

'Maybe,' he said. 'But, even if they listened to me about my job, that's only half the problem dealt with. There's still the sensible wife they want me to have.'

She shrugged. 'You could always tell them you'd like a sensible husband.'

He grinned. 'You mean, ask Tarquin to pretend that he's my life partner as well as my business partner? I think Rupert—his other half—might have something to say about that.' Then his smile faded. 'I don't want a sensible wife. Or husband, for that matter.'

'What do you want?' she asked.

What did he want?

Never to have his heart broken again.

Which meant no more serious relationships. And it

had suited him just fine over the few months, dating casually and making sure that all his girlfriends knew that a diamond ring and a change of name were never going to be on offer. That he was looking for fun, not for for ever. And most of the time he didn't even bother with that. He concentrated on work. Though it wasn't quite the work of his heart any more. Not since he'd stopped writing music.

'What I want right now,' he said, 'is to get through Nigel's engagement party without being nagged about my choice of career or lifestyle.'

'You know that's not going to happen,' she said. 'That's the thing about families. They're interested in what you do, so of course they're going to ask questions and give their opinions, whether you ask for them or not. It's part and parcel of family life.'

Clearly she didn't mind about that as much as he did. Then again, she'd said that her family just wanted her to be happy. And she'd gone straight to her sister's rescue last week; he had a feeling that Grace would've come straight to Bella's rescue, too, if the positions had been reversed. His brothers certainly weren't batting his corner. They thought he ought to give in and join them in the family business.

She shrugged. 'So. Realistically, what's the best you can hope for?'

'That an outrageous girlfriend will distract them enough to stop them nagging me about when I'm going to settle down. Just for the weekend,' he added, wanting to make it clear that this wasn't a long-term thing.

'Weekend? I thought you said it was a party?'

'It's a weekend thing,' he explained.

She looked shocked. 'You're telling me that this engagement party is going to last for a whole *weekend*? Wow. I thought that my friends and I could party pretty hard, but we're all amateurs compared to that!'

'It's not that big a deal,' he said. 'We turn up for afternoon tea and cake on Saturday with the older relatives, and then we have a cocktail party in the evening. It's black tie, by the way.'

She looked thoughtful. 'So you want me to wear an unsuitable dress to the tea party bit, and something even more outrageous for the evening do rather than a proper little black dress.'

Oh, good. She understood and she wasn't going to give him a hard time about it. 'That would do very nicely.'

'And then what?'

'Um, we stay overnight—but you'll have your own room, don't worry. I'm not expecting you to share with me or anything,' he added swiftly. 'We'll have breakfast in the morning, go for a walk, stay for Sunday lunch because Ma will insist—except that'll be just my brothers and their partners and us, plus maybe an aunt and uncle or two—and *then* we can go home.'

'A whole weekend,' she repeated.

'The food will be excellent,' he said. 'And there will be pink champagne.' And then a nasty thought hit him. 'Unless last weekend put you off champagne?'

She rolled her eyes at him. 'That's mean. I already told you, my sister doesn't normally drink more than one glass. Last weekend was exceptional circumstances.'

'I apologise. Again.'

'Apology accepted, but I have a three strikes and you're out rule,' she warned. 'Do it again and I'll stand on your foot. In spike heels. I might be only five feet four, but I'm heavier than I look.'

'Got it.' The more time Hugh spent with Bella, the more he liked her. She made him feel different—she brought back the crazy, spontaneous part of him that he'd kept locked away since Jessie. Which was dangerous. Maybe he should call this whole thing off. For safety's sake.

'So what colour do you want my hair to be?' she said, cutting into his thoughts.

'Any colour you like. It's your hair.'

She smiled. 'Good answer. You're learning.'

'I'll pay for your frocks,' he said, 'and your shoes, and whatever else you want. Just tell me how much you need.'

'It's very tempting to say yes and drag you off to the fashion department in Selfridges with your credit card,' she said, 'but I guess it'd be more believable if I wore a charity shop find.' She paused. 'Or am I playing a gold-digger who expects you to bankroll her fashion habit?'

'I don't think you'd be a believable gold digger, because you're too independent,' he said. Again, so unlike Jessie, who'd always had an eye on the main chance. Except he'd been so in love with her that he hadn't seen it at the time. With Bella, what you saw was what you got—and that was refreshing. It tempted him to relax the rules where she was concerned. Part of him thought this was a bad idea; but part of him was intrigued enough to want to know where this could take them. 'A charity shop find would be good, but I meant it about paying for your clothes and what have you. Just get anything you need and I'll pick up the bill. You shouldn't be out of pocket when you're doing me a favour.'

'OK. I'll make sure I get receipts for everything. So I need outfits for a tea party, a cocktail party, breakfast, a walk and lunch.' She raised an eyebrow. 'I hope your car has room for a lot of luggage.'

'The brasher the better—and add that to your shopping list,' he said with a grin. 'And thank you. I think I'm actually going to enjoy this now.'

'Is it really going to be so bad, spending time with your family?' she asked.

And now she'd wrong-footed him again. He wrinkled his nose. 'I love them, but they don't see me for who I am. They don't listen to me. They want me to fit in their nice little box. That's the thing I find hardest to deal with.'

'So my job is to be their wake-up call. To make them see that by pushing you so hard, they're actually making you run just as hard in the other direction. Whereas, if they leave you be, you might just come up with a compromise that will keep you all happy.'

'I'm beginning to think that you should swap places with me and be head of strategy at Insurgo,' he said.

'Hardly.' She scoffed. 'I was working on design principles.'

'They work for strategy, too.' He paused. 'Thank you. I think I'm in your debt.'

'Strictly speaking,' she said, 'and, as you pointed out, I was in yours—you rescued Grace and me when we needed help. This is my chance to return the favour. And then we're quits—right?'

'Quits,' he agreed. 'That sounds good to me.' He reached over to shake her hand, then rather wished he hadn't when his palm started tingling. He really shouldn't start thinking about Bella in that way. He'd learned from Jessie that business and love didn't mix, and he didn't want to repeat his mistake. He was attracted to Bella—she was gorgeous and vibrant and she would make any man look more than twice—but he really shouldn't take this any further. They were going to keep this strictly professional. 'I'll let you get back to whatever you were working on,' he said. 'And thank you.'

'Last thing,' she said. 'What about an engagement present?'

'It's all taken care of. And the card.'

'How much do I owe—?' she began.

'It's all taken care of,' he repeated, cutting in. 'Really. I don't expect you to pay a penny towards this.'

'Can I at least take your mother some flowers, as we're staying at your parents' place?'

He frowned. 'That's very *suitable* behaviour, Bella.'

'Actually, it's common courtesy to take a present for your hostess,' she corrected. 'I don't mind people thinking I'm an airhead and unsuitable, but I *do* mind them thinking I'm rude and selfish. So. Flowers or chocolates?'

'She's a chocolate fiend. Dark. But you don't have to—'

'Yes, I do,' she cut in. 'Or the deal's off.'

And hadn't he asked her to help him partly because she was so outspoken and independent? 'OK,' he said.

'Good. And now I'm going back to what you pay me to do,' she said, and sashayed out of the room. As much as you could sashay in jeans and flat canvas shoes.

But the images in his head wouldn't shift all day. The curve of her backside. The confident, brisk way she moved. That spark of merriment in her blue, blue eyes. The curve of her mouth.

How would her mouth feel against his? Would she make his lips tingle as much as his skin? And how would it feel to lose himself inside her?

There suddenly wasn't enough air in the room. He

walked over to the window, opened it and shoved his head out. Maybe the noise from the traffic would clear his head.

It didn't.

'Get a grip, Moncrieff,' he warned himself.

This was strictly business. Letting his imagination loose was a seriously bad idea. He wasn't going to let himself think about what it would be like to touch Bella. To kiss her. To hold her close. This pretend girlfriend business was just to get him off the hook with his family. And, the more he kept telling himself that, the quicker he'd start to believe it.

CHAPTER FOUR

'ARE YOU SURE this is a good idea, Bel?' Grace asked.

'Going to Oxfordshire and pretending to be Hugh's unsuitable girlfriend? Possibly not,' Bella admitted. 'I did tell him I thought it'd be a better idea to be straight with his family and get them to see his passion for his work. But he's adamant that this is the best way to get them off his back—and I guess they're his family, so he should know the best way to handle them.'

'I don't mean just that,' Grace said gently. 'I mean getting involved in your boss's personal life.'

'I'm not getting involved in his personal life,' Bella insisted. 'Apart from the fact that I'm officially off men for good, I'm just doing this as a favour.'

Grace winced. 'To make up for me throwing up over him in the taxi?'

'No,' said Bella firmly. 'No.' Though he had hinted at it. Which had made it easier for Bella to say yes. Not that she wanted Grace to worry about it, so she kept that information to herself. 'He just needs someone to help him make his family back off. And I kind of fit the bill.'

'So you're going to a posh afternoon tea party wearing a skin-tight leopard-print dress,' Grace said.

'Yup. And I've got tiny, tiny shorts and high-heeled

mules for the country walk the next day. And, best of all, for the cocktail party… Meet my alternative to the little black dress.' Bella produced the curtains she'd found in one of the charity shops, flapped one with a flourish and draped it over one shoulder. 'Ta-da!'

Grace blinked. 'You're wearing a *curtain* to a cocktail party?'

'Not quite—it's going to be a proper dress. Only I'm making it from a curtain instead of from normal dress fabric. Em said she'd come round tomorrow, measure me, and we'll cut it out and run it up together.' Bella grinned. 'This is where going to art school comes into its own. I know loads of people who can help. I just thought, what could be gaudier and more unsuitable for a black tie cocktail party than a mini-dress made out of a curtain?'

Grace eyed the orange flowers. 'Um. Very nineteen-sixties.'

Bella's grin broadened. 'And it's so *The Sound of Music*, don't you think?' She draped the curtain over the back of her sofa, pulled Grace to her feet, and danced her sister around the tiny living room, all the while singing, 'How Do You Solve a Problem Like Maria?' but substituting her own name in the song.

'You're impossible,' Grace said, but she was laughing.

'I'm a genius. And I've just had another great idea. We can have takeaway pizza tonight and watch *The Sound of Music* together. I love that film so much. And we can sing "Do Re Mi" in harmony—I'll even let you pick your part.'

Grace hugged her. 'I know what you're doing, Bel. You're trying to distract me. But I'm OK. Really. The hard bit was last weekend and breaking up with Howard. The temp agency's found me some work, I've got a couple of weeks to find a new flat before I have to move out of mine, and you've been the best sister and most brilliant support anyone could ask for. My new life starts now, and it's going to be just fine.'

'I still worry about you,' Bella said. She didn't quite dare ask if this was how Grace felt about her, most of the time. Grace had had to rescue her often enough from some scrape or other.

'I'm fine,' Grace reassured her again. 'But, yes, we can order a pizza and watch a film tonight. That sounds good.' She took a deep breath. 'And if this engagement party goes horribly wrong next weekend, just ring me and I'll drive straight down to get you, OK? It's only an hour and a bit from London to Oxford.'

'It won't go wrong,' Bella said. 'I'm just playing a part. Even if I wasn't officially off men, Hugh Moncrieff is the most unsuitable man in the world for me. He's my boss, and dating him would make everything way too complicated.'

'So why,' Grace asked, 'are my big sister antennae suddenly twitching like mad?'

'Force of habit,' Bella said with a smile. 'But nothing's going to go wrong.'

The following weekend, Bella's confidence in that statement had evaporated.

Had she gone too far with her outfit?

What if Hugh's family had a blazing row with him over her unsuitability and it ruined the engagement party? That really wouldn't be fair on Hugh's brother and his fiancée.

Maybe she ought to pack some suitable clothes as well, in case she needed to change at the last minute. Or borrow Grace's car so she could make a quick getaway if she needed to, rather than letting Hugh drive her down to Oxfordshire. Or maybe she should just make sure her mobile phone was fully charged and she'd got the number of a reliable local taxi firm.

Plus she and Hugh hadn't set any real ground rules. What did playing his unsuitable girlfriend actually mean? Holding hands, draping herself over him—or even kissing him?

The idea of kissing Hugh sent her into a flat spin.

He was her boss. She shouldn't even flirt with him, let alone entertain ideas about kissing him. Even if he was the most attractive man she'd met in years. Kissing was totally off the agenda.

So why, why, why couldn't she get the idea out of her head?

Her stomach was in knots by the time her doorbell rang, just after lunch.

When she answered the door, Hugh was standing there, wearing one of his business suits. He looked utterly gorgeous—and Bella felt completely out of place in her outrageous get-up. Particularly when his eyes widened in apparent shock as he took in what she was wearing: a tight leopard-skin mini-dress with a wide shiny belt cinched round her waist and spindly high heels, a chunky bead necklace, and she'd styled her hair so her normally sleek bob was in wild curls.

'This is a bit too much, isn't it?' she asked, indicating her outfit.

'It's, um, *interesting*,' he said. 'Very eighties. Especially the hair.'

In other words, he hated it. She'd gone way over the top. There was cutesy retro, and there was a total mess.

She'd clearly crossed the admittedly narrow line between the two. She took a deep breath. 'Sorry. Give me ten minutes and I'll change.'

He caught her hand. 'No, Bella, you're perfect as you are.'

A shiver ran through her at the feel of his skin against hers. She had to remind herself sharply that she was doing this as a favour to him—acting the part of his unsuitable girlfriend—and that was all. Any attraction she felt towards him was totally inappropriate and needed to be squashed. Like yesterday.

'Are you sure this isn't too much?' she asked, doubt still crawling through her. 'Are you quite, *quite* sure it wouldn't be better to switch to Plan B?'

'Which is?'

'Go to the party on your own and tell your family how much you love Insurgo, that you're perfectly happy being single and that you don't need a romantic partner to feel that your life's complete.'

'I could, but they wouldn't listen, so it has to be Plan A,' he said softly. 'And I want you to know how much I appreciate this, Bella. I don't know anyone else who could've carried this off.'

'Really?'

'Really. I'm not flannelling you.'

She could hear the sincerity in his voice. He really thought that she could do this. And to have someone believing her on a personal level, someone other than her family... That made her feel better about herself than she had in a long time.

'I'm truly grateful,' he said. 'Now, where's your luggage?'

She picked up her large, bright pink suitcase and

faked a confidence she didn't quite feel. 'OK. I'm ready. Let's go.'

His car was gorgeous—sleek and low-slung, with leather seats that were amazingly comfortable—and she wasn't surprised to discover that he had a really good sound system, too. She was happy enough to listen to music until they were out of London and on the motorway, and then she turned to him.

'Can I ask you some questions?'

'Sure you can ask,' he said, sounding as if he reserved the right not to answer.

'We'll start with your family,' she said. 'Even an unsuitable airhead girlfriend would know who she was going to visit. I know you're the youngest of four boys, and we're going to your brother Nigel's engagement party somewhere in Oxfordshire. Everyone else in your family is a stockbroker. And that's *all* I know. Do you not think that I might need to know everyone's names, at the very least?'

'I guess,' he said. His voice was totally expressionless, so she had no idea what was going through his head. 'OK. My parents are Oliver and Elizabeth. Pa's recently retired and spends half of his day on the golf course. Ma's in the WI and does charity work. My brothers—Julian's the oldest, married to Poppy, and they have a baby girl, Sophia. Alistair's the next and he's married to Harriet. Nigel's about to get engaged to Victoria, and they're getting married at Christmas. I'm the youngest, and I'm taking my new girlfriend Bella Faraday to meet the folks. Anything else?'

'Yes. Ground rules. What does playing your girlfriend actually mean?' she asked. 'Holding your hand? Draping myself artfully over you?'

He blew out a breath. 'I hadn't thought that far ahead, to be honest. I suppose they'd expect us to hold hands. And for me to dance with you at the cocktail party. Which is a point. Can you dance?'

She couldn't help smiling because he'd set up her answer so beautifully. And, with any luck, it would make him laugh and relax a bit, too. 'Would that be with or without a pole, Mr Moncrieff?'

As she'd hoped, he laughed. 'Without.'

'I don't really tend to go clubbing,' she said. 'But I go to a dance aerobics class, so I can move in time to music.'

'That's good enough for me.'

But he hadn't answered her question fully. 'Anything else?' she asked.

He frowned. 'Such as?'

'Normally, people who are dating tend to, um, kiss each other,' she said. 'Especially when dancing and parties are involved.'

'Ah. Yes. Kissing.'

The car suddenly felt way too small. And was it her imagination, or had the temperature just shot up by ten degrees?

'Chaste kissing would be acceptable,' he said.

Right at that moment, she didn't feel very chaste. And she wished she hadn't brought up the subject, because she could just imagine what it would be like to kiss Hugh Moncrieff. To cup his face in her hands and brush her lips against his, teasing at first, and then letting him deepen the kiss. Matching him touch for touch, bite for bite, until they were both dizzy with desire and he carried her off to his bed...

'Bella?'

'What?' She'd been so lost in her fantasy that she

hadn't heard him say anything to her. She felt colour flood into her cheeks.

'I said, are you OK with that?'

No. It was way too risky.

But she'd agreed to play his unsuitable girlfriend. And she was the one who'd brought up the question of kissing in the first place.

'I guess,' she said, trying to sound cool and calm and completely unbothered. 'Next question.'

'Hit me with it,' he said dryly.

'Why are you single?'

He blew out a breath. 'You're very direct. Why are *you* single?'

Because she'd put her trust in the wrong people. 'I asked you first.'

He shrugged. 'I was seeing someone and it didn't work out.'

That was obviously the need-to-know version of the story, she thought. She didn't think Hugh was the type to be a selfish love rat—someone like that wouldn't have come to her and Grace's rescue when they'd needed help, the other week—so she assumed that he hadn't been the one to end the relationship. Had his ex broken his heart? But there was no point in asking him. She knew he'd stonewall her.

'You?' he asked.

'You summed it up for me, too. I was seeing someone and it didn't work out,' she said. She didn't want to tell him the whole messy story. More precisely, she didn't want him knowing that she was so naïve and had such poor judgement in relationships. Her best friend and her live-in boyfriend. Just how had she managed to keep her eyes so firmly closed to what was really going on between them?

'Was it recent?' he asked.

'Six months ago,' she said. 'And you?'

'A year.'

'And you haven't met anyone else since?' That surprised her. When he wasn't being grumpy in the office, Hugh was good company. And he was very easy on the eye. Surely he had women lining up for him in droves?

'I've been too busy concentrating on my business.' He paused. 'You?'

'The same.' Except it hadn't just been her romantic relationship that had crashed. Kirk had dumped her for the woman Bella had believed was her best friend since sixth form, taking that support away from her, too. And Kirk had quietly cleaned out their joint bank account, the morning he dumped her—which was why Bella hadn't had her normal safety cushion of the equivalent of three months' salary when her best client went bust, and why her finances were in such a mess now.

And there had been next to nothing she could do about it, because the money had been in their joint names. She'd talked to the bank, but they'd said that any signatory to a joint account had the right to withdraw however much money they liked, no matter how much they'd actually put in.

Bella would never make that mistake again. And she was really glad that she'd listened to Grace's advice and put her tax money to one side in a different account rather than keeping it with her 'salary', or she'd be in debt to the Inland Revenue as well.

'Let's just say I'm tired of always dating Mr Wrong and I'm happier being single,' she said.

'Works for me. Any more questions?'

He was definitely in his Monday morning office mode now. Grumpy and difficult. She decided that any other questions could wait. 'I guess we've covered the basics.'

'Good. If you don't mind, I'd better concentrate on my driving.'

Given that they were going to his family home, he probably knew the route blindfold, so Bella was pretty sure that this was just his way of avoiding any more questions. And she supposed he had a point. She knew enough to play her role. Asking him anything else would be intrusive, wouldn't it? She let him concentrate on his driving and fiddled quietly with her phone, until he turned off the main road and drove them through narrower country roads to the outskirts of a village.

'Here we are, then,' he said as he turned into a driveway. The fences on either side were in perfect repair, and huge lime trees lined the fences and cast dappled shade on the driveway.

Bella had known that Hugh was from a posh background, but she hadn't realised just how posh. At the end of the half-a-mile-long driveway was the most beautiful house she'd ever seen: an Elizabethan manor house built from mellow Cotswold stone, with floor-to-ceiling sash windows on the ground floor, mullioned windows on the top floor, wisteria climbing the walls which wasn't in bloom yet but would look stunning in a couple of weeks, and a wide front door with a spider-web fanlight above it.

'That's gorgeous,' she said. 'And I've got this weird sense of déjà vu—I know I've never been here before, but somehow I feel as if I have.'

'You've probably seen the house on TV,' he said. 'It's been used as a location for a few period dramas.'

Before she had the chance to ask which ones, he parked on the gravelled area outside the house.

'I see my brothers are already here,' he said.

There were two sports cars similar to Hugh's parked outside the house, along with a Range Rover, a Daimler and a Bentley. It felt almost as if she was walking into one of the period dramas he'd mentioned. And it was a million miles away from her own background. Was she really going to be able to pull this off?

'The grandparents and the aunts are here, too, by the looks of it,' he said. 'We might as well go in and say hello. There probably isn't enough time to give you a proper guided tour of the house before tea's served, but I promise I'll do it tomorrow. Ma's probably in the kitchen fussing about. She said afternoon tea would be in the dining room and the cocktail party tonight's in the ballroom.'

'Your parents have a ballroom?' She smiled to hide the panic that trickled through her. 'That's very Jane Austen.'

'It's probably been in one of the Austen adaptations. I can't really remember,' he said with a shrug. 'Which sounds terribly snooty, but it isn't meant to be.'

'Of course not.' Bella had the feeling that he was much more nervous about this than he looked, and somehow that made her feel a little less nervous. A little less alone.

'Imagine the kind of house parties they had back in Austen's time,' he said. 'I'd be off fishing or hunting with my brothers, or playing cards and drinking. But the women in the house party wouldn't be allowed to do much more than read or play the piano. They'd be under constant scrutiny, and there were all the intricate manners…' He shuddered. 'I hate that kind of stuff. I'm glad it's not like that now.'

'Isn't it?' she asked softly—because that bit about constant scrutiny and manners sounded personal.

'No.'

'It was for my sister.' The words were out before she could stop them.

He looked at her. 'How?'

'I…' She sighed. 'OK. You're unlikely to meet her again, but if you do and you tell her you know why she drank all that champagne that night I might have to kill you.'

'Noted. What happened?' he asked, sounding curious.

'She was at the golden wedding anniversary party for her fiancé's parents. Let's just say that Cynthia of the Concrete Hair—'

He blinked. 'Who?'

'Howard's mother. You know the sort of woman I mean. Everything's all about appearances and she's so polished that her hair is set like concrete.' Bella waved a dismissive hand. 'And she watches you like a hawk and judges you—usually unfairly.'

'Yes, I've come across people like that,' he said.

'So I think Gracie finally realised that if she went ahead and married Howard, her life was going to be seriously miserable.' She grimaced. 'She tried to blot it out by drinking champagne. It didn't work. So, for the first time ever, I was the sister who did the rescuing—with a lot of help from you.' She bit her lip. 'The wedding was meant to be next weekend.'

'So Grace was a runaway bride?' He looked surprised.

'No. She didn't jilt Howard at the altar—she'd never do anything that mean. But they'd been engaged for four years and he never swept her off her feet, not *once*.'

'Being swept off your feet is overrated,' Hugh said. 'You're more likely to fall into a puddle of slurry.'

'Slurry?' she asked, not understanding.

He grinned. 'You're definitely a townie, then. Slurry is liquid manure. Used as fertiliser on fields.'

She pulled a face. 'That's vile.'

'Exactly how it smells. You always know when it's muck-spreading season.'

'It's not muck-spreading season now, is it?'

He laughed. 'No.'

'Good.' She took a deep breath. 'Righty. Time to play my part, I guess. Ditzy and unsuitable girlfriend with a terrible taste in clothes—that's me, right?'

'Right. And thank you for saving my bacon. I appreciate this. Even if it might not seem that way.'

He took their bags from the car and they went into the house. Bella noticed the sweeping staircase coming into the hallway and the Regency striped paper on the walls; the house really was gorgeous, and she itched to explore, though she knew it would be rude to ask.

Three dogs came rushing down the hallway to meet them, their tails a wagging blur.

'I forgot to warn you about the mutts,' he said. 'Sorry. Are you OK with dogs?'

'Very OK. I grew up with a dog,' she said, and bent down to make a fuss of the chocolate Labrador, Westie and Cocker Spaniel.

'This lot are Lennie the lab, Wilf the Westie and Sukie the spaniel,' he introduced them.

The dogs wriggled and shoved each other and tried to get closer to Bella. 'They're lovely,' she said, laughing. 'Hello, you ravening beasties. I'm sorry, I don't have any treats for you because I wasn't expecting to meet you, but

I can rub your ears and scratch your backs for you, and I'll play ball with you for a bit if you want.'

'Do that and they'll pester you for the whole weekend,' Hugh warned.

She smiled up at him. 'And that's a problem, how?'

A woman who looked so much like Hugh that she had to be his mother came into the hallway and hugged him. 'Darling, I'm so glad you could make it.'

OK, so now she had to be Miss Ditzy. Breathe, Bella reminded herself, and stay in character. She stood up and gave her best attempt at a goofy smile.

'Bella, this is my mother, Elizabeth Moncrieff,' Hugh said.

'Libby will do nicely,' Hugh's mother said. 'We don't stand on ceremony in this house.'

'Ma, this is my friend Bella Faraday,' Hugh continued.

'Like the scientist?'

Libby had perfect manners, Bella thought, and didn't even look the remotest bit fazed by Bella's outlandish dress. 'Yes, like the scientist,' she agreed, before remembering that she was supposed to be playing the part of someone who would probably never have heard of Michael Faraday, let alone known who he was.

'I'll just show Bella up to her room,' Hugh said hastily.

'She's in the Blue Room, next to yours. I hope that's all right?'

'Thank you, Mrs Mon—' Bella began.

'Libby,' Hugh's mother reminded her.

'Libby.' Bella opened her bag and took out the beautifully wrapped package of dark chocolates she'd bought earlier. 'And these are for you, to say thank you for having me.'

'How lovely.' Libby went pink. 'And I recognise that

packaging. These are my absolute favourites. That's very kind of you.'

'My pleasure. I'm glad you like them,' Bella said. 'Don't let Hugh anywhere near them. He's a chocolate fiend. But I guess, as his mum, you already know that.'

'Oh, I do,' Libby said feelingly.

'Let's go and put our things upstairs,' Hugh said.

'Come down when you're ready. Everyone will be in the dining room,' Libby said. 'And it's a pleasure to meet you, Bella.'

Bella followed Hugh up the sweeping staircase and all the way to the end of a corridor.

The Blue Room was enormous. It was very plain, with cream walls and a polished wooden floor with a navy rug in the centre, but what really caught Bella's attention was the ancient wooden four-poster bed. She'd always wanted to sleep in a bed like that. 'This is amazing,' she said.

'I'll put my things next door. I'll call for you in a few minutes,' he said.

Was Hugh's bedroom anything like this? she wondered. Were there things from his childhood that would give her a clue about what made him tick?

Not that she should be thinking about any of that. She was simply doing him a favour and playing a part. None of this was *real*, she reminded herself.

To distract herself, she went and looked out of the window. The room overlooked the garden at the back of the house: a perfectly striped lawn, with borders all full of tulips, and a stone wall at the end of the lawn with what looked like espaliered trees full of blossom. It was a million miles away from her own suburban upbringing. How wonderful it must have been to have a garden like that to run around in and explore as a child.

Then there was a knock at the door. 'Bella?'

'Come in.'

Hugh remained in the doorway. 'Ready?'

She nodded. 'I was just looking at the view. It's gorgeous.'

'Yes, it's pretty good. I guess I didn't really appreciate it when I was younger.' He took a deep breath. 'Let's go and face the hordes.'

She walked over to join him. 'Though you might have to roll your eyes at me to remind me to be Miss Ditzy. I already made a couple of mistakes with your mum.'

'It'll be fine,' he said. 'I know you're going to do a great job. That's why I asked you.'

'So you didn't ask me just because you were desperate?'

His eyes crinkled at the corners. 'That, too. But mainly because I think you'll do this brilliantly.'

Funny how the compliment warmed her all the way through. Maybe that was because he was being sincere.

Then again, she hadn't spotted Kirk's lies, had she? For all she knew, Hugh could be lying, too.

She took a deep breath. '"Once more unto the breach, dear friends."'

He laughed. 'It won't be that bad.'

Once they got downstairs, Bella wasn't so sure. The dining room held the biggest table she'd ever seen in her life. And every place was already filled, except two.

Hugh introduced her swiftly to everyone before they sat down. She'd already met his mother, but now there was his father, his brothers and their partners and baby Sophia, various aunts and uncles, and his grandparents. And it was all just a little bit overwhelming—especially as Bella could see the shock on all their faces, even though it was quickly masked and everyone was very polite to her.

She knew that she was playing a part and Hugh's intention had been to bring someone home who was so out of place that his family would stop pressuring him to settle down, but even so she didn't enjoy their scrupulous politeness. It looked as if this was going to be a very long weekend.

A maid came in carrying a tray with silver teapots and what Bella guessed were silver jugs of hot water to refresh the tea. Porcelain jugs of milk and dishes with slices of lemon were already on the table, along with a selection of finger sandwiches, tiny pastries, slices of cake and what looked like still-warm scones. A butler followed the maid, carrying a magnum of champagne; once everyone's glass was filled, Hugh's father made a brief speech and proposed a toast to Nigel and his new fiancée, Victoria.

The food was amazing, and in other circumstances Bella knew she would've really enjoyed it. It was a shame that she had to play a part. Until she'd had a chance to work out who was who and the best way to play it, she decided to keep quiet.

But then the old lady sitting next to her—Hugh's great-aunt Lavinia—went very pale and looked as if she was about to faint.

'Are you all right?' Bella asked her, worried.

'I do feel a bit odd,' Lavinia admitted.

'Can I get you a glass of water?'

Lavinia looked grateful. 'Yes, please.'

Miss Ditzy might not know what to do, but Bella couldn't possibly keep playing that part when the old lady clearly wasn't very well and needed help. Hugh wouldn't mind her breaking out of role for this, would he? So she had a quiet word with the maid to get some water, persuaded Lavinia to eat a sandwich, and sat quietly with the old lady until the colour had come back into her face.

'I think I might go and have a little lie-down,' Lavinia said.

'I'll see you up to your room,' Bella said. 'As long as you can direct me, that is. I'm afraid I don't know my way round the house.'

Lavinia patted her hand. 'Thank you, dear. That's very good of you.'

'My pleasure.' Bella helped the old lady back to her room, and stayed with her for a little while to make sure she was quite all right.

'You're a lovely girl, very kind,' Lavinia said. 'I can see what Hugh sees in you.'

Which was totally the opposite of what Bella was supposed to be doing. And she knew that Hugh didn't see anything in her anyway, apart from her being his graphic designer who was probably too outspoken and had been crazy enough to agree to help him in his even crazier scheme. She'd have to hope that her outrageous clothes would distract everyone else from seeing who she really was.

But going back to face everyone in the dining room felt really daunting. She didn't have a clue what to say. To her relief, Hugh met her in the hallway. 'Thanks for looking after my great-aunt. Is Lavinia OK?'

'She's fine—just having a little rest,' Bella said, and gave the same reassurances to Hugh's mother when Libby asked her the same question.

Libby gave her a searching look, then a nod of what looked very much like approval.

Oh, help. She'd really have to work at being unsuitable now. Hugh's mother wasn't supposed to approve of her. She was meant to stick out like a sore thumb.

After the tea party, everyone disappeared to get changed for the cocktail party.

'Come and knock on my door when you're ready,' Hugh said when they reached her bedroom door.

'OK.' Bella wished again that she'd brought a normal black dress with her, rather than going along with Hugh's plans, but it was too late now.

When she'd changed, she knocked on Hugh's door.

'Come in,' he called.

When she pushed the door open, she could see that he was sitting on the end of the bed, checking something on his phone. He looked up and burst out laughing. 'Well. I really didn't expect that. You actually found that in a charity shop?'

'The material, yes—it was originally a pair of curtains. One of my friends from art school specialised in textiles, so she ran this up for me.' She narrowed her eyes at him. 'Why didn't you expect it?'

'I guess I really ought to give you advance warning,' he said. 'The curtains in the ballroom are, um, exactly the same material as your dress.'

'The same material?' She stared at him in shock. 'No way. You're *kidding*.'

He coughed. 'Afraid not.'

She covered her face with her hands. 'Oh, no. I thought I was being so clever, having a Maria moment. It never occurred to me your parents might have curtains like this. I should've run this past you before we came. And I haven't got a spare dress with me.' She blew out a breath. 'Oh, well. I'll just have to change into the leopard-skin thing again.'

He came over to her and rested his hand on her shoulder. Again, her skin tingled where he touched her. 'Relax. Stay as you are. It'll be fine,' he soothed.

She rolled her eyes at him. 'I can hardly go to a party wearing a dress made out of the same curtains that are in the room, can I?'

'Actually, you can,' he said. 'You're the one person I know who can pull this off.'

She really wasn't convinced. And it didn't help that Hugh was wearing a dinner jacket with grosgrain silk lapels that matched the fabric on the buttons, a white pleated-front shirt, and a properly tied black grosgrain silk bow tie. He looked sleek, elegant and perfect.

She blew out a breath. 'You look very nice. Very James Bond, though I think you might actually have the edge on Daniel Craig.'

'Thank you.' He inclined his head in acknowledgement of the compliment. 'You look very nice, too.'

'In a dress that matches your parents' curtains and clashes with my hair?' she asked, raising her eyebrows. 'Hardly.'

'Remember, you have chutzpah,' he said.

'Maybe I should stay here. You could say I drank too much champagne earlier and have a headache.'

He shook his head. 'Have the courage of your convictions, Bella.'

She scoffed. '*Your* convictions, you mean. If we'd done it my way, I wouldn't be here and you would've shown your family how great you are at your job.'

'Let's agree to disagree on that one, because I know you can do this,' he said. 'Ready?'

No. But she had no other choice. 'Sure,' she said. 'Let's go.'

CHAPTER FIVE

BELLA'S FACE WAS pale beneath her make-up, but she lifted her chin high and pulled her shoulders back.

For a moment, Hugh thought about calling this whole thing off—someone in the house was bound to have a spare dress that she could borrow for the evening—but they'd agreed that the idea was to present Bella as Miss Totally Unsuitable. To the point where his family would all breathe a collective sigh of relief when he announced next week that the relationship was over, and they'd stop nagging him about settling down.

Bella was the only woman he knew who could pull off an outfit like this one. And he knew he was asking a huge amount from her. When they were back in London, he'd do something nice for her to make up for what he was putting her through right now. Maybe he could send her on a spa weekend with her sister or something.

He suppressed the thought that he'd like to take her away and make a fuss of her himself. She'd made it clear that she was single and wanted to stay that way. The same was true for him. Bella Faraday might make his pulse beat that little bit faster: but she was his employee, and that made her completely off limits.

They went downstairs and he ushered her into the ballroom. As they walked through the doorway, he felt her hand tighten on his arm just a fraction. And the gasps of surprise as people saw her and took in what she was wearing were actually audible.

The ground obviously wasn't going to open up and swallow her, and turning back time wasn't physically possible either. Bella glanced at Hugh for a cue about how to react and what to do—after all, this was his family and he knew them way better than she did—but he seemed to have frozen.

Nothing fazes a Faraday girl. The mantra she shared with Grace echoed through her head. Wrong. This had definitely fazed her.

Then again, Hugh had asked her to play the part of his unsuitable girlfriend. Which was exactly how she felt right now—awkward and out of place, absolutely not fitting in. What would an unsuitable girl do when she was the centre of attention? The only thing Bella could think of was to draw even more attention to her gaffe and ham it up a little.

She walked over to the curtains and did a little curtsey. 'I promise I didn't make my dress from these,' she said, gesturing to the curtains. 'Because my name isn't Maria and I'm fairly sure you're the Moncrieffs and not the von Trapp family—right?'

There was still an uneasy silence.

Had she gone too far? Or did she need to go further still? 'Well, then,' Bella said, and began to sing 'Do Re Mi' very softly.

Hugh looked at Bella, totally stunned. He'd had no idea that she could sing—especially this beautifully. It made him think of Jessie, and how his ex had bewitched him with her voice.

But Jessie wasn't half the woman that Bella Faraday was. Jessie was an ambitious, lying cheat, whereas he knew that Bella was completely open and honest. Even though at the moment she was playing a part: that was solely because he'd asked her to do it.

And right now all the heat was on her—Hugh's unsuitable new girlfriend in her even more unsuitable dress. He could hear Bella's voice faltering and he knew he ought to rescue her. Especially because this whole fiasco was his fault. He needed to step in and take the heat off her. Now.

She'd even given him the perfect cue.

Yet that would mean performing in public. Something he hadn't done since Jessie had walked out on him. And singing a duet… The whole idea of it made him feel sick to his stomach, bringing back the misery and disappointment he'd felt when he'd learned the truth about how much of a fool he'd been, and the dismay when he'd realised the ramifications for Insurgo. He really didn't want to do this.

Yet how could he be a snake and leave Bella to face everyone's disapproval alone? This whole thing had been his idea, and she was doing him a favour. It wasn't fair that she should bear the brunt of it.

It left him no real choice.

Taking a deep breath, he walked over to Bella and took her hand. 'Von Trapp, you said? I believe that's my cue.' And then he began to sing 'Edelweiss'.

Bella smiled, and to his surprise she joined him in the song.

It had been a long, long time since Hugh had sung a duet with someone. Jessie. Who'd sung like an angel, promised him paradise, and left him in hell. This should've made him want to run for the hills as fast as possible. Instead, it felt as if something in the region of his heart had just cracked a tiny bit, enough to let in some unexpected warmth. His hand tightened just that tiny bit more round hers; and when she squeezed his fingers back the crack around his heart grew just that little bit wider.

When the song finished, everyone clapped and the tension in the ballroom had dissolved.

Then Nigel came over to him. 'Hugh, I need a favour.'

Considering that he'd just almost wrecked his brother's engagement party, Hugh felt guilty enough to agree to whatever it was. 'Sure. What do you need?'

'Excuse us, Bella,' Nigel said, and led Hugh off to a quiet corner. 'The band I hired for tonight just called to say that their van's broken down and they're running an hour late. Would you play for us until they get here?' He inclined his head towards the baby grand piano in the corner of the ballroom.

'You could've had the pick of my artists. And they would've been here on time,' Hugh said mildly.

'I know, but the singer of the band happens to be Vicky's friend. Vicky asked her to do it before I had a chance to suggest asking you to recommend someone.'

Hugh laughed. 'Nice save.'

'I know I'm asking a lot of you,' Nigel said softly. 'I know why you don't play in public any more.'

Because of Jessie's betrayal. It had sucked all the joy out of music for him. He didn't write songs any more. Today was the first time he'd sung in public since she'd left. Right now though, he was punch-drunk, not quite sure how he felt—happy and sad were all mixed up together, with him smack in the centre of the whirlpool.

'Yeah.' Hugh took a deep breath. This was a big ask. But, in the circumstances, there wasn't a nice way to say no. And Hugh did love his brother. This was his chance to help, to do something nice for his family. How could he turn that down? 'All right. I'll play until the band gets here. But I'm not singing any more, and neither is Bella, OK?'

'OK.' Nigel patted his shoulder. 'Thanks. I appreciate it.'

Hugh walked back over to Bella. 'Will you be OK if I play the piano for Nigel and Victoria until the band turns up?' he asked.

'Sure,' she said, giving him what looked like a brave smile. Clearly she didn't think she'd be OK at all.

'Of course she will. I'll look after her,' his mother said, coming over and catching the end of the conversation.

That was almost what Hugh was most afraid of.

But before he could say anything his mother had swept Bella away and Nigel was looking anxiously towards the piano. What could he do but give in and sit down at the baby grand? 'Let's get your party started, O brother mine,' he said and began to play.

'I think you need some champagne after that, Bella,' Libby said, and snaffled a glass from the nearest waiter.

'I'm so sorry, Mrs Moncrieff,' Bella said, accepting the glass. 'About the dress. And... And...' She shook her head, not knowing where to start. Just that she needed to apologise. She'd thought she was being so clever, making a dress out of a curtain. And she'd ended up being horrifically rude. This wasn't who she was. At all. And it made her squirm inside. She'd come here under false pretences and she'd behaved appallingly.

'It's Libby,' Hugh's mother reminded her gently. 'My dear, I can see exactly why Hugh fell for you.' Libby patted her arm. 'What you did just now—that was very brave.'

'Or very foolish in the first place,' Bella said softly. There was a huge lump in her throat. She really hadn't expected Hugh to come to her rescue like that. The last time a man had left her in a sticky situation, he'd left her to deal with it alone. Yet Hugh had been right there by her side, supporting her and sorting it out with her. 'I didn't know Hugh could sing like that—or that he could play the piano.' Considering that Hugh owned a record label and he'd told her how much he loved producing the songs and turning them from raw material to the finished product, she should've guessed that music was more than just a money-making venture to him. But Hugh wasn't listed on Insurgo's website as one of the label's artists, and nobody in the office had even hinted that he'd ever been any kind of performer. He hadn't even sung along with the music in the car on the way to Oxfordshire.

But she'd overheard Nigel saying something about knowing why Hugh didn't play in public any more. Something really awful must've happened. And there was no way she could possibly ask Hugh about it, not without opening up what might be some very painful scars. She'd have to tread very carefully.

'Hugh was very cagey when I asked him about how you'd met,' Libby said. 'Are you one of his artists?'

Bella winced. 'Not *quite* in the way you think. I'm not a singer and I don't play an instrument.'

Was it her imagination, or did Libby Moncrieff suddenly look relieved? And why? Did that have something to do with the reason why Hugh didn't play in public?

'So how did you meet?' Libby asked.

Bella could hardly be completely honest about that, either. Not unless she wanted to tell a story that made her sister look bad, and that wasn't fair. The best she could do was give the bare bones of the truth. Which would probably be the safest thing in any case, because then she wouldn't have to remember which fibs she'd told and end up in a muddle. 'I'm an artist—and by that I mean a graphic designer, not a recording artist—and Tarquin interviewed me for the job at Insurgo.'

'Ah.'

That earlier look of relief hadn't been her imagination, then, because Libby suddenly looked wary again.

Was Insurgo the problem? Hugh had said that his family worried about him because the music business was so risky. Maybe this was her chance to bat his corner for him and get his mother to see just how good he was at his job and how much the recording label meant to him.

'As I said, I'm not a singer,' Bella said, 'but I do like music, and Insurgo produces some of the very best music around. I used to be a freelance designer, but my best client went bust a few months ago, owing me rather a lot of money. My parents would've bailed me out if I'd told them, but I wanted to stand on my own two feet rather than rely on them—so that's why I applied to Insurgo when I saw the job advertised. Hugh had nothing to do with me getting the job. Tarquin interviewed me.' She spread her hands. 'I didn't even meet Hugh until after I'd accepted the job.'

To her relief, Libby looked a bit less wary again.

She took a sip of champagne. 'It's a good place to work. I've never been anywhere with a sense of team spirit like there is at Insurgo. Everyone looks out for each other. And the musicians all love coming in to the office because they feel we listen to them. Hugh doesn't treat them just as cash cows or as if they're stupid. He listens to what they want, and he gives them advice—and they listen to him because they know he wants to help them be the best they can be. They know he'll take their raw material and polish it—but he'll still keep their vision.'

Libby nodded, but said nothing.

'Insurgo wouldn't be the success it is without Hugh. He's its heart,' Bella said. 'And he really loves what he does. There aren't many people who can say that nowadays.'

'But the music business is so precarious,' Libby said.

'It is,' Bella agreed. 'But Hugh doesn't take stupid risks. He's really sharp and he makes exactly the right business decisions—though nobody in the office will ever ask him anything on a Monday morning.'

'Why not?'

'He's, um, not really a Monday morning person. Though I guess, as his mum, you already know that.' She smiled, and told Libby about the name-cards she'd made for everyone in the office.

Libby laughed. 'You didn't do that on a Monday morning, I hope.'

Bella laughed back, feeling properly at ease for the first time since she'd arrived. 'I wouldn't have dared. No, it was a Thursday. And he was still pretty grumpy.'

'So you can sketch people really quickly?'

'Not just people.' Bella fished in her bag and took out a pen and a small spiral-bound notebook. 'Give me a few seconds,' she said with a smile. She sketched swiftly. Then she handed the notebook with the line drawing to Libby. Sitting patiently next to a cake and wearing hopeful expressions as they stared at it were Lennie, Wilf and Sukie.

'Oh, that's wonderful,' Libby said. 'May I keep it?'

'Of course.' Bella detached the page and handed it to her.

'Thank you. So what exactly did you draw on Hugh's name-card?' Libby asked, sounding intrigued.

'You're his mother. I can hardly show you.'

Libby laughed. 'I used to have to get him out of bed on Monday mornings when he was a teen. I think I've seen him at his very grumpiest.'

'Well, if you put it that way,' Bella said, 'how can I resist?' She drew another sketch. And, before she realised it, she had a circle of people around her, all wanting to see her drawings and all asking for a sketch.

Oh, help. She was supposed to be playing Miss Ditzy and Unsuitable, not making friends with everyone the way she always did. Hugh was going to be furious. She'd just have to work out how to extract herself from this before the band turned up and he could leave the piano.

Hugh finally managed to get away from the piano when the band turned up, all flustered and apologetic. He went to rescue Bella from his mother, only to find her right in the middle of a crowd. Everyone around her was laughing and joking, and he noticed that she had a pen and paper in her hand.

She looked as if she belonged.

Oh, no. That wasn't supposed to happen. His bright idea was going completely pear-shaped. His family had obviously seen way beyond Bella's surface unsuitability. And Bella herself had clearly forgotten that she was playing the part of Miss Ditzy and Unsuitable.

Then again, hadn't he also told her just to be herself? Which was exactly what she was doing. Bella, the graphic artist, the woman who'd fitted in to their team at the office as if she'd been there since day one.

Right now, she lit up the room. Which scared him and drew him in equal measures. He wanted her—but he didn't want to risk his whole life imploding again, the way it had after Jessie. He needed to be sensible about this. And right now the sensible thing to do would be to get her out of there before she said anything that made his family guess at the truth.

And she was meant to be his girlfriend, so everyone would expect him to walk over and drape his arm round her shoulders. 'Sorry to desert you like that, darling.'

She looked up at him, her beautiful blue eyes wide. 'Hugh!'

'But I'm here now. Shall we dance?'

'I...' She looked flustered. Which was pretty much how he felt, too, so close to her that he could smell her perfume and feel the warmth of her body against his.

'May I finish my sketch first?' she asked.

'Sure.' He took a step back. Putting a bit of distance between them was probably a good idea, given that right now he wanted to pull her closer.

Hugh had seen what she could produce at the Insurgo office, but he'd never actually watched her working before. And he was amazed by how deft her hands were. He also noticed how she caught the tip of her tongue between her teeth when she was concentrating, and it made him want to kiss her.

Maybe dancing with her would be a bad idea after all. It would make her way, way too tempting.

But then she finished a sketch of Lennie with his father—lightning fast and seriously good—and handed it over to Oliver with a smile.

'Thank you, my dear. That's marvellous.' Oliver kissed her cheek. 'And maybe I could ask you to sketch Libby with Sukie for me, later?'

'Of course,' Bella said, smiling back. 'But I'll require payment in advance, you know. You'll have to dance with me first.'

He positively beamed at her. 'With absolute pleasure, my dear.'

Amazing. Even wearing a dress made out of a curtain which matched the ones in the ballroom and which clashed badly with her bright red hair—two things that Hugh was sure should've annoyed Oliver Moncrieff immensely—Bella had still managed to charm his father. Just, Hugh thought, by being herself. She couldn't help it. Bella was the kind of woman who brought out the best in people.

He led her off to the other side of the dance floor. 'I was going to apologise for throwing you to the wolves, but it looks to me as if you've managed to turn them all into little fluffy-wuffy lapdogs.'

She laughed. 'Hugh, don't be so mean. Your family's nice.'

He scowled. 'Maybe. When they're not nagging me.'

'Really, Hugh. They're *nice*.' She blew out a breath. 'And I should be apologising to you. I'm afraid I kind of forgot to be unsuitable. I was telling your mum about the name-cards I did in the office last week, and I ended up drawing the dogs for her, and…' She bit her lip, and Hugh had to suppress the urge to kiss the sting away. 'It snowballed a little bit. Sorry. I'll remember to be dim and scatty and unsuitable for the rest of the weekend, I promise.'

'Hmm,' Hugh said. He didn't think she'd be able to remember it for very long. Because he realised now that Bella wasn't a natural deceiver. What you saw was what you got. There were no hidden agendas. 'It's as much my fault as it is yours. I shouldn't have left you on your own.'

'But you couldn't have refused to help your brother.' She paused and gave him a curious look. 'I didn't know you could play the piano.'

'Lavinia taught me.'

'Lavinia, as in your great-aunt I sat next to this afternoon?'

He nodded. 'Before arthritis wrecked her hands, she was an amazing pianist.'

She frowned. 'So your family does understand about music, then.'

'Lavinia does,' he admitted. 'The rest don't. They still think I should give it up and join the family business.'

She looked thoughtful. 'So you play and you sing—I've heard that for myself. I'm guessing that you probably write your own stuff, too.'

He had. Once upon a time. Not any more.

She wasn't letting it go. She ignored his silence. 'And you own a record company. Do you ever record anything of your own?'

'No,' he said, knowing that he sounded abrupt and rude, but not being able to help himself.

But it didn't seem to put Bella off. 'Why not?' she asked. 'You're good. And I'm not just saying that because you're my boss. You, a piano and a love song—you'd have women swooning all round the globe. You'd make gazillions for the label.'

Hugh had written songs for Jessie, and he'd thought about recording them as duets with her. Then Jessie had dropped her bombshell that she was moving to another record label instead of signing the new contract with Insurgo, and by the way she'd met someone else…who just so happened to be the head of her new label.

And then Hugh had realised that maybe Jessie had never loved him at all. She'd just seen him as a stepping stone in her career, and it looked as if she was doing exactly the same with her new man. He'd been so shocked and hurt that he hadn't written anything since, and he couldn't remember the last time he'd touched the piano; the joy he'd once found in playing felt tainted with memories of her betrayal. Tonight was the first time he'd sung with anyone since he'd broken up with Jessie. The first time he'd played in public again.

And he didn't want to analyse that too closely. Or why it had felt so natural to sing with Bella, after the initial shock.

'I don't want to be a performer,' he said. 'I prefer being a producer. Seeing the rough diamond of the songs and how I can make them shine. You know, like Lacey's album—putting the cello in and a double bass made it just that bit more haunting and gave the sound some depth.'

'Fair enough.' She shrugged. 'I think I understand where you're coming from, because for me it's the other way round. I absolutely love designing, but I wouldn't want to own or run a gallery. The idea of having to organise a bunch of creative people…' She groaned. 'It'd be like herding cats. No, thanks.'

He smiled. 'It's very satisfying when it goes right.'

'Each to their own,' she said.

Hugh danced with her all evening, only stepping to

one side when his three brothers and his father all demanded a dance with Bella. And then he found himself dancing with his sisters-in-law and his mother, all of whom were singing Bella's praises loudly.

'She's perfect for you,' Victoria said. 'Even if her dress sense is a little, um, unusual.'

There was nothing he could say to that. If he protested, everyone would take it as a token protest; if he agreed, they'd have a date set for the wedding within the hour.

'I really should rescue her from Pa,' he said, and fled in Bella's direction.

'Is everything all right?' Bella asked when Hugh was dancing with her again.

'I think our plan might have crashed and burned a bit,' he said ruefully.

She winced. 'Sorry. That's my fault.'

'No. You were right. It was a daft idea in the first place.'

'I'm glad you can admit when you're wrong,' she said with a smile. 'That's a good thing.'

'Mmm.' He wasn't convinced.

She stroked his face. 'Hugh. Let's just forget it for now and enjoy the party.'

Her touch made every nerve-end sit up and pay attention. He had to stop himself from turning his head and pressing a kiss into her palm. Distance. He needed a tiny bit of distance between them, before he lost his head completely and gave in to his body's urging. He snagged a couple of glasses from one of the waiters and toasted her. 'I still can't believe you stood up there in front of those curtains, in that dress, and sang "Do Re Mi".'

'Says Captain von Trapp,' she retorted with a grin.

'Oh, please.' He rolled his eyes. 'Ma loves *The Sound of Music.*'

'So do I. It's one of the best films ever.' She hummed a snatch of 'My Favourite Things'.

'I hated that film,' Hugh said.

She blinked at him, clearly taken aback. 'Why?'

'The way the guy just ignored his kids made me so angry. And it wasn't so much a stick the guy had up his backside as a whole tree.'

'And you don't?' she teased.

What? Hugh stared at her in surprise. Was she saying that she thought he was stuffy? 'No, I don't,' he said, faintly put out.

'Prove it,' she challenged.

He narrowed his eyes at her. 'How?'

'Dance the samba with me.' She raised her eyebrows at him. 'After all, this is a party, and the samba is the best party dance I know.'

'Sorry.' He spread his hands. 'I would, but I'm afraid I don't know the steps.' It was a feeble excuse, but a valid one. If the samba meant dancing close to her and touching her… That would be way too risky. He needed to be sensible about this, not getting closer to her.

'It's easy. I'll teach you. Gracie and I go to a dance aerobics class where half the moves are based on samba.' She grinned. 'Just follow my lead.' Then she paused, batted her eyelashes at him, and drawled, 'Unless you can't take direction from a woman?'

He had the distinct impression that she was flirting with him. Even though he knew he ought to resist, he found himself flirting right back. 'I can take direction.' He stared at her mouth. 'When it's *appropriate.*'

Her skin heated, then, clashing spectacularly with her hair. 'Hugh!'

And her voice was all breathy. He was about to tease her when he realised that he couldn't speak, either, because right now his head was full of the idea of kissing her. And that breathiness in her voice was incredibly sexy. His mouth was actually tingling. All he had to do was lean forward and touch his lips to hers...

They ought to stop this.

Right now.

As if she was channelling his thoughts, she muttered, 'Back in a moment.'

But what she did next was to go and speak to the band. He recognised the song from the first couple of bars: 'Livin' la Vida Loca'.

So Bella wasn't going to let him off. To pay him back for making her blush, she taught him how to samba, making him repeat the basic steps and arm actions until his movements were fluid. He was surprised by how much he enjoyed the bouncy, shimmery nature of the steps.

Other people were watching them, but when Bella realised that she was having none of it. As the band continued to play songs with a similar beat, she went round and taught everyone else in the room how to do the basic steps. The women seemed to cotton on much quicker than the men—which didn't surprise him that much, because hadn't Bella said something about learning this kind of thing at an aerobics class?—but finally the whole room was dancing. Including relatives Hugh had never actually seen get up on the dance floor before.

How on earth had she managed that?

'You certainly know how to get a party going,' he said when she came back over to him.

She laughed and tossed her hair back. ‘I *love* parties.’

He could tell. She was really lit up from the inside, and it was infectious. Being with her made him smile and forget just about everything else. How long had it been since he’d last felt this happy and carefree?

Then the band slowed it all down again. He held out one hand to her. ‘May I have this dance, Ms Faraday?’

She gave him a shy smile and took his hand. ‘Of course, Mr Moncrieff.’

He drew her into his arms and held her close, swaying with her. Weird how she fitted perfectly into his arms, all warm and soft and sweet. Maybe the romance of the engagement party had got to him, or maybe he’d drunk too much champagne, but he couldn’t resist holding her just that little bit closer, dancing cheek to cheek with her. He could smell the soft floral scent she wore—gardenia, perhaps? It was enchanting: much like Bella herself.

And from dancing cheek to cheek it was the tiniest, tiniest move to kissing her. All he had to do was twist his head ever so slightly and brush the corner of her mouth with his lips.

Should he?

And what would she do if he did?

If she moved away, he’d stop, he promised himself.

Except she didn’t move away. When he kissed the corner of her mouth, she twisted her head ever so slightly towards him, so her mouth brushed against his properly.

And Hugh was completely lost.

He tightened his arms round her and kissed her again, teasing her mouth with tiny, nibbling kisses until she let her lips part and he could deepen the kiss. It felt as if he were floating on air. Every sense was filled by her. And it had been a long, long time since he'd felt anything even approaching this.

He wasn't sure how long it was until he broke the kiss. But her mouth was reddened and her eyes were wide and bemused; he was pretty sure he looked in a similar state.

They needed to get out of here, before someone noticed or commented.

'Come with me?' he asked softly. 'Away from the crowd?'

She nodded, and he tangled his fingers with hers and led her quietly out of the ballroom and down the corridor to a room he knew would still be in darkness.

'Where are we?' Bella asked when Hugh led her into a darkened room.

'The orangery,' he said.

Once her eyes grew accustomed to the light, she realised that one whole wall was made of glass, and the moonlight shone through onto an ancient chequered red and cream flagstone floor. All along the walls were massive terracotta pots containing what she presumed were citrus trees; there were a couple of what looked like wrought-iron benches between the pots.

'Wait,' hc said, and let go of her hand.

A few moments later, she heard a soft click, and then suddenly the room was glowing softly with dozens of tiny fairy lights twined round the stems of the trees.

'Hugh, this is amazing,' she said in delight. 'It's magical.'

'Isn't it just?' he said. 'We had a film crew here when I was in my teens, and the set designer said this was where people would sneak off for some privacy at a Regency house party, among the lemons and limes and oranges.

She reckoned they'd have had candles and it would've been beautiful.'

'Just like this.'

He nodded. 'Someone suggested fairy lights as a modern take on it without the fire risk. Since then, we've often sat out here after the sun sets, just watching the stars, with the fairy lights on. And a heater, in winter, because otherwise it's absolutely freezing.' He came back to hold her hand, and drew her over to one of the benches. 'This is probably my favourite place in the house. Even in the daytime, it's lovely.'

He'd promised her a guided tour of the house tomorrow, and she intended to hold him to that. But right now, when he sat down on one of the wrought iron benches and drew her onto his lap, she couldn't think straight. All she could do was to put her arms round his neck for balance. And from there it was one tiny step to kissing him again.

Time seemed to stop. It was just them, the moonlight and the fairy lights. Nobody came out to find them or ask Hugh to play the piano or Bella to sketch. They could've been light years away from anywhere.

But they could still hear the music.

'Dance with me?' he asked.

Even though part of her knew that this wasn't sensible—it was too intimate, just the two of them in the orangery among the fairy lights—how could she resist?

They swayed together in the room.

Any moment now, she thought, he'd say something to remind her that they were both playing a part.

And yet he didn't. He just danced with her. Held her close. Cherished her.

It was so long since she'd been held like that. It made her feel warm inside. Warm all over. And when Hugh rested his cheek against hers, even though she'd promised herself she'd be sensible, she found herself moving that little bit closer to him. Turning her head so her mouth made contact with the corner of his. His arms tightened round her and he moved his head too, so his lips brushed against hers. Once, twice: and then he was kissing her with abandon, and she was kissing him right back.

She was dizzy with desire when he broke the kiss.

'Hugh—I, we...' She couldn't think straight. There was something important she had to say, but for the life of her she couldn't remember what it was. She just wanted him to kiss her again.

She trailed her fingertips across his cheek, liking the very faint scratch of stubble. 'You're beautiful,' she said. 'Poster-boy beautiful.'

He turned his head and pressed a kiss into her palm. 'Less of the boy, thank you.'

Oh, yes. He was all man. 'I didn't mean it that way,' she said. 'Just that you're beautiful.'

'So are you.' He kissed her again. 'You make me ache.'

She dragged in a breath. 'Ditto.' An ache of wanting, of need. He was driving her crazy with his nearness.

'I know this isn't supposed to be happening, but right now,' he said softly, 'I don't want to go back and join the others. I want to carry you up the stairs to your bed.'

The big, wide four-poster.

'I want to make love with you, Bella.'

A shiver of pure desire ran down her spine.

She knew they shouldn't be doing this. It wasn't what they'd agreed. She was his pretend girlfriend, not his real one. He was her boss. It could have major repercussions and she could end up in another financial mess. They really ought to stop this right now and remember who and where they were. She opened her mouth, intending to say that they shouldn't.

Then again, this wasn't real. And she knew neither of them was looking for for ever. Kirk had wiped out her trust in relationships, and from the little Hugh had said about his ex she was pretty sure that he felt the same way. He wasn't looking for The One, any more than she was.

They were both adults.

There was no reason why they shouldn't act on the attraction between them, just for one night.

So instead, she said softly, 'Tonight's just tonight. A one-off.'

His eyes looked almost navy blue in the soft light. 'No strings.'

'No promises.' She didn't believe in promises any more. 'No for ever.'

'No promises and no for ever,' he echoed.

'Then do it,' she said softly.

He kissed her once. Hard. And then he scooped her up into his arms, pausing only to switch off the fairy lights, and carried her down the corridor and up a quiet flight of stairs to her bedroom.

CHAPTER SIX

THE NEXT MORNING, Bella woke to find a warm body curled round hers. For a moment, she couldn't place where she was and why on earth a naked male body would be in her bed at all, let alone wrapped round her.

Then she remembered.

Hugh.

She went hot as she thought about the previous night. The way he'd kissed her in the orangery among the fairy lights until she'd been dizzy. The way he'd actually carried her up to her bed. The way he'd undressed her, and then made love to her until she'd seen stars.

Right now, the way he was holding her made her feel special. Even though she wasn't really Hugh's girlfriend, and they weren't in any kind of relationship other than that of employee and boss—just for a moment, Bella could imagine what it would be like if this was the real deal instead of an elaborate fiction. She'd spent the last six months feeling stupid and useless and pathetic, after Kirk's betrayal. Last night, Hugh had made her feel good again. Not just the sex, either. He'd danced with her, laughed with her—*believed* in her.

Would last night have changed everything between them? They'd agreed that this was a one-off. No strings.

No promises. No for ever. But could they still work together after this? Or would she have to resign?

They'd have to talk—*really* talk—and maybe redraw the ground rules.

Nothing fazes a Faraday girl, she reminded herself.

Except the mantra felt hollow.

Right now, she really didn't know what to do. Did she stay where she was and wait for him to wake up? Or did she creep out of bed and get dressed—or would that make facing him even more awkward?

Hugh woke to find himself curled round a warm female body.

Bella.

He remembered the previous night in full Technicolor, and panic slid down his spine. Why had he been so stupid?

It was a physical thing, that was all, he told himself. It was obvious why it had happened. He hadn't satisfied any physical urges for a while. Maybe it'd been the same for her. They'd both drunk too much champagne, they'd danced together, they found each other attractive, and they'd just given in to the temptation.

He sighed inwardly. Just who was he trying to kid?

If he was honest with himself, he'd been attracted to Bella since the first moment he'd met her. Her bright blue eyes, her bubbly personality, the way she opened her mouth and just said what was in her head without thinking it through. Not to mention the way she'd been there for her sister; Bella Faraday had a good heart. He really liked that about her.

But he still shouldn't have let things go this far between them. They were going to have to talk, *really* talk, and redraw the ground rules. Because Bella was a great designer, perfect for Insurgo, and Tarquin would have his guts for garters if she left the company just because Hugh hadn't been able to keep his hands—or anything else, for that matter—to himself.

He lay there, trying to think what to say. Even though they'd both agreed that last night was a one-off, would she feel differently this morning? And, if she did, how was he going to handle it?

He knew that Bella wasn't like Jessie. But he just didn't trust his own judgement any more. He didn't want to take the risk of getting involved with anyone, so it was easier not to start something that was likely to end up in a mess.

Eventually he became aware that Bella's breathing was no longer deep and even, and her body was slightly tense. Clearly she was awake.

Was she, too, remembering what had happened?

Did she, too, think about turning round and kissing him hello, the way he wanted to kiss her right now?

Or was she full of regrets and awkwardness and embarrassment?

Right now, he didn't have a clue. But he knew he was going to have to do the right thing rather than ignoring the rest of the world and making love with her all over again. They had to talk.

'Bella?' he whispered.

'Uh-huh.' She sounded worried.

He resisted the urge to kiss her bare shoulder. No matter how much he wanted to touch her, taste her, he had to keep himself in check. Carefully, he withdrew his arms from round her. Odd how cold it made him feel. 'I think we need to talk.'

'Uh-huh,' she said again, and turned to face him. 'OK. I'll say it first. I know we agreed that last night was a one-off, but it really shouldn't have happened at all.'

Relief coursed through him. If she knew it, too, then it meant that things weren't going to be awkward between them. They could still work together. He wouldn't have to find another designer.

He tried to ignore the fact that another emotion underpinned the relief. It was ridiculous to feel disappointed, especially as he didn't want to risk starting another relationship. He knew he was better off on his own, concentrating on his business.

'Last night was last night,' he said.

'Exactly. You know the Vegas principle?'

'The Vegas principle?' he asked, not quite following her train of thought.

'You know—what happens in Vegas, stays in Vegas,' she explained.

'Ah. Yes.'

'I think we should apply that to last night,' she said carefully.

He agreed. Completely. 'So you're not going to resign because I couldn't keep my hands to myself?' he asked.

'And you're not going to sack me because I didn't stick to our plan?'

Clearly she didn't want to leave her job, either. Which was a very, very good thing. 'Apart from the fact that I don't have any grounds to sack you, you're good at your job. Tarquin would kill me if I made you leave.'

Was it his imagination, or was there a flash of disappointment in her eyes?

He wasn't going to analyse that too closely. Much better to let each other off the hook instead than to get tied up with all the complications. And he definitely shouldn't tell her that he didn't want her to leave because he liked having her around. That'd be way too much pressure on both of them.

'What happened last night—we don't talk about it ever again. And it's not going to be repeated,' she said.

'Agreed,' he said.

She took a deep breath. 'So we stick to the plan from here on, and I'm back to playing Miss Ditzy this morning.'

'Uh-huh.' Even though he knew she wasn't very good at it. Yesterday, although she'd tried, her true self had just shone through the play-acting. And his family had responded in kind: warmth generating warmth.

If only he'd met her years ago. When he was still able to trust. But there was no point in wishing for something he couldn't have.

'What's the agenda for today?' she asked. 'You promised me a guided tour of the house.'

And he'd make very sure that the orangery wasn't part of that. Because then he'd remember how it had been last night and he'd want to kiss her again. It would be very stupid to put himself back in the path of temptation. 'Of course,' he said, 'and everyone's going for a walk between breakfast and lunch.'

'I have a really unsuitable outfit for that,' she said. 'Totally impractical spike-heeled mules that I can totter about in.'

'They sound perfect.' He paused. 'I guess we ought to, um, get up and face everyone downstairs for breakfast. I'll, um, go next door and have a shower.' Even though part of him would much prefer staying here and having a shower with her.

'Uh-huh.'

Was she relieved or disappointed that he was going? He hadn't a clue. And he wasn't going to ask. 'I'll knock for you when I'm ready, shall I?'

This time she definitely looked relieved. He winced inwardly. Did she really think that he'd leave her to find her own way through the house, and then face his family on her own? Or maybe that was the way her ex had treated her. Again, he couldn't really ask. Not without maybe ripping open some scars, and he didn't want to hurt her.

'See you in a bit, then,' she said. And then she closed her eyes.

Was she feeling shy? Or was she trying to spare his blushes?

He climbed out of bed, pulled on his boxer shorts, grabbed the rest of his clothes—and then made the mistake of glancing back at the bed. She looked so cute, lying there. Warm and sweet. He almost dropped his clothes back on the floor and climbed back in beside her again. Especially as he remembered last night so clearly. Touching her. Tasting her. The look of sheer pleasure in her eyes just before she'd fallen apart. The soft little cry she'd made when she'd climaxed in his arms.

No, no and absolutely no.

Common sense won—just—and he managed to get back to his own room without bumping into anyone in the corridor.

Showering helped to restore a little more of his common sense, once he'd turned the temperature of the water right down. Once he'd dressed, he stripped the bed, threw everything into his case, and knocked on Bella's door.

'Come in,' she called.

She was just closing the lid of her suitcase, and she was wearing a strappy top and the shortest pair of denim cut-offs he'd ever seen. Her legs went on for ever. And his tongue felt as if it was glued to the roof of his mouth.

It grew even worse when she gave a little wiggle. Her bottom had the most perfect curve, and it made him want to touch her again.

'Is this ditzy enough?' she asked with a grin, seemingly oblivious to the desire coursing through him.

'Uh—yeah.' And now he sounded like a total troglodyte. He didn't want her to guess the effect she had on him, particularly as he knew she wasn't doing it deliberately. Bella wasn't a game-player. 'I need some coffee,' he gabbled wildly. 'You know I'm not a morning person.'

'Coffee sounds good. Would you mind, um, showing me where I can make some?'

'There's probably already a pot on the go downstairs.'

Though now they had to face his family at the breakfast table. Please don't let any of them start asking questions about where he and Bella had disappeared to last night, he begged silently.

When he ushered Bella into the kitchen, his brothers and their partners were all sitting there, along with Sophia in her high chair; his mother was bustling around and his father was deep in the Sunday newspapers. He narrowed his eyes at them all in warning that they were absolutely not to say a single word, and to his relief they actually went along with him, saying nothing more awkward to her than a cheerful, 'Good morning.'

Without another word, he pulled out a chair at the table for Bella, then sat down next to her.

'Would you like tea or coffee?' Libby asked, coming over to them.

'Coffee, please,' Bella said. 'Can I do anything to help?'

'No, sweetie, it's fine. Bacon sandwich? I'm just about to do another batch.'

'Yes, please.' Bella smiled. 'Bacon and sandwich have to be the two most perfect words for a Sunday morning.'

'And coffee,' Nigel added with a smile. 'Don't forget coffee. Especially where Hugh's concerned.'

'I reckon it'll be another twenty minutes before we get a civil word out of our Hugh,' Julian teased.

'And the rest! He only ever grunts before midday,' Alastair added. 'Even *with* coffee.'

'Now, now, children,' Libby said, mock-warning.

Bella was really enjoying the byplay between Hugh and his brothers. She missed chatting in the kitchen with her mum and her sister on Sunday morning, when her dad would be deep in the Sunday papers in the living room and they would talk about anything and everything—from films to books to seriously girly stuff that would make her dad squirm.

Then her smile faded. If any of her family knew what had happened last night… Well. Nobody would be surprised. If there was a way to mess things up, Bella would be the one to find it. But she and Hugh had agreed that they'd act as if last night hadn't happened.

She just hoped that he meant it.

The kitchen was amazing, a huge room with cream cupboards and tiled floors, with an Aga and an island workstation as well as the breakfast area with the massive table looking out onto the garden. There were comfortable-looking dog beds next to the Aga, but Bella had already worked out that the Labrador, the Westie and the spaniel were all sitting under the table, waiting patiently for treats to be sneaked down to them. 'Your kitchen's really lovely, Libby,' she said.

'Thank you,' Libby replied, putting a plate of bacon sandwiches onto the table. 'Has Hugh shown you the rest of the house yet?'

Only the orangery. And Bella had to fight to prevent the blush that threatened to betray her. 'Not yet,' she said.

'I promised I'd do that before we go out for our walk,' Hugh drawled.

'Make sure you do,' Libby said.

Bella noticed that little Sophia was fussing in her high chair; both Poppy and Julian looked exhausted, and she guessed that Sophia had slept badly during the night, meaning that so had her parents. 'Can I give her a cuddle?' Bella asked.

Poppy looked torn between wariness and gratitude.

'One of my friends does music classes for babies and toddlers,' Bella said. 'So I know a few things that might help distract her—then you might be able to have your breakfast in peace.'

'You haven't had your own breakfast yet,' Poppy said.

'I'll be fine.' Bella shrugged and smiled. 'So can I?'

Poppy smiled back at her. 'Thank you.'

Bella didn't quite dare look at Hugh as she scooped Sophia out of the high chair and then settled the baby on her lap. But Sophia clearly enjoyed being bounced to 'Humpty Dumpty' and 'Row, Row, Row Your Boat' and the other nursery songs Bella could remember, and she was gurgling with delight when Julian picked her up from Bella's lap again.

'Eat your bacon sandwich before it gets cold,' he said, patting her shoulder. 'And thank you for cheering up Miss Grumpy here.'

'Any time,' Bella said with a smile.

'Can I help with the washing up?' Bella asked when she'd finished her sandwich.

Libby shook her head. 'No, sweetie. Thank you for the offer, but it's fine.'

'The kitchen is Ma's domain,' Nigel explained.

'My mum's the same, except we all pitch in and help when we have family over for lunch, because it's really not fair to make someone peel all the veg on their own,' Bella said.

'Well, if you really want to, you can help me with the veg,' Libby conceded. 'But let Hugh show you round first.'

'Hint taken,' Hugh said and stood up. 'Come on, Bella.'

She took his hand and let him lead her out of the kitchen.

He dropped her hand again, the minute they were out of sight. 'Guided tour,' he said, and proceeded to whisk her through the house. The house was glorious, with mullioned windows upstairs and floor-to-ceiling windows downstairs.

'Hugh,' she said when he'd taken her swiftly through the library, not even letting her browse a single shelf in the acres of shelving.

'What?'

'What did I do wrong?' she asked.

'Nothing.' But his voice was clipped.

She sighed. 'Was it because I cuddled the baby? I *like* babies, Hugh. And I like your family.'

'You're meant to be unsuitable,' he reminded her.

'Even unsuitable girlfriends can like babies.'

'Hmm,' he said. 'Drawing room.' There were comfortable chairs and amazing artwork on the walls, and a den with a state of the art television and music system.

'Dining room.'

She'd already seen this the previous day, and the ballroom—though it was much less intimidating now it was empty. She was almost tempted to ask him to play something for her on the piano, something soft and gentle for a Sunday morning, but there was an odd expression on his face and she didn't quite dare.

So much for the Vegas principle. He was clearly finding it hard to ignore what had happened between them.

And that was probably why he didn't show her the orangery in daylight. It would've been too much of a reminder of how reckless they'd been.

'Do you want your family to think we've had a fight?' she asked when he'd finished the tour and was leading her back to the kitchen.

'Fight? Oh.' The penny clearly dropped, and he took her hand again.

Except it felt grudging.

Considering that *he'd* been the one to come up with the idea of the unsuitable girlfriend in the first place, Bella wanted to shake him by the scruff of his neck. 'You have to be the most difficult man in the universe,' she muttered.

He didn't disagree with her. And she had the nasty feeling that she was going to be looking for another job, pretty soon. She just hoped that Tarquin would give her a decent reference—she certainly wasn't going to ask Hugh. And she wasn't telling Grace about any of this. So much for standing on her own two feet and getting her life in shape. She'd just messed up again. Big time.

In the kitchen, everyone was still drinking coffee.

Libby looked at her shoes. 'You need to borrow some wellingtons, Bella, or you'll risk ruining those lovely shoes.'

'I guess they're probably not that suitable for a walk in the garden,' she said, playing Miss Ditzy—though her heart really wasn't in this any more.

'Hugh will find you something in the boot room,' Oliver said.

She blinked. 'You have a room just for *boots*?' Hugh hadn't shown her that.

'It's for boots, coats and muddy dogs to dry off in,' Hugh explained.

The boot room turned out to be just off the kitchen. The room had a stone chequered floor that reminded Bella a bit of the orangery, teamed with white tongue and groove panelling on the cabinets. There were shelves of wellington boots, pegs for coats, and a couple of wicker picnic baskets on shelves; there were also a washing machine and tumble dryer, and she guessed that there would be an iron and ironing board in one of the cupboards.

Hugh checked her shoe size and came up with a pair of green wellington boots and an ancient waxed jacket that was too big for her. 'You'll need socks,' he said, and rummaged in one of the wicker baskets for an old but clean pair of what looked like rugby socks.

And at least borrowing a jacket meant she had pockets to shove her hands into and she wouldn't have the temptation of being hand-in-hand with Hugh—or the awkwardness if she tried to hold his hand and he rejected her, which she thought would be the most likely outcome.

Hugh's brothers and their partners all joined them on the walk, along with Sophia in her pushchair, and the dogs romped along happily beside them.

'So we're going for a walk in the nearby woods or something?' she asked.

Hugh nodded. 'They're part of the estate.'

Well, of course a huge manor house like this would come with an estate rather than just a garden. How stupid of her not to think of that before.

But her awkwardness turned to delight when they walked through the narrow paths in the woods and she could see bluebells everywhere. 'That's gorgeous!'

'It's still a bit early for them yet,' Hugh said, 'but they're like a blue haze when they're fully out.'

'A real bluebell carpet—how lovely,' she said. It made her itch to sit out here with a pad of cartridge paper and a box of watercolours. 'I love the colour of new leaves, that really bright lime-green that means spring's really here.'

'Yeah.'

Somehow, Hugh was holding her hand again, and it sent a shiver of pure desire through her.

He met her gaze. 'I'm not coming on to you,' he said in a low voice. 'Everyone will expect me to hold my girlfriend's hand.'

'Of course,' she said, but she had to swallow her disappointment. Which was ridiculous in any case. She didn't want a relationship and she didn't want to mess up her job. Hugh was off limits and this was simply a bit of play-acting for his family's benefit. They'd agreed. And the fact that he was holding her hand simply meant that the bluebells had just got rid of his Monday morning-itis, which was actually more like *every* morning-itis.

Back at the house, the others all disappeared to sort out various things, and Hugh's father called him to come and help with something. Feeling a bit like a spare part,

Bella went in search of Libby in the kitchen. 'I promised to help you with the vegetables.'

'You really don't have to,' Libby said. 'You're a guest.'

'Even so,' Bella said. 'Is that beef I smell roasting?'

'Yes.'

'I could make the Yorkshire puddings, if you like.' She laughed. 'I admit I'm a terrible cook, but I'm actually quite good at cupcakes, pancakes and Yorkshire puddings. I guess it's because they're light and fluffy, like me.'

Libby gave her look as if to say that she knew there was much more to Bella than that, or Hugh wouldn't be dating her. 'You're playing a part, this weekend, aren't you?'

Uh-oh. She hadn't expected Libby to call her on it. 'A part?' Bella asked, trying not to panic. 'What makes you say that?'

'Because the real you keeps shining through. The way you brought me my favourite chocolates, the way you looked after Lavinia yesterday afternoon, the way you drew those pictures for everyone, the way you haven't minded a muddy dog draped all over you, the way you sat and cuddled Sophia this morning during breakfast and sang nursery songs to her.' Libby ticked them off on her fingers. 'If you were the dreadful airhead that you and Hugh clearly want us all to think you are, I'm not so sure you would've done any of that.'

There was no way she could keep up the pretence any more. 'Busted, I guess. But please don't tell Hugh you know.'

'I won't,' Libby said softly. 'But what I don't understand is why you both feel that you have to play a part.'

'I did tell him Plan B would be better,' Bella said with a rueful smile.

Libby's frown deepened. 'What's Plan B?'

Bella held up both hands in a surrender gesture. 'Just ignore me. I'm rambling.'

'No, I think this is something I need to know,' Libby said.

Bella bit her lip. 'Please, please don't shoot the messenger, because you've all been so kind and I don't want to be rude and ungrateful. Even though I've already been rude and obnoxious.'

'Now you're really worrying me,' Libby said. 'What's plan B?'

'To tell you the truth about his job and make you see how he feels. Hugh isn't a stockbroker at heart,' Bella said, 'he's a music producer. He loves his job and he's really, really good at it. I really don't mean to be rude or to offend you, but he seems to believe that you all want him to toe the line—to sell Insurgo Records to the highest bidder and join the family firm instead. If he does that, you're going to break his heart and his spirit. He'd hate it so much and he'd spend all his time wishing he was somewhere else. And then he might grow to resent you all instead of loving you like he does now.'

Libby was silent for so long that Bella thought she'd gone too far.

'Mrs Moncrieff? Libby?' she asked anxiously.

Libby's eyes were glistening with tears. 'Those were very wise words,' she said softly. 'And they came from the heart.'

Hugh was halfway down the corridor to the kitchen when he heard his mother ask, 'So are you his real girlfriend pretending to be his fake girlfriend?'

What?

Oh, no. He knew his mother was perceptive. He needed to go in and head her off. Or had Bella already caved in and told her the truth?

To his horror, he heard Bella say, 'That all sounds so complicated. But I was telling you the truth when I said I'm the designer at Insurgo.'

Oh, hell. She *had* caved in. She'd blown their cover completely. And he was shocked by how hurt and disappointed he was. He'd been telling himself that Bella wasn't like Jessie—and yet she'd let him down, too. She'd promised to play a part and she'd gone back on her word. Betrayed his trust. Ratted him out to his mother, so his subterfuge was well and truly uncovered. So much for thinking that she was different. Obviously his judgement was still way off.

'That,' Libby said, 'figures.'

'What does?' Bella asked.

Hugh went cold. Please don't let his mother start talking about Jessie. He only realised he was holding his breath when Libby said, 'If he hasn't told you, I won't break his confidence.'

'That's not very fair, given that I've just done that,' Bella said.

She'd even admitted what she'd done. And it made him feel sick. How far had she gone?

He strode into the kitchen. 'Breaking my confidence?' he asked.

Bella went white. 'Hugh. I didn't know you were there.'

'Obviously.' He shook his head in disgust. 'Well, thanks a bunch. I guess that'll teach me to trust you. So do you blab Insurgo's business all over social media, too, the same way you've just blabbed my personal business to my mother?'

'Hugh, that's not fair,' Libby said. 'She was trying to help.'

'She was gossiping about me.' And that hurt.

'I wasn't gossiping at all,' Bella said. 'Right now, I want to tip this Yorkshire pudding batter all over your stupid head. But I'm not going to waste food and put your mum in an awkward position. Instead I'm going to walk outside in the garden, in this stupid outfit I found to fit your even more stupid idea. And *you*,' she said, walking over to him and stabbing her finger into his chest, 'are going to sit down with your mum and talk. Really talk.'

He was too taken aback to say anything. Not that he could've got a word in edgeways, because Bella was on a roll.

'You're going to tell her how you feel about your business and how it's not just your job, it's your passion, and for you it's like breathing. And you're going to tell her that you're great at business and you don't take unnecessary risks—that you save being a total idiot for the other bits of your life. You three,' she added to the dogs, 'you're coming with me and we're going to find some tennis balls, and I'm going to pretend they're Hugh's head and kick them as hard as I can.'

'Bella—' he began, knowing that he needed to apologise.

'No. Talk to your mum,' she said. 'Right now, I don't want to talk to you. I'm going out with the dogs.'

'Take whatever you need from the boot room, love,' Libby said. 'And I'll shout at him for you.'

Bella shook her head. 'I'd much rather you listened to him,' she said softly. 'Even though right at this moment I don't like him very much, I respect him when it comes to business—and I think you both need to listen to each other.' And she walked quietly out of the kitchen, followed by the dogs.

Hugh found himself talking—*really* talking—to his mother about the most important thing in his life. And she listened. Understood. Just as he could now see that the worrying and fussing were driven by love rather than a need to make him toe a family line that didn't actually exist.

Without Bella's intervention, this would never have happened, and he knew it.

When he'd finished, Libby said, 'You owe that girl—'

'—a huge apology,' he cut in. 'I know.'

She hugged him. 'You're my youngest son, Hugh, and I love you, but I don't like you very much today.'

'I don't like myself very much, either,' he admitted.

'She isn't Jessie,' Libby said softly.

'I know.' Jessie would never have offered to help prepare the vegetables. Yes, musicians had to look after their hands, because an accidental cut or burn would affect their ability to play an instrument—but Jessie wouldn't have offered to do something that didn't risk her hands, either. She wouldn't have played with Sophia. He knew that his family hadn't taken to her—they'd been polite but reserved. But everyone had instantly warmed to Bella, from his great-aunt to his brothers and even his father. 'I need to go and talk to her.'

'Be nice,' Libby said softly. 'She's got a good heart. She didn't break your trust. She found a better way to deal with things than any of us did.'

Hugh hugged his mother back. 'I know.' And he'd messed this up. Big time.

He went outside to find Bella. She looked as if she'd

been crying, and he felt a total heel. How could he have been so unkind to her?

'Bella. I'm sorry,' he said.

'Hmm.' She didn't look in the slightest bit mollified by his apology.

'You were right and I was wrong.'

She folded her arms. 'That's rather stating the obvious.'

'And I'm sorry I was obnoxious to you. I shouldn't have said any of that.'

'Also stating the obvious,' she said.

'I can't even blame it on Monday morning-itis.' He sighed. 'How do I make it up to you?'

'You've made it clear that you don't trust me. So, actually, I don't think you can,' she said.

He blew out a breath. 'I don't have a clue what to say or what to do. Only that I'm sorry for hurting you. And, without you, I don't think my family would ever have understood what Insurgo means to me. And I wouldn't have understood how they really feel, either. I appreciate that.'

She shrugged. 'Even so, I'm not your personal punchbag. Hugh, I don't enjoy people lashing out at me. I was only playing Miss Ditzy because you asked me to. I'm not an actress. Your mum saw right through the whole thing. And I did tell you it was a stupid idea.'

'You were right,' he said again. 'I know you probably want to be a million miles away from here right now, so if you want me to drive you straight home, then I'll do it. But I think my family would like you to stay for lunch. They like you. And I mean they like the *real* Bella Faraday,' he clarified. 'The one who looks out for elderly aunts, cuddles babies, plays ball with the dogs, is an amazing artist and brings out the best in everyone. The woman who really is the life and soul of the party—because I've never seen my entire family get up on the dance floor before you came along.'

Her eyes sparkled with tears; he brushed away the single one that spilled over her lashes.

'They don't hate me for lying to them?' she whispered.

'No. They really, really like you.' And so did he. Though now wasn't the time to say so. After the way he'd hurt her, she wouldn't believe him—and he couldn't blame her.

'Come and have lunch,' he said.

'For your mum's sake. Not yours.'

'I know,' he said softly. 'And thank you.'

Although Bella didn't say much to him once they were back in the house, she sparkled all the way through Sunday lunch. She insisted on helping to clear things away and on cuddling Sophia again when his niece had another fit of the grumps. And when his family said goodbye to her, it was with a warm, heartfelt hug rather than the formal handshakes they'd always given Jessie.

'Come back soon,' Libby said. 'And I mean *really* soon. You have to see the bluebells when they're at their best.'

'I'd love to,' Bella said, hugging her back. 'Thank you so much for having me.'

His brothers and their partners all got hugs, too, along with the baby. And so did his father, who then shocked Hugh immensely by saying, 'Come and paint the bluebells for my study, and I'll cook you my famous chicken biryani.'

Since when had his father ever cooked? Let alone something as exotic as biryani?

Hugh was so stunned that he didn't say a word until they were halfway home. And then it was only because Bella was the one to start the conversation.

'I think we need to talk,' she said carefully.

'Talk?'

She took a deep breath. 'I'm sorry I messed up your plans. If you want me to resign and go quietly from Insurgo, I'll accept that and write you an official resignation letter as soon as we're back in London.'

'No, that's not fair.' And he didn't want her to leave.

'You asked me to play your unsuitable girlfriend, and I didn't do it right.'

'I also told you to be yourself,' he said. 'And you were. Though I don't get how you do it.'

'How I do what?' she asked, sounding confused.

'Fit in so effortlessly. When you joined Insurgo, within a couple of days it was as if you'd been one of the team right from the start. And my family. They took to you like they never did to—' He stopped abruptly.

'Never did to whom?' she asked softly.

'Never mind.'

'The girl who broke your heart? The one you worked with?'

He gave her a sidelong glance. 'Fishing, Bella?'

'No—but I can hardly ask you straight out about it, can I? You're not exactly approachable.'

'My past isn't any of your—' he began, then stopped, knowing that he was being completely unfair to her. 'Sorry. That was rude and unkind. Especially as you've just given up your whole weekend to do me a favour, and I've already treated you badly. I apologise unreservedly. And you have the right to stamp all over me in spike heels.'

'Spike heels?'

'Your "three strikes and you're out" rule. I've broken that several times.'

'That's bravado,' Bella said, sounding sad. 'I don't really stomp on people.' And he felt even guiltier when she added, 'Besides, you're right. Your past isn't any of my business.' She sighed. 'Did you hear everything I said to your mum?'

'Only from when she asked you if you were my real girlfriend pretending to be my pretend girlfriend.' He gave her another swift look. Guilt was written all over her face. 'Is there more I should know about?'

'I told her that you're Insurgo's heart—and joining the family firm would break your spirit and make you resent them instead of loving them and being exasperated by them as you do now.'

If Hugh hadn't been driving, he would've closed his eyes in horror. 'We never talk about that sort of stuff.'

'I think you might do, in future,' Bella said softly. 'But, as I said earlier, I understand if you want me to resign.'

'Right now,' Hugh said, 'I think the best thing would be if neither of us said another word until we get back to London.'

'OK,' Bella said, and lapsed into silence.

Which made Hugh feel even more mean and guilty. He knew she'd said everything with the best of intentions. But his head was in a whirl. Bella Faraday knocked him seriously off balance, and he didn't trust himself to say what he really meant. He wasn't even sure what he really felt, other than being completely mixed up, so it was better to say nothing.

It didn't help that he could still smell her perfume, and

that made him remember kissing her in the orangery last night. That kiss—and what had happened afterwards—was something he really couldn't dare to repeat. So it was better to put a little bit of metaphorical distance between them. Wasn't it?

Finally he pulled up in the road outside her flat. 'I'll see you to your door.'

'There's no need,' Bella said. 'Thank you for the lift. And I won't ask you in. Not because I'm being rude, but because I'm sure you're busy. And, tomorrow morning, when we're back in the office, this weekend never happened.'

'Agreed,' he said.

Even though he didn't see her to the door, Hugh waited until she'd closed her front door behind her before he drove away. That was the very least he could do. And as for the damage to their working relationship… He'd better hope that he could fix it. Because the only way he could keep Bella in his life was as a colleague—and he didn't want to lose her.

What a weekend, Bella thought as she closed the front door behind her.

She changed swiftly into a more comfortable—not to mention demure—pair of jeans and a normal T-shirt, and bustled about sorting out things in her flat. There was a message on her phone from Grace.

Give me a ring when you're back and let me know how it went xxx

Yeah, right. Bella rolled her eyes. She could hardly admit to her sister what she'd done: slept with her boss, gone completely off brief, interfered and told his mother the truth, and then had a huge row with Hugh. Even though he'd apologised, she still hated the fact that he thought he couldn't trust her. Maybe his ex had broken his ability to trust, the way Kirk had broken hers; but it still hurt that he could think of her in that way. Did he not know her at all?

So she left it until late in the evening to text a reply to Grace: Just got back. That was stretching a point, but it was only a tiny fib. Too late to call. That bit was true. All fine. That bit might not be true. But she hoped that Grace wouldn't push her for more details—and that things would be OK in the office tomorrow. That she and Hugh could pretend that nothing had ever happened. Because, otherwise, she'd be looking for another job.

And, if she left Insurgo, it wasn't just the job she'd miss.

CHAPTER SEVEN

On Monday morning, Bella was slightly nervous as she walked in to the Insurgo offices. She bought a double-shot cappuccino from the café downstairs to give her courage. Would Hugh be the same with her as he usually was, or would he avoid her? Would he be more difficult than he usually was on Monday mornings?

But he wasn't in the office. He'd left Tarquin a message to say that he was in a meeting across town and probably wouldn't make it in to the office until very late that day, if at all. Bella wasn't sure if she was more relieved at not having to face him or disappointed at missing him; though she knew that she couldn't let anyone guess how she was feeling. Nobody knew she'd been in Oxfordshire with Hugh, and it had to stay that way. As far as everyone at the Insurgo offices was concerned, he was the boss and she was simply the graphic designer. Full stop.

By Wednesday, Hugh knew that he had to show his face in the office or Tarquin would start working things out for himself. But he wasn't sure if he could do what Bella had suggested and work on the Vegas principle.

On paper, it was easy. What had happened in Oxfordshire should stay in Oxfordshire.

The problem was, he could still remember what it felt like to wake up wrapped round her. And, worse still, he wanted to do it again.

But he couldn't see a way of making this work. He already knew that from his experience with Jessie. Even though Bella wasn't anything like Jessie, the equation was the same: business plus relationship equals disaster.

So either he dated her and she left the company—which wouldn't be good for Insurgo, because she was a great designer—or she stayed in her job and he'd have to keep a lid on his feelings. It made business sense for it to be the latter. Plus he was used to keeping a lid on his feelings.

But that had been before Bella Faraday exploded into his life. Before he'd taken her home as his 'unsuitable' girlfriend. Before she'd turned his world upside down.

Bella was aware of every time Hugh walked into the room, even when her back was to the door.

She looked up several times from her work when he was in the main office, talking to Tarquin, and caught his eye. He looked away again almost immediately. And, because Hugh was so good at being impassive, she didn't have a clue what he was thinking.

Was he thinking about what had happened between them? Did he feel the same pull, the same awareness, as she did? Or was he regretting every single moment?

She was half tempted to text him and suggest that they talked. But that would be needy and pathetic, and that wasn't who she was. She'd got through Kirk's betrayal, and this situation with Hugh wasn't anywhere near that on the scale of awfulness.

Things would all settle down, soon enough. She

would get to the stage where she could look at Hugh without remembering how it had felt when he'd touched her and kissed her. Where she could look at him without wanting him to kiss her again. It would just take a bit of time, that was all. Until then, she'd just have to keep a lid on her feelings. This wasn't appropriate, and she wasn't in a position where she dared do anything to jeopardise her job.

Hugh sat in front of his computer with his elbows resting on the desk and his chin propped in his hands. This was ridiculous. He never, ever let anything distract his focus from his work.

But he couldn't stop thinking about Bella.

Maybe he should call her. Text her. Tell her he'd like to change his mind about the Vegas principle and see her now they were back in London. Ask her out to dinner or to a show.

But then things would start to get complicated in the office, and he didn't want that. He knew that keeping his distance from her was the sensible thing to do.

All the same, he was antsy. He couldn't settle to anything. And he knew it was making him snappy with everyone.

On the Thursday, he was glad that one of his artists was in the studio in the basement, recording an album. It gave him an excuse to stay out of the office and focus on producing the music—the part of his job he loved most. That would keep his head too busy to let him think about Bella Faraday.

And he actually managed it...until lunchtime, when Tarquin brought Bella down to meet the band and talk about the cover art concept.

She'd changed her hair colour again, Hugh noticed. Today she was brunette. It was a huge change from the almost fire-engine-red she'd sported in Oxfordshire, but it suited her and it brought out the depths of her eyes. It made her look seriously pretty.

How he wanted to twirl the ends of her hair round his fingers. Feel how soft and silky it was. And then touch his mouth to hers…

What made it worse was that she was dressed in faded jeans which hugged her curves, and spike-heeled ankle boots. She'd teamed it with a black T-shirt with the Insurgo logo on the front, clearly going for the rock chick look. And she carried it off beautifully.

He wasn't surprised that she charmed the band as quickly as she'd charmed his family. Just by being herself: bright, vivacious Bella with her ready laugh, and the way she touched people's hands or arms or shoulders when she spoke. She was very tactile; and yet she didn't make you feel as if she'd invaded your personal space. It felt natural. Easy.

Hugh caught her eye. Was it his imagination, or was there the faintest blush in her cheeks as she looked at him? Probably his imagination, he decided, because she was totally professional and almost cool with him. Clearly she didn't have a problem with the Vegas principle.

They discussed the album concept and cover with the band, and Bella made a few sketches and notes. Hugh could barely take his eyes off her hands. He remembered how they'd felt against his skin, and it made him ache.

When would he stop wanting her?

Tarquin had also organised a buffet lunch for all of them, sent down by the café on the ground floor. Being together in a more social setting would be awkward, Hugh thought, but no way could he or Bella get out of this. He hadn't said a word to Tarquin about the situation and he was pretty sure that she hadn't said anything, either, or his business partner would've had quite a lot to say about it.

Well, they'd just have to roll with it and pretend that everything was normal. Even though it wasn't.

He noticed that Jet, the band's lead singer, was flirting with Bella during lunch. She wasn't encouraging him at all; she was professional and polite and made sure that she included the rest of the band in the conversation. Hugh couldn't fault her behaviour. But he really wanted to snarl at Jet and tell him to back off, because Bella wasn't available. Which would put her in an impossible situation, so he kept his tongue firmly under control.

But then he reached for the plate of sandwiches at the same time as Bella did. As his fingers brushed against hers, he felt the heat zing through him. And when his gaze caught hers, her pupils went just that little bit darker and wider. So was it the same for her, too? This crazy, raging need that sent him into a flat spin?

And just what were they going to do about this?

The more time Hugh spent with her, the more he wanted her—and this wasn't fair to either of them. But right at that moment he couldn't see a way of making things better. Not without complicating things or risking things getting a whole lot worse.

To his relief, after lunch Bella made an excuse to go back up to the office with Tarquin, which left him to concentrate on the music and the band and working on the arrangements.

Jet turned to him at the end of the next song. 'I was going to ask you—could you give me Bella's number?'

'To discuss the album cover?' Hugh asked, deliberately misunderstanding the other man. 'Just call the usual office number and someone will put you through to her.'

'No, I meant...'

'What?' Uh-oh. He really hoped that Jet hadn't picked up how short his tone was.

But the singer didn't seem fussed in the slightest. 'Dating her, man,' he said with a grin. 'I know you're dedicated to your work, Hugh, but surely even *you* have noticed how hot she is?'

Of course he'd noticed. More than noticed. 'She's my colleague,' he said crisply. 'I never mix business and relationships.'

Jet gave him a look as if to say, *more fool you*. 'So can you give me her number?'

'She might already be involved with someone.'

Jet held his gaze. 'And she might not.'

'I'll let her know you asked, and leave it up to her if she wants to call you,' Hugh said. And he seriously hoped she didn't. Even though he knew he was being a complete dog in the manger, given that he wasn't actually in a relationship with Bella. For all he knew, she might actually want to date Jet. But he'd be much happier if she didn't. 'Now, let's get back to work and go through the next song, shall we?'

Later that afternoon, when the band had left, Hugh walked back into the office. Bella was working at her desk, but he knew by the sudden tension in her shoulders that she knew he was there.

'Jet asked for your number,' he said abruptly.

Her head snapped up and she stared at him. 'Jet?'

'The lead singer of the band. You were talking to him at lunch.' And Jet had most definitely been flirting with her. Surely she'd been aware of that?

'Oh.'

'I told him to ring the office and someone would put him through, if he wants to discuss the album cover.'

'Uh-huh.'

He couldn't tell anything from her expression. Which left him with no choice; he'd have to raise the issue. 'Jet didn't want to discuss business.'

'Then what did he want?'

He gave her a speaking look. Wasn't it obvious? 'I told him that relationships and business don't mix.'

And now there was the tiniest, tiniest glint in her eyes. Amusement? Anger? Pity? He wasn't sure. There was no way he could ask without betraying himself, and until he knew what was going on in her head he didn't want her to know what he was feeling.

'Did you, now?' she drawled.

'I said I'd tell you he'd asked.'

'I might,' Bella said, 'already be committed to someone.'

'So you might,' he said. And he had to suppress the wish that it was him.

'I'll make sure he knows that,' she said.

So she wasn't going to date the guy? He was shocked by the way it made him feel as if a massive weight had been lifted from his shoulders. 'Thank you.' But he didn't want her to realise he was glad for selfish reasons. 'I like the office to run smoothly,' he added coolly.

'Noted, Mr Moncrieff.'

And then she did something that nearly finished

him off. She moistened her lower lip with the tip of her tongue, so her lips looked as shiny as if she'd just been kissed. *Just as she'd looked when he'd kissed her.*

'Right,' he said, and left for his own office. While he still could.

Back at his desk, he rested his elbows on the table and propped his face in his hands. When was he going to stop wanting this woman? When was his common sense going to come back? He knew it wouldn't work between them. It couldn't.

Yet he still wanted her.

By the end of the next week, Hugh was near to going insane. Throwing himself into work wasn't making any difference at all. And when he was at home he actually found himself sitting down with a guitar in his hand or at the piano, something he hadn't done in a long time. There were little snatches of songs buzzing round in his head—nothing he recognised, so he knew they were his own compositions. There were bits of melodies, bits of introductions, and bits of a middle eight. None of them fitted together and none of the melodies had proper words to go with them, but Hugh knew that he was starting to write songs again.

And that worried him even more.

It had taken him a year to get over the mess that Jessie's betrayal had caused. He didn't want to leave himself open to the risk of feeling that low ever, ever again—even though part of him was glad that the music he loved so much was bubbling up inside him again, and he knew it was all due to Bella.

But this was all too complicated.

He was just going to have to get over these growing

feelings for Bella and ignore them. And ignore the hints from his parents that the bluebells were starting to look really pretty and the dogs would love to go for a run with him. They might just as well have texted him in capitals to say WE WANT TO SEE BELLA.

Well, it wasn't happening.

What happened in Oxfordshire, stayed in Oxfordshire. They'd agreed it. Their relationship had been strictly business from that Sunday afternoon onwards.

So why couldn't Bella get Hugh out of her head? Why could she still feel the warmth of his body wrapped round her? Why, every time she closed her eyes, did she remember him kissing her among the fairy lights until they were both dizzy?

'Are you OK, Bella?' Tarquin asked.

'Fine.' She smiled at him. 'Just a bit of a headache.' A headache called Hugh Moncrieff. Not that she would ever admit that to anyone at Insurgo. Since they'd been back, Hugh's cool and professional behaviour towards her had made it clear that their relationship was strictly business. And she didn't want to cause tension in the office. Even so, she couldn't help asking, 'Tarq, have you known Hugh for very long?'

'We were at school together, so yes. Why?'

'I just wondered,' she said, 'why he has this thing about not mixing business and relationships.'

'Ah. That's not my story to tell, sweet-cheeks,' Tarquin said softly. 'Why? Are you…?'

Oh, no. He hadn't guessed how she felt about Hugh, had he? 'No, no, not at all,' she fibbed hastily. 'It's just something he said when Jet from the band asked for my number.'

'OK.'

But Tarquin looked curious, and Bella wished she hadn't said anything. 'Just being nosey,' she said sweetly. 'Obviously something's happened in the past that made things difficult for everyone in the office, so he doesn't want people to get involved with people they have to work with. I get it.'

'Something like that,' Tarquin said.

But he still looked oddly at her, and she knew she had to do something to distract him. 'I'm going to do a tea and coffee run. What do you want?' Even if that did mean going upstairs to the staff kitchen and being even closer to Hugh's office, it would hopefully distract Tarquin and he wouldn't start working things out or leaping to conclusions.

'I'd love a coffee, thank you, sweetie,' Tarquin said, and to her relief the sticky moment was over.

On Friday evening, Tarquin walked into Hugh's office and tapped the face of his watch with an exaggerated motion. 'Right, you. Time to turn the computer off.'

Hugh frowned. 'Not now, Tarq. I've got a couple of things to do.'

'They can wait. We're meeting Ro, or had you forgotten?'

Roland was their other best friend from school. And both Hugh and Tarquin had been worried about him for months; their regular fortnightly meeting was their way of keeping an eye on him, under the guise of rescuing Hugh from being a total workaholic. 'I'd forgotten what today was,' Hugh admitted. He glanced at the screen. 'OK. Let me save the file and shut the computer down, and we'll go.'

* * *

Roland walked into the bar at roughly the same time they did, and raised his hand to show he'd seen them.

But although Hugh had thought this was all about keeping an eye on Roland, he was in for a surprise when Tarquin turned to him after ordering two beers and a mineral water for Roland.

'All righty. You're being more of a nightmare than usual in the office, Hugh. I'm pretty sure it's got something to do with your brother's engagement party—and, as I haven't been able to get it out of you, Ro's going to do the thumbscrews.'

Roland spread his hands. 'That pretty much sums it up. So you can tell us now, or we can nag you until you tell us. Your choice, but I'd advise saving all the drag of us droning on at you and just telling us.'

Hugh raked a hand through his hair. 'Nothing's wrong.'

'Or,' Roland suggested, 'I could call your mother and tell her that Tarq and I are worried about you. She'll tell us what you're not saying.'

Which was what Hugh and Tarquin had done to Roland, the previous year, out of sheer desperation. It had worked, but they'd had an unspoken pact since then that calling any of their mothers was off limits.

'No. *Don't* call Ma. Please.' Hugh had been avoiding his mother's calls, too, returning her answering machine messages with a brief text to say he was up to his eyes at work and would call her soon. If his two best friends tag-teamed her and she told them the information he'd been keeping back, he wouldn't stand a chance. He put his hands up in a gesture of surrender. 'OK. I'll talk.' At least then maybe he could do some damage limitation.

Tarquin handed him a beer and gestured to one of the quieter tables in the corner.

They really weren't going to let him off this, were they? He suppressed a sigh and went to sit down.

'Tell us, sweet-cheeks,' Tarquin said. 'What happened at Nigel's party?'

Hugh blew out a breath. 'I thought I was being so clever. I took someone with me. A pretend girlfriend. Someone unsuitable. The idea was that they'd all be so horrified by her that they'd be glad when I told them it was all over—and then they'd back off.'

Tarquin and Roland exchanged a glance. 'But?' Tarquin asked.

Hugh grimaced. 'They saw through it. And they liked her. A lot.'

'Hmm. If you liked her enough to ask for her help, and she liked you enough to go along with it, and your family all liked her, then it sounds to me as if you're looking at this from completely the wrong direction,' Roland said. 'Why don't you just date the girl properly?'

'You know why,' Hugh said. 'After Jessie, there's no way I'm getting involved with anyone again. Nothing serious. I'm concentrating on the business. That's how I like my life.'

'Not all women are like Jessie,' Tarquin said. 'There's no reason why you can't try again with someone else.'

Hugh folded his arms. 'I *know* not all women are like Jessie. But I don't trust my own judgement any more. I was stupid enough to let her fool me, so what's to say I won't make the same mistake again?'

'Because you're too bright to do that,' Tarquin said. 'Think about it. You earned a first class degree.'

'Plus you own the hottest indie record label in the

country and the business is going from strength to strength,' Roland said.

It was now. Thanks to a lot of hard work—and Roland's investment. But Hugh knew just how much damage had been done to his business by letting his heart rule his head over Jessie.

'Tarq has a point,' Roland continued. 'It's been a while. Surely you're lonely?'

Yes. He was. And he wanted Bella. Hugh's temper flared. 'That's rich, coming from you.'

'That's a different kettle of fish altogether,' Roland said, his voice very quiet.

Hugh saw the emptiness in his best friend's eyes and flinched. 'Ro, I'm sorry—that was way, way below the belt. I apologise unreservedly. I shouldn't have said that.' Roland was single, but not from choice; his wife had died in a car crash eighteen months ago, and he was still mourning her. Some well-meaning friends had tried matchmaking over the last few months, but every attempt had failed spectacularly.

'Apology accepted.' But Roland's voice was completely neutral, and Hugh knew he'd overstepped the mark. Big time. Exactly the way he'd lashed out at Bella—and for exactly the same reason.

The only way he could think of to make amends was to tell the truth. Well, some of it. 'I *am* sorry, Ro. This whole thing makes me antsy, and I shouldn't have taken it out on you. I'm just as horrible at work, and...' He shrugged. 'I hate being like it. Everyone else hates it just as much. But I don't seem to be able to stop myself.'

Tarquin patted his arm. 'You're in Monday morning mode. We get it. Now spill.'

'I like her. A lot. And it scares me stupid,' he admitted. 'The way I feel about her is like nothing else I've ever known. Not even Jessie. I just can't get her out of my head.'

'Are you going to tell us anything about her?' Roland asked.

Hugh squirmed. How could he do this without giving away too much? 'She's bright, she's funny, and she makes me feel as if the world's full of sunshine.'

'Which sounds perfect. So why aren't you dating her officially?' Tarquin asked.

'It's complicated,' Hugh hedged.

'Complicated how?' Roland asked.

Hugh put his face in his hands. There was no way out of this, any more. He was going to have to bite the bullet. 'Because she works for Insurgo,' he muttered. '*Now* do you get why it's a problem?'

Tarquin groaned. 'No. Please. Not Bella. Tell me you didn't take Bella with you to Oxfordshire.'

'Who's Bella?' Roland asked, looking mystified. 'And why would it be so bad if Hugh was with her?'

'Bella's our new designer,' Tarquin explained. 'She's really good at her job, and she makes everyone in the office laugh for all the right reasons. She fitted in from the moment she walked in to Insurgo. She's adorable. If I was straight, I'd be tempted to ask her to marry me. Which gives you an idea of just how great she is.' He looked at Hugh, unsmiling. 'All righty. Bottom line. How does she feel about you?'

'I don't know.' Hugh looked away.

Tarquin groaned. 'I've got a bad feeling about this. I thought she'd been a bit wary of you in the office, this last week or so. And you've been grumpier than usual. I assumed it was because of your family—but it's not, is it?'

'Bella Faraday and I are not an item,' Hugh said calmly. 'Don't worry, Tarq. It'll be absolutely fine. Things will settle down. We talked about it.'

'Did you tell her about Jessie?' Roland asked.

'No. The subject didn't come up.' Which was a big fat lie. The subject *had* come up, but his family hadn't told her quite enough for her to work it out for herself, and Hugh had refused flatly to discuss it. He'd even been rude to Bella when she'd asked. Unkind. Unfair.

Tarquin rolled his eyes. 'Great. So now I'm going to have to scour London for a new designer—one as good as she is and who'll fit in as quickly as she has. Which is practically impossible. You *idiot.* I could shake you until your teeth rattle.'

'It's fine,' Hugh repeated. 'She's staying. We understand each other.'

'You mean you've both said all the right words,' Roland said. 'And neither of you have said what you're really thinking.'

'Neither of us wants any complications,' Hugh insisted.

'But you complicated it anyway?' Tarquin asked dryly.

'Yes,' Hugh admitted. He told them about her dress and the curtains in the ballroom, making them both laugh. 'And I sang with her.'

His best friends both went still. 'She sings?' Roland asked, his voice very soft.

'Not professionally,' Hugh said. 'Tarq already told you that she's a graphic artist. She really loves what she does. She doesn't want to be a pop star.'

'Ro, this isn't a re-run of the Jessie situation,' Tarquin said. 'Bella's nothing like Jessie at all. If someone came and offered her ten times her salary to work for them instead of for Hugh, she'd tell them to get lost. She's loyal, she's sweet and she's utterly lovely.' He looked at Hugh. 'And you know it, too. Actually, now I think about it, she's absolutely perfect for you and she might even make you into a nicer man. Except you're such an idiot that you won't give her a chance.'

Hugh folded his arms. 'You know how I feel about the situation, and you know I'm right. Mixing business and your love life is a recipe for disaster.'

'No. Getting mixed up with Jessie was a recipe for disaster,' Roland corrected. 'How many people meet their partners at work and there's a happy ending?' He paused. 'I met Lynette at work. And, if it hadn't been for the car accident, we'd still be together now.'

Hugh patted his shoulder awkwardly. 'What happened to her was beyond awful, Ro.'

'Yeah. But,' he said, surprising Hugh, 'I've decided it's time to make the effort. Lyn wouldn't have wanted me to spend the rest of my life on my own, missing her and being lonely. She would've wanted me to live life to the full.'

'So you're going to date again? Have you actually met someone?' Tarquin asked.

'No. But I'm going to try,' Roland said. 'Jessie, on the other hand, would want you to be on your own and miserable, Hugh. Which is because she's totally self-absorbed and wants the universe to revolve round her. Are you really going to let her make the rest of your life as lonely and empty as it's been for the past year, when you've met someone you actually like and you have a chance of grabbing happiness with both hands?'

'You,' Hugh said, 'are trying to pull a guilt trip on me.'

'No,' Tarquin said. 'He's telling you that it's OK to feel let down by Jessie, but it's not OK to wallow in it. Talk to Bella. Find out how she feels about you. Then, if she feels the same way you do, just sweep her off her feet.'

Could he?

Should he?

Would it all go wrong anyway?

'Maybe,' Hugh said. 'Now, can we please change the conversation and lighten this evening up a bit?'

'Flowers for the best sister in the world,' Bella said, dumping a large bunch of flowers into Grace's arms. 'And pudding.' She swung the carrier bag from one finger, and added with a grin, 'I bought it rather than made it, so it'll be edible.'

Grace simply laughed. 'Oh, Bel. You're going to have to learn to cook, one day, you know.'

'No, I won't. I have an excellent plan. I'm going to win a million on the lottery and have a housekeeper,' Bella retorted.

'In your dreams,' Grace teased back. 'Come and sit down. The kettle's on.'

'Just what I wanted to hear. So how's the flat-hunting going?' Bella asked.

Grace wrinkled her nose. 'I'm still looking. But when I have to leave here at the end of the week, Charlene's letting me use her spare room because her flatmate's spending a month in Australia. And that'll hopefully give me enough breathing space to find somewhere.'

'You can stay at mine, any time,' Bella said. 'I know it'll be a squeeze, but I'll never see you out on the streets, Gracie.'

Grace hugged her. 'I know. And the same goes for you.'

Bella enjoyed dinner—until Grace made them both a cappuccino and said, 'So when are you going to tell me?'

'Tell you what?' Bella asked, feigning innocence and trying frantically to work out how she could distract her sister.

'About what really happened in Oxfordshire? You've been way too quiet about it.'

Bella laced her fingers together. 'There's nothing to tell.'

Grace coughed. 'Try the truth.'

'I messed it up,' Bella confessed.

'So does that mean you're looking for another job?'

'Yes and no,' Bella hedged.

'You're not making a lot of sense.'

'I know.' Bella sighed. 'I don't know where to start.'

'Try the beginning?' Grace suggested gently.

'OK. I managed the afternoon tea bit OK, and I looked after his great-aunt when she wasn't feeling well.'

Grace frowned. 'That doesn't sound like messing up, to me.'

'It's not what an unsuitable girlfriend would do,' Bella pointed out.

'I guess—but it's what a decent person would do, and I know you, Bel. You couldn't have just left her to be unwell. So then what?'

'My dress for the cocktail party.' Bella blew out a breath. 'It turned out that the curtains in the ballroom were the same material as my dress.'

Grace put her hands up in a 'stop' gesture. 'Wait. Let me get my head round this. They have a *ballroom* in their house?'

Bella nodded. 'They live in an Elizabethan manor house—it's been used as a location for a few period dramas, Hugh said. Oh, Gracie, the house is utterly gorgeous, and his family's so lovely. Libby—his mum—

she's so like our mum. And his oldest brother and sister-in-law have the cutest baby, and they have three dogs.'

'I think I'm beginning to see what you meant about messing up,' Grace said. 'They didn't think you were unsuitable at all, did they?'

'Um—no.' Bella squirmed. 'I guess they kind of liked me.'

'Of course they liked you. Everyone who meets you likes you,' Grace said.

'Except Mrs Concrete Hair,' Bella said, referring to Grace's almost mother-in-law.

Grace laughed. 'I don't think she likes anyone. So his family are nice and you get on. Was that a problem for Hugh?'

'Possibly,' Bella said. 'We haven't exactly spoken much since we've been back.'

'It's difficult between you at work?'

'We pretty much ignore each other—unless we're in a meeting together, which isn't that often,' Bella said. 'And I'm just hoping that nobody in the office has noticed that it's a bit strained between us.'

'Maybe they haven't,' Grace said. 'So—back to your dress. What happened?'

'I brazened it out,' Bella said. 'I said I hadn't cut it from their curtains because they weren't the von Trapps—and then I sang "Do Re Mi".'

Grace laughed. 'That's *so* you, and I bet everyone joined in.'

'No. It was a bit awkward. And then Hugh sang "Edelweiss".' She bit her lip. 'That's something else odd, Gracie. The band his brother booked for the party was late, so Hugh played the piano until they turned up. He's really talented. And he has a gorgeous voice. I can't understand why he doesn't release records as well as produce them—and his brother said something about knowing why Hugh doesn't sing or play in public. His mother kind of let something slip, too. And Tarquin in the office, this week… I was subtle when I asked.'

Grace laughed. 'Bel, you don't do subtle.'

'Subtle for *me*, then.' She frowned. 'I might be putting two and two together and making ten, but I think Hugh fell for someone he worked with and it went pear-shaped.'

'Have you asked him about it?'

'Sort of—and he said it was none of my business. Which is quite right,' Bella added hastily, seeing Grace's eyes narrow in annoyance. 'It was rude of me to ask. And I wasn't subtle when I asked him. Anyway, we danced together. And he sneaked me off to the orangery—Gracie, it was the most romantic place ever, just the two of us and the darkness outside and fairy lights wrapped round the base of the orange trees, and he k—' She stopped, realising that maybe she shouldn't have admitted that much.

But Grace had clearly realised anyway. 'He kissed you?' she asked softly.

There was no point in trying to deny it. Especially as Grace was sensible enough to help her work out how to deal with it, and her sister could only do that if Bella told her the truth. She nodded. 'And it was like seeing stars—it's never been like that for me before.'

'Me, neither,' Grace said, sounding wistful. Then she frowned. '*Just* kissing?'

Bella winced. 'No. But we took precautions. And the next morning we agreed it'd be like the Vegas principle—what happened there, stayed there.'

'Uh-huh,' Grace said. 'So what's the situation now?'

'I don't really know,' Bella admitted. 'I like him, Gracie. I mean *really* like him. Which is crazy. We've only known each other for a few weeks. And yet in some ways I feel I've known him for ever. He's a good man. Look at the way he rescued us. And I know from talking to some of the artists that he's gone way beyond the call of duty for them. He's one of the good guys. He'd never do anything like what Kirk did.'

'Not if he wanted to keep all his bits intact, he wouldn't,' Grace said crisply.

Bella gave her sister a wan smile. 'I don't know what to do, Gracie. After Kirk, I don't really believe in love any more. And I don't want to mess up my job by falling for my boss, knowing that he doesn't believe in mixing work and relationships. One of the bands came in to record an album and the lead singer wanted to ask me out, and Hugh told him straight out that work and relationships don't mix.'

'Because he wants you for himself?'

That was the big question. Bella dragged in a breath. 'I don't actually know,' she said miserably. 'I don't know what to do, Gracie. I mean, I know I'm scatty and disorganised outside work and it's usually fine, but right now I feel as if I'm in the middle of a whirlwind, and it's really not very comfortable. I don't like feeling this way.'

'I think, love, you're going to have to take a risk and talk to him,' Grace said. 'If he likes you and you like him, then it's simple.'

'But what if he doesn't like me?'

'Bel, you're sweet and you're warm and you're funny and you're beautiful. What's not to like?'

'You're my sister. You're supposed to think that.' Bella folded her arms. 'And I don't know what he thinks of me.'

'For what it's worth,' Grace said, 'you've already said he's not like Kirk. And from what you said he's not like Howard, either—he was right there by your side when you sang "Do Re Mi". So it sounds to me as if he likes you.'

'And his family's definitely not like Mrs Concrete Hair and Mr Toad,' Bella added, referring to Howard's parents.

'Well, then. Talk to him. What's the worst that could happen?'

'That he turns me down and then it's too awkward to work with him,' Bella said.

'But isn't it already awkward working with him?' Grace asked.

'A bit,' Bella admitted. 'So I've been half thinking that I might need to find another job anyway.'

'And if you don't say anything, what's the worst that could happen?' Grace asked.

Bella knew that her sister wouldn't let her get away with being feeble. 'I'll always regret not talking to him and seeing if we could make a go of it. And maybe he'll meet someone else, and he'll never know how I felt about him because I was too much of a coward to try.'

'And you're not a coward, Bel. You're brave and you're honest and you're lovely,' Grace said. 'Talk to him.'

'I'll try,' Bella promised.

But would Hugh talk to her? Or would he keep himself shut off?

CHAPTER EIGHT

'ARE YOU SURE you don't want to leave this until the morning, sweet-cheeks?' Tarquin asked, the following Tuesday evening. 'It's late and you've already put in a lot of hours.'

'I'm sure,' Bella said firmly. 'It won't take me very long to get this finished and I really hate leaving things.'

'OK. Just let Hugh know when you leave, so he can lock up,' Tarquin said. 'I'll let him know you're working late so he doesn't accidentally lock you in or anything.'

A frisson went through her. So she and Hugh would be alone in the building?

Well, not completely alone—she knew that there would be people downstairs in the café—but there would be just the two of them in the office.

Maybe she could be brave and talk to him tonight...

'See you tomorrow, Tarq,' she said brightly. 'Have a nice evening.'

'You, too—and don't work too late, do you hear?'

She smiled and blew him a kiss; smiling back, Tarquin left her to it. Bella managed to concentrate on what she was doing and finished the piece of art she'd been working on all day. Once she'd turned off her computer and checked all the other switches in the main office, she paused by the staircase. Time to face Hugh.

Would she have the nerve to talk to him about the unfinished business between them?

She took a deep breath, headed upstairs and rapped on Hugh's closed door.

'Yes?' he called.

She opened the door and leaned against the door jamb. 'Tarquin said to tell you when I was leaving so you could lock up.'

'OK. Thanks.' He barely glanced at her, concentrating on a file on his desk.

He looked tired, she thought, as if a gazillion things were on his mind and stopping him sleeping. She knew the feeling. He clearly wasn't going to bring up the subject, because he was too stubborn. Which meant that she'd have to be the one who initiated the conversation. She walked over and sat on the edge of his desk. Hugh looked up at her again and glowered. 'What?'

She wasn't fooled by the brusqueness. 'You were in earlier than everyone else, and you're here later than everyone else. It's been like that ever since we got back from Oxfordshire. Carry on like this and you're going to risk burn-out.'

'Thank you for your concern, but my mother doesn't need anyone to help her nag me.'

His tone was snippy enough to make her back off. Except she'd seen that tiny glint of vulnerability in his eyes before he'd looked away. So maybe Grace was right and he was feeling as antsy as she was, and for the same reasons. She knew she was taking a huge risk here and it could all go horribly wrong, but on the other hand if she didn't try then she knew she'd always regret it. She leaned over and stroked the hair back from his forehead. 'Hey,' she said softly.

He looked at her again, and his pupils were huge. So he *did* react to her then.

'You've done enough for today,' she said. 'Come and have dinner with me.'

He was silent for so long that she thought he was going to refuse. She was about to back away and tell him to ignore anything she said because she was sleep-deprived and that meant her mouth wasn't in sync with her brain, when he asked softly, 'Are you asking me out on a date, Bella Faraday?'

His voice was deep. Slightly raspy. Just as he'd sounded when he'd made love with her and whispered her name. And it sent a thrill right the way through her.

'I'm asking you back to my place,' she said. 'There's not going to be anything super-fantastic on the menu, just a stir-fry, because I'm really *not* a very good cook. But it does mean that you won't have to make anything for yourself when you finally leave here and go home.'

He looked at her, wide-eyed with surprise. 'You're mothering me?'

She gave him a rueful smile. 'As you said, your mother doesn't need any help.'

He grimaced. 'Sorry. That was rude and unfair of me.'

'And a defence mechanism. You're snippy when you want people to back off.'

He raised an eyebrow. 'So you're a psychologist as well as an artist, now?'

'Nope. Just someone who also uses a defence mechanism. Except mine's sunshine rather than grumpiness.'

He smiled, then, and rested his hand against her cheek. 'Bella. Go home.'

His touch made heat zing throughout her body. And

maybe short-circuited her brain, because she said, 'Not without you.'

'Bella—I've already told you, I don't do relationships.'

'Neither do I.' She dragged in a breath. 'But you and I, we've been circling each other in the office ever since we went to Oxfordshire. And I think we need to...'

He was staring at her mouth. 'Need to what?'

She twisted her head to one side and pressed a kiss into his palm. 'Talk.'

His pupils dilated even more, making his eyes seem completely black. 'Uh-huh.'

'Maybe among other things,' she admitted. Because talking wasn't all she had in mind. Particularly when he was this close to her.

He moistened his lower lip with the tip of his tongue. 'Do you really think it's a good idea for you and me to be alone in a room that might have a bed nearby?'

She smiled. 'Who needs a bed?'

He groaned. 'Bella, you're killing me.'

'Maybe,' she said, 'we need to get this out of our systems. Unfinished business and all that.'

'I don't do for ever,' he warned.

'Neither do I.' And this time she leaned forward and touched her mouth to his. Really, really lightly. Every nerve-end in her lips tingled.

Was he going to kiss her back? Pull her into his arms and really kiss her? Anticipation danced through her. Any second now. Any second...

Hugh dragged in a breath. 'Bella. Right now, my self-control is hanging by the thinnest thread. We can't do this. Go home.'

It was enough of a confession to give her the courage to ignore his protests. She curled her thumb and fingers into her palm and widened the gap between her first and middle finger, as if her hand were a pair of scissors, then smiled at him and 'snipped'. 'Come home with me,' she said softly.

She could see the struggle in his face. Hugh the honourable man, who wanted to do the right thing and keep his employee at a respectable distance, versus Hugh the lover, who remembered how in tune their bodies had been and wanted to do it all over again.

Then he pulled her into his arms and she knew that the lover had won.

When she surfaced from the kiss, she whispered, 'Ready?'

'Not in a million years.' He kissed her again. 'We need to lock up.'

His head and heart were still warring, she guessed.

She waited for him to lock up, then took his hand.

'My car's outside,' he said.

She nodded, and followed him out to the tiny car park behind the offices. He actually opened the passenger door for her; she loved his old-fashioned good manners.

Then he drove her home and parked outside the road by her flat.

'Do I need a parking permit or anything?' he asked.

Yes, but she didn't want him to have time to think about this and change his mind. 'There won't be any traffic wardens around at this time of night,' she said.

He kissed her. 'I wouldn't bet on that, but OK. You're worth a parking ticket.'

She grimaced. 'Now you've made me feel guilty.'

'Good.' He gave her a slow, sensual smile. 'You can make it up to me.'

He held her hand all the way between the car and her

front door. Once they were inside, he slid his hands into her hair and kissed her until she was dizzy. 'I can't get you out of my head,' he said, holding her close.

'Me, too,' she admitted. She slid her hand under the hem of his T-shirt and splayed her hands against his abdomen. 'Every time I close my eyes, I see you. And I want you, Hugh. It's driving me crazy.'

'Me, too,' he admitted. 'Let's do something about it.'

She took his hand and led him to her room. Slowly, she took off his T-shirt; then she took a step backwards, looked at him and sucked in a breath. 'I want to paint you.'

'Oh, yes?'

'Like Michelangelo's David.'

He grinned. 'I'm hardly a fourteen-foot-tall statue.'

'Scaled down,' she said, grinning back. 'But you're still wearing too much.'

'So are you,' he pointed out.

She spread her hands. 'Do something about it, then.'

He kissed her, then stripped off her T-shirt; and then it was her turn to get rid of his jeans. He followed suit, stroking every inch of skin he uncovered as he removed the soft denim, then making her whimper when he kissed the soft undersides of her breasts and drew a path downwards.

Bella wasn't sure who finished stripping whom, but finally they were naked and in her bed and he was inside her. And the world felt very right indeed.

As they lay curled up together afterwards, her stomach rumbled. 'Sorry,' she said, feeling the heat flare into her cheeks.

He laughed and kissed her. 'It's not just you. Sorry. I was hungrier for you than I was for food.'

'Me, too,' she admitted. 'It's been driving me crazy this last couple of weeks, seeing you in the office and knowing I was supposed to keep my hands off you.'

'That's why I've been skulking in my office instead of coming downstairs with the rest of the team,' he said, and kissed her again. 'Bella, we need to talk. We need to work out how we're going to deal with this.'

'The Vegas principle again?' she asked.

'Maybe,' he said.

'Let's eat, first,' she suggested. 'It might get some brain cells working properly.'

'Good idea.' He climbed out of bed and started to get dressed.

Bella was tempted to tell him not to bother putting his T-shirt back on, but a wave of shyness stopped her; she, too, scrambled out of bed and pulled on her clothes.

'Take a seat,' she said in the main room of her flat, gesturing to the little bistro table in her kitchen area.

'Now I think I know why your desk is so untidy,' he teased.

'Because there's more room on it than there is in my flat?' she asked wryly.

'It's, um, bijou,' he said.

'I like it.'

He stroked her face. 'It's a nice flat.'

'But the whole thing's hardly bigger than the boot room in the house where you grew up.'

'Isn't there a saying that lovely things come in small packages?' he asked. He kissed her lightly. 'Starting with you.'

'Hmm. Sit down and I'll feed you,' she said.

Except when she was making the stir fry, she managed to burn the chicken slightly, and then the noodles caught on the bottom of the wok as well, and the vegetables had somehow gone watery. The whole thing looked disgusting and smelled disgusting—and she dreaded to think what it would taste like. Even a sachet of sweet chilli sauce wouldn't be able to disguise the burned or watery bits.

No way could she serve him this.

'I'm so sorry,' she said, and bit her lip. 'This has all gone a bit wrong. I wish I was more like Gracie—she's a great cook and I've never got the hang of anything more than cupcakes, pancakes and Yorkshire puddings,' she finished miserably.

Hugh came over to her, gave her a hug and kissed her frown away. 'It's no big deal. Actually, I'm an OK cook. Ma taught us all before we left for uni. Do you mind me taking over your kitchen?'

'But I was supposed to cook for you, because you're tired. I can't make you cook for me.'

He kissed the tip of her nose. 'The thought was there, and it's appreciated. But right now you're stressed, and cooking relaxes me anyway. Let me do this for you.'

'OK. And thank you. But I need to get rid of this mess first.' She gestured to the wok.

'Sure.'

She scraped the ruined stir fry into the bin and put the burned pan to soak in the sink. 'Would you like a glass of wine?' she asked.

He shook his head. 'Thanks for the offer, but I'm driving.'

Obviously he wasn't planning to stay the night, then. Well, she shouldn't have expected it. He'd made it very clear that he didn't do relationships. Neither did she, really; so this was just unfinished business to get it out of their systems. 'You'd still be under the limit with one glass,' she pointed out.

'My best friend's wife was killed by a drunk driver, eighteen months ago,' he said softly. 'Since then, none of our group of friends touches a drop of alcohol if we're driving.'

Her eyes widened. 'Oh, poor Tarquin! But I thought he was...' Her voice faded. 'Um. Well.'

'Not Tarquin,' he said. 'His partner—who is indeed male—is just fine. I was talking about Roland. He went to school with Tarq and me. He's a silent partner in Insurgo.' He gave her a sidelong look. 'Though I guess it's a bit greedy, having two best friends.'

Just lucky, Bella thought. She'd been perfectly happy with one—until it had all gone wrong. 'There's nothing wrong with having two best friends,' she said. 'So can I get you a coffee instead?'

'Thanks. That'd be good.'

'I'm afraid it's instant,' she warned. Because Kirk had taken their posh coffee machine as well, and replacing it had been a wee bit out of her budget.

'Instant's fine,' he reassured her.

She made coffee for them both while he rummaged in her cupboards and her fridge. Within ten minutes he'd made the best pasta carbonara she'd ever eaten in her life.

'Is there anything you're not good at?' she asked.

He laughed. 'My ego says thank you.'

'Seriously. You're good at business, you're good at music, you can dance, you're good in b—' She stopped, feeling her face heat. 'Well.'

'Have you gone shy on me, Bella?' His eyes glittered with amusement, but she knew he was laughing with her rather than at her.

'I'm going to shut up and eat my dinner. Which really I should've made for you, except there's no way I could produce anything as excellent as this.'

They ate in silence that wasn't quite companionable but wasn't quite awkward either, then shared a tub of posh ice cream from her freezer.

'I guess,' he said when they'd sorted out the washing up, 'we need to deal with the elephant in the room.'

'You and me.'

'Yeah.' He blew out a breath. 'Bella, I don't do relationships—nothing more than casual, anyway. And I never, ever mix work and relationships.'

'Something obviously happened to make you feel that way,' she said. She'd picked up that much from his family and Tarquin. But would he trust her enough to tell her?

There was a long, long pause. Then he nodded. 'It was a couple of years ago. Insurgo had just hit the big time, and this woman came to the offices to ask if I'd sign her. I said no, because right at that moment my list was full, and she asked me for two minutes to change my mind. And then she sang for me.' He looked away. 'She sang "The First Time Ever I Saw Your Face". She was good. Seriously good. I fell in love with her voice.'

'I love that song,' Bella said. 'There was a version a while back that I really liked—who sang it?' She thought about it. 'Oh, I remember now. Jessie Harrison.'

'That would be her,' Hugh said softly.

'Jessie Harrison? Seriously?' She stared at him. 'But she isn't one of your artists.' Jessie wasn't on the list that Tarquin had given her. Bella would've recognised her name.

'Not any more, she isn't.'

Bella had a nasty feeling where this was going. 'You were dating her?'

'Yes. It happened one night when we were in the studio. She'd been working on a song and couldn't get it right, and she wanted my help.' He paused. 'I played piano for her and did the harmonies, and suggested a few changes to the music—and then somehow I ended up taking her home. A couple of months later, she moved in with me.'

Now Bella was beginning to understand what his brother had been getting at. Obviously the reason why Hugh didn't play the piano or sing in public was because it reminded him of being with Jessie. Working with her, loving her, having his heart broken by her.

Yet he'd sung 'Edelweiss' with Bella, to take the heat off her when their plan to make her his unsuitable girlfriend had gone wrong. And she realised now that it must have brought back memories and hurt him.

'I'm sorry,' she said softly.

'I loved her, and I thought she loved me,' Hugh said, 'but it turned out I was her stepping stone to a bigger label and a bigger career. Six months after she moved in with me, I did something very stupid. Because I was in love with her, I assumed she was just being scatty and hadn't got round to signing her new contract. I'd already put a lot of work into her new album, and I'd put a lot of money into promotional stuff.'

'And it didn't happen?' Bella asked softly.

'It didn't happen,' he confirmed. 'She told me she was leaving Insurgo for another label.'

'What about all the work you'd done—all the things you'd paid out for?'

'It was her word against mine. She hadn't signed anything and I'd gone ahead on an assumption I should never have made. There was nothing I could do except absorb the losses.' He dragged in a breath. 'But it was a really bad business decision that put the label at risk for a while, until Ro decided to invest. I hate that I let everyone down because I let my heart rule my head.'

'I know that feeling,' Bella said. 'It's not much fun.'

'Jessie didn't just leave Insurgo. She left me, too.' He shrugged. 'I found out she'd been having an affair with the head of her new label. That's how, she, um, got him to sign her.'

'That's a really vile way to treat someone.' Bella could understand now why Hugh didn't want to mix work and relationships. He'd been badly burned. But she wasn't Jessie and she would never behave like Jessie had. Surely Hugh could see that?

'I've kind of lost my faith in relationships since then,' he said.

She could appreciate that, too. 'Yeah. It's hard to get your trust back when someone lets you down.'

'That sounds personal.'

She nodded. 'You told me the truth about your past, so I guess I should tell you about mine. Even though it makes me feel so stupid.' She sighed. 'I'd been living with Kirk for six months, though we'd been dating for a year before that. He'd gone all secretive on me for a few weeks. I thought he was going to ask me to marry him, and he was planning this amazing proposal—which was why he was acting oddly, because he wanted it to be a surprise—and I was so happy. I was going to say yes.'

She blew out a breath. 'Except it turned out he'd been seeing my best friend. Instead of proposing to me, he went off with her.'

Hugh winced. 'Your boyfriend and your best friend? That's a double betrayal. Nasty.'

She might as well tell him the worst. Just so he knew how naïve and stupid she'd been. 'He cleared out our bank account as well. Which is why it hit me so badly when my client went bust a couple of months back.' She grimaced. 'Thankfully Grace is an accountant. When I went freelance, she told me that I should always put my tax money to one side in an account I never touched as soon as a client's payment cleared, and to keep a cushion of three months' salary in my bank account. So, although Kirk wiped out my cushion, at least I can still pay my tax bill without worrying where to find the money.'

'But how did he manage to take all the money out of your account?' he asked.

'Online banking—he just transferred all the money to a different account. When you have a joint current account, it seems it doesn't matter how much you each put in to the account; you can both take out however much you like because the bank treats it as jointly owned money,' she explained. 'The bank said if it'd been a savings account, that would've been different and I could've taken him to court for theft. But it was a current account, so I couldn't because he had as much right to the money as I did.' She sighed. 'And how stupid does that make me?'

'Not stupid. Naïve, perhaps,' Hugh said. 'But you loved him and you had no reason not to trust him. Were there any signs that he was going to take all your money?'

'No. He'd been seeing a lot of my best friend, but I thought it was all to do with the secret proposal and that she was helping him plan it. It was the same as you and Jessie, really. You loved her and you had no reason not to trust her, either.' She looked levelly at him. 'You and I—we both made the same kind of mistake, and we both paid for it.'

'Very true.'

'So where does that leave us now?' she asked.

He blew out a breath. 'I'm attracted to you, Bella. Seriously attracted.'

And it was mutual, she thought.

'You're the first person I've really wanted to date since Jessie.'

'And you're the first person I've wanted to date since Kirk.' The first person she'd slept with since Kirk. 'But?' she asked. Because it echoed as loudly in her head as if he'd actually said the word.

'But,' he said softly, 'I learned from my mistakes. I'm never going to mix business and relationships again.'

She narrowed her eyes at him. 'Are you saying, if we start dating then I have to find another job?'

He paused for a long, long time. And then he said, 'Yes.'

She frowned. 'That's totally unreasonable, Hugh. I'm not Jessie, just as you're not Kirk.'

'I know.'

'We can keep it strictly business in the office and see each other outside. There's no reason why we can't separate our relationship from work. We're both grown-ups.'

'You came up to my office tonight and kissed me,' he pointed out.

She blinked. 'So you're saying that this is all my fault?'

He raked a hand through his hair. 'No. Just that it's not negotiable. If we see each other, we can't work together.'

'So I have to choose between seeing you and keeping my job.' She frowned. 'Can you not see how unreasonable that is?'

'Yes,' he said. 'But it doesn't stop me feeling it. I can't keep working with you and seeing you.'

'I admire the fact you have strong principles,' Bella said, 'but actually, right now I think you're being really stubborn and inflexible. You're not taking into account that life doesn't stay the same all the time. Things *change*, Hugh.'

'Not this.'

She stared at him. 'Think about this, then: whatever I decide to do, I lose something. According to your rules, I have to give something up—either you or my job.'

'We can't work together,' he said again.

And he didn't have to give anything up. Admittedly, Insurgo was his company and his last relationship had put it all at risk, so she could understand why he was so antsy about getting involved with someone he worked with. But she was going to be the one making all the sacrifices—which wasn't fair. 'I need time to think about this,' Bella said. 'And I think you, do, too.'

'Yes.' He looked at her, unsmiling. 'So I guess I'll see you tomorrow. Or not.'

Depending on whether she chose him or his job. Or neither, though he hadn't seemed to consider that as an option. Which made her even antsier.

'I guess,' she said.

Unless she could find an argument to convince him

that there was another way. One that didn't involve either of them making a sacrifice. But would he be able to compromise? Or had he been hurt too badly to let himself try again?

CHAPTER NINE

BELLA SAT MISERABLY on the sofa with her knees drawn up and her arms wrapped around her legs for half an hour after Hugh left. Then she pulled herself together and went to splash her face with water.

She needed to think about this—and, better still, to think aloud and work out what to do. Right now there was only one person she knew who'd let her talk and help her see her way through this. She picked up the phone and called her sister. 'Gracie? It's Bella.'

'Are you OK, sweetie?' Grace asked.

'Sure,' Bella fibbed.

'You don't sound it. What's happened?'

Bella sighed. 'I talked to Hugh.'

'I'm coming straight over,' Grace said. 'Hold on. I'll be with you in twenty minutes.'

'You don't have to—' Bella began, but the phone line was already dead.

Twenty minutes later, Grace used her spare key to Bella's flat, walked in and gave her a hug.

'You didn't have to come over,' Bella said.

'I most certainly did,' Grace corrected her. 'You're my little sister, and there's no way I'm letting you cry yourself to sleep.' She hugged Bella. 'Right. Cake and hot chocolate.'

'I don't have any cake,' Bella said miserably.

'I do,' Grace said, and took a wrapped cake from her bag. 'Emergency ginger cake.' While the milk for the hot chocolate was heating in the microwave, Grace cut them both a slice of cake, then finished making the hot drinks and sat down with Bella on the sofa. 'Right. Tell me everything.'

Bella did so, ending with, 'So it seems I have a choice. Either I lose him or I lose my job.'

'Maybe,' Grace said carefully, 'you might be better off without both of them.'

'How do you mean?'

'If you choose the job, it's going to be hard to work with him.'

Bella sighed. 'He's being totally unreasonable about this.'

'Which is why I'm worried,' Grace said. 'Supposing you choose him and you find another job—and then he lets you down?'

'I'm not exactly planning to live with him and open a joint bank account with him,' Bella said dryly.

'OK. You've already told me he's not like Kirk. And, although I wasn't in a fit state to remember much when I met him, you've said he has a good heart and I trust your judgement. So I guess, when it comes down to it, the real question is what do *you* want?' Grace asked.

'I want Hugh,' Bella said. 'But, because he's being stubborn about it, that means losing my job—which I can't afford to do.'

'I've got savings,' Grace said immediately. 'I can cover

your bills. So you don't have to worry about money. Not now and not ever.'

'That's so lovely of you, and I appreciate it,' Bella said, 'but I'm going to say no. Not because I'm an ungrateful, spoiled brat, but because I want to stand on my own two feet. I want to be able to hold my head high, instead of having to rely on you or Mum and Dad to bail me out all the time.' She sighed. 'I want Hugh, but I can't be with someone who's not prepared to even consider meeting me halfway. Having principles is a good thing—something that Kirk didn't have—but Hugh's at the opposite extreme of the spectrum. And if he can't learn to compromise, then we don't stand a chance.' She looked plaintively at her sister. 'Why can't life be simple?'

Grace squeezed her hands. 'I wish I could wave a magic wand for you, Bel.'

'You already have. You came straight over when I called, you brought me cake and you listened.' Bella swallowed hard. 'The only person who can sort this out is me.'

'Together with Hugh.' Grace bit her lip. 'I feel guilty, because I'm the one who told you to talk to him in the first place.'

'No. You were right. We needed to talk.' Bella lifted her chin. 'And now I have to think about it. Long and hard. And then...' She sighed. 'Then I need to make a decision.'

'Sleep on it,' Grace advised. 'And if you want to talk to me about it, even if it's stupid o'clock in the morning and you've just woken up, then just pick up the ph—. No, actually, scratch that,' she corrected. 'You don't need to call me, because I'll be right here. I'll stay with you tonight.'

Bella hugged her. 'I love you. But you really don't

have to stay.' Her bed was only big enough for one and her sofa wasn't big enough to sleep on, which meant that one of them would have an uncomfortable night on the floor. And she knew that Grace would be the one to insist on taking the floor.

'I can sleep on the fl—' Grace began, unconsciously echoing her younger sister's thoughts.

'No, you can't. And, although I can lend you pyjamas and toiletries, my clothes would be totally unsuitable for a day at your office. Not to mention the fact that you're four inches taller than I am, so nothing I own would fit you properly anyway,' Bella pointed out.

'True,' Grace said. 'In that case, go and have a shower and get into your pyjamas. We're going to snuggle up on your sofa under a throw and watch a rerun of *Friends* for a bit.'

Exactly what Bella had done with Grace on the very first day she'd met Hugh—the day when Hugh had rescued them from the Fifty Shades of Beige party. And she was pretty sure her sister remembered that, too. Tears pricked her eyelids. 'Oh, Gracie.'

'It'll work out,' Grace said gently. 'You're strong and you're brave, and you'll make the right decision when you've slept on it.'

Snuggling up with her sister on the sofa—with the help of their favourite comedy, more cake and more hot chocolate—made Bella feel marginally less miserable. But she knew that Grace needed to be up early tomorrow for work and it wasn't fair to keep her up late. Especially as she could see her sister's eyelids drooping.

'Go home, sweetie,' she said. 'You've got work tomorrow.'

Grace shook her head. 'I don't want to leave you.'

'I'll be fine,' Bella reassured her. 'Really. I'm already a lot better than I was.'

'I'll go,' Grace said, 'but only on condition you promise to ring me if you need me. Any time. And I mean *any* time.'

Bella knew she meant it. 'I will, and thanks.'

'And I meant it about covering your bills. Even if you insist on it being a temporary loan,' Grace said. 'If you decide to leave Insurgo, I can help you out until you find another job. It doesn't mean you're stupid or pathetic or needy—it's what sisters do. You had my back when I called off my wedding to Howard. And I've got yours now.'

Bella had to blink back the tears. 'I love you,' she said.

'I love you, too.'

'Text me when you get home.'

Grace laughed. 'You sound as if you're turning into me.'

Good, Bella thought. Maybe Grace's capable, calm togetherness would rub off on her and help her make the right decision.

She didn't sleep much that night. Every time she looked at the clock, the minute hand barely seemed to have moved. The next morning, she felt groggy and her head ached. She washed her hair, drank two big glasses of water and took some paracetamol.

Time to make her decision. Hugh or her job? Whatever she did, she'd lose.

She thought about it for a long time, and eventually came to the conclusion that this was the only way forward. She typed a text to Hugh on her phone, but didn't send it; she needed to bite the bullet, first.

She rang the Insurgo office, hoping that Hugh wouldn't

be the one to answer. She actually crossed her fingers as the call connected and she heard the ringing tone, and then to her relief Tarquin answered.

'Hi, Tarq, it's Bella.'

'You sound terrible,' he said immediately. 'Are you calling in sick?'

'I, um—no, actually.' She sighed. 'I'm, um, afraid I'm resigning. For personal reasons. With immediate effect. Anything of mine in the office, just give to the local charity shop if nobody else wants it.'

'What?' He sounded utterly shocked. 'Bella, sweetie, are you all right? What's happened? Is there anything I can do, anyone I can ring for you?'

His concern and kindness nearly undid her. But she lifted her chin. She needed to do the right thing and stand on her own two feet. 'No, I'm fine.' As fine as you could be with a broken heart. 'I'm sorry to let you down. To let everyone down.'

'Sweetie—I don't know what to say, but I'm worried about you.'

'I'll be fine. Really. And I've loved working at Insurgo. I'm sorry to let you all down.' She'd call the café later, wield her credit card and get them to deliver cake to the team on her behalf to say goodbye. 'I need to go now, Tarq.' Before she let herself down by bursting into tears. 'All the best.'

Once she'd hung up, she pressed the button on her phone to send the text to Hugh.

And then she switched off her phone.

Hugh's phone buzzed as he was walking up the stairs to his office. He checked the screen.

Bella.

His heart skipped a beat. So she'd made her decision? He flicked into the message.

Am leaving Insurgo

She'd chosen him. Thank God. He closed his eyes with relief, realising just how much he'd wanted her to make that choice.

His phone beeped again, and he looked at the screen. Another message from Bella.

Am leaving Insurgo but I can't be with someone who gives me impossible ultimatums. I wish it could've been different. Sorry.

What the hell? But she'd just said…

He looked at the previous message. At the bottom, in a different script, it said: This message has only been partially downloaded.

Yeah. And how.

He really hadn't expected this. He'd given her the choice of a working relationship or a proper relationship. He'd never dreamed that she'd pick a different option: neither.

He was still trying to get his head round it when his best friend stormed in to his office and slammed the door behind him.

'What the hell did you do?' Tarquin asked. 'Bella's resigned and, after the conversation we had with Ro, I know it's your fault. What did you do?'

'Something very stupid. Don't worry. I'll find you another designer,' Hugh said wearily.

'Not like Bella, you won't. And nobody can believe

she's just left like that. Just what did you do?' Tarquin asked again.

Hugh shook his head. 'You know how I feel about things. I can't mix work and relationships.'

'So you're seeing her?'

That had been the plan. But he'd got that wrong. 'No.'

'Then what the...?' Tarquin shook his head. 'I don't understand what's going on.'

Hugh handed over his phone. 'Here. Read it for yourself.'

Tarquin read the text, then stared at Hugh with narrowed eyes. 'What was the ultimatum?'

'Work and relationships don't mix,' Hugh said.

'You mean you actually asked her to choose between you and Insurgo?'

Hugh winced. 'Put like that, it sounds bad.'

'Sounds bad? It *is* bad, Hugh. Really bad,' Tarquin said. 'I can't believe you did that.'

Hugh was rather beginning to wish that he hadn't, either.

'You,' Tarquin said, 'are my best friend as well as my business partner. Which is why I can tell you that you're also the most stupid, stubborn, *unreasonable* man I've ever met, and right now I don't want to work with you. I don't want to see your face in the office this week. I don't want to speak to you—and, quite frankly, you're lucky the rest of us aren't all walking out on you as well. As of now, you're taking a week's leave.'

Hugh coughed. 'I'm the senior partner.'

'True. But I'm in charge of personnel,' Tarquin reminded him, 'which means that in this case *you* do what *I* say.'

Hugh had never seen his best friend so angry. And he

knew he only had himself to blame. 'I can't take a week off. We've got people in the studio.'

'Most of them are outside bookings. There's only one Insurgo artist due in, and I'll rearrange that for at least a week's time—when your head might be in a fit state to deal with it. I'm not letting you do any more damage this week,' Tarquin said firmly.

'Ouch,' Hugh said, but he knew that he deserved it—and that Tarquin was telling the truth. 'OK. Call me if you need anything.'

'From you? I'll tell you what I need,' Tarquin said. 'I need you to go and have a long, hard think. Look at yourself, look at your life, and think about what you really want. And when you come to your senses and realise that Bella Faraday is the best thing to happen to you—as in the best thing *ever*—you'd better find a fantastic way to apologise to her. And you'd better hope that she's a better person than you are and will actually forgive you. In her shoes, I'm not so sure I would.'

'Noted,' Hugh said dryly.

'Don't you try your Mr Grumpy-in-the-mornings act on me,' Tarquin said, scowling at him. 'Now go home and sort your life out.'

Sorting his life out was easier said than done.

By the time he got back to his house, Hugh was half surprised not to have had a barrage of calls from his family to ask him what he thought he was doing. He was grateful that Tarquin clearly hadn't told his mother or his brothers; though he knew Tarquin had told Roland because his other best friend simply sent him a text saying, You are *such* a moron.

Nothing felt right. Everything felt two-dimensional.

And he knew exactly why: it was because Bella had walked out of his life.

He picked up the phone and called her. A recorded message informed him that her mobile phone was switched off, so please try later or send a text. He tried her landline next, but it went through to voicemail. Which didn't exactly leave him much of an option. Awkwardly, he said, 'Bella, it's Hugh. I'm sorry. I've been a complete idiot. Can we talk? Please call me.'

But she didn't return his call.

He tried both lines again later, several times, with the same result: her mobile was switched off and her landline was switched through to voicemail. Was she avoiding him? Or was she just busy?

Going to her flat in person didn't help, either. Although he rang the bell, there was no answer. He knew Bella wouldn't refuse to answer the door, so clearly she was out. He had no idea where she was and no idea how else to contact her; she was close to her sister, but an internet search to find a phone number for Grace Faraday in London when he couldn't narrow it down to any particular part of the city left him frustrated and grumpy.

It looked as if he'd just have to wait for Bella to contact him. Even though waiting wasn't something that sat well with him.

He paced round the house for a bit, flicked through various television channels without finding anything remotely interesting, and couldn't even lose himself in music. Though he found himself wide awake at three a.m. with music filling his head. He lay there for a bit, trying to ignore it, but the urge was too strong.

In the end, he pulled on a pair of jeans and padded downstairs to his piano. Luckily the houses in his road were well insulated, and he'd installed soundproofing in his music room when he moved in, or the neighbours wouldn't be too happy with him playing the piano at stupid o'clock. He grabbed a manuscript book and a pencil, scribbled down the words in his head, and then started to work out the tune to go with them. By the time it was light again, he'd finished the song.

And he knew exactly what he was going to do.

He showered and changed, though he didn't bother shaving; he just wanted the rest of his life to hurry up and start now. He drove to Bella's and rang the doorbell. There was no answer, but the curtains were still closed—so surely she was there? He rang again and waited, but there was still no answer. Panicking slightly, he leaned on the doorbell.

She opened the door abruptly, rubbing her eyes. 'All right, all right, give a girl time to wake up… Oh,' she said, taking in who was standing on her doorstep.

'I'm sorry. I'm an idiot, please forgive me and—' He broke off, not quite ready to say the three little words yet. 'Come for breakfast.'

'Breakfast?' She blinked, looking confused.

'Breakfast,' he confirmed. 'At my place, and I'm cooking.'

'Hugh, it's the crack of dawn,' she protested.

'It's half past seven,' he pointed out.

'Same thing.'

'No, it isn't. I saw the sun rise this morning, and I'm pretty sure it was about five o'clock.'

She frowned. 'But you're not a morning person. What on earth were you doing up at five o'clock?'

'Finishing.'

'Finishing what?'

'Come for breakfast and I'll show you.'

'Hugh…'

'You don't have to dress up,' he said. 'Just grab some clothes. Please.'

She paused for so long that he thought she was going to say no. But then she gave a weary nod. 'Come in and make yourself a coffee while I have a shower.'

'Thank you.' Though he didn't bother with coffee. He simply paced around her tiny flat, music running through his head. He felt more alive than he'd been in months. Than he'd ever been, if he was honest with himself. And once he'd opened his heart to Bella, told her how he really felt about her, he just hoped she'd give him a second chance.

At last, Bella emerged from the bathroom wearing jeans and a T-shirt. Clearly she'd taken the time to shower, as her hair was damp and not styled, but she hadn't bothered with make-up—and she'd never looked more beautiful to him.

'Ready for this?' he asked softly.

She nodded, and he drove her back to his house. Once he'd made coffee and they'd gone through a stack of pancakes with maple syrup, he said, 'We need to talk.'

'I thought we did all our talking the other night, back at my flat,' she said.

'No, we didn't, because I wasn't thinking straight,' he said. 'I was wrapped in panic because I was so scared of repeating my past mistakes—even though I know you're not Jessie and you'd never behave like her in a million years.' He dragged in a breath. 'I wrote a song for you.'

She looked surprised. 'You wrote a song for me?'

'That's why I was up in the middle of the night. I had music in my head—music you inspired—and…oh, look, why am I blathering on about it? I need you to hear something. That's why I brought you here.'

He led her into his music room and she curled up on his easy chair. Then he sat down on the piano stool and played the song to her.

It was the most beautiful song Bella had ever heard and she knew it came straight from the heart. Hugh's voice kept catching with emotion as he sang, 'You're the missing piece of my heart.'

When the last chord had died away, he turned round to face her. 'I love you, Bella. Yes, I have issues, and I'm probably not going to be the easiest person to share your life with, but I love you and that's not ever going to change. I think I fell in love with you when I saw you bouncing out of Insurgo and into my taxi, that Friday night. I love everything about you—your warmth and your vitality and your brightness. You make my world feel a better place. And I meant everything I sang to you, because you really are the missing piece of my heart,' he said simply.

She simply stared at him. 'I can't believe you wrote this song for me.'

'You took down all the barriers I'd put round myself and set the music free again.' He smiled at her. 'I'm a nicer person when I'm writing music. And you make me a better man.' To Bella's shock, he moved off the piano stool and dropped to one knee in front of her. 'I was totally wrong about not being able to mix business and a relationship. With you by my side, I can do anything; and without you everything just feels wrong. Will you marry me, Bella Faraday?'

She stared at him, not quite sure she was really hearing this. 'But the other night you wanted me to choose between you and my job.'

'Because I was scared. Because I was stupid. But a few hours on my own to think about it and what I could be losing means I've worked through that,' he said. 'I admit, you might still need to tell me I'm stubborn and unreasonable at various points in the future, but I promise I'll listen to you and I'll take it on board—and, more importantly, I'll talk things over with you instead of brooding. So will you give me a second chance? Will you come back to Insurgo?'

'You really think you can work with me?'

'I work a lot better with you than without you. And you're a great designer. Everyone misses you. And they're all pretty mad at me for being an idiot and driving you away,' he admitted.

'So do I still have to choose between you and my job?' she checked.

He shook his head. 'And you took the option I never even considered—not because I'm arrogant but because being without you in any way is so unthinkable. I was wrong, and I'm sorry. Please come back to Insurgo. And—even more importantly—please will you marry me?'

Words she'd expected to hear six months ago from someone else—from a man she'd thought she'd known but she'd been so wrong. So foolish.

And now Hugh—a man she'd known for only a few weeks—was saying those words to her. Offering her for ever. Sweeping her off her feet.

She knew he'd still be grumpy in the mornings. And obstinate. There would be days when he'd drive her crazy.

But, the very first time she'd met him, he'd been there

for her. He'd given her help when she'd needed it, without any strings. And he'd believed in her, been there right by her side when the pretend girlfriend plan had gone wrong.

With Kirk, she'd had dreams. Castles built on sand.

With Hugh, she had reality. Something solid.

'We haven't known each other very long,' he said, as if picking up on her worries, 'but I think you know when you've met the right one. It feels different with you. Like nothing else I've ever known.'

'Me, too,' she whispered.

'And I think that's why I asked you to come home to Oxfordshire with me,' he said. 'Because, even then, I knew you were the right one. The woman who'd just be herself and my family would love her as much as I did—even though I was in major denial at the time.'

'And you let me wear a dress made out of the same curtains your parents had.'

'That's when I knew.' He coughed. 'May I point out that I'm still on one knee, waiting for an answer?'

She leaned over and stroked his face. 'You're not Kirk. You're not going to run off with my best friend and the contents of my bank account. Though you did run off with my heart. Which I guess is why I agreed to go to Oxfordshire with you instead of sending you off with a flea in your ear.' She smiled. 'The answer's yes.'

'To coming back to Insurgo? Or to marrying me?'

'Both,' she said, 'because I love the job—and I love you.'

'I love you, too. So much.' Hugh kissed her, then stood up, scooped her out of the chair, sat down in her place and settled her on his lap. 'One thing. You might have noticed that I'm not very good at waiting.'

'Meaning?' she asked.

'Meaning that I don't want this to be a long engagement.'

'Gracie was engaged to Howard for four years,' she said.

'Way, way, way too long,' he said. 'This is going to be a very short engagement. As short as we can possibly make it.'

'So you're telling me I don't get an engagement party like Nigel and Victoria's—a tea party with your older relatives, a dress made out of curtains and a sneaky dance in the orangery?' she asked.

'How about a wedding in a tiny parish church in Oxfordshire, a party afterwards in my parents' ballroom, and as many sneaky dances as you like in the orangery and a walk in the bluebell woods with the full carpet out?' he countered.

She blinked. 'But the bluebells are out now.'

'And they'll still be out for the next three weeks,' he said softly. 'I reckon we can organise a wedding in three weeks—don't you?'

She grinned. 'I see what you mean about not being good at waiting. Yes, we probably can organise a wedding in three weeks, but we're going to need help.'

'I have a feeling that the Moncrieffs and the Faradays are all going to be very happy if we ask them to help us sort things out,' he said. 'Plus Tarquin and Roland.'

'Hmm. It sounds to me as if we're going to have two best men,' she said.

'Is that OK?' He looked worried.

She kissed him. 'It's very OK. I haven't met Roland yet, but if he's anything like Tarq we'll get on famously. Though, Hugh, if we're working to a deadline of three weeks, we're going to have to start asking people now.'

He grabbed his phone. 'OK. We'll start with a synchronised text to our parents, siblings and best fr—' He stopped. 'Um. Sorry.'

'Don't apologise. You haven't brought back any bad stuff. I do still have a best friend,' Bella said softly, 'but she's usually known to the world as my sister.'

'And I hope also as our chief bridesmaid.' He paused. 'How many bridesmaids can we have? Can we ask my sisters-in-law? Because, um, they all told me you were perfect for me at Nigel and Victoria's engagement.'

'Oh, bless.' Bella smiled. 'Of course. And we need Sophia—she'll be perfect as the flower girl.'

'You are utterly wonderful. And I intend to tell you that every single day. As well as telling you how much I love you.' He typed in a message on his phone.

Bringing Bella to see the bluebells this weekend. Need everyone there for family meeting to plan our wedding.

'How about this?' he asked, and handed the phone to her.

She read it swiftly. 'Perfect. OK.' She handed his phone back and grabbed hers from her pocket. '"Going to see the bluebells at Hugh's parents' in Oxfordshire at weekend. Need you to come with us as is also family meeting to plan our wedding,"' she said as she typed.

'Perfect,' he said.

They both put all the phone numbers in to the right place and smiled at each other. 'Ready?' he asked.

She nodded. 'Go.'

Simultaneously, they pressed Send.

'What do you think—maybe ten seconds before we get a response?' Hugh asked.

'About that,' Bella agreed.

They counted.

On cue, both their phones started ringing and beeping with texts from the people who were obviously trying to call and discovering that the line was engaged.

'And let the wedding planning craziness begin,' Bella said with a grin.

EPILOGUE

Three weeks later

WHEN THEIR PARENTS had gone down to the hotel reception to wait for the other bridesmaids to arrive, Grace turned to Bella. 'Are you absolutely sure about this? Because if you've got even the *slightest* doubt, you walk away now and we'll all support you.'

'I'm absolutely sure,' Bella confirmed. 'Hugh's everything I want.'

'Then I wish you both a lifetime of happiness together,' Grace said softly. 'And you look amazing.'

'So do you. And I can't believe we've organised everything in less than three weeks.'

Grace laughed. 'With Team Faraday and Team Moncrieff joining together—of course we've managed to organise everything in the shortest space of time possible between us!'

'You're all pretty awesome,' Bella agreed.

'And your new in-laws are fantastic,' Grace said. Neither of them said it but both were thinking, the Moncrieffs were so unlike the Suttons, and how nearly Grace had been trapped in a lifetime of misery.

'Thankfully you're not a Bridezilla, so it was relatively easy to sort everything out,' Grace said.

'It's not the dress or the food or even the venue that's the most important bit of a wedding,' Bella said. 'It's the vows and the people there.'

'Totally,' Grace agreed. 'Though I have to admit I'm glad it's the perfect day for an early summer wedding—much better to have bright sunshine than trying to dodge the showers.'

Bella hugged her. 'Sorry. I'm being selfish. This must be so hard for you, considering that right now you should've been just back from your honeymoon.'

'Actually, no,' Grace corrected. 'You're not selfish at all, and today's confirmed for me that I did the right thing. When you and Hugh are together, you both glow—and that's not how it was for Howard and me. I think we both owed it to each other to let ourselves find the person who'd make us light up and who we could light up in return.'

'But you just blinked away tears,' Bella pointed out.

'Those are tears of happiness,' Grace said softly, 'because I'm so glad for you. You've got the kind of love you deserve.'

There was a knock on the hotel room door and their parents came in, followed by Hugh's sisters-in-law and little Sophia, all dressed up in their wedding finery.

'Look at you all—you're gorgeous,' Bella said in delight.

'Bel-Bel,' Sophia cooed, and Bella scooped her up for a kiss.

'My little Sophia.' She grinned. 'We're so going to do "Row, Row, Row Your Boat" later.'

'Bo!' Sophia said happily.

'Careful,' Poppy said, 'or she'll have us all singing that down the aisle.'

'What an excellent idea.' Bella laughed. 'So are we all ready to get this show on the road?'

'We certainly are,' Harriet said. 'Even though we still can't quite believe how fast this is all happening.'

'Sorry. I did kind of steal your and Nigel's thunder, Victoria,' Bella said.

'No, you didn't. It's good to see Hugh happy,' Victoria said. 'And it could be worse. You could've made us all wear bridesmaid dresses made out of curtains.'

In response, Poppy started singing 'Do Re Mi', and everyone joined in, ending in gales of laughter.

Finally it was time to go downstairs, where the bridal cars were waiting to take everyone to the tiny country church where Hugh and Bella were getting married—the church where Hugh's parents had been married and Hugh himself had been christened.

'I'm not even going to ask you if you're sure about this,' Bella's father said when they were in the car. 'Apart from the fact that I know Gracie's already asked you, I can see it in your eyes. Hugh's the right one for you.'

'Absolutely yes,' Bella said.

'Will you please stop checking your watch, sweet-cheeks?' Tarquin asked in exasperation. 'She'll be here. She might be a couple of minutes late, because it's traditional, but she'll be here.'

'She loves you to bits,' Roland added.

'I know. I'm just antsy.' Hugh dragged in a breath. Standing here by the altar, waiting, was much more nerve-racking than he'd anticipated. He'd been there before as Roland's best man, but being the groom gave you a totally different perspective. The ancient Cotswold stone church was full to bursting, there were flowers everywhere he looked, and the sun was shining through the stained glass in the windows, spilling pools of colour over the congregation. Everything was perfect.

Or it would be, when Bella was here.

And then a memory surfaced that made him even more antsy. 'Did I ever tell you, her sister cancelled her wedding three weeks before the big day?'

'And you've had three weeks to organise yours,' Tarquin said. 'But, from what Bella told me, Grace would've been donning a ball and chain instead of a wedding ring, and she did absolutely the right thing in calling it off.'

'Even so, cancelling it just three weeks before the actual day—surely she must've known earlier that she didn't want to get married?' Roland said with a frown. 'She sounds a bit princessy to me. Obviously she's nothing like her sister.'

'Grace is all right, actually—but she is pretty much the opposite of Bella,' Tarquin agreed.

'You would've met her and found out for yourself if you hadn't been off on a conference when the rest of us were doing wedding organising stuff,' Hugh pointed out mildly.

Roland rolled his eyes. 'If you will insist on getting married with practically no notice, Moncrieff…'

'We wanted the rest of our lives to start as soon as possible,' Hugh said softly. 'There was no reason to wait.'

'Hang on. You're not…?' Tarquin asked.

'Expecting a baby?' Hugh finished. 'No. We just didn't want to wait. Because we're sure this is the right thing for us.'

'I remember that feeling,' Roland said softly.

Hugh patted his shoulder. 'I know. And I'm sorry.'

'Don't be sorry. It was the best day of my life. Just as this will be yours,' Roland said.

Suddenly, the organ music changed from Bach to the processional music from *The Sound of Music*.

'So very Bella to choose this one to walk down the aisle to,' Tarquin said with a grin. Then he looked over his shoulder. 'Oh, my. Ro. Look.'

Roland looked. 'Hugh, you definitely need two best men, one either side—because otherwise your knees are going to go weak and you'll fall flat on your face when you turn round and see her. She looks incredible.'

Fortified by their warnings, Hugh looked round to see Bella walking down the aisle towards him on her father's arm. She looked absolutely amazing. Being Bella, she'd made a few alterations to the traditional wedding gown. Her dress was in cream silk and chiffon, with a strapless sweetheart neckline and a ballerina-type skirt which came to just above her ankles and showcased her strappy high heels—which were exactly the same dark red as the bouquet of sunflowers she was holding, the bridesmaids' dresses and the waistcoats and cravats of the men in the wedding party. He knew that Grace had talked her out of dyeing her hair the same colour as the sunflowers, but today she'd gone back to being platinum blonde. Just like the first day he'd seen her.

And she looked like an angel.

'I love you,' Hugh mouthed at her as she joined him at the altar, and was rewarded with a smile that felt as if it lit up the whole church.

They both pledged to love, honour and cherish each other, in front of a whole church full of family and friends. And then came the bit he'd been waiting for. The moment when he could kiss his beautiful bride.

Signing the register and walking back down the aisle as man and wife passed in a blur, and then they were walking on the path outside the church with dried white delphinium petals raining down on them. Hugh's face was aching, but he didn't care because he couldn't stop smiling. Even posing for endless photographs, both at the church and back at his parents' home under the wisteria, didn't try his patience: Roland had been absolutely right, he thought, because this was really the happiest day of his life.

'Libby, Oliver, this is so perfect—thank you so much,' Bella said, hugging them both inside the marquee on the lawn in the back garden.

'It was a team effort between the Moncrieffs and the Faradays,' Oliver said. 'The men put up the marquee and the women did the flowers and the table arrangements.'

'And what gorgeous flowers,' Bella said happily. There were alternating arrangements of red and yellow sunflowers in the centre of the table.

'Come and see the cake,' Hugh said. 'Victoria says the top tier is red velvet, the middle one's vanilla and the bottom one's chocolate.'

In keeping with the rest of the theme, red sunflowers made from fondant icing spilled down the side of the cake in a cascade. 'Just brilliant,' Bella said. 'We're so lucky, Hugh. We have the best joint family in the entire world.'

'We do indeed,' Hugh said.

The meal was perfect, too, and Roland and Tarquin did the perfect double act for the best man's speech, teasing Bella about her ever-changing hair colour and Hugh about having to learn to be less grumpy in the morning now he was married. Oliver welcomed Bella to the Moncrieff family. 'Though I still have to stop myself calling her Maria,' he teased at the end, 'and I'm going to have to check the curtains for cut-outs before she and Hugh leave tonight.'

Bella laughed and raised a glass to him. 'I promise—no scissors, so your curtains are safe. For today, at least!'

Ed welcomed Hugh to the Faraday family. And Hugh's own speech was simple but heartfelt. 'I do enough talking in my day job, so I just want to say that Bella's made me the happiest man alive and I intend to make her the happiest woman alive, I'm glad you're all here to celebrate with us, and I hope everyone else has as happy a day as we're having.'

After the speeches were over and the cake had been cut, the party moved to the ballroom for the dancing. Oliver and Libby had decorated the room with fairy lights, so it looked completely romantic and utterly gorgeous.

Hugh took Bella's hand. 'You know we don't always do things the traditional way,' he said, 'and the first dance is no exception—because we're not actually going to dance to the first song. We also know most of you are pretty sure we're going to use "Edelweiss" or something else from *The Sound of Music* as "our song", because of the first time a lot of you met Bella in this very room. But instead,' he said, 'it's this.' He sat down at the baby grand piano, pulling Bella onto his lap, and began to play the song he'd written for her—'The Missing Piece of My Heart'.

She joined him when he sang the chorus.

And there wasn't a dry eye in the house when they'd finished.

'That's our song,' Hugh said softly. 'The one Bella

inspired. Because she really is the missing piece of my heart. Now, please, I want you all to dance and drink champagne and enjoy yourselves—because today's all about celebrating.'

'Today and the rest of our lives,' Bella said softly.

'The rest of our lives,' Hugh echoed.

* * * * *

Kiss his best friend?

His whole body hummed with desire. Her eyes reflected the same heat. Had it always been there and he'd been too blind to notice it?

"Katie," he whispered, "I want to kiss you."

He expected her to walk away. To be the voice of reason.

Instead she leaned forward and kissed him. She nipped at the corner of his mouth then traced her tongue along the seam of his lips.

Where had homebody Katie Garrity learned to kiss like this? He pulled her against him, deepened the kiss and fell back against the couch, taking her with him.

His hands hiked up her sweater to the clasp of her bra. With one quick movement he unhooked it.

Katie giggled against his mouth. "Somehow I knew you'd be good at that. Loads of experience, I imagine."

To his embarrassment, Katie didn't have to imagine. Noah made no secret of his no-commitment flings. What was he doing? This was his friend. "We shouldn't—"

"We should." She pressed her hand over his mouth. "I want to know what else you're good at."

* * *

Crimson, Colorado:
Finding home—and forever—in the West

A BABY AND A BETROTHAL

BY

MICHELLE MAJOR

First Published in Great Britain 2016
By Mills & Boon, an imprint of HarperCollins*Publishers*
1 London Bridge Street, London, SE1 9GF

ISBN: 978-0-263-91969-1

23-0316

Our policy is to use papers that are natural, renewable and recyclable products and made from wood grown in sustainable forests.The logging and manufacturing processes conform to the legal environmental regulations of the country of origin.

Printed and bound in Spain
by CPI, Barcelona

Michelle Major grew up in Ohio but dreamed of living in the mountains. Soon after graduating with a degree in journalism, she pointed her car west and settled in Colorado. Her life and house are filled with one great husband, two beautiful kids, a few furry pets and several well-behaved reptiles. She's grateful to have found her passion writing stories with happy endings. Michelle loves to hear from her readers at www.michellemajor.com.

To the Special Edition readers.
You are the best ever, and I feel blessed
to be part of your world!

Chapter One

It was pretty much a given that a first date was a disaster when getting ready for it had been the best part of the evening.

Katie Garrity picked at the pale pink polish on her fingernails as she tried to look interested in the man sitting across from her. Owning a bakery was tough on her hands, so she'd tried to make them look more feminine tonight. She'd blown out her hair, applied makeup and even worn a dress and heels. All to look datable, the kind of woman a man would want to marry and have babies with. Her stomach squeezed at the time and effort she'd wasted. Or maybe it was her ovaries clenching.

Her date tapped his fingers on the table and her gaze snapped to his. "I have a couple of friends who are on gluten-free diets," she said, hoping she was responding to the question he'd asked. "I've been working on some recipes that would appeal to them."

"I'm talking about more than gluten-free." Her date

shook his head. "I mean a full overhaul to a raw-foods diet. You would not believe how fast your colon cleans out when—"

"Got it," Katie interrupted, looking over his shoulder for the waitress. The man, Mike, the project manager from nearby Aspen, had already given her too many details on what happened to his digestive system after a few bites of bread.

Why had she agreed to this date in the first place?

Because one of her customers had offered to set her up, and Katie wanted a date. A date that might lead to more, might give her the future she so desperately craved but couldn't seem to manage on her own.

She knew almost everyone in her hometown of Crimson, Colorado, but her popularity hadn't helped her love life in recent years. Men might be addicted to the pastries she created in her bakery, Life is Sweet, but that was where their interest in her ended.

"You should think about changing your shop to a raw-foods restaurant. The one in Aspen is doing quite well."

Katie focused on Mike, her eyes narrowing. "Are you suggesting I close my bakery? The one I inherited from my grandmother and has been in my family for three generations?" She had nothing against vegetables, but this was too much.

"Sugar could be considered a drug," Mike continued, oblivious to the fact that steam was about to start shooting from her ears. "It's like you're running a meth lab."

She felt her mouth drop open. "Okay, we're done here." She stood, pulled her wallet out of her purse and threw a few bills on the table. "Thank you for an enlightening evening. Have a safe drive back to Aspen."

Mike blinked, glanced at his watch then up at her. "Should I call you?"

"I'll be busy," she answered through gritted teeth. "Baking in my 'meth lab.'"

She turned for the bar. Although they'd met for dinner at the brewery that had opened in downtown Crimson a few months ago, Mike had insisted they both order water while droning on about the contaminants in microbrewed beer. She needed a good dose of contaminants right about now.

The doors to the brewery's patio were open, letting in fresh mountain air on this early-summer night. The days were warm in Crimson in June, but because of the altitude the temperatures dropped at night. Still, there was a crowd out front, and Katie was glad for it. Crimson was a quaint, historic town nestled at nine thousand feet deep in the Rocky Mountains, with streets lined with Victorian-era houses. Crimson attracted a fair number of visitors, and anything that brought more people into downtown was good for all the local businesses, including her bakery.

Turning back to the bar, her gaze snagged on a set of broad shoulders hunched over the polished wood. Katie felt her ovaries go on high alert. *Down, girls*, she admonished silently.

She walked closer, ordered a pale ale from the bartender and nudged the shoulder next to her. "Hey, Noah. When did you get to town?"

"Katie-bug." Noah Crawford's deep voice washed over her. Then he smiled, turning her insides to mush. Of course, she'd had this response to Noah since high school, so she was used to functioning as a glob of goo. "I got in a few days ago to see my mom. What are you doing out tonight?"

"I had a date," she mumbled, taking a drink of the beer the bartender set in front of her.

"A date?" Noah's cobalt blue eyes widened a fraction. He normally had a good six inches on her, but while sitting on the bar stool while she stood, they were the same height.

"Yes, Noah, a *date*." She grabbed a handful of nuts from the bowl on the bar and popped a few in her mouth. "It's when a man and a woman go out together in public. It usually involves more than alcohol and meaningless sex, so you might not be familiar with the term."

"Ouch." He shifted toward her, turning on the bar stool so his denim-clad knee grazed her hip. She felt the connection all the way up her body and gripped her beer glass harder, gulping down half the amber liquid.

"Did I do something to you, Bug? Because I thought we were friends. Hell, you've been one of my best friends since we were sixteen. Lately… I'm not the most observant guy, but it seems like you kind of hate me."

She took a breath through her mouth, trying to ignore the way Noah's scent—the smell of pine and spice—washed over her. "We're still friends, Noah," she whispered. "But stop calling me Bug. That was a nickname for a kid. I'm not a kid anymore."

"I know that, *Katie*." His tone was teasing and he poked her shoulder gently. "How was the date?"

"Stupid." She glanced at him out of the corner of her eye, not trusting herself to look straight at him and keep her emotions hidden. One beer and she was tipsy. She signaled the bartender for another.

Yes, she and Noah were friends, but she'd always wanted more. Noah had never acknowledged her silly infatuation. She wasn't sure he'd even noticed.

"Stupid, huh?" She felt rather than saw him stiffen. "Do I need to kick his butt? Was he out of line?"

"Nothing like that. Just boring."

"So why'd you go out with him in the first place?" The bartender brought refills for both of them. Katie watched Noah's fingers grip the pint glass. His hands were big and callused from the work he did as a division chief for the United States Forest Service. He spent his days outside, and she knew he was in great shape. She did *not* sneak a glance at the muscles of his tanned forearm as he raised the glass to his mouth. Nope, that would get her nowhere except more frustrated than she already was.

"I'm going to have a baby." She took a sip of beer as Noah choked and spit half of his beer across the bar. "I should say I want to have a baby."

"*Going* to or *want* to?" Noah pulled on the sleeve of her lightweight sweater, spinning her to face him. "There's a big difference."

She rolled her eyes. "Want to. Would I be in a bar drinking if I was pregnant now?"

"Good point." He lifted the hem of his olive green T-shirt to wipe his mouth just as she handed him a napkin. His lips quirked as he took it from her. His dark blond hair was longer than normal, curling a little at the nape of his neck. The top was messed as though he'd been running his hands through it. Which she knew he did when he was stressed. "Aren't these things supposed to happen naturally?"

"Easy for you to say." She took another drink, the beer making her stomach tingly and her tongue too loose. "You smile and panties all through the Rocky Mountains spontaneously combust."

He tilted back his head and laughed then flashed her

a wide grin. A glass shattered nearby, and Katie turned to see a young woman staring slack-jawed at Noah. "See what I mean?"

He winked at the woman then turned his attention back to Katie. "Are your panties combusting?" He leaned in closer, his mouth almost grazing her jaw.

Katie resisted the urge to fan herself. "My panties are immune to you."

"That's why we can be friends," he said, straightening again.

Katie felt a different kind of clenching than she had earlier. This time it was her heart.

"Seriously, though, why would you agree to a date with a loser?"

"I didn't know he was a loser when I agreed. I'm at the bakery by four every morning and in bed most nights by nine. My social life consists of pleasantries exchanged with customers and the occasional girls' night out."

"Have one of your girlfriends set you up."

"I've asked. They're looking." She propped her elbows on the bar and dropped her head into her hands. "Everyone is looking. It's a little embarrassing. People are coming out of the woodwork with men for me to date. I feel like a charity case."

"It's not that." His hand curled around the back of her neck, massaging the tight muscles there. It shamed her how good even such an innocent touch felt. How it ignited the rest of her body. "Locals in Crimson love you, just like they loved your grandma when she ran the bakery. You help everyone, Bug. It's time to let them return the favor."

She started to correct his use of the nickname he'd

given her so long ago when he added, "You deserve to be happy."

Something in his tone made her head snap up. Through the haze of her slight buzz, she studied him. Fine lines bracketed his blue eyes, and although they were still brilliant, she realized now they also seemed tired. The shadow of stubble across his annoyingly chiseled jaw looked not careless but as if he'd been too busy or stressed to shave.

"What's going on, Noah? Why are you in town?"

"I told you, to visit my mom."

She'd seen that look in his eyes before. A decade ago, the year his father died of cancer. "Because..."

He crossed his arms over his chest, the soft cotton of his T-shirt stretching around his biceps. He was wound tight enough to break in half. "She has a brain tumor." The words came out on a harsh breath, and she could tell how much it cost him to say them out loud. A muscle throbbed in his jaw.

"Oh, no. I'm sorry." She closed her eyes for a moment then met his guarded gaze.

For all her mixed emotions toward Noah, she loved him. Not just romantically, but deep in her soul, and she hated to see him hurting. Katie knew better than most how difficult his dad's illness had been, the toll it had taken on the entire Crawford family and Noah in particular. She reached out and wrapped her fingers around his wrists, tugging until she could take his hands in hers. Despite the beating her hands took in the bakery, they looked delicate holding his. "What can I do?"

"It's okay." He shook his head but didn't pull away. "It's called a meningioma. Based on the results of the MRI, it's benign. Apparently she'd been having symptoms for a while and finally went to Denver for an MRI.

She didn't call Emily or me until she had the results so we wouldn't worry."

"That sounds like your mom." Meg Crawford was one of the strongest women Katie had ever met. She'd seen her husband, Noah's father, Jacob, through stage-four pancreatic cancer with grace and optimism. No matter how bad things got, Meg's attitude had never wavered. "Is Emily back in town, too?" Noah's younger sister lived on the East Coast with her attorney husband and young son.

"I picked up her and Davey in Denver earlier today."

Katie had never met Emily's four-year-old son. "How long will the two of you be here? What's the treatment? Your mom's prognosis?"

"Slow down there, Bug." A hint of a smile crossed his face. "I mean Katie."

"You get a free pass tonight. Call me whatever you want." She squeezed his hand.

"I'll take her to Denver early next week for a craniotomy. They'll biopsy the tumor to confirm that it's benign. She'll have follow-up cognitive testing. The first couple of weeks are when she'll need the most help, but it'll be at least six until she's back to normal. If all goes well, it's just a matter of regular MRIs going forward."

"She'll recover completely? No long-term side effects?"

"That's what her doctor is saying now, although there are a lot of variables. The brain is complex. But she's... We're hopeful."

"She's going to be fine, Noah. Your mom is strong."

"So was my dad."

"Do you two want another round?" The bartender spoke before Katie could answer.

"Not for me." She drew her hands away from Noah's,

suddenly aware of how intimate they looked sitting together. She caught the jealous glare of the woman who'd dropped her drink earlier. That woman was Noah's type, big bust and small waist—a girl who looked as if she knew how to party. Opposite of Katie in every way.

Noah followed her gaze and the woman smiled.

"Your next conquest?" Katie couldn't help asking.

"Not tonight." He stood and took his wallet from the back pocket of his faded jeans, tossing a few bills on the bar. "I'll walk you home."

"You don't have to—"

"I *want* to." He shrugged. "Sitting here drinking is doing me no good. I…I don't want to be alone right now, you know?"

She nodded. "Want to watch a movie?"

"*Elf*?" he asked, his expression boyishly hopeful.

"It's June, Noah," she said with a laugh. The two of them shared a love for all things Will Ferrell.

"Never too early for some holiday cheer."

"*Elf* it is, then."

He flashed a grateful smile and chucked her on the shoulder. "What would I do without you, Bug?"

Katie ignored the butterflies that skittered across her stomach at his words. Noah was a friend, and no matter what her heart wanted, she knew he'd never be anything more.

Chapter Two

As they walked along the street that led away from downtown, Noah couldn't think of anyone he would have been happier to see tonight than Katie. His yellow Lab, Tater, clearly felt the same way. The dog stuck close to Katie, nudging her legs every few steps. He'd adopted Tater after some hikers found the tiny puppy sick and shivering near a trailhead outside of Boulder almost five years ago. Katie had been the one to name the dog when Noah had brought the pup to Crimson for Christmas that year, saying she looked like a golden tater tot. She was still his go-to dog sitter when he traveled to DC for meetings or conferences.

Now Katie laughed as Tater trotted in front of them, flipping the tennis ball she carried out of her mouth then rushing forward to catch it again. He was relieved the tension between them had disappeared. His work for the United States Forest Service kept him busy and normally he was in the Roosevelt National Forest, about two hours east of Crimson near Boulder. He tried to get back to his hometown on a regular basis to visit his mom, but Katie recently made excuses as to why she couldn't hang out like they used to in high school and college.

Although he wasn't in town often, he loved Crimson. Tonight the sky above the mountain was awash in shades of purple and pink, soft clouds drifting over the still-snowcapped peak. At least he'd be able to enjoy the view this summer. It had been too long since he'd spent any time in the forests in this part of the state, so he tried to focus on the only positive in this whole situation with his mom's illness.

As if reading his mind, she asked, "What are you doing about your job?"

"I've been transferred temporarily to White River. I'll be running the division office out of Crimson for the summer."

"Oh." Her step faltered, and he glanced at her. "That will make your mom happy."

"But not you?"

Her smile didn't meet her eyes. "I'm swamped at the bakery right now and helping to coordinate the bake-off for the Founder's Day Festival."

"Plus you have to make time for dating all the men being offered up." A horn honked and he waved to one of the guys he'd been friends with in high school as a big black truck drove by.

"No need to make it sound like they're lambs being led to the slaughter."

"Marriage and fatherhood..." He gave a mock shiver and was rewarded with a hard punch to his shoulder. "I'm joking. Any guy would be lucky to have you."

She huffed out a breath and increased her pace, flipping her long dark hair behind her shoulder. Now it was Noah's step that faltered. The thought of Katie Garrity belonging to another man made a sick pit open in his stomach. He wasn't lying when he said any guy would be lucky. Katie was the kindest, most nurturing person he knew.

Now, as he watched her hips sway in her jeans, he realized she was also gorgeous. The pale yellow sweater she wore hugged her curves and its demure V-neck highlighted her creamy skin. For so long she'd been like a sister to him, but the way his body was reacting to her all of a sudden made his thoughts turn in a totally different direction. He shook his head, trying to put brakes on the lust that rocketed through him. This was Katie-bug.

She wanted more than he was willing to give.

Deserved more, and he'd do well to remember that.

"Are you staying at your mom's farm?" She turned, her brows furrowing as she took in his expression.

He quickly schooled his features and took a few steps to catch up to her. "No. Tonight I'm using the garage apartment at Logan and Olivia's place. I have to spend a few days out on the trail starting tomorrow to get caught up on things in this section of the forest. There will be no nights away for me once Mom has the surgery. When I get back from this survey trip, I'll move out to the farm but…"

"You haven't stayed a night at the farm since your father died."

There were good and bad things about someone knowing you so well.

"Every time I'm there it reminds me of how much I failed him when he was sick."

"You didn't—"

"Don't make excuses. I couldn't handle watching him die. I spent as much time away from home as possible our senior year."

"You were a kid." They turned down the tree-lined street where Katie lived. Noah had been to the house only once since she'd inherited it from her grandmother. That spoke poorly of him, he knew. He'd been a lousy son and was quickly realizing he was also a lousy friend.

"Bull. Emily had just turned sixteen when he was diagnosed. She was there, helping Mom with his care every step of the way."

"You're here now." Katie turned down the front walk of a cute wood-shingled bungalow and Noah stopped. He barely recognized her grandmother's old house.

Katie glanced back at him over her shoulder and seemed pleased by his surprise. "I made some changes so it would feel more like mine."

The house was painted a soft gray, with dark red shutters and a new covered front porch that held a grouping of Adirondack chairs and a porch swing painted to match the maroon trim. "I like it. It fits you."

A blush rose on her cheeks. "Thanks. I hope Gram would approve."

"In her eyes you could do no wrong." He followed her up the steps and waited as she unlocked the front door.

"I miss her," she said on a sigh then crossed the threshold into the house. She pointed toward the cozy family room off the front hall. "The DVDs are in the TV cabinet. Will you set it up while I get snacks together?"

Noah felt his remaining tension melt away. There was something about this house and this woman that put him at ease. Always had.

She made hot chocolate to go with the Christmas theme

of the movie and brought in a plate of the bakery's famous chocolate-chip cookies. They watched the movie in companionable silence. It was nice to forget about his life for a couple of hours. "I can't even count the number of your grandma's cookies I ate that last year of high school." On the screen, Will Ferrell as Buddy the Elf was working his magic in the movie's department-store Santa display.

Katie gave a small laugh. "Every time you and Tori had a fight, you'd end up here or at the bakery."

Noah flinched at the name of his high school girlfriend. The girl he'd expected to spend the rest of his life with until she broke his heart the weekend before graduation. "It made her even madder. Since the two of you were such good friends, she felt like you belonged to her."

"I'd get in trouble for taking your side. Tori and I lost touch after she left for college." Katie used her finger to dunk a marshmallow in her mug of hot chocolate. "I've heard her interior-design business is successful. Someone said she was working on a project in Aspen this summer."

"Huh." That was all Noah could think to answer. He'd purposely put his ex-girlfriend as far out of his mind as possible for the past decade. Now, watching Katie lick the tip of her finger, he could barely even remember his own name. He concentrated on the television, where Santa's sleigh was flying over the rooftops of New York City.

When the movie ended, Katie flipped off the television. His whole body was humming with desire, inappropriately directed at the woman next to him, but he couldn't seem to stop it. He didn't move, continued to watch the dark screen that hung on the wall above the antique pine cabinet where the DVD player sat. Clearly misunderstanding his stillness—maybe believing it had something to do with memories of Tori or thoughts of his mother—Katie scooted closer and placed her fingers on his arm. That simple touch set him on fire.

"If there's anything you need, Noah," she said into the quiet, "I'm here for you."

He turned, studying her face as though he was seeing her for the first time. The smooth skin, pert nose and big melted-chocolate eyes. Her bottom lip was fuller than the top, and there was a faint, faded scar at one edge from where she'd fallen out of bed as a girl. That was what she'd told him when he'd asked about it years ago, but now he wanted to know more. He wanted to explore every inch of her body and discover each mark that made her unique.

As if sensing his thoughts, she inhaled sharply. His gaze crashed into hers, and her eyes reflected the same flame of desire he felt. Had it always been there and he'd been too blind to notice it? Now he couldn't see anything else.

But this was Katie, and her friendship meant something to him. More than any of his casual flings. She mattered, and despite his raging need for her, Noah didn't want to mess this up. Which was how it worked with him—as soon as a woman wanted more than he was capable of giving, he bailed.

He couldn't do that with Katie, but would he be able to offer her anything more?

He lifted his hand, tracing his thumb across her bottom lip. "Katie," he whispered, "I want to kiss you right now."

Her eyes widened a fraction and he expected her to jump up or slap away his hand. To be the voice of reason when he couldn't.

Instead she leaned forward, her eyes drifting shut as

he moved his hand over her face then wound his fingers through her mass of thick hair. His own eyes closed, anticipating the softness of her lips on his. They flew open again when she nipped at the corner of his mouth then traced her tongue along the seam of his lips.

Although he didn't think it was possible, his need for her skyrocketed even more. Where the hell had Katie Garrity, who claimed not to have time for a social life, learned to kiss like this? He pulled her against him, deepened the kiss further and fell back against the couch, taking her with him.

His hands ran down her sweater before hiking up the hem so he could touch her skin. He smoothed his callused palms up her back until he felt the clasp of her bra strap under his fingers. With one quick movement, he unhooked the clasp.

He felt Katie giggle against his mouth. His hands stilled as she lifted herself on her elbows, amusement mingling with the desire in her eyes. "Somehow, I knew you'd be good at that."

"At unhooking a bra?"

She nodded, her tone teasing. "Loads of experience, I imagine."

To his embarrassment, Katie didn't have to imagine. Noah made no secret of the fact that he loved women. He'd had more than his share of no-commitment flings and one-night stands, many of which Katie had witnessed, at least from a distance. Now he felt a niggling sense of shame that he traded quantity for quality in his relationships with the opposite sex. Once again, the thought that Katie deserved better than him filled his mind.

He shifted and she sat up, straddling his hips in a way that made it hard to do the right thing. "Maybe we shouldn't—"

She pressed her hand over his mouth. "I want to know what else you're good at, Noah." Her voice caught on his name, and the fingertips touching his lips trembled.

Before he had time to form another halfhearted protest, Katie yanked up her sweater and whipped it over her head, taking her unfastened bra along with it. She held her arms over her breasts.

"You are beautiful," he said softly, amazed that he hadn't noticed it before. "Drop your hands, Katie."

She did as he asked, revealing herself to him. He covered her with his hands, running his thumbs across her nipples and hearing her sharp intake of breath as he did.

He leaned forward and pressed his mouth to her puckered skin as she pulled off his T-shirt. He shucked it off and drew her to him once again, flipping her onto her back then easing his weight onto her. "The bedroom," he managed on a ragged breath.

"Here, Noah," she said against his mouth. "Now."

Katie watched as Noah dropped to his knees next to the couch and tugged on the waistband of her jeans, undoing the button and pulling the fabric, along with her underpants, down her hips. She wasn't sure where she'd got her courage in the past several minutes. Stripping off her sweater as Noah watched? That was totally unlike her.

But when Noah had said he wanted to kiss her, something in Katie's world shifted. It was all she could ever remember wanting, and there was no way she was going to let this moment pass her by, no matter how out of her element she felt. She knew if she revealed her doubts and insecurities, Noah would stop. The women she'd watched him choose throughout the years were experienced and worldly, able to keep up with him and his desires. Katie found that what she lacked in experience, she made up for in the magnitude of wanting him. It made her bold, and she wasn't about to let this night end now.

She bit down on her bottom lip as his jeans and boxers dropped to the floor. She hadn't seen his bare chest since the summer after college and Noah had filled out every bit of the promise his younger body had held. He was solid muscle, broad shoulders tapering to a lean waist and strong legs. She tried to avoid looking too closely at certain parts of him—big parts of him—afraid she'd lose her nerve after all.

A tiny voice inside her head warned her this was a mistake. Noah had been drinking and he was an emotional wreck between worry over his mother and memories of his father. The thought that she might be taking advantage of him slid through her mind and she fervently pushed it away. If anyone was destined to be hurt in this situation, it was Katie. Yet she couldn't stop.

He pulled a wallet from the back pocket of his jeans and took out a condom before tossing the wallet onto her coffee table. He sheathed himself as he bent toward her again. "You're going to hurt that lip biting it so hard," he said, drawing her attention back to his face.

"Give me something better to do with my mouth," she told him, amazed at her own brazenness.

His answering smile was wicked and he kissed her again, his hand sliding along her hip then across her thighs. She loved his hands on her, warm and rough. He seemed to know exactly how much pressure she wanted, how to make her body respond as though she'd been made for him. His fingers brushed her core and she squirmed then let herself sink into the sensation he evoked. She moaned, gasped then shifted, arching off the sofa as his rhythm increased.

"Not enough room," she said on a gasp, flinging her hand toward the edge of the sofa.

"You're so ready, Katie." Noah kicked at the coffee table with one leg, shoving it out of the way then rolling off the couch, pulling her with him onto the soft wool rug as he went. They fell in a tangle of limbs and he eased her onto her back once more, cradling her face in his big hands as he whispered her name. "I want you so much."

"Yes, Noah. Now." She grabbed on tight to his back, loving the feel of his smooth skin and muscles under her hands. He slid into her and for a moment it was uncomfortable. It had been an embarrassingly long time since she'd been with a man. Then it felt good and right. Perfect like nothing she could have ever imagined. Noah groaned, kissed her again then took her nipple between his fingers. It was enough to send her over the edge. She broke apart, crying out his name as he shuddered and buried his face into the crook of her neck.

A long time later, when their breathing had slowed and she could feel the sweat between them cooling, he placed a gentle kiss against her pulse point then lifted his head.

Katie was suddenly—nakedly—aware of what they'd done, what she'd instigated. How this could change their friendship. How this changed *everything*.

"I guess practice *does* make perfect," she said softly, trying to show with humor that she was casual and cool.

"*You* make it perfect," Noah answered, smoothing her hair away from her face.

Her eyes filled with tears before she blinked them away. How was she supposed to keep cool when he said things like that? When he looked at her with something more than desire, deeper than friendship in his gaze? He might as well just open up the journal she'd kept for years and read all her secret thoughts.

He reached up and grabbed the light throw that hung over the back of the couch. He wrapped it around them both, turning on his side and pulling her in close. "But the floor? I should be ashamed of myself taking you like this. You should be worshipped—"

"I feel pretty worshipped right now," she said, running her mouth across his collarbone. "I like being with you on the floor."

"Then you'll love being with me in bed," he answered. He stood, lifting her into his arms as he did, and carried her down the hall to her bedroom.

Chapter Three

Katie blinked awake, turning her head to look at the clock on her nightstand. 3:30 a.m. She woke up every morning at the same time, even on her day off. Her internal clock was so used to the extreme hours of a baker, they had become natural to her.

But today something was different. She wasn't alone in bed, she thought, shifting toward where Noah slept beside her. Except he wasn't there. The empty pillow was cool to the touch. It had been only a couple of hours since he'd made love to her a second time, then tucked her into his chest, where she'd fallen asleep.

She sat up and thumped her hand against her forehead. That was exactly the kind of thinking that would get her into trouble. Noah hadn't *made love* to her. They'd *had sex*. An important distinction and one she needed to remember. She knew how he operated, had heard enough gossip around town and witnessed a few tearful outbursts by women he'd loved then left behind.

Still, she hadn't thought he would be quite so insensitive when it came to her. Love 'em and leave 'em was one thing, but they were supposed to be friends. She climbed out of bed, pulling on a robe as she padded across the hardwood floor. Her limbs felt heavy and a little sore. She found herself holding her breath as she made her way through the dark, quiet house. Maybe Noah hadn't been able to sleep and had come out to the kitchen. Maybe he hadn't rushed from her bed the moment he could make an easy escape.

The rest of her house was as empty as her bedroom. He'd put the coffee table back and straightened the cushions on the couch. Without the aches from her body and the lingering scent of him on her, Katie wouldn't quite have believed this night had happened. She'd imagined being in his arms so many times, but nothing had prepared her for the real thing or the pit of disappointment lodged deep in her gut at how the morning after dawned.

She glanced at the glowing display on the microwave clock and turned back for her bedroom. There was no time for prolonged sadness or a free fall into self-pity. It was Friday morning and she had the ingredients for her cherry streusel coffee cake waiting at the bakery.

She had a life to live, and if Noah didn't want to be a part of it, she had to believe it was his loss. She only wished that knowledge could make her heart hurt a little less.

When Noah climbed out of his Jeep four days later, he was hot, sore and needed a shower.

It was a perfect early-summer day in Colorado, clear blue skies and a soft breeze. The weather had been great on the trail, too, and normally Noah would have relished the time in the forest. As he'd climbed the ranks of the United States Forest Service, more of his time was spent in meetings and conference rooms than outside. Since he'd be town-bound once his mom had her surgery and started treatment, he'd taken the opportunity to check out a trail restoration project on the far side of Crimson Pass. He didn't want to think about the other reasons he might have disappeared into the woods for a few days—like worry over his mom's health or what had happened between him and Katie the night before he'd left.

Because if he'd wanted to escape his thoughts, he should have known better than to try to do it with the silence of the pristine forest surrounding him. It was as if the rustling of the breeze through the tall fir trees amplified every thought and feeling he had. Most of them had been about Katie. The tilt of her head as she smiled at him, the way her lips parted when he was buried inside her, the soft sounds she'd made. He'd been consumed by visions of her, catching the sweet smell of vanilla beneath the pine-scented air around his tent.

He knew he should have talked to her before he left. Hell, he had the start of two different notes wadded up in the glove compartment of the Jeep. But he hadn't got more than a few words past *Dear Katie* either time. She was worth more than pat lines and unconvincing excuses as to why he couldn't stay. As much as he wanted her, he should have never given in to his desire. Katie wanted more than he would ever be able to give her.

Maybe he'd left like a coward because he wanted to prove to both of them that, despite his best intentions, he couldn't change who he was. She wasn't a one-night stand, although that was how he'd treated her. Regret had been his faithful companion during his time on the mountain. Katie had always seen more in him than most people, and the worry of ruining their friendship weighed heavily. He owed her an explanation, and that was the first thing on his agenda this morning. After getting cleaned up.

"Do you smell as bad as you look?" a voice called from behind him.

He turned to see his friend Logan Travers coming down the back steps of the house he shared with his wife, Olivia. It was midmorning, and Logan held a stainless-steel coffee mug and a roll of paper—no doubt construction plans for one of his current renovation projects.

"Probably." Noah hefted his backpack from the Jeep's cargo area. Tater jumped out and trotted over to Logan, rolling onto her back so that Logan could access her soft belly.

Shifting the plans under his arm, Logan bent and scratched. "You made someone very happy taking off like that."

Noah's gaze snapped to Logan before realizing that his friend was talking about the dog. "She loves being out on the trail."

"A perfect match for you."

Noah didn't like the idea that the only female he could make happy was of the canine variety. "Thanks for letting me use the garage apartment." He took the rest of his supplies from the backseat and set them near the Jeep's rear tire. He'd need to air everything out once he got to his mom's house. "I'm going to pack up later and head out to the farm. Emily will want to skin me alive for showing up at the last minute."

Logan straightened, ignoring the thump of Tater's tail against his ankle. "The surgery is tomorrow."

Noah gave a curt nod in response.

"I've cleared my schedule so if you need company in the waiting room I can be there."

"No need." Noah tried to make his tone light, to ignore the emotions that roared through him when he thought of his mother's scheduled five-hour surgery. "There won't be much to do except..."

"Wait?" Logan offered.

"Right." He slung the backpack onto one shoulder. "I appreciate the offer, but I'm sure you have better things to do than hang out at the hospital all day."

"We're friends, Noah. Josh and Jake feel the same way," he said, including his two brothers. "Not just when it's time to watch the game or grab a beer. If you need anything, we're here for you."

"Got it." Noah turned away, then back again. It was difficult enough to think about being there, let alone with his friends, who knew him as the laid-back, fun-loving forest ranger, an identity he'd cultivated to keep people in his life at a safe distance. A place where they couldn't hurt him and he wouldn't disappoint anyone. But he was quickly realizing that being alone wasn't all it was cracked up to be when life got complicated. "I'll call tomorrow and update you on her condition. If you want to swing by at some point, that would be great."

Logan reached out and squeezed his shoulder. "Will do, man."

He waited for his friend to offer some platitude about how everything would be okay, the clichéd phrases of support he'd grown to resent during his dad's illness. But Logan only bent to pet Tater behind her ears before turning for his big truck parked in the garage.

Noah headed for the steps leading up to the garage apartment, letting out a shaky breath as he did. He'd like to run back to the forest, to hide out and avoid everything that was coming. But his mom needed him. He owed it to her, and he'd made a promise to his father over ten years ago to take care of the family. He hadn't been called on to do much more than change an occasional lightbulb or fix a faucet drain until now. This summer would change that, and during his few days away he'd realized who he wanted by his side as he managed through all of it.

He walked into Life is Sweet forty-five minutes later and inhaled the rich scent of pastries and coffee. The morning crowd was gone, but the café tables arranged on one side of the bakery were still half-full with couples and families.

Crimson was the quirky, down-home cousin to nearby Aspen and benefited from its proximity to the glitzy resort town when it came to tourism. That and the fact that the town was nestled in one of the most picturesque valleys in the state. He knew the bakery was popular not only with locals, but also with people visiting the area thanks to great reviews on Yelp.

His gaze snagged on Katie, bent over a display of individually wrapped cookies and brownies near the front counter. Today she wore a denim skirt that just grazed her knees, turquoise clogs that gave her an extra inch of height and a soft white cotton T-shirt with a floral apron tied around her waist. He wanted nothing more than to run his hand up the soft skin of her thighs but didn't think she'd appreciate that in the middle of her shop or after how he'd left her.

Her hair was tied back in a messy knot, a few loose tendrils escaping. The scent of her shampoo reached him as he approached, making him want her all the more.

"Hey, gorgeous," he whispered, trailing one finger down her neck.

"What the—" She whipped around and grabbed his finger, pinning it back at an angle that made him wince.

"It's me, Bug," he said through a grimace.

"I know who it is," she said, lessening the pressure on his hand only slightly. "Your free pass is over, Noah. Don't call me Bug. Or gorgeous." She leaned closer. "I'm not interested in your bogus lines. What you did was lousy. We were friends and now..." Her voice broke on the last word and she dropped his hand, turning back to the cookies. "Lelia's taking orders today." She nodded her head toward the young woman at the register. "If you want something, talk to her."

"What I *want* is to talk to you." He reached out, but she moved away, stepping behind the counter, her arms now crossed over her chest. He knew he'd messed up leaving the way he had but didn't think Katie would be this angry. There was nothing of the sweetness he usually saw in her. The woman in front of him was all temper, and 100 percent of it was directed at him. "Let me explain."

"I know you, Noah. Better than anyone. You don't have to explain anything to me. I should have seen it coming." She waved a hand in front of her face, bright spots of color flaming her cheeks. "Lesson learned."

"It wasn't like that." He moved closer, crowding her, ignoring the stares of the two other women working behind the counter and the sidelong glances from familiar customers. "Being with you—"

"Stop," she said on a hiss of breath. "I'm not doing this here."

"I'm not leaving until you talk to me."

Katie huffed out a breath but grabbed his arm and pulled him, none too gently, through the swinging door that led to the bakery's industrial kitchen. She'd prepared herself for this conversation for the past four days. Actually, she'd wondered if Noah would even try to talk to her or if he'd just pretend nothing had happened between them. Maybe that would have been better because prepared in theory was one thing, but having him in front of her was another.

Her heart and pride might be bruised by the way he'd walked away, but her body tingled all over, sparks zinging across her stomach at the way he'd touched her—at least until she'd almost broken his finger. She had to keep this short, or else she'd be back to melting on the floor in front of him.

Once the door swung shut again, she released him and moved to the far side of the stainless-steel work counter that dominated the center of the room.

Suddenly Noah looked nervous. Which didn't seem possible because he was never nervous, especially not with women. "I'm sorry," he said simply, as if that was all he had to offer her.

"Okay," she answered and began to rearrange mixing bowls and serving utensils around on the counter, needing to keep her hands busy.

"Okay?"

"Fine, Noah. You're sorry and you don't want me to be mad at you." An oversize pair of tongs clattered to the floor. She bent to retrieve them then pointed the tongs in his direction. "You've apologized. I've accepted. You can go now."

"What if I don't want to go?"

"You sure weren't in a hurry to stick around the other night." She tossed the tongs into the sink across from the island. "How long after I fell asleep did you sneak out? Ten minutes?"

Her eyes narrowed when he didn't answer. "Five?" she said, her voice an angry squeak.

"I didn't sneak out," he insisted. "You have to get up early and I didn't want to wake you." He leaned forward, pressing his palms on the counter's surface, his dark T-shirt pulling tight over his chest as he did. "You knew I was heading out on the trail for a few days."

Her mouth went dry, and she cursed her stupid reaction to Noah Crawford. His hair was still damp at the nape of his neck and she could smell the mix of soap and spice from his recent shower. He'd got more sun while in the woods, his skin a perfect bronze, and there was a small cut along one of his cheeks, like a branch had scraped him. Despite her anger, she wanted to reach out and touch him, to soothe the tension she could see in his shoulders. She had to get him out of her bakery before her resolve crumbled like one of her flaky piecrusts.

"I get it. But I was disappointed in you..." He flinched when she said the word *disappointed*, but she continued. "Mainly, I'm furious with myself." She lowered her arms to her sides, forced herself to meet his blue eyes. "I know who you are, how you treat women. I shouldn't have expected it would be any different with me."

He shook his head. "You are different—"

"Don't." She held up one hand. "We've been friends too long for you to lie to me. It was one night and it was good."

One of his brows shot up.

"Great," she amended. "It was great and probably just what I needed to bolster my confidence."

"Your confidence?"

"My confidence," she repeated, suddenly seeing how to smooth over what had happened between them without admitting her true feelings. "It had been...a while since I'd been with a man. Truthfully, I was kind of nervous about how things would go…in the bedroom." She forced a bright smile. "But now I feel much better."

"Are you saying I was a rehearsal?"

"For the real thing." She nodded. "Exactly."

"That didn't seem real to you?" His gaze had gone steely, but Katie didn't let that stop her.

"What's real to me is wanting a husband and a family." She bit down on her lip. "Great sex isn't enough."

"And that's all I'm good for?"

"You don't want anything else." She fisted her hands, digging her fingernails into the fleshy part of her palms. "Right?"

He didn't answer, just continued to stare. So many emotions flashed through his gaze.

"This is a difficult time for you. I went to see your mom yesterday."

"I talked to her on the way here," he answered on a tired breath. His shoulders slumped as if he carried a huge weight on them. "She told me."

"She's worried about you and Emily. About the toll this will take on both of you."

Noah scrubbed one hand over his face. "Did you meet Emily's son?"

"Davey?" Katie nodded. "I did."

"Then you know Em's got her hands full."

"You both will after tomorrow."

"We'll get through it. I'm sorry, Katie," he said again. "Disappointing the people I care about is something I can't seem to help."

"I'm fine. Really." She stepped around the counter. "I need to get back out front. There will be enough talk as it is."

"Mom's cooking lasagna tonight. She insisted on a

family dinner before her surgery." He lifted his hand as if to touch her then dropped it again. "Would you join us? She thinks of you as part of the family."

"I can't." She offered a small smile. "I have a date tonight."

She saw him stiffen, but he returned her smile. "You really do deserve a good guy." He shut his eyes for a moment, and when he opened them again his mask was firmly back in place. This was the Noah he showed to the outside world, the guy Katie didn't particularly like—all backslapping and fake laughter.

As if on cue, he gently chucked her shoulder. "If this one gives you any trouble, he'll have to deal with me." He turned and walked out to the front of her shop, leaving her alone in the kitchen that had been her second home since she was a girl.

Katie stood there for several minutes, trying to regain her composure. She was too old for girlish fantasies. She'd held tight to her secret crush on Noah for years, and it had got her nowhere except alone. She *did* deserve a good man, and no matter how much she wanted to believe Noah could be that man, he clearly wasn't interested.

It was time she moved on with her life.

Chapter Four

"Do you want another glass of milk?" Noah's mother was halfway out of her chair before she'd finished the question. "More salad?"

"Mom, sit down." Noah leaned back in his chair, trying to tamp down the restlessness that had been clawing at him since he'd moved his duffel bag into his old room at the top of the stairs. "You shouldn't have gone to so much trouble, especially the night before your surgery. You need to rest."

His mother waved away his concerns. "I'll have plenty of time to rest during my recovery. I want to take care of the two of you..." His mom's voice broke off as she swiped at her eyes. "To thank you for putting your lives on hold for me. I'm so sorry to put this burden on either of you."

A roaring pain filled Noah's chest. His mother, Meg Crawford, was the strongest person he knew. She'd been the foundation of his family for Noah's whole life. Her love and devotion to Noah's late father, Jacob, was the stuff of legend around town. She'd been at her husband's side through the diagnosis of pancreatic cancer and for the next year as they'd tried every available treatment until the disease finally claimed him. She'd been the best example of how to care for someone Noah could have asked for. As difficult as it was to be back in this house, he owed his mother so much more than he could ever repay in one summer.

He glanced at his sister, whose gaze remained fixed on the young boy sitting quietly next to her at the table. Something had been going on with Emily since she'd returned to Crimson with her son. Normally she would have rushed in to assure their mother that everything was going to be fine. That was Em's role. She was the upbeat, positive Crawford, but there was a change in her that Noah didn't understand.

He cleared his throat. "We want to be here, Mom. It's no trouble. *You* are no trouble." That sounded lame but it was the best he could do without breaking down and crying like a baby. The surgeon had reassured them of the outcome of tomorrow's surgery, but so many things could go wrong. "It's all going to be fine," he said, forcing a smile as he spoke the words. "Right, Em?"

Emily started as if he'd pinched her under the table, a trick he'd perfected at family dinners and during Sunday church services when they were growing up. She focused her gaze, her eyes the same blue color their father's had been, first on Noah then on her mother. "Of course. You're going to get through this, Mom. We're all going to get through it together. And we're happy to spend a summer in Colorado. Henry's family will be in Nantucket by now. The beach is great, except for all that sand. Right, Davey?" She ruffled her son's hair then drew back quickly as he pulled away.

"Can I play now, Mommy?" Davey, Emily's four-year-old son, stared at his plate. He looked like his father, Noah thought. He'd only met his brother-in-law, Henry Whitaker, the weekend of Emily's wedding in Boston four years ago, but he knew Davey got his thick dark hair from his father. The boy's eyes, however, were just like Emily's. And his smile… Come to think of it, Noah hadn't seen Davey smile once since they'd arrived in Colorado.

Emily's own smile was brittle as she answered, "You've barely touched your meatballs, sweetie. Grandma made them from scratch."

"Don't like meatballs," Davey mumbled, his dark eyes shifting to Noah's mom then back to his plate. He sucked the collar of his T-shirt into his mouth before Emily tugged it down again.

"Not everyone likes meatballs," Meg told him gently. Noah couldn't think of one person who didn't like his mother's homemade meatballs and sauce but didn't bother mentioning that. "I think it would be fine if you went to play, Davey. If you're hungry later, I'll make you a bowl of cereal or a cheese sandwich."

Before Emily could object, the boy scrambled off his chair and out of the room.

"He can't live on only cereal, cheese and bread," Emily said with a weary sigh. She picked up the uneaten spaghetti and passed it to Noah. "No sense in this going to waste."

Noah wasn't going to argue.

"When you were a girl, there was a month where you ate nothing but chicken nuggets and grapes. Kids go through stages, Emily."

"It's not a stage, Mom, and you know it. You know—"

Noah paused, the fork almost to his mouth, as Emily looked at him then clamped shut her mouth. "What does she know?" He put the fork on the plate and pushed away the food. "What the hell am I missing here? Is Davey homesick?"

Emily gave a choked laugh. "No."

"Then what gives?" Noah shook his head. "I haven't seen you since last summer but he's changed. At least from what I remember. Is everything okay with you and Henry?"

"Nothing is okay, Noah."

Emily's face was like glass, placid and expressionless. Dread uncurled in Noah's gut. His sister was always animated. Whatever had caused her to adopt this artificial serenity must be bad.

"Davey started having developmental delays in the past year—sensory difficulties, trouble socializing and some verbal issues." Meg reached out for Emily's hand but she shook off their mother's touch, much like her son had done to her minutes earlier. "I wanted to get him into a doctor, figure out exactly what's going on and start helping him. Early intervention is essential if we're dealing with…well, with whatever it is. But Henry forbade it."

Noah took a deep breath and asked, "Why?" He was pretty sure he wouldn't like the answer.

Emily folded the napkin Davey had left on his seat. "He said Davey was acting out on purpose. He started punishing him, yelling at him constantly and trying to force him to be…like other kids." She shook her head. "But he's not, Noah. You can see that, right?" Her tone became desperate, as if it was essential that he understand her son.

"I can see that you love Davey, Em. You're a great mother. But where does that leave your marriage? You also loved Henry, didn't you?"

"I don't know how I feel," Emily said. "You have no idea what would have happened if I'd stayed. Henry is going to run for Congress next year. The Whitakers are like the Kennedys without the sex scandals. They're perfect and they expect perfection from everyone around them. Davey was… Henry couldn't handle the changes in him. I had to get him away from there. To protect him. Our divorce was finalized a month ago."

"Why haven't you come home before now?" Noah looked at his mother. "Did you know?"

Meg shook her head. "Not until a few weeks ago."

"And neither one of you had the inclination to tell me?"

The two women he cared about most in the world shared a guilty look. "We knew you had a lot going on, that it was going to be difficult for you to stay here for the summer," his mom answered after a moment. "Neither of us wanted to add any more stress to your life. We were trying to protect you, Noah."

He shot up from the table at those words and paced to the kitchen counter, gripping the cool granite until his fingertips went numb. "I'm supposed to protect you," he said quietly. He turned and looked first at his mom then his little sister. "Dad told me to take care of you both."

"Noah." His mother's tone was so tender it just about brought him to his knees. "Your father didn't mean—"

He cut her off with a wave of his hand. "Don't tell me what he meant. He said the words to *me*." It was the last conversation he'd had with his father and he remembered everything about it in vivid detail. Hospice workers were helping to care for his dad in the house and a hospital bed had been set up in the main-floor office. His memories of those last days were the reason he'd spent so little time in his parents' house since then. Everything about this place, the smells, a shaft of light shining through the kitchen window, reminded him of his dad's death. He thought he'd hid his aversion to home with valid excuses—his work, travel, visiting friends. But it was clear now that Katie hadn't been the only one to understand his cowardice.

"I'm here," he told them both. "Now and for the long haul. Don't hide anything from me. Don't try to *protect* me. I don't need it. If we're going to get through this it has to be together."

His mom stood and walked toward him, her eyes never wavering from his. The urge to bolt was strong but he remained where he was, took her in his arms when she was close enough and held her tight. "Together," she whispered.

He looked at his sister across the room. "Come on over," he said, crooking a finger at her. "You know you want to."

With a sound between a laugh and a sob, Emily ran across the room and Noah opened up his embrace to include her, too. He'd made a lot of mistakes in his life, but he was at least smart enough to try to learn from them. His first lesson was sticking when things got tough. Nothing like starting with the hard stuff.

"I want you to tell me more about Davey," he said against Emily's honey-colored hair. "What he needs, how to help him."

He felt her nod, and then her shoulders began to shake with unshed tears. His mother's crying was softer, but he heard that, too.

Noah tightened his hug on the two of them. "We can

get through anything together," he said, lifting his gaze to the ceiling and hoping that was true.

"I had a good time tonight."

Katie glanced at the man sitting in the driver's seat next to her and smiled. "I did, too. Thank you for dinner."

"It was smart to choose a restaurant outside of town. We got a little privacy that way. Everyone seems to know you around here." Matt Davis, the assistant principal and swim-team coach at the local high school, returned her smile as he opened the SUV's door. "I'll walk you to your door."

"You don't have to—" she began, but he was already out of the Explorer.

He was a nice guy, she thought, and their date had been fun—easy conversation and a few laughs. Matt was relatively new to Crimson. He was a California transplant and a rock-climbing buddy of her friend Olivia's husband, Logan Travers. It was Olivia who'd given Matt her number. He was cute in a boy-next-door kind of way, medium height and build with light brown hair and vivid green eyes. He'd been a semiprofessional athlete in his early twenties and had trained briefly at her father's facility near San Diego. Now he seemed safe and dependable, although he'd made a few jokes during dinner that made her think he didn't take life too seriously.

She liked him, a lot more than her carb-police date from Aspen last week. And if her stomach didn't swoop and dip the way it did when she looked at Noah, it was probably for the best. Katie didn't want head-over-heels passion. She was looking for a man she could build a life with, and although this was only a first date, Matt Davis had definite potential.

He opened her door and she stepped out onto the sidewalk in front of her house. Bonus points for being a gentleman. She'd left on the front porch light and stopped when they came to the bottom of the steps, just outside the golden glow cast by the Craftsman-inspired fixture. She could hear the sounds of her neighborhood, a dog barking in the distance and music playing from the rental house at the end of the block.

For a moment she debated inviting Matt in for a drink, not that she had any intention of taking this date too far, but it had been nice. *He* had been nice. Something stopped her, though, and she didn't dwell too long on the thought that Noah had been the last man in her house or why she might not want to let go of her memories of that night.

"Thank you again," she said, holding out her hand. That was appropriate, right? Didn't want to give him the wrong impression of the kind of girl she was.

He shook it, amusement lighting his eyes. He really did have nice eyes. There was that word again. *Nice.* "I hope we can do it again sometime," he said, still holding her hand.

A dog whined from nearby. A whine Katie recognized, and she went stiff, glancing over her shoulder toward the darkness that enveloped her house.

Misunderstanding her body language, Matt pulled away. "If you're not—"

"I'd love to," she said on a rush of air. "See you again, that is."

He brightened at her words, placed his hands gently on her shoulders. "I'll call you, then." He leaned closer and Katie's eyes shut automatically then popped open again when the crash of a garbage can reverberated from her side yard.

Matt jumped back, releasing her once more.

"Probably just a bear," she said, her eyes narrowing at the darkness. "They can be *annoying* sometimes." Her voice pitched louder on the word *annoying*.

"Do you want me to take a look?" Matt asked at the same time he stepped back. It took a while to get used to the wildlife that meandered into mountain towns, especially for those who'd moved to Colorado from the city. Besides, Katie had no intention of allowing him to discover exactly what—or who—was lurking in her side yard.

"It's fine." She crossed her arms over her chest. "I keep the regular can in the garage. There's nothing he can mess with over there. I'd better go in, though. Early morning at the bakery."

Matt kept his wary gaze on the side of her house. "I had a great time, Katie. I'll call you soon. You should get in the house." He flashed a smile but waited for her to climb the steps before turning to his Explorer.

Katie waved as he drove away. She stood there a minute longer until his taillights disappeared around the corner. Blowing out a frustrated breath, she tapped one foot against the wood planks of the porch. "You can come out now," she called into the darkness. A few seconds later, Tater trotted onto the porch, tail wagging. Katie bent and scratched the dog's ears. Tater immediately flipped onto her back.

"Slut," Katie whispered as she ran her fingers through the Lab's soft fur. She didn't want to think about how much she had in common with Tater, since Katie's instinct was to beg for loving every time she thought about Noah. Even at her angriest she wanted him, which made her more pathetic than she was willing to admit.

She commanded herself to *woman up* as Noah hopped onto her porch and leaned against the wood rail.

"Are you afraid to come any closer?" she asked, straightening. Tater flipped to her feet and headed into the box spruce bushes that ran along the front of the house.

"Should I be?" His voice was low and her body—stupid, traitorous body—immediately reacted. The darkness of the night lent a sort of intimacy to their exchange that Katie tried her best to ignore.

She forced herself not to look at him standing in the shadows. She was stronger than she had been a week ago, committed to moving on from her silly girlhood crush. The fact that the object of that crush had just crashed a very promising first date was irrelevant. "What are you doing here, Noah?"

"Protecting you."

She huffed out a laugh. "From a really nice guy who might actually be interested in me?" She turned for the house, opening the screen door. "Excuse me if I forget to thank you."

Her fingers had just touched the door handle when Noah was beside her, reaching out to grab her wrist. "I'm sorry," he whispered, releasing her when she tugged away from his grasp. "I *did* want to make sure you were okay."

"Why wouldn't I be?"

"I don't know." He raked his fingers through his blond hair, leaving the ends sticking out all over. It should have made him look silly, but to Katie it was a reminder of running her own hands through his hair when he'd held her. "I've been a lousy friend, and this isn't my place. I've told you I can't give you what you want. We both know that. But…you're *alone* here, Katie."

Her lungs shut down for a second as sharp pain lanced through her at his words. Then she gasped and his gaze met hers, a mix of tenderness and sympathy that had her blinking back sudden tears. He knew, she realized. Her biggest fear, the one nobody recognized because she kept it so hidden. As busy as she was, as much as everyone in this community needed her, at the end of the day Katie was alone. Alone and afraid that if she didn't make herself useful, they'd toss her aside. It was irrational, she knew, but she couldn't seem to stop herself from believing it. Without the bakery and her volunteering and offers to help wherever it was needed, where would she be? Who would want her—who would love her—if she didn't have something to give them?

Could Noah possibly understand? And if he did, how could she ever look at him again?

He paced to the edge of the porch and back. "When was the last time you saw your parents?"

Her mouth dropped open and she clapped it shut again. "Two summers ago. They had a layover in Denver. Dad had just finished an Ironman in Europe."

"They didn't come to Crimson?"

She shook her head. "He wanted to get back to his business. His coaching business has exploded in the past few years. He still races but spends more time training other elite athletes." He continued to watch her, so she added, "Mom and Dad haven't been here since my grandma's funeral."

"So no one in your family has seen the changes you've made to the bakery? How successful you've made it."

"It was successful when Gram ran it."

"Not to the level it is now. Do your parents have any idea?"

"They wanted me to sell the shop and the house after Gram died. Mom never liked me working at the bakery. You know that." She smoothed a hand across her stomach. "She didn't think it was good for me to be near all that sugary temptation. She was afraid I'd get fat again."

"You weren't fat."

She almost smiled, but the memory of so many years of being ashamed about her weight and having every mouthful of food analyzed by her mother drained any wistful humor she felt about the past. "You don't remember when I first moved to Crimson. By the time you started dating Tori in high school, I was halfway to the goal weight my parents set for me."

"I remember you just fine." Noah shrugged. "I just never saw you like that."

Katie suppressed a sigh. Was it any wonder she'd fallen in love with him back then? She bit down on her lip, forcing herself to keep the walls so newly erected around her heart in place. "You never saw me at all."

As if he needed that reminder, Noah thought, as Katie's words hung in the air between them. He should walk away right now. It had been a stupid, impulsive idea to show up at her house when he knew she had a date. He had no business intruding on her life.

"I'm a jackass, Katie-bug," he said with a laugh then cringed when she didn't correct him. "But I wasn't lying when I said I wanted you to be happy. I came here because… I guess it doesn't matter why. I want to be a better friend if you'll let me." He shut his eyes for a moment, clenched his fists then focused on her. "Even if that means vetting your dates for you."

She arched one eyebrow, a look so out of place and

yet so perfect on her he had to fight not to reach for her again.

"Matt Davis is a good guy."

Her eyes narrowed. "How do you know my date's name?"

"I asked around." He shrugged. "I'm sorry if I cut your night short. I'm sorry I keep doing things that make me have to apologize to you." He flashed a smile. "Good night, Katie."

He stepped around her onto the porch steps.

"Noah?"

He turned. His name on her tongue was soft. The same tenderness that had annoyed him earlier from his mother now made him want to melt against Katie. To beg her not to give up on him.

"I'll be praying for your mom tomorrow." She wrapped her arms tight around herself as if she was also trying to hold herself back. "And you."

He gave a quick jerk of his head in response then took off into the night. He couldn't stand there and let her watch his eyes fill with tears. Her kindness slayed him, made him want and wish for things that weren't going to be. Even now, as he moved down the quiet street, Tater's breathing soft at his side, he wanted to run. The feelings that had bubbled to the surface at his mom's house earlier were still churning inside of him. It was part of what had driven him to Katie tonight.

After his mom and Emily had gone to bed, the farmhouse had been so quiet that Noah's mind had gone into overdrive. Thinking and remembering. Two pastimes he'd tried like hell to avoid the past decade. His job kept him moving and he surrounded himself with friends—and women—during his downtime. Noah was always up for a good time as long as there were no strings attached. It was what had affected his friendship with Katie. Like his mom, she wanted more from him. She knew the serious stuff, the demons that haunted him, and it had been easier to keep her at arm's length than to see himself fail at living up to her expectations.

But he couldn't run any longer. He was tethered to this town and to the women in his life by an unbreakable, invisible thread. He wasn't sure whether he had it in him to become what each of them needed, but it was past time he tried.

Chapter Five

The next morning dawned far too early. Noah moved on autopilot as he drove his mother along with Emily and Davey toward Denver. His mom tuned the radio to her favorite station, all of them silent as music filled the SUV. He expected Emily to initiate some sort of conversation, but when he glanced at her in the rearview mirror, all her attention was focused on Davey watching a movie on his iPad. Normally the winding drive down into the city calmed Noah, but he hardly noticed the scenery. His mom worked quietly on her knitting until they arrived at the hospital.

She'd already had her pre-op visit and filled out most of the paperwork, so it was only a short wait at registration before she was admitted. They stayed with her until she was moved to the OR, emotion lodging in Noah's throat as she kissed his cheek.

"I love you, Mom," he called as they wheeled her through the double doors.

She waved, her smile cheery as she disappeared.

He felt Emily sag against him and wrapped one arm around her shoulders. "She's going to be fine."

His sister's response was to punch him lightly in the stomach. "I know you're as scared as I am. Don't act like you aren't."

He sighed and closed his eyes, allowing his fear to wash through him for just a moment, testing how it felt, how much of it he could handle. When the feelings rose up and threatened to choke him, he forced them down again. "I'm acting like I believe she's going to make it through this, Em. I can't stomach the alternative right now."

"That's fair," she answered softly. "We *will* get through this."

"I need to go potty," Davey announced. The boy stood just a foot away from them, his arms straight at his sides, his gaze fixed on the linoleum squares of the hospital's tiled floor.

"Let's go, then, little man." She glanced at Noah with a halfhearted smile.

"I'll be in the waiting room." He watched his sister guide Davey around the corner toward the restrooms, and then he turned and made his way down the hall to the surgical waiting area.

A man stood as he approached. "What are you doing here?" Noah asked.

Jason Crenshaw shrugged. "Where else would I be?" He stepped forward and gave Noah a quick hug. "Meg is the closest thing to a mom I had. You're like a brother to me. Of course I'm here."

Jase had been Noah's best friend since they started second grade, assigned to sit next to each other alphabetically. Noah hated to admit how many tests he'd passed by looking over his friend's shoulder. Jase had been smart, motivated and intent on doing the right thing all the time—a perfect teacher's pet and the exact opposite of Noah. But the two had forged an unlikely bond that had seen them through both good times and bad.

Like Katie, Jase saw past his good-old-boy act. Unlike Katie, most of the time he let Noah get away with it. Although Jase hadn't been athletic as a kid, he'd grown into his body and now stood an inch taller than Noah's own six foot two. Whenever Noah was in town, he and Jase would find time for some type of extreme outdoor activity—rock climbing in the summer and fall or backcountry snowboarding in the winter. With Jase's dark hair and glasses covering his hazel eyes, they didn't look like family, but Jase had always felt like a brother to Noah.

But he'd purposely kept his communication with Jase to texts and voice mails this trip. Jase had been raised by an alcoholic single father and had spent many afternoons, most weekends and even one extended stay with Noah's family when his dad had finally ended up doing jail time after too many DUIs. Noah knew their close relationship should have made him reach out to Jase, but instead the idea of sharing his pain with his friend had been too much.

Now he realized he'd probably hurt Jase by not including him—another fence to mend during his time in Crimson.

"I'm sorry I haven't—"

"No apologies," Jase interrupted. "You get to deal with this however works for you. But I'm going to be here one way or another."

Noah bit the inside of his cheek and nodded. "I'm glad."

"How's your mom holding up?" Jase asked as Noah sat in the chair next to him. The waiting room was almost empty at this early hour, only an older man in a far corner reading the newspaper. That should be his father, Noah thought with a sense of bitterness. His dad should be here now, and the old loss tugged at him again.

"She's a trouper, like always. She's happy to have Emily and me under her roof again, even if it's for such an awful reason."

"Emily's here, too?"

Noah glanced up at his friend's sharp tone. "She came in last week with her son."

"What about her husband? The politician, right?"

"I hear you're the local politician now." Both men looked at Emily, who walked up to where they sat, Davey following close at her heels but still not touching her.

Jase scrambled to his feet. "Hey, Em." He shoved his hand forward and ended up poking Emily in the stomach as she leaned in to hug him.

Noah hid a smile as his sister grunted, rubbed at her belly and stepped back.

"Sorry about that," Jase mumbled, reaching one of his long arms to pat her awkwardly on the shoulder. "It's good to see you, but I'm sorry this is the reason for your visit." He continued to thump her shoulder until Emily finally pulled his arm away.

Noah cringed for his buddy. Jase's crush on Emily was well-known to everyone but Noah's sister. She'd never seen him as anything but one of Noah's annoying friends.

He thought about Katie and how feelings could

change in an instant. Still, he couldn't imagine his lively, sophisticated sister with a hometown boy like Jase. Emily had always wanted more than Crimson could offer, even more so after their father died. But life didn't always pan out the way a person expected. The gauzy circles under his sister's eyes were a testament to that.

"It's nice of you to be here, Jason," Emily said in a tone Noah imagined her using at fancy society dinners where she'd lived with Henry in Boston. "And congratulations on your success in Crimson. I'm sure you'll make a great mayor."

Color rose to Jase's neck. "The campaign's just started, but I'm cautiously optimistic."

Emily glanced at Noah. "We know that feeling."

"Is this your son?" Jase crouched down to eye level with Davey. Noah saw Emily's eyes widen and wondered what he'd missed. "What's your name, buddy?"

"Davey, say hello to Mr. Crenshaw." Her voice was wooden as she threw Noah a helpless look. Davey continued to hide behind her legs.

"Hey, Jase," Noah said quickly. "Tell me more about your plans for the campaign. Maybe I can help while I'm home."

Jase glanced up at Noah then straightened. Emily took the opportunity to duck away, leading Davey over to the far side of the waiting area and taking out a LEGO box from the shopping bag slung over her shoulder.

"She really doesn't like me," Jase muttered. "Something about me literally repels her. Always has."

"It's not like that." Noah placed a hand on his friend's back. "She's dealing with a lot right now."

Jase's gaze turned immediately concerned. "Like

what? Is she okay? Is that East Coast prick treating her right?"

Noah squeezed shut his eyes for a moment. This was the last conversation he wanted to have right now, and he couldn't share Emily's story with Jase anyway. It wasn't his to tell.

He looked at Jase again, ready to offer an excuse and change the subject, when something made him glance down the hospital's hall. Katie walked toward him, balancing a large picnic basket in her arms. She wore a pale blue sundress and a yellow cardigan sweater over it. A well-worn pair of ankle-high boots covered her feet, and the few inches of pale skin between the top of the leather and the hem of her dress were the sexiest thing he'd ever seen. Her hair was swept up, tiny wisps framing her face. He caught her eye and she gave him a sweet, almost apologetic smile.

He stepped forward, heart racing, to greet her.

"Sorry I wasn't here earlier," she said, lifting the basket. "I wanted to bring—"

Before she could finish, he grabbed the picnic basket from her hands, set it on the ground and wrapped his arms tight around her. He buried his face in her hair, smelling the sugar-and-vanilla scent that was uniquely hers. With Katie in his arms, a sense of peace flooded through him. Suddenly he had hope—for his mom and for himself. Everything else melted away, from his sister's hollowed eyes to Jase's unwanted concern. He'd deal with everything. But all that seemed to matter at the moment was that Katie hadn't given up on him.

Katie tried to keep her heart guarded as the warmth of Noah's big body seeped through her thin sweater and dress. She hadn't even been sure she should come to the hospital today after how their last conversation had ended.

But she'd known his family forever and she wasn't the type of person to desert a friend in need, even if it took a toll on her emotions. Who was she kidding? She couldn't possibly have stayed away. People in need were Katie's specialty. She'd gone extra early to the bakery this morning to make fresh scones and sandwiches for later. Food was love in her world, and she was always ready to offer her heart on a plate—or in a picnic basket.

But Noah dropped the food to the floor as if it didn't matter. Right now, he was holding on to her as though she was his rock in the middle of a stormy sea. Funny that for years she'd wanted to be that person for Noah, but he'd been unwilling to look at life as anything but a continual party. Now that she'd decided to give up on her unrequited love for him, he wanted her for something more.

For how long? she couldn't help but wonder. Even as his breath against her neck made her stomach dip and dive, she could already see the ending. His mom would make it through the surgery—there was no question in Katie's mind about that. And as soon as Meg recovered fully, Noah would go back to his party-boy ways and leave Katie and Crimson behind once again.

She knew he was friends with many of the women he'd dated over the years. In his heart, he loved women—all women—he just couldn't commit to one. When things got serious, he'd move on. Yet Katie'd always been amazed at the warmth between him and most of his former flames. It was impossible to remain angry with Noah for long. He couldn't help who he was. But Katie had to keep the truth about him fresh in her mind so she wouldn't make what was happening between them into something more than it was.

When she caught both Jase and Emily staring at them, she pulled away, quickly picking up the picnic basket and holding it in front of her like a shield. "Is everything okay?" she asked, thinking maybe there was a reason for his uncharacteristic display of affection toward her. "Have you heard something?"

He glanced at the clock hanging above the elevator doors across the hall and shook his head. "It's too early. The doctor estimated close to five hours for the surgery." His blue eyes were intense as he looked back at her. "Thank you for coming. It means…a lot to me."

She swallowed, her throat dry. Why did she ever think she could keep her heart out of the equation with this man? As much as she wanted to support Noah and his family, this was dangerous territory for her. "I wanted to bring by some food. There's breakfast and lunch in here."

"Katie, I—"

"By breakfast, I hope you mean something you baked this morning." Jase Crenshaw stood and moved forward, as if he could sense how hard this was for Katie. Jase was one of the nicest guys she knew, and at this moment, Katie appreciated the rescue.

"Cranberry-orange-and-cinnamon scones," she answered with a smile, beginning to lift the cover off the basket.

"Thanks." Noah quickly took it from her and handed it to his friend. "Here you go, Jase. Give us a minute."

Jase took the basket and Katie clenched her palms together in front of her stomach, feeling exposed without something separating her from Noah. She gave a small wave to Emily, who nodded but stayed with her son on the floor in one corner of the waiting room.

Jase peeked in the basket. "Looks and smells delicious, Katie."

"There are paper plates and napkins on the bottom." She took a step around Noah but he grabbed her wrist.

"A minute," he said again to Jase, who lifted his brows but turned away with the basket of food.

As if realizing he was holding on to her in a way that seemed almost proprietary, Noah released her arm. "You didn't have to bring the food."

She flashed a bright smile. "Have you eaten anything today?"

He looked at her for a long moment before shaking his head.

"You have to keep up your strength for your mom. She's going to need you."

"I need…" he began then shook his head. "You're right, as usual."

"Josh and Logan are planning on coming down later. They don't want you and Emily waiting here alone."

"Logan told me, but they don't have to do that."

"They're your friends, Noah. They want to be here." She gestured to where Jase stood with Emily. "I'm glad Jase is with you. He cares about your family a lot."

Noah continued to watch her, as if anticipating her next words.

"I only wanted to drop off the food. I have some things for the bakery I need to pick up in Denver and—"

"Stay."

Her lips parted as he breathed out the one word, as if she could catch the air whispering from his lungs. "You don't—"

"I don't want your food, Katie." He stopped, ran one hand through his thick blond hair. "It was sweet and generous of you to bring the basket of stuff. I'm sure it will help while we're waiting. But I want… I need…" His gaze slammed into hers and she almost took a step back at the intensity in his blue eyes before he blinked and shuttered his emotions once more. "Just stay," he whispered.

"Okay," she answered and could almost feel the tension ease out of him. His shoulders relaxed and he flashed her his most charming smile.

He put his arm around her shoulders and led her toward the chairs where he and Jase had been sitting. It was as if he thought she might make a run for it if he didn't hold on to her.

She couldn't have walked away if she wanted to, not when he was finally giving her a glimpse into the soul she knew he kept hidden behind his devil-may-care mask. Even if she ended up with her heart crushed, this was where she belonged right now. It wouldn't change her future, she told herself fiercely. This momentary vulnerability didn't make Noah a long-term type of guy. But if he would take what she was able to give him right now, that would be enough. She'd move on with her life when this was finished, find a nice man and live as happily ever after as she could manage. Right now she was going to follow her heart.

And her heart had always belonged to Noah.

Chapter Six

By the time the doctor came out almost four hours later, the waiting room was filled with Noah's friends. Jase was still there, helping Emily's son to build an elaborate LEGO structure on the floor. Logan and Josh Travers had arrived an hour earlier. Josh was sprawled on one of the small couches in the waiting room while Logan paced the hallway. Each time a hospital staff member walked through the doors to the OR, all conversations and movement in the waiting room stopped. So far there'd been no word on Meg.

Katie had expected Noah to leave her in order to hang out with his friends. His normal role was the jokester of the group, and she figured he had plenty of steam to let off during these hours of waiting. Instead, he'd stayed by her side or kept her near him when he got up to pace the hall. Even now, he sat silently staring at the ceiling, and while none of his friends had left, they'd given up on pulling him into any sort of conversation.

Katie shrugged her shoulders at the questioning glance Jase threw her from across the room. She'd never seen Noah so quiet, and unfortunately, Katie wasn't the type to fill the silence with light conversation. As she shifted in her chair, Noah's hand took her wrist in a vise-like grip.

"Where are you going?" he asked, his voice hoarse. His fingers gentled, his thumb tracing a circle over the pulse point on the inside of her wrist.

"Nowhere." She moved again. "My foot fell asleep from crossing my legs too long."

"Give it to me." Noah smoothed his palm down her dress and over her thigh, inching up the fabric between his fingers.

"Stop," Katie squeaked. She swatted away his hand, color rising in her cheeks as everyone in the waiting room turned. "Noah, what are you doing?"

He looked baffled. "Give me your foot. I'll massage it until it's back to normal."

She swallowed. "In the middle of the hospital? Are you crazy?"

To her surprise, he seemed to ponder the question seriously. "I don't know, Bug. But I can tell you sitting here without a damn thing to do is testing my sanity."

"Noah," she whispered, reaching up to place her hand against the rough stubble darkening his jawline. Their friends were still watching, but she didn't care. "We'll hear something soon."

As if she'd conjured him, an older man in blue scrubs came through the double doors that led to the operating rooms. Noah jumped to his feet and both he and Emily rushed forward.

"How is she?" Noah asked as Emily added, "When can we see her?"

"Your mother is a strong woman," the doctor told

them. He glanced at the crowd of people gathering behind the two, but didn't comment. "The surgery was a success. We did an initial scan in the OR and it appears we were able to remove all of the tumor without impacting any of her nerve centers. We'll do a biopsy and will have to rescan once the swelling goes down. Plus she'll still need a course of radiation to make sure it's totally gone." He paused, took a breath, scrubbing his fingers over his eyes. "But it's a positive outcome. The best we could have hoped for."

As a cheer went up from the assembled group, Katie watched Noah's shoulders rise and fall in a shuddering breath. Logan and Josh patted him on the back and high-fived each other.

Emily started to cry, wiping furiously at her cheeks even as she laughed. "I cry at everything these days."

Katie noticed Jase take a step forward then stop himself.

"Can we see her?" Emily asked again, her voice more controlled.

The doctor glanced from Emily to where Davey still sat on the carpet with his LEGO bricks. "Yes. They're moving her up to the Neuro ICU now. Come with me and the nurses will take you. But no children allowed."

"I'll stay with him," Jase offered immediately. He folded his long legs down to the carpet. "We can't stop in the middle of the construction project anyway." He picked up a handful of colored blocks.

Emily looked as if she wanted to argue, but Noah took her hand. "Just for a few minutes," he said, "so we can see that she's really okay."

She turned to Jase, almost reluctantly. "Thank you," she whispered and followed Noah and the doctor toward the double doors.

Katie watched, knowing she should get her things and leave before they got back. Although it felt wrong, she loved being here for Noah when he needed her. But his mom had made it through surgery, and she'd served her purpose. She had people covering at the bakery all day, but it wouldn't hurt to check in.

She saw Noah say something to the doctor then turn back as the physician and Emily disappeared through the double doors. He walked toward her, his expression unreadable until he took her face in his hands. The look in his eyes was at once tender and fierce, as if he couldn't quite figure out his own feelings.

Katie opened her mouth to speak, but he pressed his lips to hers. The kiss was gentle yet possessive, and there was no confusion in it. He pulled back after a moment and whispered, "Thank you for getting me through today."

As he walked away, a strange silence descended on the waiting room. Katie felt the stares from Josh, Logan and Jase. She shook her head, pressing her fingers to her lips and not making eye contact with any of them. "I don't want to talk about it," she said, then gathered her purse and the picnic basket and hurried toward the elevator.

Katie glanced at the clock on the wall behind the bakery's counter as a demanding knock sounded on the door. They'd been closed for almost an hour, and she was alone in the empty shop.

The urge to ignore the group of women she could see gathered on the sidewalk in front of the bakery was strong, but it would only postpone the inevitable. In truth, she was surprised it had taken them this long to descend.

She turned the lock on the door and opened it, plastering a smile on her face. "Why do I feel like I'm being visited by *Macbeth*'s Three Witches?" she asked as she stepped back to allow the women to enter.

Sara Travers, Josh's wife, was the first to enter. "Nice reference. Going classic with Shakespeare. I like it." Sara not only helped Josh run a guest ranch outside of town, but she was a Hollywood actress who was enjoying a resurgence in her career in the past few years.

Natalie Donovan followed her. Another Crimson native, Natalie and she had forged a true friendship in the past few years, despite not having been close growing up. Until she reconnected with her high school sweetheart, Liam Donovan, Natalie had been a divorced mom raising her son by herself. Katie had helped with babysitting nine-year-old Austin on a regular basis but didn't see him as often now that Natalie and Liam were married and Nat wasn't working so many hours and juggling multiple jobs.

"Do you have brownies?" Natalie asked as she threw Katie a "what were you thinking?" glance. "We're going to need chocolate for this conversation."

"I left a plate on top of the display counter." Katie had anticipated this visit.

The last woman in their trio was Millie Travers, who had married the eldest Travers brother, Jake, earlier this year. "Olivia says not to pay attention to Natalie," she told Katie, giving her a quick hug after she shut the door. "She's been having morning sickness all day long, otherwise she would be here."

"Poor thing," Katie murmured as she followed Millie to the table where Natalie had set the brownie plate. "I'll text her later and see if I can bring her anything."

She didn't pretend to wonder why her friends had

come today. "It wasn't my fault," she told them, focusing on Sara and Millie, who were more likely to be sympathetic than Natalie.

Of course, it was Nat who answered. "Right. His mouth just ran into yours."

"It wasn't like that," Katie murmured, sinking into a chair. She pointed a finger at Natalie. "And I won't share my sweets if you're mean."

With an exaggerated eye roll, Natalie snagged a brownie off the plate. "I'm never mean."

Millie snorted as Sara filled water glasses from the pitcher on the counter. "It was probably just a strange reaction to stress. You and Noah have always been just friends, but today had to be hard on him."

"I saw plenty of people dealing with stress when I worked at the nursing home." Natalie broke off a piece of brownie. "They didn't start making out with their friends in the hallway."

Katie gasped. "We weren't making out. It was… I don't know what it was."

"A reaction to stress," Millie said firmly.

"A mistake?" Sara's tone was gentle.

"A kiss from the guy you've been in love with since high school." Natalie didn't form her response as a question, and while the other women stared, she sucked a bit of chocolate off her finger then pointed at Millie and Sara. "You two may be newer to town, but you can't ignore our girl's feelings for the ever-gorgeous man-boy Noah."

Man-boy. Katie almost snorted at that description but didn't bother to deny Natalie's assessment. It was pathetic that so many people knew about her crush on Noah when he'd always been oblivious. Even if he had been interested in settling down, Noah was way out of her league, another fact she'd pushed aside when he'd wrapped his arms around her. Now she could imagine the reaction from the locals. Noah was well-known for dating gorgeous, wild women. There was no shortage of those on the outskirts of a fancy ski town like Aspen. Katie didn't fit that bill. "I'm an idiot," she muttered, dropping her head into her hands.

"Josh said Noah kissed you." Sara placed four waters on the table and sat in the last empty chair. "The way he described the scene, I would have loved to be there."

"How did he describe it?" Katie asked, trying not to cringe as she lifted her gaze to meet Sara's.

"Well…" Sara answered with a smile. "He said it was 'pretty crazy,' and Josh has seen plenty of crazy, so that's a big deal for him. I don't think any of the guys saw it coming."

"Join the club," Katie said. "They probably think I'm a slut."

All three of her friends laughed. "You are the least slutty woman in Crimson," Millie told her.

"Only on the outside." Sometimes Katie hated her sainted reputation. The pressure to live up to what people thought about her could be enough to drive her crazy. "If you knew what I was thinking and feeling on the inside…"

Natalie wiggled her eyebrows. "Which is?"

"That I'd like to get Noah into the bedroom." She reached for a brownie and added, "Again."

"Again?" three voices chorused.

Katie ignored the heat rising in her cheeks, both from revealing the secret to her friends and from the memory of Noah's hands all over her body. "We didn't plan it the first time, and I know it was a mistake based on his reaction."

"Let me guess." Natalie pushed back in her chair. "He freaked out."

"Took off into the woods for several days," Katie said with a nod. "He couldn't handle it."

"I don't know him well," Sara said, "but it doesn't seem like Noah does long-term relationships."

"Noah's idea of *long term* is a second date," Natalie confirmed.

Millie placed a gentle hand on Katie's wrist. "And you're ready to settle down with the right guy. That's the whole reason for Project Set Up Katie."

"I'm a project? That's depressing."

"Not if it gets you the future you want," Sara argued.

"Unless what you want has changed," Natalie suggested. "Because I thought you were moving on from how you feel about Noah. You know he's not the type of guy to settle down. You want hot sex, I bet he can serve that up on a silver platter. Nothing more, Katie."

"I get it," she agreed then paused. "But if you saw how he looked at the hospital, how alone he was… He needs more in his life than a string of one-night stands. He needs…"

"You?" Sara asked.

Before she could answer, Natalie sat forward. "No. He needs to grow up and take responsibility for his own stuff. You've been available to him for years, and he suddenly realizes you're there just when his mom is sick and he's back in Crimson for the summer. Too much of a coincidence for my taste."

"But if she cares about him, maybe this is the opportunity they've needed." Millie absently brushed the brownie crumbs into her palm. "Maybe she's what Noah needs."

"Of course she is," Natalie agreed. "Any guy would be lucky to have our Katie. But he doesn't deserve her."

"Stop talking like I'm not here." Katie stood abruptly and grabbed the empty brownie plate. "I know all about Noah. I know he's not a long-term bet, but I do care about him. I can't turn that off. It doesn't matter anyway. He has me on such a pedestal, he couldn't handle something real between us."

"Does that mean more kissing and stuff?" Sara asked with a wink.

"Or does it mean no more dates with other men?" Millie asked. "Because Olivia had high hopes for Matt Davis."

"Matt is a great guy." Katie walked behind the counter and set the plate in the sink. "I told him I'd go out with him again."

"And Noah?"

She shook her head. "No more kissing and stuff. You're right. I want something more. Something Noah is unwilling and unable to give me."

Millie looked as if she wanted to argue, but Natalie spoke first. "I'm glad that's settled. Which one of the guys is nominated to straighten out Noah?"

"I'll handle Noah." Katie flipped off the lights behind the counter and checked to make sure all of the baked goods were put away for the night.

Millie stood and gave Katie a tight hug. "Speaking of needing you," she said with a hopeful smile, "any chance you're free on Saturday to keep Brooke for the night? Jake and I are supposed to go to Denver. Sara and Josh have a family reunion arriving to the ranch, and with Olivia not feeling well..."

"I'd love to watch her. We'll have a girls' night."

"Are you still able to help with the brunch at the ranch on Sunday morning?" Sara asked.

"Sure," Katie answered automatically. "I'll bring Brookie with me to deliver everything. She'll love it."

"Thanks, sweetie." Millie gave her another hug. "What would we do without you?"

"I hope you'll never have to find out." She grabbed an envelope off the counter. "Can I give these to you?" she asked Sara. "They're the Life is Sweet donations for the Founder's Day Festival." Sara was chairing the silent-auction portion of the event.

"Gift cards for the bakery?" Natalie looked interested. "Perhaps a year's worth of brownies delivered to my door?"

Katie laughed. "A couple of gift certificates for merchandise," she explained. "Also a private baking lesson for a group of up to six friends." She pointed to Natalie. "In case you ever want to learn to make your own brownies."

Nat mock shuddered. "I pride myself on helping to keep you in business."

"But Katie *gives* you the brownies half the time," Millie pointed out with a smile.

"Only half the time," Natalie said.

"Thanks for these." Sara hugged Katie. "We can always count on you."

The statement was true and normally comforting. Today it gave her an empty feeling in the pit of her stomach. She didn't say this to her friends, though. She was the even-keeled, dependable one in their group. They didn't need another reason to worry about her. Katie hated the feeling of being any kind of burden, especially emotional, on someone else.

Satisfied she wasn't headed down a dark and crazy

path with Noah, the three women said goodbye and headed out into the late-afternoon sunshine.

Katie finished checking things in the shop then stood staring at the baked goods tucked away in the refrigerated display cabinet. For the first time in as long as she could remember, she had the almost uncontrollable urge to open up the glass and stuff as many cookies in her mouth as would fit.

She took a couple of deep breaths, but the smell of sugar and vanilla that permeated the air of the bakery didn't help suppress her craving. She quickly locked up the store and started walking away from Crimson's town center, where Life is Sweet was located. There was a bike path along the edge of town, next to the bubbling Crimson Creek, and she made her way to the crushed gravel path. It would take her longer to get home on this route, but she counted on the familiar sound of the water to help smooth her tumbling emotions.

When she and her parents had first moved to Crimson, her dad was still competing in Ironman triathlons and other distance sporting events. Katie had felt as out of her element in the small mountain town as she did in her own family. The only thing her mother had ever been dedicated to in life was Katie's father. Monica Garrity didn't have much use for her family's small bakery or her sweet, unassuming mother who ran it. But she'd liked the convenience of being able to leave Katie with her grandma so she could travel with Katie's father, Mike, as he competed and trained.

Neither of her parents could accept the fact that Katie hadn't inherited either their natural athleticism or their need for adrenaline. Katie had eaten to stuff down the feelings she had of being unworthy to even be a part of her immediate family, although she hadn't known that was why she was doing it back then. All she'd understood was being in her grandma's kitchen, both at Gram's house and in the bakery, felt like where she belonged.

But when her weight had become too much of an issue for her mother to ignore, Monica had threatened to ban Katie from Life is Sweet so she wouldn't be tempted to overindulge. Katie had quickly learned to limit her weakness for bingeing on baked goods and had found that it made her a better apprentice baker. When she wasn't constantly shoving food in her mouth, she actually appreciated the flavors more. Katie's time in the bakery had always bothered her mother, but once she lost the extra weight there wasn't much of an argument Monica could give to keep her away.

Although the scale and mirror might not reflect it, Katie still felt like the same chubby girl she'd been so many years ago. She'd traded stuffing her own face for giving her baked goods away to friends and for charity events, like the Founder's Day silent auction. But when her emotions threatened to get out of hand, food was always the first place she turned for comfort.

Add that to the growing list of reasons to stay clear of Noah. She liked being in control of her emotions. Mostly. Sometimes the pressure of always being stable, friendly and ready to lend a helping hand was too much. She'd chosen this, as clearly as she'd decided to take the bike trail back to her house. Straying from her path now would be very messy. And Katie wasn't one for mess.

Chapter Seven

Noah spent two nights at the hospital with his mother before she finally sent him away.

"I love you, Noah," Meg said from where she was propped up against several pillows, flipping through a gardening magazine. "But you're making me nervous with all that pacing." As was her habit at home, she woke early in the hospital. Much of the normal color had returned to her face and they'd removed the bandage from her head. The angry red of the scar from her surgery was beginning to fade to a lighter pink color already.

"I'm not pacing," he countered and forced himself to stop moving back and forth across her small room.

"And you smell," she added, folding back the page of an article she wanted to keep. One of his trivial but vivid memories from childhood was the stack of magazines always piled in the corner of his mother's bedroom, all with folded pages she'd never look at again. She'd saved them for years, from magazines she looked at during road trips and throughout the endless hours she spent on the sidelines of the various sports he played as a kid. The morning after his father's funeral, she'd emptied out her entire bedroom, packing up his dad's clothes to donate and loading stack after stack of magazines into the back of the pickup truck to be recycled. He remembered watching in numb silence, too swept up in his own sorrow to either stop her or offer to help.

It was odd to watch her with a magazine again.

He started to argue about his need for a shower then lifted his T-shirt and took a whiff. She was right. "I'll drive up to the farm, shower and come back. Tater is fine out at Crimson Ranch, but I don't want you to be alone here for too long."

"That's at least five hours round-trip. It's too much. Emily texted a few minutes ago. She and Davey are on their way. She got a hotel room in Denver for the night." His mother let the magazine fall to her chest and sighed. "I'm worried about her, Noah."

"She's fine," he answered, although he didn't believe that was true. "You need to focus on yourself."

Meg waved away his concern. "All the scans are clear. The doctor is happy with my progress. I'm going to be discharged in a few days. There will be plenty of time for your hovering once I'm back home."

"I'm not hovering." Except he was. Hovering and pacing. He couldn't seem to stop himself.

"I'm not going to die, Noah." His mother flashed a wry smile. "Not yet, anyway."

"Don't joke about that," he snapped automatically then forced himself to take a breath. "I'm sorry. I know you're going to be fine. You have to be fine."

"I think you're avoiding going back to Crimson."

He laughed, although it sounded hollow to his own ears. "That's crazy. I just don't want to leave you."

"Emily told me about the kiss."

"Emily should worry about her own problems."

"A minute ago you said she was fine."

He scrubbed a hand over his face. "If it means we don't have to talk about me, I've changed my mind."

"Katie is a good friend," his mother said, unwilling to be distracted. "She cares for you."

"But I'm too messed up to deserve her," he interrupted.

"I didn't say that."

"You're thinking it." He turned toward her then sank down on the edge of the hospital bed. "I'm thinking it. Everyone must be."

"You're my son, Noah." She nudged his hip with her foot. "I think you deserve everything you want in life."

"Thanks, Mom." He shifted closer and took her hand in his, running his fingers along the hospital bracelet that circled her wrist. His mother's hands had never been delicate. Her nails were short and rounded, the top of her palm callused from work on the farm. Maybe that was the reason women with ornately manicured nails and dainty hands always made him suspicious. Katie had strong hands, too, he realized. Still feminine, but not delicate thanks to her hours in the bakery.

"The question is, do you *want* Katie?"

"If you'd asked me that two weeks ago, I would have said you were crazy for even asking me. She was Tori's best friend all through high school. I never thought of her that way. In the years since then…"

"You're my son," his mother repeated. "But you have horrible taste in women."

"I haven't brought a woman home in years."

"No one since Tori," she agreed.

"So how do you know anything about my taste in women?"

"It's a small town. For that matter, it's a small state when it comes to gossip. I still have friends in Boulder. I hear things."

"You've been keeping tabs on me?"

She shrugged. "Worrying is what mothers do. Your father's death—"

"Has nothing to do with the women I date."

"My surgeon asked me to dinner," she said quietly, picking up the magazine again.

"Are you kidding?" Noah shot off the bed and stalked to the edge of the room, something close to panic creeping up his throat at the thought of his mom with a man who wasn't his father. "That's got to be a breach of the doctor-patient relationship. I'll file a complaint with the hospital. I'll kick his—"

"I'd like to go out with him, Noah."

His righteous indignation fled as quickly as it had come. "Why would you want to do that?" He tried and failed to keep his voice steady.

"It's been more than ten years since your dad died." Unlike his own, Meg's voice was gentle. "He was my whole world, and for a while I wished I'd died right along with him. If it hadn't been for you and Emily, I'm not sure I could have kept going." She placed the magazine on the rolling cart on the far side of the bed. "But I haven't been with a man in all this time."

Noah grimaced. "Mom, I can't have this conversation with you."

"Get your mind out of the gutter," she said with uncharacteristic impatience.

As difficult as this was for him, Noah realized it was just as hard for his mom. He owed her more than he was giving right now. This was why he was here, he reminded himself. To support her.

"I'm sorry." He walked back to the bed, pulled up a chair and sat across from her. "You want to go on a date with the doctor? I'm okay with that. Emily will be, too."

"Sweetie, I appreciate that, but it's not the point. Each of us was deeply affected by losing your father. I've spent too many years with a ghost as my only company. Emily just wanted to get away however she could. And you—"

"I tried, Mom." He interrupted her before she could delve too far into his demons. That was the last thing he needed right now. "I was going to ask Tori to marry me. I wanted to be with her forever." He shrugged, rubbed his hands along his thighs. "Before she cheated on me, that is. Maybe my reluctance to get into another serious relationship has more to do with finding my girlfriend with her naked legs wrapped—" He stopped, stood again. "I can't have this conversation, either."

Meg laughed. "I may be your mother, but I'm a grown woman. I know what teenage couples do in the back of a car."

He turned, narrowed his eyes. "How did you know I found them in the back of a car?"

"Small town," she repeated. "Don't let your father's death or what happened with Tori stop you from believing in love or your capacity for it."

"I think my track record speaks for itself."

She sighed. "I can't stop you from believing the worst about yourself. But it's not how I see you. I don't think it's how Katie sees you, either."

"She should. I haven't done right by her."

"You can't change the past." His mother leaned back against the pillow, closed her eyes. "But you can choose how to move forward."

He thought about that for a moment then leaned forward and placed a soft kiss on her forehead. "Have you always been this smart?"

"Yes." She cracked open one eye. "Take a shower, Noah. Take Tater for a hike. Talk to Katie. I'll be fine here and I'll call if I need anything."

"I'll come back—"

"Tomorrow," she finished for him.

"Tomorrow," he agreed. "I love you, Mom."

"You too, sweetie."

He walked to the door then looked over his shoulder. "And your new Dr. Love better treat you right. I meant what I said about kicking his butt otherwise."

With his mother's smile in his mind, he walked out of the hospital to head toward the mountains.

"Have dinner with me?"

Katie whirled around from where she was stapling a flyer for the Founder's Day Festival onto the community bulletin board outside the bakery.

Noah crossed his hands in front of his face and ducked. "Maybe you want to put down the weapon before you answer."

She lowered the arm that held the staple gun. "How's your mom?" she asked, ignoring his question.

Some of the stress had eased from his face. In fact, he looked much better than he had when she'd last seen him in the hospital. Almost perfect, damn him. He wore his Forest Service uniform, and the gray button-down shirt stretched across his muscled chest while the olive-colored pants fit his long, toned legs perfectly. Okay, she needed to not think about his body. At all.

"She's good," he answered, one side of his mouth kicking up as if he could read her mind's wayward thoughts. "Healing up nicely and itching to be out of the hospital and back home. She's due to be released on Friday."

"You've been staying at the hospital?"

He gave a quick nod. "She finally got sick of me and sent me home. I need to get caught up on some paperwork at the office and thought I'd pick up a dozen cookies to take in with me."

"Lelia's working the counter," Katie told him. "She can help you. I want to hand out a few more flyers along Main Street."

"Mind if I keep you company?"

Mind if I plaster myself across your body?

"Sure." She handed him half the stack of papers in her hand. "You take this side of the street. I'll do the other and meet you on the corner."

Before he could argue, she dashed across the street, narrowly avoiding being hit by a minivan with Kansas license plates pulling out of a parking space. She heard Noah shout her name but didn't look back, ducking into the outdoor-equipment store in the middle of the block. She made a few minutes of small talk with the shop's owner then proceeded to the next storefront. She took her time, part of her hoping Noah would give out all of his flyers and leave for the Forest Service headquarters near the edge of town.

Instead he was waiting for her at the corner, leaning back against a light post with his head tilted up to the sun. He wore his usual wraparound sunglasses and the ends of his golden hair curled at the nape of his neck.

How long would she have to tell herself she'd got over him before her body believed it was true?

"Getting hit by a car is a little extreme as a way to avoid talking to me," he said as she approached.

"I didn't plan that part of it," she answered, taking the remaining flyers he handed to her. His finger brushed her wrist and she pulled back, sucking in a breath. This had to stop or he was going to drive her crazy. "What do you want, Noah?"

"You didn't answer my question about dinner." He smiled at her, a grin she recognized from years of experience. It was the devil-may-care smile he gave to women in bars, at parties or in general as he easily charmed his way into their hearts and beds. It wasn't going to work on Katie, even if her toes curled in automatic response to it.

"No."

She moved around him, looked both ways on the street and stepped off the curb.

It was only seconds before he caught up with her. "You don't mean that."

"I do."

"You can't."

"And why is that?" she asked, glancing at him out of the corner of her eye.

He was staring at her and wiggled his brows. "Because you want me."

"Wow." She shook her head, almost tripped over her own two feet. "Your ego never fails to astound."

"I want you even more." He leaned closer, his breath tickling the hair that had fallen out of her long braid. "It was too good between us. I haven't been able to stop thinking about you. The way you touched me… the sounds you made when I—"

"Stop!" She turned and pushed him away, hating the way her body had caught fire at his words. "I can't do this anymore." She crushed the flyers to her chest, as if she could ease the panic in her heart.

"So what if I want you?" She poked at his chest with one finger. "Every woman you've ever been with—and don't forget I know many of them—still wants you. You've got skills." Her eyes narrowed as she glared at him. "Unfair, maddening skills. But you're…you're… a man-boy."

"Man-boy?" His body went rigid. "What the hell does that mean?"

"We've been over this. You want a good time. I want a future. I'm not going to deny that I'm attracted to you. Eighty-year-old women and babies are attracted to you. But I want more. The only way I'm going to get it is to move on. How am I supposed to do that if I hop back into bed with you?"

"I asked you to dinner, Katie. A date. I'm not looking for friends with benefits. I could find that anywhere."

She gasped, and he cringed in response. He ran one hand through his hair, blew out a breath. "Let's start over. I'm messing this up and that wasn't part of my plan." He took off his sunglasses and the intensity of his piercing blue eyes captured her. She couldn't have moved if she'd wanted to. "Would you please have dinner with me, Katie Garrity? A real date." He smiled, but this time it was hesitant and a little hopeful.

The catch in her heart made her sure of her answer. "No," she whispered.

Noah's head snapped back as if she'd struck him. She expected him to stalk away. Noah liked his women agreeable and easy. And Katie wanted to be, not just because of her feelings for him but because she liked making people happy. She was agreeable to a fault, but somewhere inside, her instinct for self-preservation wouldn't allow her to succumb to Noah's charms. She'd promised herself she was moving on, and that was what she was going to do.

But he didn't move. He didn't speak, just continued to stare at her as if she was a puzzle he wanted to solve.

"I'm going out with Matt again," she offered into the silence. Katie hated awkward silences. "You and I are friends, Noah. That's how it's been for years and it's worked just fine."

"Has it?" He reached out and rubbed a loose strand of her hair between two fingers. She shivered. "I'm not sure—"

"Well, isn't this cozy," a voice said from behind Noah.

His hand dropped at the same time Katie felt her stomach pitch and roll.

He flipped his sunglasses down before turning away from her. "Hey, Tori," he said to the woman glaring at the two of them. "Welcome back to Crimson."

Noah wanted to see his ex-girlfriend at this moment like he wanted to be stuck on the side of a mountain in a lightning storm.

The analogy seemed to fit as he could almost feel the tension radiating between the two women. He didn't understand that at all. Katie had been Tori's shadow and best friend throughout high school. Yes, she'd taken his side in the breakup. But since he'd caught Tori in the act with one of his football buddies, Noah wasn't sure how she could fault Katie for not being more sympathetic. As far as he knew, the two hadn't spoken in all these years.

Now he wished he would have questioned that more. Hell, there was a lot more he wished he'd paid attention to over the years. Katie had just always been there, consistent like the sun rising, and he'd never thought about the possibility of that changing. Or how he'd feel if she wasn't a part of his life.

He wasn't going to give up on her, even if he knew he should. His mom was right—Noah may have not done his best in life up until now, but there was no better time to change his future. Of course, he needed to convince Katie of that before it was too late. He'd seen the way Matt Davis had looked at her the night of their date. But as far as Noah was concerned, Katie was his and always would be.

"How long are you in town?" Katie asked, her voice shaky. Noah saw her dart a glance between Tori and him. She couldn't possibly think he still had feelings for his old girlfriend.

"At least a month," Tori answered, bitterness blazing in her eyes as she glared at Katie. Noah had to resist the urge to step between the two of them. If memory served, Tori could be vicious when she wanted to. "I'm redesigning a residence in Aspen. My client is wealthy enough to want me on-site for the whole project. I'm visiting my parents while I'm here." She leaned forward and placed a hand on Noah's arm. "I've been thinking about both your mother and you. There are so many reminders of our time together here."

As Katie let out a snort, Tori's eyes narrowed further. "Let's grab a drink sometime while we're both in town. There's so much I'd like to explain to you about that night, Noah. Details you've never heard."

He shook out of her grasp, noticing that Tori's fingers were long, the nails bright red and perfectly manicured. "I saw enough detail to last me a lifetime, Tori. Let's leave the past where it belongs."

She bit down on her lip, the corner of her mouth dipping into a pout he used to find irresistible. Now it made her seem as if she was trying too hard. "If that's what you want, but I'd still be interested in that drink."

He felt Katie shift behind him. He wasn't about to let her get away. "I'm busy these days, Tori. But maybe we can work something out."

Her smile was immediate. "Why don't we—"

"I'll catch you later." Without waiting for a response, he turned and jogged to catch up to Katie. "What's the matter?"

"Nothing," she said on a hiss of breath. "But I think you just proved my point. It hadn't been a minute since I said 'no' and you were making a date with your ex."

They were back in front of the bakery. He took Katie's arm as she reached for the door. "I could care less about Tori, and you know it. I wanted to get away from her without making a scene. I didn't make a date. A *date* is where I pick up a woman at her house and buy her dinner. A date is what I want with *you*."

She looked so lost standing there, as if his simple request to take her to dinner was tearing her up inside. This wasn't what he wanted for Katie. He wanted a chance to make her happy, not to cause her more pain.

"I don't trust—"

"Katie?" A petite woman with shoulder-length brown hair poked her head out of the storefront. "Marian Jones is on the phone. She forgot to order a cake for her husband's retirement party and needs something by tomorrow."

"I'm coming, Lelia." She closed her eyes for a moment, and when she opened them again, her expression was carefully blank. "I've got to go, Noah. We're friends and it works. Let's not jeopardize that."

He started to speak but she held up a hand. "Tell your mom I'll be over to see her as soon as she gets back home." She stood on tiptoe, leaned forward and kissed his cheek. Her mouth was sweet, and he wanted to turn his face and claim it. But he didn't move and a second later she disappeared into the bakery. He pressed his fingertips to the skin where her lips had been, as if he could still feel their softness. That kiss had felt like goodbye, and no matter how much he wanted to, Noah didn't know how to change that.

Chapter Eight

The sun was warm on her back when Katie climbed the steps of the Crawford family farmhouse the following week. Emily appeared a moment later, wearing a faded T-shirt and sweatpants and still managing to look more sophisticated than Katie did on her best day. If it wasn't for the shadow of sadness in Emily's ice-blue eyes, Katie might be jealous of the other woman.

Emily had been only a year behind them in school, but Noah's sister never had much use for anyone in Crimson. Even before Jacob Crawford had got sick, it was clear Emily was destined for a bigger future than this town could give her. Once her father had died, it seemed to Katie that Noah's sister had become more frenetic in her quest to get out of town.

But now she was back, just like Noah, and it bothered Katie to see how out of place Emily looked. Katie could relate to that feeling.

The smile Emily gave Katie was genuine, if drawn.

"Come on in." She stepped back to allow Katie room to enter. The Crawfords had done quite a bit of renovations to the property when Noah and Emily were kids. Most of the first floor was covered in shiplap siding that had been painted warm gray. A colorful rug sat on top of slate tile floors, making the entry seem both modern and as if it would have fit the decade the house was originally built.

"Noah's not here right now. He's—"

"In Boulder," Katie finished, then nervously scraped at a bit of dried frosting near the hem of her shirt. She'd been working crazy hours at the bakery and was wearing the same clothes as yesterday. "He mentioned heading down for a meeting." Actually, she hadn't spoken to Noah since they'd run into his ex-girlfriend. She'd wanted to visit Meg but hadn't been able to deal with him again so soon. The older woman who answered the phones for the Forest Service office in town stopped in almost every day for a muffin and coffee, and it hadn't been difficult to get her to share Noah's schedule for the week.

One of Emily's delicate brows arched. "And you picked today to come out to the house?"

"Well, I thought…it seemed…" Katie could feel color heating her cheeks as she stumbled over an explanation. "Yes," she said finally. "I'm here today."

Emily looked at her another moment. "Most women fall at Noah's feet without him even lifting a finger."

"I've borne witness to that phenomenon more than once," Katie agreed.

"He needs more of a challenge than that."

"I'm not trying to challenge him."

"But you do." Emily nodded. "It's good for him."

"We're just friends, Em."

Katie had been here a few times over the years and always thought the house displayed not only Meg's design taste but the love of the family that lived here. Now it seemed almost too quiet.

"I watched him kiss you."

Katie shrugged. "He was…worried about your mom. It was an emotional response, and I happened to be there."

"I don't think my brother has ever had a truly emotional response to anything. He isn't built like that."

"Not true." Katie wasn't sure why she needed to defend Noah but couldn't seem to stop herself. "He cares too much, and it scares him. That's why and when he makes some of his more brilliantly stupid decisions. If he could learn to deal with what he feels…" She stopped, frowned at the knowing look Emily gave her.

"If someone could help him with that…" Emily flashed a hopeful smile.

Katie shook her head. "I can't be that person."

"Can't or won't?"

"Same outcome. I didn't come here for this. I care about Noah and your whole family, but Noah and I are only friends. How is your mom doing?" she asked, needing to steer the conversation to a safer topic. "If this isn't a good time—"

"She's feeling good and will be happy to see you." Emily started toward the back of the house. "Noah moved her bed down into Dad's office on the first floor. We thought it would be easier not to have to deal with steps." She looked over her shoulder. "According to Mom, he'll be moving it back upstairs by the end of the week. Home from the hospital three days and she wants everything back to normal."

They paused outside a closed door. Emily straightened her shoulders and reached for the handle.

"How are you, Em?"

The other woman turned, her hand still on the doorknob. "What has Noah told you?" Her expression had turned wary.

"Not a lot. He respects your privacy. I'm asking you."

"Things are peachy." Emily pushed her hair away from her face. "My marriage is over. I have no job and no prospects since I left college to pursue my dream of becoming a trophy wife." She smiled, but her voice dripped sarcasm. "I'm back in a town I couldn't wait to leave behind, friendless, penniless and living with my mother. I'm now fighting my ex-husband to get our son the treatment he needs for problems I barely understand. So, yeah, 'peachy' about sums it up."

"Emily, I'm sorry—"

"Don't." When Katie reached for her, Emily shook off the touch. "If there's one thing I can't take right now it's pity. I'm sure this whole town is talking about how the girl who was too good for Crimson has come crawling back with her tail between her legs."

"I don't think that's true and I certainly don't pity you. I remember how much you helped with your father's care. You're strong. You'll get through this."

Emily met her gaze, her blue eyes sparkling with bitterness and unshed tears. "You don't know me at all."

"Maybe not," Katie agreed, "but I'd like to. I'm helping with the committee for the Founder's Day Festival—more than I'd planned because my friend Olivia, who was chairing the celebration this year, is having a tough go with morning sickness. It's her first baby."

"Olivia Wilder?" Emily asked. "The wife of the mayor who skipped out of town?"

"She divorced him and married the youngest of the Travers brothers—Logan."

Emily shook her head. "The one with the twin who died? I thought he was trouble."

"People change. Logan came back to town for his brother's wedding and met Olivia. They're good for each other. He has a thriving construction business and she runs the community center now and took over the festival as an offshoot of her work there. Most of the plans are in place and it's going to be a lot of fun."

"That's quite a reinvention for both of them."

"The people in Crimson are more forgiving than you think, Emily. It's a great town, actually. If you got involved—"

"Don't push it, Katie. I'm happy for you to help Noah, but I don't need saving."

Emily's words stung, but Katie pressed on. She'd bet a pan of brownies that Noah's sister needed more help than she would admit. "I'm only trying to include you while you're in town."

"I'll think about it," Emily said then sighed. "I appreciate the offer." She opened the door then held out a hand. "Give me your cell phone and I'll put in my number. Text me the time of the next meeting and we'll see."

"Katie, is that you?"

Handing off her cell to Emily, Katie smiled and entered the room. "I'm sorry I haven't been by sooner, Mrs. Crawford. You look wonderful."

Noah's mother smiled and put aside the book she held in her hands. "No apologies. I understand how busy you are with the bakery." She waved Katie forward. "Your grandmother would be so proud of you, sweetheart. I'm proud of you."

Tears stung the backs of Katie's eyes. It had been a

long time since anyone had given her that kind of praise. One problem with being a fixture in town for so long was the expectation she'd do well with the bakery, plus help out wherever needed. Her grandma had held the role and Katie'd taken it over without question. Only recently, since she'd decided she wanted something of a life for herself besides her business, did she wonder if there was more to her than the dependable girl next door everyone in Crimson saw. Hearing Meg say that her grandmother would be proud made the long hours and sacrifice worth it. Gram had been the most important person in her life, and there was nothing Katie wouldn't sacrifice to live up to her legacy.

"From what I hear, you're the one who deserves the praise," she said as she took the seat next to the head of the bed. "Your recovery has been amazing so far. I know both Noah and Emily are thrilled you're doing so well."

Meg waved away her words. "They worry too much. Noah especially, although he'd never admit it. Now tell me what you brought me."

Katie bit back a laugh. "What makes you think I brought you something?"

"Because 'life is sweet' isn't simply the name of your shop. It's what you do—you make life sweeter for the people around you."

Katie's heart swelled at the words, and she reached into the cloth shopping bag she'd carried in with her. "Cinnamon rolls," she said with a wink.

"My favorite," Meg whispered and took the box, opening it and licking her lips. "How do you remember everyone's preferences?"

"You're not just anyone, Mrs. Crawford."

"Call me Meg." She lifted the box as Emily walked

up to the bed and handed Katie her phone. "She brought cinnamon rolls."

As Emily leaned forward to breathe in the scent, a deep voice called from the doorway, "You're planning to share those. Right, Mom?"

Katie's phone clattered to the tile floor and she heard a crack as the screen shattered. "Damn," she muttered, bending forward to retrieve it. Noah's long fingers wrapped around hers as she picked up the phone. "I've got it." As soon as she said the words, he released her. "I thought you were in Boulder today."

He quirked one brow at her statement. "Checking up on me?"

"Katie is my guest today, Noah," Meg said. "And you owe her a new phone."

"It's fine," Katie said quickly. "My fault."

"It was clearly Noah's fault," Emily said.

"Because I came home?" he asked, his voice incredulous.

"You made her drop the phone," Emily insisted.

Katie shifted in her chair, focusing her gaze on Emily and Meg. "He didn't."

"I'm sorry, Katie," Noah offered after a moment. "I'll gladly buy you a new phone if you'll make eye contact with me."

Katie sucked in a breath, shocked that he'd call her out publicly in front of his mom and sister.

Her eyes snapped to his, but before she could speak, Meg said, "Noah, would you please put on a pot of water for tea?"

"Emily can do that." He kept his blue gaze on Katie, who fingered the cracks on the screen of her phone. A dozen hairline fissures radiated out from the center.

Splintered just like her heart felt since Noah had returned to Crimson.

"I'm going to check on Davey." Emily hitched a thumb toward Noah. "Save one of those for me. Don't let Noah eat them all."

"I may not let him have one if he doesn't do what I ask." Meg lifted a brow at her son. Katie kept her head down.

"Fine," he mumbled and followed Emily out of the room.

"I should go," Katie said when they were alone.

"You just got here," Meg argued.

Katie stood, dropped her ruined phone into her purse. "I really only came to drop off the cinnamon rolls to you. I came because…"

"Because you thought Noah was in Boulder today." Meg slowly shut the white cardboard box that held the cinnamon rolls. "He's my son and I love him. That doesn't mean I'm unaware of how he operates."

"He didn't mean for my phone to break."

"He wouldn't mean to break your heart, either."

Katie swallowed, nodded. "But he could."

"Or he could make it whole."

"I can't take that chance." She dropped a kiss on Meg's cheek, unwilling to consider the possibility of trusting Noah with her heart. "I'll be by to see you again. I hope you'll be well enough to attend some of the Founder's Day Festival events. I'd like Emily to help out with the committee."

Meg nodded. "That would be good for her. You're good for this family, Katie. For Noah. I hope you know that."

Katie didn't know how to answer, so she flashed a

smile she hoped didn't look as forced as it felt. "Take care, Meg."

She slipped from the room and down the hall. She could hear Noah banging cabinet doors shut and china rattling in the kitchen as she sneaked by as quietly as she could.

Her foot hit the first step of the porch when the front door slammed. "Is this what it's come to?" Noah's voice rang out in the silence of midafternoon. "We go from friends to lovers to you running away from me? I'm used to being the person disappointing everyone around me. Now I understand how they've felt on the receiving end of it all these years."

He'd meant to rile her—because misery loved company, and Noah was miserable and angry right now. The anger was mostly self-directed. He'd finished his meetings early in Boulder and left before lunch to beat rush-hour traffic coming out of the city. When he'd pulled up to his mom's house and seen Katie's Subaru parked in front, a flash of pleasure and anticipation had surged through him. He couldn't think of a better way to spend the afternoon than on the front porch of the farmhouse with a cold beer in his hand and Katie on the porch swing next to him.

Except it was obvious she not only hadn't expected his return but was upset by it. Katie, who had always been ready with a smile and a hug, didn't want to see him and tried to sneak out to avoid him.

Oh, yeah. He was pissed. But as he watched her stiffen while strands of hair blew around her shoulders in the summer breeze, he wondered if he'd gone too far.

All Noah wanted to do was get closer, but the only

thing he seemed to manage when he opened his mouth was push her further away.

"I came to see your mom." Katie turned, her fingers gripping the painted railing. "This has nothing to do with you."

"I don't believe you."

Her eyes narrowed. "Have you had that drink with Tori?"

He shook his head. "I won't if it upsets you."

"It's none of my business."

"It matters what you think, whether it's your business or not. You said it yourself—we're friends." And more, even if she wouldn't admit it and he barely understood his changing feelings about their relationship. He felt alive with Katie, his body electric in its response to her. Her blue cotton T-shirt hugged the curves of her breasts and her slim waist, and he knew how her skin felt underneath it. That was the thing making him so crazy. It was knowing her in a way no one else did. People in town saw her as the dependable, caring baker they could count on in any situation. But he wanted more of the passionate woman who had nipped and teased him, responsive to every kiss and touch. He wanted to close the distance between them and place his mouth on her throat, where a tiny patch of dried icing stuck to her skin. The idea of sucking it off, imagining the sugar on his tongue mixed with her unique taste made him grow hard.

"Friends," she repeated, drawing him back to the moment.

"If that's all you'll give me." He cleared his throat, doing multiplication facts in his head to keep his heated thoughts in check.

She tilted her head, pulled her hair over one shoulder

as if deciding whether she could trust him. He knew the answer to that but wasn't about to share it with her.

"I need your help," she said after a moment.

"Anything." He stepped forward. "What is it? Founder's Day? The bakery? Something at your house?"

"Slow down, Noah," she said with a small smile.

Something in him fizzed and popped at the sight of that smile. He ran one hand through his hair, needing to pull it together.

"I'd like you to teach me to swim."

His brain tried to compute that request. "You know how to swim. I've seen you at the hot springs."

She shook her head. "In open water. I haven't been to the reservoir since I freaked out during the triathlon my dad signed me up for when I was twelve."

"Why now?" He braced himself for her answer, confident he wasn't going to like it.

"Matt invited me out on his boat for the Fourth of July. A group of his friends is going to Hidden Canyon."

He bit back the irritating urge to growl at the mention of the other man's name. "He's a swim coach, right? Why not have him teach you?"

"What if I panic again? My stomach feels sick just thinking about going in the water. I don't want him to see me like that."

"But it's okay if I see you like that?"

"We're *just* friends," she said softly.

"You want me to help you overcome your fear so you can go out with another guy?"

She looked at him for a moment then shook her head. "Never mind. I'll deal with it on my own." She turned and headed toward her car, dust from the gravel driveway swirling behind her.

"Katie, wait." When she didn't stop, Noah cursed and

ran after her, his hand slamming against the driver's-side door as she reached for the handle. "I'll help you. Of course I'll take you swimming."

"Forget it. I shouldn't have asked you. It's stupid anyway. It's not as if I'm going to hide who I am from him forever. I don't even own a bathing suit."

"Let me help you with this." He crouched down so they were at eye level. "Please."

She met his gaze then pressed a hand to her eyes. "I feel like I'm going to throw up."

"You won't throw up." He took her hand in his, gently peeling it away from her face. "We can get you through this."

Her gaze turned hopeful. "I want to be the fun girl. The one who can hang out with a guy's friends. The one you call for a good time."

Noah kept a smile plastered on his face, although the thought of some other guy having a "good time" with Katie just about sliced him open. "I have one condition."

She rolled her eyes. "Seriously?"

He nodded. "Your bathing suit needs to be one piece. The one you wear on July Fourth, anyway. With me, I'd recommend a string bikini."

"Right," she said, choking out a laugh. "Can you see me in a string bikini?"

"I'm picturing it right now," Noah whispered then groaned when she bit down on her bottom lip. "Definitely a string bikini with me."

"But only you?"

He shrugged, tried to look nonchalant. "I'm thinking of you. Everyone goes cliff jumping at Hidden Canyon Reservoir over the Fourth. You don't want to lose your top in front of all those partyers."

"Oh, no." She slapped her hand back over her eyes. "I forgot about the cliff jumping."

"You don't have to—"

"And get left on shore serving snacks when they return?" She shook her head. "I'm tired of being the town's mother hen. I'm going to jump off the highest rock out there." She swallowed, hitched a breath. "Or the second-highest."

"That's a girl." Noah couldn't help himself. He reached out a finger and touched the bit of icing dried to her skin. "I can get time off next Tuesday. It's supposed to be warm. We can go then when it won't be crowded."

"Okay. Thank you." She fingered the base of her throat. "I'm covered in frosting. What a mess."

"You're beautiful," he answered.

She swayed closer and for an instant he thought she might kiss him. Damn, he wanted her to. Instead she blinked and pulled back.

"I'll see you next week."

Removing his hand from her door, he balled it into a fist at his side as she got in her car and drove away. He tried to tell himself this was progress, although helping her win the affection of another man was hardly a step in the right direction. But it would allow him more time with her, which had to count for something.

Katie didn't need to become more adventurous or change in any way as far as Noah was concerned. She was perfect exactly the way she was. He only wished it hadn't taken him so long to realize it.

Chapter Nine

"Are you sure you want to do this?" Jase asked him two days later.

"Absolutely. Hand me that microphone stand." Noah was in the park at the center of town. It was a block wide with picnic tables and a covered patio area on one side and an open expanse of grass and a playground on the other. He was helping Jase set up the temporary stage for the concert that would take place tonight. The Founder's Day committee had organized it as a teaser for the big festival, to get both locals and tourists vacationing in the area excited about the upcoming event.

"Thanks, man. I know you're juggling a lot between your mom and work. It means a ton that you'd come out to help."

Noah didn't answer, just lifted an amplifier into place.

"Katie's more involved with the committee this year."

"Emily might have mentioned that," Noah admitted. He saw Jase shake his head. "But that's not why I'm here."

His friend laughed. "Uh-huh."

"It's not the *only* reason I'm here," Noah amended. "I hate being in that house."

Jase continued setting up the stage but asked, "Is everything okay with your mom?"

"Yes. She's amazing. As always. Made me promise I'd move the bed back upstairs tomorrow. She has a date next week with one of her doctors."

"She's led a pretty solitary life since your dad died."

"I didn't realize that until I came back to stay. Don't get me wrong, it's been good to see her and Emily. Em and I were close as kids, you know? Really close. I thought I understood her. Since she's come back I can't figure out what the hell she thinks about anything. She's so overwhelmed with Davey and her divorce but won't open up."

"Some things take time."

"I guess Katie's asked her to help with the baking competition—coordinating judges or something like that."

"Maybe that will help." Jase turned to him, unlooping a microphone cord as he spoke. "Is that why you hate being in the house—because of Emily and her son?"

"No," Noah answered quickly. "Not at all. I like the kid, actually. He's quirky but in an interesting way. Tater adores him." Noah ran a hand through his hair. "If I was anyplace else with them, maybe it would be different. It's that house. The memories there. How I failed my father. All the mistakes I made."

"I doubt your mother sees it that way."

"She's my mom. Of course she'll support me no matter what."

"That's no guarantee," Jase said softly.

"Damn. I'm sorry."

"It's old news. Just don't take her love for granted."

Now Noah felt like an even bigger jerk. Jase's mother had deserted her family when Jase was only eight. He'd grown up with only an alcoholic father to parent him.

"I get it, and I love my mom and Em. But I can't stand being reminded of how much I wasn't around when Dad needed me."

"You're here now."

"Funny," Noah said with a chuckle. "That's exactly what Katie said."

"She's smart." Jase unrolled a colorful Oriental rug across the wood of the stage floor.

"Smart enough to be done with me." Noah blew out a breath. "I can't let that happen, Jase."

"Why now?" his friend asked. "Katie's been a part of your life forever. She's put up with you for years and suddenly you realize she was worth looking at all this time."

"Yes." Noah helped straighten the rug then leaned back on his heels. "I mean no. I don't understand it. All I know is now that I've seen her—really seen her—I can't give her up."

"She's coming to the concert with Matt Davis."

"You know that for sure?" Noah let out a string of curses. "I thought since she was on the committee she'd be here working."

"Making her easy pickings for you?"

"Why are you giving me a hard time? You've got to be on my side."

"I *am* on your side." Jase jumped off the stage onto

the grass. "You think you failed your father and that belief has haunted you for over a decade. If you hurt Katie, it's going to be just as bad. For both of you. Don't go down that path."

"But I need her," Noah whispered. "I want her even if I don't deserve her."

"Be careful and be sure." Jase glanced to the pavilion end of the park, where people were gathered in front of the barbecue food truck parked near the sidewalk. "We have a few more things to unload before everyone heads this way."

Noah nodded. "Put me to work. Whatever my motivations for being here, I'm definitely cheap labor."

"Bless you for that." Jase smiled and led the way to his truck.

Noah worked without a break for the next two hours. He helped set up the four-piece bluegrass band's instruments and moved trash and recycling cans around the perimeter of the lawn. He saw quite a few people he knew and found it was good to catch up with most of them. The universal sentiment seemed to be that he was the golden child for coming back to Crimson to help take care of his mom. He tried to downplay it as much as he could since his first instinct was to clarify how much he had to make up for from his father's illness. By the time the concert started, he was wrung out emotionally and ready to retreat to the back of the stage to watch the show. It was out of character since he never walked away from a party. Being around other people was the best way he knew to avoid dealing with his own thoughts. But tonight he craved a little solitude.

As he moved through the crowd, he saw Katie along with Matt Davis and another couple laying a blanket across the grass. The same picnic basket she'd brought to the hospital was tucked under her arm. She wore a lemon yellow shirt with thin straps and a pair of tight jeans and platform-heeled sandals. She looked fresh and beautiful, like sunshine come to life.

He slapped his hand against his forehead as Matt draped a sweater over her shoulders. No matter how warm it got during the day, the temperature in the mountains almost always cooled by at least fifteen degrees in the evening.

Noah hated the idea of another man touching her, even in such an innocent way, but he couldn't stop it. All he could do was stick it out, something he'd never excelled at, and hope that she would understand his feelings were real.

"Stop staring at me." Katie planted her feet on the grass and crossed her arms over her chest as she glared at Noah. Feeling his gaze on her was making it hard to remember she was on a date with another man this evening.

He sat alone behind the stage, his face obscured by shadows. "How's the date going?" he asked gently, not bothering to get up or face her. Darkness had fallen completely over the town, and the music coming from the stage was loud and boisterous.

The four-piece bluegrass band had driven over from Breckenridge to play this concert. Their songs ranged from slow ballads to livelier tunes like the one they were playing now. If she tilted her head, Katie could see the crowd in front of the stage, many of them on their feet dancing and swaying to the beat. The lights strung across the green gave the whole scene a warm glow.

But the heat she'd felt had been from Noah's gaze on her. She'd seen him when her group had first settled on the grass but had expected him to join Jase and his other friends once the concert started. Instead, he'd remained alone—something Noah never did.

"The date would be going a lot better if I wasn't being watched." She took a step forward, wanting to see him. She couldn't explain the reason. "Why are you back here by yourself anyway? Jase is out there with Josh, Sara and a whole group of your friends."

"I'm not in the mood for a big group tonight." He stood, turned to face the stage but didn't step out of the shadows. "You weren't dancing."

"Matt isn't much of a dancer."

"But you love it. Do you want me to ask you to dance, Bug?"

Oh, yes. Her body ached for him to twirl her into his arms. "No," she said through clenched teeth. "Why are you watching me?"

"Because you're beautiful," he answered simply.

Katie felt a current race through her, as if her whole body was electric. She tingled from head to toe, a sensation she seemed to feel only with Noah. It was dangerous, exciting and she should hate it. Instead, it drew her to him and away from her plan, her date and her idea of what life should look like.

"I'm trying to move on."

"I should let you go?"

She sighed. "You never had me in the first place."

"Didn't I?" He moved suddenly, reaching for her. He took hold of her arm, pulled her in front of him. He wrapped his arms around her, pressed her back to his chest. His breath tickled her ear as he spoke against her skin. "Because when I see you with him, all I can think is *mine*."

"I'm not," she argued, but her voice was breathless

and she loved the feel of his body against hers. The band started a slower song, the guitar and fiddle playing a mournful tune as the singer sang words of longing for a lost love. Goose bumps rose along Katie's bare arms as Noah pressed a kiss on her shoulder.

"You need your sweater," he whispered, wrapping his arms more tightly around her, enveloping her in his heat. He swayed with her, almost dancing but more intimate. Just the two of them, moving together.

God, she was a slut. No, that wasn't true. She only wanted to be when it came to Noah. Her willpower faded along with the chill she felt from the cool night air as he turned her in his arms and kissed her. His mouth molded to hers and every ounce of intelligence she possessed disappeared. She didn't care that it was wrong or that she would be hurt in the end. All that mattered was this moment and the man making her senseless with his touch.

"This is wrong," she whispered, pulling away as far as he'd let her. "You don't want me."

He laughed, the sound vibrating against her skin as he ran his lips over her jaw. "I want you so much, Katie."

The sound of applause from the front of the stage brought her back to reality. "No." She took two steps away, trying to get her breath, her emotions and her heart under control. "Not the way I'm looking for. You've said so yourself."

"Maybe I can change. For you."

She wanted to trust him, but what if it didn't work out? Katie knew what it was like to be rejected by the people you cared about most in the world. She'd spent most of her adult life overcoming the pain of not being the person her parents wanted her to be. With Noah it could be even more heartbreaking.

"We won't know unless you give me a chance."

She'd loved him almost half her life, but it was easier to love in secret than risk him seeing all the things she'd hidden about herself from the world. Her doubts, her fears, her moments of anger and pettiness.

Noah had the same perfect image of her as most people in town. The one she'd cultivated through the years, but which now weighed her down with its limits. That was why she was trying to start fresh with someone like Matt—a man who had no preconceived notions about her. She could be anyone she wanted with him—wild, impetuous, or selfish when it suited her. Although nothing about him brought out her wild side like Noah did.

She wanted someone to see her as real, more than the supportive friend or generous local shop owner. Yet Katie didn't know who she was without those labels. What if she peeled back her layers for Noah and he didn't like the person she was underneath?

That would do more than break her heart. It would crush her soul.

"I've got to go," she said. "Matt and the others will be waiting for me."

"Katie..." Noah's voice was strained, as if he was holding back so much of what he wanted to say.

"I don't want to ruin our friendship," she told him. "It's too important to me."

She turned and fled, unable to look at him for one more second without launching herself into his arms.

The next several days Katie spent in the kitchen at the bakery, tweaking the new recipe for her parents' superfood bar and finishing up orders for several events taking place in Aspen over the weekend.

She had just enough time to deliver a final round

of cupcakes before hurrying back to Crimson for a Founder's Day Festival committee meeting. As much as she wanted to help out Olivia, what Katie really needed was to take a nap. As she drove along the highway that ran between the two towns, her eyes drifted shut for one brief moment—or so it felt—and she almost swerved across the median. Between her work on the festival, late nights at the bakery and losing sleep over thoughts about Noah, Katie was exhausted. Maybe she should pull back a bit.

Fighting back a yawn, she got out of her car and climbed the steps to the community center, planning to tell Olivia exactly that before the meeting.

Her friend was waiting for her near the receptionist desk in the lobby.

"Katie, you're a lifesaver," Olivia said as she approached. She looked pale and more fragile than ever leaning against the wall behind the desk. "I don't know what we'd do without you stepping in on the committee."

"I wanted to talk to you about that." Katie hugged her purse close to her body. She never said no or reneged on a commitment, so the thought of letting Olivia down almost made her physically nauseous.

"Can it wait?" Logan came around the corner at that moment and Katie took a step back. Logan was big, with the broad, strong body of a man who made his living doing physical labor all day. He could be intimidating, but Olivia's presence had softened him a great deal since his return to Crimson. Now the expression on his face was downright scary.

"I've got time," Olivia said gently, laying a hand on his arm.

"You need to get to the hospital."

"The hospital?" Katie stepped forward, swallowing around the worry that crept into her throat. "Is everything okay with the baby?"

"Yes," Olivia answered at the same time Logan said, "We don't know."

Olivia waved away his concern. "It's a routine appointment. My doctor wants me to go in for a blood test and some monitoring they can't do in his office."

"Plus IV fluids," Logan added.

"She thinks I'm dehydrated." She smiled, but it looked strained. "The morning sickness isn't getting better."

Logan took her hand. "And it lasts all day."

"But it isn't an emergency." Olivia stepped forward, swayed and leaned into her husband. "Really, Katie. I'm tired and weak. It's not life threatening."

Logan glowered. "Not yet."

"You two go on." Katie gave Olivia a quick hug and patted Logan awkwardly on the shoulder.

"But if you need something—"

"It can wait." Katie felt embarrassment wash through her. She was worried about needing a nap when Olivia could be in the middle of a real crisis. "I'll drop off dinner to your house so that it's there when you get home."

"You're doing so much already," Olivia said, pursing her lips.

"But we'd appreciate it." Logan shrugged when his wife threw him a disapproving look. "What? You need to eat something besides crackers and I know she's a great cook." He turned to Katie. "I'm parked on the next block. Would you stay with her while I pull up my truck?"

"Of course."

He gave Olivia a quick, tender kiss on the top of her head and jogged toward the front door.

"He worries too much," Olivia said when the door shut behind him.

"He loves you." Katie linked her arm in her friend's. "Does Millie know you're going to the hospital?"

"Please don't say anything," Olivia answered, shaking her head. "I promise I'll text if we find anything serious." She squeezed Katie's hand. "I love this baby so much already. I know it's wrong to become attached so early in the pregnancy. So many things can go wrong, and I'm not exactly a spring chicken."

"Don't be silly." Olivia was in her early thirties and Logan a couple of years younger than Katie. Although an unlikely couple, they were actually perfect for each other. "Have the tests and I'm sure the news will be good."

"Of course. You're right."

They walked out of the community center just as Logan pulled to the curb. He jumped out of the truck and came around to open Olivia's door for her. The love in his eyes as he looked at his wife made Katie's heart ache.

"Thanks, Katie," they both said as Olivia climbed into the truck.

Katie waited until they'd disappeared down the block then turned back toward the community center. Tori Woodward stood on the sidewalk in front of her.

Katie smothered a groan. The last thing she needed today was a run-in with her former friend. "Hey, Tori." She went to step around the other woman. Tori, as always, looked Aspen chic in a pair of designer jeans with elaborate stitching on the pockets, a silk blouse and strappy sandals. Katie glanced at her own utilitarian clogs, part of her standard work uniform. The pair she wore today were bright purple, shiny like a bowling ball and totally clunky in front of Tori's delicate sandals. "I've got a Founder's Day Festival meeting right now. Good to see you."

Tori moved, blocking Katie's way again. "Of course you do, Saint Katie. I see you're still using the same martyr routine to ingratiate yourself with people. Does anyone have a clue as to who you really are?"

Katie's head snapped back at Tori's words. "This is who I am," she said, wishing her voice sounded more sure.

"Right. You're also the person who would ruin her supposed best friend's chance at love."

Katie swallowed. It would be simple to think Tori was talking about present day and the change in Katie's relationship with Noah, but she knew that wasn't the case. "You're the one who cheated, Tori. You made that choice."

"Noah would have never found out if you hadn't given him that note."

"The note he received wasn't signed."

"Don't play dumb," Tori said with a snort. She lifted her Prada sunglasses onto the top of her head, her green eyes boring into Katie's. "You were the only person who knew about my fling with Adam."

"You can't know that for sure. And if you were so committed to Noah, you wouldn't have fooled around with someone else."

"I was eighteen and stupid, I'll grant you that. Mainly stupid to trust you with my secret. You had a crush on Noah even then. It killed you that he was in love with me."

"I was happy for you," Katie argued, shaking her head. She felt her breathing start to come faster, bile rising in her throat. "But it wasn't fair to him."

"He wasn't himself that year," Tori shot back. "When his dad got sick, Noah couldn't focus on anything else."

"He was going to ask you to marry him."

"Exactly," Tori practically hissed. "I would have said yes. We were going to be happy together. Noah was my first, you know." She shook her head, gave a bitter laugh. "Of course you knew—you were my best friend. I thought you understood I needed to make sure he was the one."

"I never understood why you needed to sleep with another guy." Katie crossed her arms over her chest. "It was wrong, just like it was wrong of you to ask me to cover it up."

"So why didn't you just tell him instead of letting him find out the way he did?"

Katie almost blurted out the truth. How she couldn't stand to be the one who hurt Noah, had been afraid Tori would turn it back on her. Katie and Tori had become friends freshman year of high school, when Tori's family moved to Crimson—her father had worked in one of the exclusive hotels in Aspen, and Tori acted as if that made her better than the local kids around Crimson. She'd been a snob, yes, but she'd also been beautiful, gregarious and so confident.

It had felt as if a spotlight suddenly shone on her when Tori chose her as a friend. Now it seemed clear Tori had liked Katie because her low self-esteem made her easy to manipulate. It was her mother all over again. Tori made small digs about Katie's weight or lack of style, and like a puppy eager to please, Katie would do more to make herself indispensable so Tori wouldn't drop her.

"You don't know it was me who left the note."

"All this time, and you're still denying it? You haven't even admitted it to him. What's Noah going to think when he finds out his perfect Katie-bug was the one to break his heart?"

Katie swallowed around the panic lodged in her throat. Yes, Tori had cheated, but Katie remembered how angry Noah had been at the anonymous note that had led him to find his girlfriend with another guy. "Why are you doing this? Do you want him back? Is that why you're here?"

Tori closed her eyes for a moment, as if she was debating her answer. "No. I'm way past wanting to be the wife of a forest ranger." She tapped one long nail against her glossy mouth. "Although I wouldn't mind a roll in the sheets for old times' sake. If Noah had mad skills in the bedroom back then, I can only imagine how he's improved over the years."

Katie felt herself stiffen. When Tori's gaze narrowed, she realized she'd walked right into a trap.

"You've had sex with him."

"I didn't mean—"

"That's why I'm going to tell him." Tori leaned closer. "You betrayed me, and no one gets away with that."

"It was ten years ago."

"Doesn't matter. In this town I'm the one who crushed Noah Crawford's already broken heart and you're the angel who picked up the pieces. But we were both responsible for his pain. I'm tired of everyone looking at me like I'm some sort of Jezebel."

"No one thinks—"

"Noah does. His friends do. Hell, my own mother reminds me every Christmas about the one that got away. Maybe I deserve it, but I'm not the only one."

Tori had started dating Noah sophomore year of high school, and Katie thought he'd always loved her more than she deserved. When Tori alienated most of her girlfriends besides Katie, she'd become more dependent on Noah's attention. But she'd always wanted Katie to tag along, almost as a buffer or proof to Noah that she wasn't the mean girl other people made her out to be. Katie knew she was, and as her feelings for Noah had grown, it became more difficult for her to watch the way Tori strung him along.

Maybe she'd taken advantage of the knowledge she had to break them up. But she'd believed it was the right thing to do. He'd been wrecked that summer, and holding tight to his relationship with his self-centered, shallow girlfriend wasn't going to make his grief over his father's death any easier.

But would Noah understand her motivations and why she'd never revealed that it was she who'd typed that note?

"Don't do this," she whispered. "I was a good friend to you and that note wouldn't have changed the outcome of your relationship with Noah."

The other woman pursed her glossy lips. "I won't say anything," she said after a moment.

Katie started to breathe a sigh of relief but Tori added, "Yet. But I'm here the whole summer. And I may change my mind. You'll never know. Any day, any moment I may decide to throw you under the bus the way you did me."

Katie shook her head. "I'll deny it. You have no proof."

"You won't," Tori answered confidently. "If he confronts you, I know you won't lie. The little *bug* doesn't have it in her."

Oh, that nickname. Noah had started calling her Bug after he heard Katie's mother chastise her for something she'd eaten at the bakery. Katie had been so embarrassed, feeling fat and sloppy. But Noah had put his arm around her shoulders and whispered that she was no bigger than a little bug, and next to his height and bulk, she'd actually felt petite.

Over the years it had become a reminder of their "buddy" relationship. Hearing Tori speak the word made her want to run home and inhale a pan of brownies in one sitting.

"I'm going to my meeting," she said after a moment. "I'm sorry you're still angry. But you need to figure out where that animosity should really be directed. It isn't at me."

"Don't be so sure." Tori adjusted her sunglasses back on her face then walked away, her sandals clicking on the sidewalk as she went.

Katie fisted her hand then pushed it against her stomach, trying to ward off the pain and dread pooling there. All she wanted was to eat and sleep right now, but she turned and started back into the community center. She had responsibilities, people depending on her, and no matter what she wanted for herself, she couldn't stand to let them down.

Chapter Ten

Noah drummed his thumbs against the steering wheel, glancing every mile marker at Katie's profile.

It was a great day for swimming, unseasonably warm for late June with the sun shining from a sky so blue it looked like the backdrop on one of Sara's movie sets. He'd borrowed a small fishing boat from Crimson Ranch so he could take Katie to the far side of the reservoir where the water might be a degree or two warmer than near the mouth of the mountain stream that fed it.

The day was perfect, other than the fact that Katie had barely said two words since he'd picked her up an hour ago.

"We're almost there," he said and adjusted the radio to a satellite station with better reception this far into the mountains.

Hidden Valley Reservoir lay on the far side of the pass past Aspen. The dirt road that wound into the hills above the valley was maintained but still rutted in places.

"Okay" was her only response.

"You nervous?" He placed one hand on her leg, squeezing softly in the place above her knee where he knew she was ticklish. Immediately she flinched away from him and he pulled his arm away from her.

"A little." She continued to look out the window for a few minutes, then added, "I'm tired. Sorry I'm bad company."

"You're never bad company, Bug."

"Noah," she said, her tone harsh.

"Sorry. It's a habit. I won't call you that." He focused more closely on the road as they passed an SUV coming from the other direction. "I mean it in a good way, you know? I always have."

"I don't like it," she snapped.

"Are you sure you want to do this?" He wasn't sure what was going on, but if swimming took her off her game this much, was it really worth it?

"If you want to turn around, go ahead." She pressed her fingers to her temples. "I'm not sure what's wrong with my mood today, but I understand if you don't want to be with me."

As he came to the opening in the trees that signaled the entrance to the state park where the reservoir was located, he pulled off onto the shoulder of the gravel road. "Listen to me," he said, moving his seat belt aside so he could face her. "I don't give a damn about your mood. Happy, sad, pissy for no reason. It happens and I'll take them all. We're friends, Katie. You've seen me at my worst. The more I think about it, I've never seen you anything but kind, generous and ready to please whoever you're with. I can take one afternoon of a bad mood without turning tail. Give me a little credit."

She looked at him as if she wanted to argue, then shocked him when she asked, "Do you think you would have been happy married to Tori?"

He felt his mouth drop open, clamped it shut again. "Where the hell did that question come from?"

"It's weird seeing her back in town for an extended period of time. It makes me wonder—"

"Don't." Noah lifted his hand to cut her off. "I'm not interested in reuniting with my old girlfriend, if that's what you want to know."

She shook her head. "That's not it. But if things had gone differently that summer, you'd have asked her to marry you."

"I was a different person back then. Young and in so much pain." He pressed his head against the seat back, looked out the front window to the endless blue sky above the treetops. "I had no business thinking of spending my life with anyone. In the end, Tori and I chose very different directions for our lives. Who knows if that would have made a marriage too difficult?"

"Maybe it was good that you broke up? I mean, in the long run?"

He let out a bark of laughter, surprised at the bitterness he felt after all these years. "I sure as hell can't say I'm glad things happened the way they did. But I don't regret not having Tori as my wife."

Memories of the pain of that summer, the sting of her betrayal when he was already so low flooded through him. The thought that people knew about what she was doing, and no one had the guts to actually talk to him about it. A stupid, cowardly note left under his windshield wiper.

As his body tensed, he felt Katie's fingers slide up his arm. "Thank you for answering the question. I know you don't like to talk about that part of your past."

"Did it help you?" He inclined his head so he could look at her, watched her bite down on her bottom lip as she thought about her answer.

"Yes," she said after a moment. "It did."

He grabbed her hand, kissed the inside of her palm then pulled back onto the road again. "Then it was worth it." He squeezed her fingers before placing her hand back in her lap. "And bad mood or not, we're doing this. You have nothing to be afraid of with me, Katie."

Her chest rose and fell as she stared at him. "You have no idea, Noah."

"Katie."

"We're going to do this. I'm going to do this." The way she looked at him, her brown eyes soft and luminous in the bright daylight, made his breath catch.

She must be talking about swimming, but he thought—and hoped—her words might have more meaning.

Best not to push her too far too fast. So he nodded and finished the drive to the reservoir.

Who would have guessed the hardest part of going swimming with Noah would be stripping down to her bathing suit in front of him?

"Turn around." They'd launched the small boat he'd borrowed into the water and now it was tethered to the small dock down the hill from the state park's gravel parking lot. Katie stood next to the back of the truck, clutching a beach towel to her chest.

"I've seen you naked, Katie." Noah grinned at her, looking every bit the modern-day rake she knew him to be. "I think I can handle a bikini."

"I did *not* wear a bikini. And it was dark that night at my house. Broad daylight is different." She reached for the wet suit he held in his hand. "Give that to me and turn around. I don't need you watching while I encase myself like a sausage."

"The water's not bad today," he said with a laugh, holding out his arms wide. "You won't need that."

"Easy for you to say." Noah wore a pair of low-slung board shorts, Keen sandals and a T-shirt with the Colorado state flag on the front. He looked like a high-mountain surf bum. Cold air and water had never bothered him, and his work for the Forest Service only seemed to make him more impervious to the elements.

He frowned as he studied her. "You're already shivering. It must be close to ninety degrees today. What's going on?"

"Nerves." She squeezed the edges of the towel tighter. "My teeth are chattering."

Noah took a step closer to her, placing his palms over the tops of her arms, his skin warm against hers. "You don't have to do this. If Matt or any other guy cares that you don't like boating or swimming, they're not worth it. This is who you are."

She shook her head. "It's not who I *want* to be. It probably seems like nothing because you aren't afraid of anything. But I'm sick of being scared and living life on the sidelines."

He bent until they were at eye level and flipped his sunglasses off his head, his brilliant blue eyes intense. "There are plenty of things I'm afraid of, and you don't live life on the sidelines. Not being the adrenaline junkies your parents are doesn't make you less of a person, Katie-bug. You have friends who care about you, a thriving business, and you're an important part of this community."

"Because I have no life so I'm always available," she muttered, although she had to admit his words soothed her a bit.

"Will boating on the Fourth of July give you a life?"

"The start of one, maybe." She shook her head. "Matt knew my parents out in California—that's where he went to college and he trained with my dad for an Ironman a few years ago."

"I thought Logan and Olivia introduced you."

"They did. My parents told Matt we wouldn't have much in common since I'm such a homebody." She tried to make her voice light. "My own parents think I'm a homebody."

Noah's eyes narrowed. "Your parents are wrong."

"I'd like to prove to myself that I'm more than who they think I am."

He placed a soft kiss on the top of her head. "I'll wait for you down by the boat. We're going swimming today."

As he turned away, Katie placed the towel on top of his truck and squeezed into the wet suit. The thick black material covered the entire upper half of her body but cut off at midthigh. Zipping it up, Katie glanced at her reflection in the passenger-side window then groaned. She looked like a cross between a rubber inner tube and a baby seal. The wet suit fit like a second skin, and while it was more coverage than her bathing suit, it still showed more of her figure than she was used to.

It was good she was doing this with Noah before she went boating with Matt and his friends. She could boost her confidence not only in the water but out of it. She made her way down to the dock and forced herself to lower the towel to her side as Noah looked up. The wet suit might be tight, but it was basically modest. She had nothing to be embarrassed about in front of him.

Nothing at all, she realized as his eyes widened in appreciation at her approach. "Damn," he said when she hopped onto the dock. "I've never seen anyone make a wet suit look sexy."

She waved away his compliment, but butterflies zipped across her belly at his words.

"Seriously, Katie." He helped her step into the boat. "Sexy. As. Hell."

"Stop." She placed the tips of her fingers in his and jumped onto one of the captain's chairs near the front then down onto the floor. Noah gave her a tug, and she landed against his chest as his arms came around her. "Just friends, Noah."

His smile was teasing. "There are many types of friends."

"We're the type who don't call each other sexy," she answered but didn't pull away.

He placed his mouth against her ear. "If you say so." His breath tickled the sensitive skin. "Still nervous?"

She heard the smile in his voice and moved away, lowering herself into one of the leather chairs. "I'm in a boat," she whispered. "On a lake."

"A reservoir, to be specific."

"I'm going swimming, and you're trying to distract me so I won't be so scared."

He tucked a lock of her hair behind her ear. "Is it working?"

"I'm not cold. That's a start."

He took the seat behind the steering wheel and reached past her to open the glove compartment. He took out a faded baseball cap. "Put this on and tighten it."

"Won't it blow off?"

It was one of his favorites and it felt strangely intimate to adjust it on her head.

"Should be fine and it'll keep your hair from tangling in the wind."

"You have a lot of experience with the long-hair issue on the water?"

Without answering, he leaned over the side of the boat to unfasten the rope looped on one of the dock's pillars. A minute later he'd motored them away from the shore and toward the mountains rising up on the far side of the water. The reservoir was calm, almost placid, and they passed only a couple of smaller fishing boats with old men casting from the sides. Over the holiday weekend, the state park would be crowded with tents and RVs in the campground on the high ridge. Over a dozen boats would dot the water, with people tubing, water-skiing and wakeboarding along the waves.

Colorado might be a landlocked state, but enough outdoor enthusiasts lived in and near the mountains to make the best of the sprinkling of man-made lakes and reservoirs throughout the high country. As popular as these areas were during the summer, Katie had managed to avoid going out on the water since she'd had her bad experience as a girl. To call it a near drowning might be exaggerating, but it had felt that way to her.

Her fear of open water was irrational, but until now she'd had no reason to confront it. She concentrated on breathing as the boat sped across the water.

Noah's hand landed on hers a moment later, and he tried to pry her fingers loose from the seat. "You're safe," he called over the hum of the motor.

She shrugged out of his grasp. "You should keep

both hands on the steering wheel," she yelled back. "And eyes on the road. I mean the water."

He laughed, his voice carrying over the noise.

She recited the ingredients for favorite recipes in her head, focusing on the familiar to distract her from how far away the dock was now. She knew Hidden Canyon Reservoir was nearly seven miles long, making it one of the larger bodies of water in the state. It wasn't as wide as Lake Dillon in nearby Summit County, a fact that comforted her a bit. She could see from edge to edge, and she watched cars drive along the state highway that bordered the park, counting the seconds between them as she tried not to hyperventilate.

After what seemed like an eternity, Noah slowed the boat and she could hear waves slapping against the aluminum side. Aluminum. Ugh. She was basically floating in a soda-pop can. The thought did not reassure her.

"We're in the middle," she said, her breath hitching. "How deep is it here?"

Noah checked the depth finder mounted near the boat's dashboard. "About eighty-five feet."

Katie swallowed.

"Water temperature is seventy-two degrees. That's like a hot tub for this time of year."

"What are those things?" She pointed to the black dots moving across the square screen.

"Fish. It tells you their depth so you know how to set the down riggers. Josh mainly uses the boat to take groups of guests fishing." He glanced at her then grinned. "The big schools of trout stick to the ten- to twelve-foot range. They won't be nibbling your toes, if that has you worried."

Katie dug her fingernails deeper into the seat cushion. "Everything has me worried." She straightened her shoulders and stood. "If I'm going to do this…" She began to step onto the side of the boat.

"Hold up, Little Mermaid." Noah grabbed her around the waist. "Don't dive in quite yet. This isn't the swimming lesson I had in mind."

Katie frowned. "Then why are we here?"

He killed the engine. "I want you to have a chance to get used to the water."

"I'd like to get this over with and get the heck off the water."

"Do you know anything about Hidden Valley?"

"It's big and black and terrifies me?"

He swiveled her chair until she faced him. "The Hidden Valley dam was one of the first to be built in this area, back in the early 1940s, under the Roosevelt administration. There's a hydroelectric power plant at the base of the dam that, along with some of the other facilities in the area, provides electricity for almost fifty thousand homes. So it's more than just a recreation area."

"Why do you know so much?"

He shrugged. "Colorado history interests me, especially how the areas that are surrounded by national forest were developed. People think of it as just another body of water, but there's more to it than that."

"My dad used to come up here after a big storm, when the water was choppy, to swim. It was the closest he could get to conditions in the ocean when he was training for the Ironman."

"But a ton colder."

"He liked that," she answered. "Thought it made him stronger. Wanted it to make me stronger."

"Is this where you had the bad experience?"

"No. My freak-out was in Lake Dillon. It was the

summer they decided I was getting too fat and needed to train for a junior triathlon. I was twelve, and I'd developed early, you know?"

His eyes stayed on her face. "I can imagine," he said gently.

"My mom always had a boyish figure, ninety pounds soaking wet. I was a mutant Amazon compared to her and my dad." She tried to smile. "It's not good when the preteen daughter wears a bigger jeans size than her father."

"You're a woman," Noah argued. "You're supposed to have curves."

"The only curves my dad approved of were muscles. I didn't have those." She shrugged. "They were helping organize the event, and I'd been swimming and running and biking all summer long. I wanted to make them proud. But I'd only trained at the high school pool. I didn't realize how different open water would be. There were so many kids, all of them more prepared and in shape than me. When the race bell sounded, my group ran for the water. But as soon as I dived in, I freaked out. I had goggles but couldn't see in front of me. Other kids were swimming into me, over me. I kept going. I could hear my dad shouting from the shore and I wanted to finish. But the farther I swam, the more fear took over. I tried to stand and catch my breath, but I was out too far and I couldn't touch. Then the next wave of swimmers came and there were too many kids around me. I couldn't keep going."

She looked into the black water and the scene came back to her again. Panic rose in her chest at the memories of trying to lift her head and being knocked to the side. Taking in big gulps of water that left her choking and struggling to tread water. She realized she was almost hyperventilating when Noah placed his hands on her knees. "Breathe, sweetheart," he whispered. "I promise I'm going to take care of you today."

"I had to signal for the rescue dinghy. They hauled me onto it—it took two men to lift me out of the water. I threw up into the bottom of the boat. It felt like everyone was disappointed. I had to watch the rest of the swimmers before they brought me to shore." She shook her head. "My dad couldn't look at me. He was a world-class athlete and his daughter couldn't even swim a quarter mile."

"You panicked. It happens. Adrenaline can sometimes have a strange effect."

"My dad got the opportunity to help establish the training center in California shortly after school started in the fall." She picked at the skin on one of her fingers. "Mom suggested it would be better for me to stay with Gram."

"I thought you chose to stay in Crimson."

Katie saw the confusion on his face. Of course that was what he thought; it was the way she'd told the story. "It was less embarrassing than saying my parents had ditched me here. Of course, Gram was wonderful. I loved living with her." She leaned over toward the edge of the boat and dipped her fingers in the cool water. It was translucent in her hands, the shallow puddle in her palm as clear as if it had come from a faucet. Not scary at all.

"I remember you visited your parents during the summer and over winter break each year."

Katie shrugged. "At first it was awkward. We all knew the reason they left me behind, but no one wanted to talk about it. Then I started baking for them—energy bars to use at the training center. My dad really got into it—he's fascinated with the perfect fuel for the body. It's the one thing that still keeps me connected to them."

Noah looked toward the mountains. "Katie, you don't—"

"I'm not going to let one incident from my childhood define me. That day in the water was a turning point for me, and not in a good way. I need to move past it, as silly as it might seem."

"It doesn't seem silly." Noah's voice was gruff. "Let's go swimming."

Chapter Eleven

She humbled him with her bravery.

Noah turned off the motor as the boat drifted toward the small inlet near the cliffs on the western side of the reservoir. As they neared the bank, he tugged his T-shirt over his head and jumped into the water, his shoes squishing in the sandy bottom. He pulled the boat close to a fallen tree and tied the rope to one of the dead branches.

"You can stand here."

Katie stared at him for a moment before her brows shot down over her eyes. "This was a terrible idea. I can't get in the water with you looking like that…" She flicked her fingers at him. "And I look like a sausage." She smoothed her hands over the black material, and not for the first time, Noah wished he was touching her.

"You're the cutest sausage I've ever seen."

She snorted in response, making him grin. "I feel ridiculous." She stood, arms crossed over her chest. "It's stupid to be afraid of getting in water that's only as high as my knees."

"Don't say that. Nothing about you is stupid." He leaned down, splashed some of the cold lake water onto his chest and arms. He was overheated, and not only because of the warming temperature and sun beating down. Katie had weathered so much rejection from her parents, but she kept moving forward. He never would have guessed the full truth of why she'd lived with her grandma, and it made him feel like even more of a failure as a friend.

He couldn't imagine being deserted by his parents—because that would have never happened in his family. Noah was the one who'd separated himself during his father's illness, pulling away by degrees when the pain of staying became too intense.

Katie thought he had no fear, but that was far from the truth. He was afraid of everything that made him feel. He'd tried to insulate himself from the pain of possibly losing someone else he cared about. The fact that she trusted him gave him hope that he could change, that it wasn't too late. For either of them.

"You're stalling." He motioned her forward. "Get in the water."

She squeezed shut her eyes for a second. "I'm stalling," she admitted and inched closer to the port side of the boat. Flipping one leg over, she balanced on the ledge. Her knuckles turned white as she clenched the metal edge.

"It's shallow. You're safe." He wanted her to believe him, and not just in this moment. He may have failed in lots of areas, but he was determined to keep her safe. Not many people took Noah seriously and with good reason. Sure, he was good at his job and had plenty of responsibility with the Forest Service, but in none of his relationships with coworkers, friends or his family did people trust him with anything deeply emotional. Katie had, and it went a long way to fill some of the emptiness inside him.

He had lost time to make up for with her. Beginning now. He walked through the water and stopped at the side of the boat. His first impulse was to tease or splash her—something to lighten the mood and break through her nerves. But this was serious, and he wanted to respect that.

"Take my hand," he told her instead. "I've got you."

A knot of tension loosened in his chest when she placed her fingers in his. She hopped down, landing in the water with a splash.

"It's cold," she said, sucking in a breath.

"You'll get used to it."

She was gripping his fingers so tight he could see the tips turning bright pink. Katie holding him like a lifeline was the best sensation he'd had in ages.

"What now?" she asked, her body stiff.

"We walk out a little farther. Only as deep as you can handle."

"I'm such a wimp," she said with a groan.

"You're doing this, Katie. That makes you a badass."

She smiled. "I've never once been described as a bad anything."

"Stick with me," he assured her and was rewarded with a soft laugh.

A moment later the water was at her waist. She stopped and closed her eyes. He could almost see her steeling herself on the inside, fighting whatever demons were left over from that long-ago fear. The cold water lapped at his hips. A benefit, he thought, since the vulnerability in her expression was having the inconvenient reaction of turning him on. He had to get a hold on himself where Katie was concerned.

Slowly he let go of her hand. Her eyes snapped open as he backed away.

"Where are you going? You can't leave me."

"Come with me," he said, sliding his fingers through the ripples on the reservoir's surface. He moved deeper into the water.

She gave her head a short shake.

"You can do this," he told her, sinking under the water. Damn, it really was cold. He resurfaced, pushed the water from his face and grinned when he saw she'd stepped out far enough for the waves to brush the underside of her breasts. Too bad the wet suit covered them up so efficiently. He leaned back and gave several hard kicks until he was out far enough not to touch the bottom.

"Swim, Katie," he called to her.

She glanced behind her at the grassy shoreline then put her arms out straight and dived forward. As soon as her face hit the water, she reared up, sputtering and coughing, wet hair draped forward over her eyes and cheeks. She swiped at it, looking both scared and angry, making his heart lurch.

"I'll come back in," he said loud enough to be heard over her panting breath. "We'll start slower."

"No." She held up a hand. "Give me a minute." She slicked her hair away from her face. Droplets of water glistened on the tips of her eyelashes. He couldn't tell if they were lake water or tears but continued to tread water and wait.

"You don't have to put your head in."

"Yes, I do."

Her lips were moving, as if she was giving herself

a silent lecture. Then she pushed off again, slower this time. He eased out a little farther as she swam for him. He shouldn't have been surprised that once she started her form was perfect. If she'd been taught to swim by her father, he would have made sure of that. Within a few strokes she was next to him.

She lifted her face out of the water and looked around. "I did it," she whispered. Her teeth were chattering but she grinned. "I sw-swam."

"Just like the Little Mermaid," he agreed, taking her hand and pulling her into him. Her arms wrapped around his neck as her legs went around his waist. Again he was grateful for the cold water. "How are you doing?"

"Freaking out. But in a good way this time." She hugged him then gently kissed his cheek. "Thank you, Noah."

He forced himself not to shift his head and take her mouth with his, not to take advantage of their position and her emotions. He was her friend today and grateful for the chance to support her. With an effort of will almost beyond him, he pushed her away. "Race you back to shore."

She splashed water in his face at the same time she yelled, "Go!"

He laughed, wiped his eyes then followed her through the water.

"I want to swim more," Katie told Noah an hour later.

"You've got to get in the boat, honey." Noah leaned over the front of the boat to where she was treading water in a different, deeper inlet. "Your lips are blue."

Katie pressed her fingers to her mouth and realized she couldn't feel her lips. She swam to the back and put her foot onto the step that hung from the edge, hoisting herself out of the water. Noah had taken her to several different parts of the park so she could gain confidence swimming in new areas. She'd stripped out of the wet suit for this last dip, since she wouldn't have it to cover her on the Fourth of July. There was too much adrenaline charging through her to be embarrassed by Noah seeing her in a bathing suit.

He took her arm to steady her as she stepped on the boat then cursed. "Your skin is like ice. Hell, you're probably halfway to hypothermia. I should have never let you stay in the water so long."

"I'm fi-ne," she told him, but her teeth were chattering so hard it was difficult to speak.

"You need to dry off." He wrapped a towel around her shoulders and she sank into one of the captain's chairs. Katie didn't care that she was freezing. She'd done it. She'd conquered her fear of the water. It felt like the first step toward something new and exciting in her life.

"Tha-at was so-o fu-un."

"Stop trying to talk." Noah picked up another towel to dry her hair. "You're shaking so hard you'll chip a tooth."

He covered her head with the towel, scrubbing it over her hair. His touch felt so good all Katie could think was the old advice of reheating someone with hypothermia by skin-to-skin contact. Just the thought of pressing herself to the broad expanse of Noah's chest warmed her a few degrees. She giggled, the sound coming out more like a hiccup with her teeth still chattering.

"What's so funny?" Noah used the edge of the towel to smooth the hair away from her face.

She shook her head, but couldn't seem to stop grinning. "I'm happy."

He dropped to his knees in front of her. “I’m proud of you, Katie. I’d like to think your dad would be proud, too, but he’s an insensitive jerk.”

She arched one eyebrow.

“And I’m learning not to be,” he added. He leaned closer, his mouth almost brushing hers as the boat dipped and swayed on the water. “Which is why I’m not going to kiss you now,” he whispered.

“You’re not?” She wasn’t sure whether to be relieved or disappointed.

Disappointed, her body cried. She expected her brain to register relief, but it shut off as she stared into Noah’s familiar blue eyes.

He gave a small shake of his head. “I want you,” he said softly. “You know I do. But you have to choose. I can’t make any promises, and my track record isn’t the greatest.”

She gave an involuntary snort and he smiled. “Right.” He traced one finger along the seam of her lips. She must have defrosted, because his touch made her whole body tingle. “You’ve got your new plan for life, and I don’t fit into that. I’m going to try to do the right thing and respect that.”

No, she wanted to shout. *Kiss me. Be with me.* But she didn’t say those things. Swimming was one thing, but taking an emotional risk was a different level of courage. One she didn’t yet possess.

“I brought lunch,” she said, trying not to sound as lame as she felt.

Something passed through Noah’s gaze, but he pulled away and stood. “Are you warming up?”

Not as much as she’d like. But with the towel wrapped around her shoulders, she nodded and pulled the insulated tote bag from under the dash. Taking out two sandwiches wrapped in wax paper, she handed one to Noah. "Chicken salad," she told him.

"My favorite. What are you having?"

"Same thing—it was easier to make two. I also have fruit, chips and homemade lemonade."

She glanced at him when he didn't move. He stood in the center of the boat staring at the wrapped sandwich resting in his hand.

"What's wrong?"

He glanced at her, his brows furrowed. "Chicken salad is my favorite, but you don't like it."

"That's not true." She pulled out the bag of potato chips from the tote. "Exactly."

He shook his head, sank down on the seat across from her. "Is this your grandma's recipe?"

"Of course." She pretended to search the bottom of the tote. "I know I packed forks for the fruit."

"Then you definitely don't like it. I remember from when she made it in high school."

"I don't *dislike* it. Why are you making a big deal over the sandwich?"

"Because you're starting a new life." He tugged the tote bag out of her grasp. "Or so you tell me. You've got to start making what you want a priority, even if it's in your choice of sandwich fillings." He placed the bag on the floor and, before she could stop him, grabbed her sandwich out of her hand. "And I bet…" He unwrapped the wax paper. "I knew it. You used the heels."

Katie felt more exposed than if she was prancing around in a string bikini. "Who cares? We don't use them at the bakery. Why waste food?"

He lifted one corner of his sandwich. "Then why not use them on mine, too? I'm not picky."

"Because…" She grabbed the chip bag, tore it open

with such force that a few chips flew out and landed in her lap. She stared at them, hating the embarrassment coursing through her. "It's habit. I use the ends of the bread for myself. Maybe I like the ends."

"No one likes the ends." Noah picked up the chips scattered across her thighs, his fingers golden against her paler skin. "You think I don't notice things, and most of the time you're right. But we've been friends for over ten years, Bug. I know how you put the needs of everyone around you in front of your own."

"You make it sound like a bad thing," she muttered, brushing her palms across her legs. Her stomach rolled, as if she was eleven years old again and her mother had caught her taking extra cookies from the jar on her grandma's counter.

Noah sighed, caught her hands in his and held them until her gaze lifted to his. "It's not, but I want to make sure you make yourself a priority." His smile was tender. "You may not think I can take care of you, but the guy you choose should put you first. You're perfect the way you are."

She wanted to believe those words were true. But she'd had a lifetime of the people around her proving they weren't. She hadn't been enough for her own parents. And as much love as Gram had given her, Katie had never been sure if it was unconditional. From the moment her mom and dad left her in Crimson, she'd made herself indispensable, working after school, weekends and summer vacation in the bakery. She'd learned the art of baking and made herself a valuable part of the business. Of course she loved it. But what if she hadn't? What if she'd rebelled or turned her back on her grandmother's legacy? What if she didn't help whenever someone needed her now? If she wasn't giving them her best, would people leave her behind just like her parents had?

Noah would never understand the deep roots of her fear of rejection. Even though he'd been through a lot with his family, he'd always had their unwavering love and support. She forced a laugh, tugged away from his grip and grabbed the sandwich from his lap. "You win," she said lightly. "No more bread ends for me."

He studied her a moment then unwrapped his sandwich. "I hope that's true," he said. "If you need somewhere to donate all those ends, my stomach volunteers." He took a bite and gave a little moan of pleasure. "Especially if the ends come with your chicken salad between them."

She appreciated that he let go of the topic. The rest of the afternoon saw them back to their normal camaraderie. She stifled a yawn as he docked the boat an hour later.

"Worn-out?" he asked, hopping onto the wood planks and tying a rope to one of the poles.

"Exhausted," she admitted. "I've been tired in general lately." She gathered her sunscreen and tote bag and stood. "I hope I'm not getting sick. There's too much to do before the Founder's Day Festival for that."

He reached out a hand and steadied her as she climbed onto the dock. "That's what I'm talking about. You work too hard, doing your part and everyone else's."

"Olivia is pregnant," she argued, exasperated they were back on this subject. "It's not like she dumped her responsibilities on me for no good reason."

"All I'm saying is you matter, too."

"Point taken." She dropped her sandals to the ground and shoved her feet in them, starting toward his truck before he could lecture her any longer. His words were especially irritating because they were true. She was pushing herself too hard, taking on more special orders at the bakery just as the summer tourist season was heating up. With the extra work for the festival, she was spread way too thin. It grated on her nerves to have Noah point it out. People praised her overzealous work ethic. They didn't chastise her for it.

Noah caught up to her as she reached the back of the truck. "Don't be mad. I only want you to take care of yourself."

The concern in his eyes was real. She knew that. He'd only said out loud what she'd been thinking the past week. "Maybe I'll put Lelia in charge of some of the smaller orders. She trained at a bakery in San Francisco, so she knows her way around the kitchen." Katie had never shared any significant chunk of responsibility at Life is Sweet since her grandma's death. But she couldn't keep going at this pace.

"Good idea," he said and opened her door for her.

"Do you need help with the boat? I didn't mean to run off and leave you with all the work."

"I've got it." He patted the passenger seat. "You probably swam a couple miles today. You deserve a rest."

The truck's interior was warm from the sun beating through the front window. Katie's eyes started to drift shut, but she managed to stay awake while Noah maneuvered the boat onto the trailer. By the time they headed back toward town, her eyelids were so heavy it was hard to fight off her need for a nap.

"Close them," Noah said softly.

With a sigh she did and immediately drifted asleep.

She woke in her own bed, the light spilling through the curtains indicating early evening. She vaguely remembered them arriving at her house and Noah carrying her to her bedroom. Rubbing her eyes, she climbed from the bed. She needed to find the new cell phone she'd got to replace hers and check messages in case anything had come up with the bakery or the festival. She found the cooler bag, her purse and her phone sitting in a neat pile on the kitchen counter. Next to them was a plate covered in plastic wrap with a note on top.

"I'm not the only one with favorites. Thanks for a great day. N."

She unwrapped the plate to find a peanut-butter-and-banana sandwich. He'd even cut off the crusts. She quickly took a bite, savoring the chewy peanut butter and sweet banana slices. So Noah remembered her favorite sandwich?

She knew it wasn't a big deal—they'd been friends long enough that he should remember that kind of detail about her. As she chewed, she tried—and failed—to convince herself that she'd be able to remain friends with Noah while trying to fall in love with another man.

Where did that leave their friendship? Katie didn't want to think about the answer. Maybe it would get easier once his mom was fully recovered and he wasn't around all the time?

She only hoped that was the case. Otherwise, she was in big trouble.

Chapter Twelve

By the time Noah checked in with the Forest Service ranger station and returned the boat to Crimson Ranch, it was almost dinnertime. When someone was sick or in trouble in Crimson, food poured forth from the community like manna from heaven. Right now there were enough lasagnas, casseroles and soups in his mother's freezer to last them another three months. He and Emily took turns defrosting food for dinner each night while his mom wrote thank-you notes for the meals, flowers and miscellaneous bits of support she'd received.

The house was empty when he walked in, however, and his mom's Toyota SUV that Emily had been driving wasn't in the garage. He hoped this meant pizza or some kind of carryout for dinner. A person could only handle so much lasagna.

His mother spent most of her afternoons reading or doing crossword puzzles on the screened-in back patio, but when he didn't find her there, Noah quickly climbed the steps to the second floor. She'd been doing great since she'd returned from the hospital, almost back to her regular self as far as Noah could tell. He also understood how quickly something could change. The pancreatic cancer that claimed his father had been sudden and ruthless, only a matter of months between the initial diagnosis and his dad's death.

"Mom, where are you?" Noah shouted as he sprinted down the hall to the master bedroom. The door was closed, and he burst through then stopped as his mother's gaze met his in the mirror over the dresser.

"What's the matter?" She whirled around, took a step toward him. "Are you okay?"

He held up one hand as he tried to catch his breath and still his pounding heart. "Of course I'm okay. It's you I'm worried about."

"Me?"

He nodded. "Why are you dressed like that?" She wore a long, flowing skirt with a gauzy tunic pulled over it. A bright beaded necklace circled her neck, a gift from his father for her fortieth birthday, shortly before his dad had got sick. Her head was covered in a silk turban, covering the scar that ran from her temple to her ear. He'd got so used to seeing her with a simple knit cap or a baseball hat, he couldn't quite make sense of her looking so glamorous. She was even wearing makeup, something he hadn't seen his ever-practical mother do in years. Suddenly his skin felt itchy. He glanced at his watch. "Where's Emily? It's her turn to make dinner."

"I'm sorry, sweetie. Did I forget to tell you?"

"Tell me what?" he said through clenched teeth.

Her smile was wide. "I have a date tonight." She spun in a circle, and Noah's mouth dropped open. His mother was twirling as if she was a teenage girl or princess-movie character. "I have to admit I'm a little nervous." She turned again toward the mirror, patted her head. "I wish my hair would grow back faster. I may have more wrinkles than I used to, but I always had good hair."

Noah felt as though his head was about to start spinning, as if he was some demon-possessed horror-movie cliché. "Where's Em?"

"She drove to Aspen to meet a friend from back East who's vacationing there. Davey went with her. It's a big step for both of them. Other than helping Katie with a few things for Founder's Day and grocery runs, your sister has barely left the farm since she got here."

"Mom, you've been home less than a week. Don't you think you should take it easy?"

"I feel great, like something in me is coming back to life. Does that sound silly?"

It would have a few weeks ago, but after spending time with Katie, especially the way it made him feel to be the one to help her overcome her fear of the water today, his mother's words struck a deep chord inside him. All of them had been wounded by his father's death and they'd each stopped living in their own personal ways. He realized now that Tori's betrayal, so soon after his father had died, had made him wall off his emotions. He might act like casual flings and random hookups were all he wanted in a relationship, but that was a lie he couldn't maintain any longer.

Seeing his mother go out with another man might be difficult, but he'd never deny her the chance to feel alive again. She deserved whatever—or whoever—could make her happiest.

Meg opened a tube of lipstick, dotted another layer onto her lips. He walked up behind her, wrapped her in a hug and kissed her cheek. The scent of the perfume she'd been wearing for years, flowery and delicate, washed over him. He couldn't remember smelling it since his father's death. She'd put away too much of herself as part of her grief. "You don't need makeup to look beautiful, Mom. You know Dad would have wanted this. For you to be happy again."

"I loved him," his mother whispered, her eyes shining with tears.

"I know."

"He was proud of you, Noah."

His arms stiffened, and he tried to pull away, but she held on to his wrists. "I know you don't believe it, but he already saw the man you were going to become. Don't ever doubt that."

"I don't doubt his vision, but my ability to live up to it."

"If you could only—"

The doorbell rang, interrupting her. "I think that's for you," Noah said with a smile and released her.

She dropped the lipstick onto the dresser and smoothed her fingers under her eyes. "I can't believe I'm nervous. It's just dinner." She gave Noah a quick hug. "Come down with me and meet John."

He followed her down the stairs and opened the front door while she gathered her purse. It was odd to see her doctor standing on the other side, not wearing a white lab coat or scrubs. Tonight the man wore a collared shirt and thin cargo pants, both carrying the logo of a well-known fly-fishing company.

"Dr. Moore," Noah said, but didn't move from the doorway. He'd never got into the "man of the house" role since his father died but felt suddenly protective of his mother.

"Please call me John." The older man smiled, almost nervously, and tilted his head to try to look around Noah. "Is Meg ready?"

"Almost." Noah stepped onto the porch. "Where are you *kids* headed tonight?" Tater ambled up to them, sniffed at the doctor, who scratched her behind the ears.

"There's a new restaurant that opened recently off the highway between here and Aspen. The owner is one of my patients."

Meg walked up behind Noah, and the doctor's eyes lit with appreciation. "You look wonderful," the man said softly then glanced at Noah, one brow raised.

Noah gave him a small nod. "Have her home at a reasonable hour. She still needs rest."

"Noah," his mother said on a laughing breath. "He's a doctor. You don't have to lecture him."

But John only nodded. "I'll take care of her," he assured Noah, as if he knew Noah's words were about more than her physical well-being.

"Have a good time, then."

She kissed his cheek, and then she and John headed for the Audi SUV parked in front of the house. It was another perfect summer night, the air holding just a hint of a breeze and the sky beginning to turn varied shades of pink and orange. Noah watched them drive away as Tater pushed her head against his legs. "I'm not the only one who's been left without dinner, huh, girl?" She nudged him again and he went back into the house and scooped kibble into her bowl.

As the dog crunched, Noah looked around the empty kitchen. He could heat up leftovers from the fridge, but he was no longer in the mood for dinner. Normally Noah craved solitude when he wasn't out with friends. It was part of what he loved about his job with the Forest Service, the ability to lose himself in the quiet of the woods. Despite being social, a piece of him needed occasional alone time to recharge. It was one more excuse he'd made for not engaging in serious relationships. He didn't want a woman to encroach on his private time. "Determined to be single," Katie had called him. While that determination had once felt like a privilege, now he realized the price he paid for it was being lonely.

It didn't sit well, and he took out his phone to start texting. Suddenly the last thing he wanted in his life was more time by himself.

"Why are we out here on the most crowded day of the year?" Liam Donovan growled as he slowed to steer his MasterCraft speedboat around another group of smaller boats on Hidden Canyon Reservoir over the holiday weekend.

Noah pulled the brim of his ball cap lower on his head as he scanned the boats dotted around the water.

"Because Noah is stalking Katie," Liam's wife, Natalie, answered with a grin.

Noah shot her a glare.

"And Noah taught me to wakeboard." Natalie's nine-year-old son, Austin, munched on a piece of red licorice, practically bouncing up and down on the seat next to Noah.

"You did great, kid." Noah ruffled the boy's dark hair.

"I could have taught you to wakeboard," Liam said, turning to look at his stepson.

Austin shrugged. "He's better than you."

"Ouch," Liam muttered.

Natalie reached over and rubbed his shoulders. "You have many other skills, dear husband."

Noah's gaze flicked to his friends. Natalie and Liam

had been a couple in high school then spent close to ten years hating each other. When Liam had returned to Crimson at the end of last year, he'd been the consummate example of the phrase "money can't buy happiness." Liam was a hugely successful entrepreneur and had recently headquartered his newest company in Crimson. But reuniting with Natalie had made the biggest change in him. Liam finally realized there was more to life than business. Noah had to admit he envied his friend. To rediscover that kind of love was a gift, he now realized.

"There she is." Noah stood, pressing his palms to the edge of the boat. She wore a two-piece bathing suit, which practically killed him, and her thick hair was tied back in a ponytail. The sight of her did strange things inside Noah's chest, so he tried to focus on what he could control. "They've got a whole group on that boat. Might be too many. Not sure if it's legal."

"Want me to call them in?" Liam asked with a laugh. "Or do you remember how many guys we used to pile on my boat in high school?"

Noah snorted. "We were lucky we didn't sink that thing." He gestured toward the red-and-silver powerboat floating near the far end of the reservoir. It was at least twenty-six feet, the bright colors and sleek lines making it look as if it belonged in Southern California instead of a mountain lake high in the Rockies. "How close can you get without them spotting us?"

Natalie looked at Austin. "Don't listen to either of them. You will never do the stupid things these guys did." She pointed two fingers at her eyes then turned them toward Noah. "I'm not sure I like what's going on here. Why are we spying on Katie? She's on a date."

"You know how she feels about water. I want to make sure she's comfortable."

"You're not looking to sabotage her?" Natalie narrowed her eyes. He didn't blame Natalie for doubting him. But even if he and Katie were only friends, Noah wanted to be the best damn friend he could.

"No one deserves happiness more than Katie," he answered, sinking back into his seat as Liam inched closer to the cliffs where Matt's boat was anchored. "I want to make sure she gets it."

"With Matt?" Natalie asked. "Because she likes Matt, Noah. It could turn into something more if given the chance."

"Nat, enough with the third degree," Liam said gently.

Noah rubbed the back of his neck, where a dull ache had been bothering him since the morning.

Austin handed him a long band of licorice. "You need this more than me."

"Thanks." He took the licorice and bit off one end, meeting Natalie's wary gaze. "I'm not going to mess it up for her. Promise."

"Okay," she said after a moment. "But that still doesn't explain why we're here."

Noah didn't understand it himself. A part of him hoped that Katie would see them on the water and realize she belonged with him instead. He squinted as they got closer, trying to identify the people on Matt's boat. He could see the woman who worked with Katie at the bakery—Lelia, he'd heard her called. There were three other guys with them, all lean and rangy, friends of Matt's, he assumed.

The truth was he liked the feeling he'd had when he and Katie spent their day on the reservoir. *He* wanted to be the one to help her if she got scared, to bolster her confidence and make her see she was more than she believed. Now she laughed at something Matt said, throwing back her head and exposing her delicate throat as that long tumble of dark hair cascaded over her shoulders. Noah felt his pulse leap at the sight and wanted nothing more than to lay Matt Davis out on the ground.

"We should go," he said suddenly. "Nat, you're right. It's stupid that I'm spying on her this way. Katie can take care of herself."

"No way," Austin whined. "Liam, you promised we could go cliff jumping."

"You promised *what*?" Natalie choked out.

Out of the corner of his eye, Noah saw someone throw an oversize rubber inner tube into the water off the back of Matt's boat. Ignoring Liam and Natalie, he turned his full attention across the water. Katie was fastening a life vest across her chest as Matt adjusted one on Lelia's tiny frame.

Katie smiled at something one of the other guys said, but her hands were balled tight at her sides. "You don't have to prove anything to them," he whispered, willing his words to carry to her.

Instead, she and Lelia climbed onto the colorful tube, stomachs down, and Matt pushed them out behind the boat. Noah glanced at the sky—perfectly blue and the air was almost still. The temperature was forecast to hit over ninety today, so conditions were perfect for tubing. Hell, he'd had a great time in the water an hour earlier helping Austin learn how to balance on the wakeboard.

He knew Katie was more confident now, but he hadn't expected her to volunteer for something like this. He hoped Matt took it easy on the two women. Depending on the boat's driver, tubing could be fun or it could be a crazy ride.

As Matt's boat sped off toward the open middle of the reservoir, Natalie came to stand next to him. "Is Katie tubing?" she asked incredulously.

"Yeah."

"You took her swimming last week, right?"

He gave a brief nod, cursing under his breath as the tube disappeared around a bend in the lake.

"She's not afraid anymore?"

"She's good," he said, more for his own benefit than Natalie's. "She can handle this."

His stomach lurched as the boat came back into view. "If that idiot will slow the hell down. He's going way too fast."

"Can we go to the cliffs now?" Austin asked.

"In a minute," Natalie said automatically. Noah heard her breath catch as the inner tube hit another boat's wake and popped into the air a few feet. Both women held on and Matt headed toward the center of the reservoir then spun the boat in a wide arc. The tube skidded across the water, bumping through the waves as slack filled the line before it jerked tight again.

"They're heading for us," Natalie murmured.

Noah shook his head and glanced past the front of Liam's boat. "He's taking them to the edge of the reservoir." The concrete dam front loomed on the other side of the cliff face. It was where the water from the mouth of the Hidden Creek River flowed into the dam. A rope and buoys floated fifty yards in front of the dam, alerting boaters and swimmers that the area was off-limits. It made that stretch of water almost empty compared to the popularity of the rest of the lake on a weekend holiday.

"Liam, head toward the dam." As his friend hit the throttle, both he and Natalie dropped into seats.

Austin leaned forward around Noah. "Is that Miss Katie?" he asked, pointing at the inner tube skimming through the water.

Natalie's smile looked forced as she turned to her son. "Sure is, bud. She's quite the daredevil, isn't she?"

Noah glanced at the boy and saw his eyes widen. "That's way faster than you went on the wakeboard, Noah."

"That's faster than anyone should be driving with the reservoir so crowded." As if his words were an omen, a small Jet Ski took a sharp turn then stalled out, stopping directly in the path of Matt's boat. Noah cursed as the boat swerved one way then the other. He could see the men in back laughing and pumping their fists as if egging on Matt's reckless driving. The tube hit the boat's wake and ricocheted into the air before slamming back down. It immediately flew up again and this time one of the women came off, bouncing across the water like a skipped stone. Lelia hit the water and popped back up thanks to her life vest, brushing her hair out of her face.

Noah's vision turned red as he saw Matt bump knuckles with one of his friends on the boat. But he didn't slow down, instead making another wide turn then a sharper one, sending the tube airborne and Katie soaring through the air along with it.

"Katie," Natalie yelled. "Liam, get to her now."

But unlike Lelia, Katie didn't pop up out of the water. Instead, her life vest immediately surfaced. Empty.

"Where is she?" Natalie screamed.

"Stop," Noah yelled and stripped off his shirt, diving in toward the place where the yellow life vest bobbed empty in the water.

Chapter Thirteen

For a few moments, Katie didn't register anything but the sensation of flying through the air. Then she hit the water with a force that tore the air from her lungs. Her arms already burned from holding on to the handles of the inner tube, so she pumped her legs, finally surfacing with a choked breath.

When she began to sink again, she patted her chest and realized with a start that the life vest had ripped off when she landed. Panic seized her as a wave splashed over her head. She focused on treading water, squinting against the sun's reflection on the lake. Surely Matt would be coming for her any second, but it was hard to see anything beyond the waves from various boat wakes swelling around her. Her heart squeezed and she struggled to rein in her hysteria. A flash of yellow caught her gaze as the water receded for a moment.

Her life vest.

Make it to the life vest.

Her arms felt like lead weights as she lifted one then the other out of the water. *You can do this*, she told herself, but the voice in her head sounded like Noah's. Coaxing her, calming her and making her believe she could overcome the fear that had been a part of her for so long. She could almost hear his voice calling to her.

Then he was in front of her, appearing over the crest of a wave, her life jacket in his hand. "Grab on," he said and she reached for it. Reached for him.

His arms went around her waist. "I've got you, sweetheart," he said against her hair, his voice thick with emotion. "Damn, you scared me."

She opened her mouth, but no sound came out. Fear and panic still lapped at the corners of her mind, just like the water rising and falling around her.

"Focus on me," he said and she did. On his blue eyes, even brighter against his sun-kissed skin, on the scruff on his jaw. His thumb brushed across her cheek, the slight pressure making her wince. "You already have a bruise forming. Just a minute more and Liam will have the boat here."

"What are you—" Water splashed into her face and she coughed again.

"Katie, are you okay?" She looked up as she heard Natalie yelling to her.

Her brain wouldn't register why her friend was peering down at her from the side of a shiny blue-and-silver speedboat.

"Where's Lelia?"

"She's fine."

"What about Matt and the boat?"

She felt Noah stiffen, his lips thinning into a tight line. "Let's get you to safety. Then we'll deal with Matt Davis."

"My arms…" she whispered. "I don't think I can pull myself out of the water."

"I'll help you." He swam them toward the back of the boat, where Liam had slung a plastic ladder next to the engine.

"Pull her up," Noah commanded, positioning Katie in front of the ladder. "Step up as he lifts you, Bug," he whispered in her ear.

Gritting her teeth against the pain, she took hold of the metal railing. With his hands on her hips, Noah held her out of the water while Liam gripped under her arms and hauled her onto the boat. She stumbled and Natalie grabbed her around the waist, helping her to one of the seats near the front of the boat as she wrapped a towel around Katie's shoulders.

"Are you okay?" Natalie repeated her earlier question.

Embarrassment washed over her. After all her preparation, she'd needed to be rescued from the water yet again. "I'm fine," she mumbled, but they all knew it was a lie.

Apparently Austin believed her because a wide grin broke across his face. "That was so cool, Miss Katie. You must have caught six feet of air." He stood on tiptoes and reached his hand above him to indicate how high the inner tube had flown. "Then you slammed down on the water."

She could return his smile now that she was safely on the boat. So many parts of her body ached, but the reality was she'd made it.

"You hit so hard your life vest came off," he all but shouted. "Wait until I tell my friends that story. They won't believe it from the cupcake lady."

"Austin, enough." Natalie's tone was firm but gentle.

"Sorry." He looked at Katie, sheepish. "No offense."

"None taken." She ran two fingers over her cheek. It hurt but not as badly now. "I was wearing one of the larger life vests because Lelia's so tiny she needed the woman's size. I thought I'd tightened it enough, but it must have slipped over my head on impact."

"Impact," Noah growled, sounding disgusted. "What the hell was he thinking taking you on that kind of ride?"

"Don't make this a big deal, Noah." Katie lifted her chin. "I mean it."

He opened his mouth to respond, but at that moment Matt's boat came closer. The guys on the boat were cheering with shouts of "Awesome, Katie," "Sweet dismount" and "You nailed it."

"You want to swim over and we'll get you back in the boat?" Matt called. Lelia stood next to him, grinning from ear to ear. It made Katie feel like an even bigger wimp.

She sucked in a breath as Noah snapped, "You're an ass—"

"We're heading to shore," Liam said, cutting off Noah midsentence. "We'll meet you over there."

Matt nodded, still smiling as Liam motored away.

Natalie reached out to take Katie's hand. "You're sure you—"

"Please don't say anything," Katie said, glancing from Natalie to Noah. "None of them knew I was nervous on the water."

"It doesn't matter," Noah yelled over the roar of the engine. "He shouldn't have been driving that fast."

Katie agreed, but she wasn't going to fuel Noah's anger by admitting it.

The ride across the reservoir to the grassy shore

below the parking lot and picnic area lasted only a few minutes. In that time, Katie took stock of what had happened. She blamed herself for letting Matt and his friends convince her to get on the tube in the first place. She liked Matt, but the more time she spent with him, the more she realized he was an adrenaline junkie like her father. As much as she wanted to fit in with him and his friends, someone like Lelia had much more in common with them. Most of the talk on the boat today had centered around the best spots around Crimson for mountain biking and rock climbing, both sports Lelia had been eager to try. Other than another inner-tube ride, Katie could think of nothing she'd want to do less.

"I need a bathroom break," Natalie said as they pulled into a space between two smaller boats.

Noah hopped into the water, hauling the boat to shore with the rope Liam tossed him. As muscles bunched in his arms and across his shoulders, Katie's mouth went dry and she dropped her head into her hands. She was pathetic.

Austin jumped into the water, too, leaving Natalie and her alone in the boat.

"Why were you guys out there?" she asked, lifting her gaze. "Liam normally hates crowds. A holiday weekend on the lake can't be his idea of a good time."

"Noah was worried about you."

"Why? Didn't he think I could handle it?"

"From what I could tell, it's because he cares about you." Natalie shook her head, one side of her mouth curving. "I've never seen him like that. He had us motoring all over the lake to find you." She held up a hand when Katie would have argued. "Not because he didn't think you could handle yourself. He wanted to look after you. Like a friend, but it was more. A lot more."

Katie sighed, looked at Noah standing on the bank talking to Liam and Austin. "This was the summer I was going to get over him, Nat. There's no future there."

"Are you sure? People change. Sometimes they only need to open their eyes to what's in front of them." She gave Katie's shoulder a squeeze. "I think the combination of seeing you with another guy then hurtling across the lake may have done that for our buddy Noah."

Katie thought about that. Yes, she'd vowed to move past her feelings for him. She wanted more from life than he was willing to give her, and the frustration at her unrequited love was beginning to take a toll on their friendship. But what if Natalie was right? Had she given up too soon? Or was he only interested in her because suddenly she was out of reach?

She glanced up as Matt's boat pulled in at the end of the line of boats docked below the picnic area. One of his friends was driving now, and Matt climbed off the front to beach the boat and tether it to a tree stump. She closed her eyes so she wouldn't be tempted to compare him to Noah. Matt was handsome, but her body didn't react to him like it had to Noah moments ago.

"That won't end well."

Katie blinked at Natalie's words. As Matt finished knotting the rope, Noah was stalking toward him, every muscle in his body radiating anger.

She scrambled forward, holding the towel around her waist as she threw her legs over the side of the boat. She made her way up the shoreline, picking her way over the rocks that dug into her bare feet.

"You're a reckless idiot," Noah yelled, pushing Matt in the chest.

The other man, several inches shorter than Noah, stumbled back, the easy smile disappearing from his face. "What the hell was that for?" He took two steps toward Noah.

"For putting those women in danger. You were driving like an idiot with them on the tube behind you."

"Who are you, the coast guard?" Matt came forward until his chest almost touched Noah's. "We were having fun, Grandpa."

Noah's head snapped back as if Matt had actually hit him. In his circle of friends, Noah was the life of the party. Katie knew he cultivated and protected that image like a coveted prize.

"Fun?" Noah all but spit the word in Matt's face. "You almost killed Katie."

Matt's expression registered shock then anger. "She was having a good time."

"She's afraid of the water," Noah ground out.

Katie was right behind them but stopped as the group took in Noah's words. Again embarrassment rolled through her. "I'm fine," she said tightly, unwilling to look at Matt's friends on the boat. She kept her gaze fixed on him and Noah.

"Is that true?" Matt backed up from Noah a few steps. "Why didn't you say anything?"

"It's not..." She trailed off. How could she deny something so much a part of her, even if she didn't want it to be? "I was having fun."

Noah cursed under his breath. "Are you joking?" He turned fully toward her, blocking Matt's view with his body. "That was the opposite of fun for you."

"I wanted to get on that inner tube, Noah. No one forced me."

"He shouldn't have been driving like that."

"I'm sorry," Matt said behind him. "Katie, you should have signaled me to slow down."

"I thought it was great," Lelia called from the boat.

Katie narrowed her eyes at the woman.

"Sorry," Lelia muttered. "But I did."

"You're enough," Noah whispered, pitching his voice low enough that she was the only one who could hear him. "Just the way you are, Katie. You don't need to try this hard."

His words cut across her, turned her insides to liquid and fire. All she'd wanted in life was to be enough for someone. Without having to try. She'd *always* had to try, as if she was inherently lacking as a person. She'd told herself she was turning over a new leaf, but it felt as if she'd traded one mask for a different guise. She'd wanted to move off the sidelines so badly that she'd pitched herself headfirst into becoming someone she was never meant to be.

"Okay," Matt said, stepping around Noah. "Now we know that you're not one for adventure." His voice was kind, but there was a note of disappointment in it she couldn't miss. He held out a hand to her. "Let's have lunch. Then you can keep the boat steady while the rest of us cliff jump."

On the boat, Lelia clapped her hands.

Noah snorted and bent so he was looking into her eyes, his gaze intense. "You're not going back out there with him," he said softly.

She bit down on her lip, glanced at Matt. "I came with them, Noah. I don't want anyone to think that ride rattled me."

"Who cares what they think?" he shot back.

"I do."

He straightened and turned on his heel. "Liam, I'm done for the day. I'll catch you back in town," he called and stomped off, heading up the hill.

Matt rubbed his hand along her upper arm. "Damn, that was intense. Makes me want a beer." When she only stared, he dropped his hand. "You brought lunch, right?"

She nodded. "In the cooler on the boat."

"Great." He chucked her on the shoulder. "That was a massive crash," he said with a boyish grin.

Katie looked between Matt's boat to where Liam's was tethered five feet away. Natalie raised her eyebrows, her silent question clear to Katie.

"I'm not going back on the boat with you." She spoke the words out loud and saw Natalie nod in approval.

Matt shrugged. "Suit yourself. Can we still keep the food?"

"Sure."

"Katie, do you want me to come with you?" Lelia spoke from the deck of the boat.

"No, you stay." She smiled. "Have fun and take tomorrow off. I'll see you at the bakery on Tuesday."

The young woman squealed with delight. "Really? Tomorrow off? You're the best boss ever."

The best boss, the best friend, the best committee chair. As long as it meant putting other people's needs in front of her own, Katie was a veritable expert.

But what about what she wanted? If she had to admit the truth, she was so unused to taking care of her own needs, she barely registered having any. Her eyes drifted to the parking lot above the reservoir.

"Take these," Natalie said behind her, and Katie whirled, unaware of her friend's approach. Natalie handed her a pair of slip-on sandals. "They'll make getting up the hill a lot easier."

Katie dropped the shoes to the ground and slipped her feet into them. "I'm sorry this day was so much trouble for you guys." She hitched her head toward Liam and Austin, who were busy tying a lure to the end of a fishing pole.

"This has been a great day," Natalie told her with a smile. "You have no idea how much I enjoyed watching Noah Crawford make a fool of himself over a woman." She winked. "Especially when that woman was you."

"He didn't—"

Natalie interrupted her with a wave of one hand. "Go on, before you miss him. Austin isn't going to leave the boat until we take him to the cliffs."

"Thanks, Nat." Katie gave her friend a quick hug and turned.

"And, Katie?"

She glanced over her shoulder.

"That landing will go down in history. It was epic."

Epic. That word had never been linked to her before, and Katie found that, despite the aches and pains that went with it, she kind of liked being epic. Even if it was an epic fail. With a laugh, she headed for the top of the hill.

Chapter Fourteen

Noah sat in the parking lot, trying to get a handle on himself. His truck had been parked in the sun all day, and the temperature inside was almost stifling. He welcomed the heavy air and the bead of sweat that rolled between his shoulder blades. He hit the automatic door lock, as if that would keep him from dashing back down the hill to pluck Katie out of the boat with Matt and his adult-frat-boy friends.

It was none of his business. The rational part of him knew that, but logic had disappeared the moment Noah thought Katie was in danger. Hearing her downplay the incident to Matt left Noah feeling like an overprotective geezer. Hell, he and Liam had done way more dangerous things over the years—on the water, on the slopes. The group mentality dumbed down their common sense to preteen-boy levels. But never Katie. Even over summer breaks, she'd been the responsible one, always making sure her friends got home safe. Maybe that was why he'd overlooked her for so long. He'd been so intent on acting out as a way to numb the regret and sadness he felt over his father's death. Katie, with her stability and sweetness, had been practically invisible to him.

Now she was all he could see. All he could feel. He wanted to share every tiny thing that happened in his day, to make up for lost time in discovering all the hidden-away pieces of her. But he was a bad bet, and he didn't blame her for rejecting him. It was payback long overdue. If nothing else, he'd take it like a man.

With a heavy sigh, he turned the key in the ignition as a knock sounded on the passenger-side window. Katie stared in at him, peering through the glass.

He rolled down the window then wiped the back of his hand across his forehead.

"I just wanted to say thank you." Her chest rose and fell as if she was having trouble catching her breath. He could barely tear his gaze away from the slight swell of her breasts peeking out from the low V-neck of the bathing-suit top. "For rescuing me. For being there when I needed you."

"You didn't need me," he answered, shaking his head. "You would have been fine. You were swimming toward the life vest when I got to you. I overreacted, and I'm sorry." He laughed, but the sound was bitter. "Again. I know you can take care of yourself."

"And everyone else in town while I'm at it?" she said, humor in her voice.

His gaze snapped to hers. "I hate that you wore a bikini today."

She looked down at herself then back at him, her eyes suddenly dancing. "It's a tankini and about an inch of skin is showing between the top and bottom."

"It's an access thing," he said irritably but couldn't help his smile as she laughed so hard she snorted. He'd bet Matt Davis never made her snort, and the feeling of accomplishment was ridiculous. But the thought of another man having access to Katie's body, to the vibrant passion he knew she hid under her placid, sweet surface, made his temper flare again. "What is this, Katie? What are you doing up here when the *fun* is down on the lake?"

She straightened her shoulders, as if steadying herself or drawing courage. "Unlock the car, Noah," she whispered.

Something had changed in her tone, and his pulse leaped in response. He flicked the button for the lock but didn't watch as she climbed in next to him. He kept his eyes straight out the front of the truck, but he was all too aware of her. Even after a dip in the reservoir, Katie smelled delicious. This time the scent of vanilla was mixed with suntan lotion. The combination made him immediately hard.

He put his hands on the steering wheel, not trusting himself to resist reaching for her.

"You told me to choose," she said softly. "I choose you."

He felt dizzy, as if every one of his secret desires was being handed to him on a platter and he didn't know which to select first. He turned to her now, his hands still on the wheel. He didn't want to ruin this moment, to push her too far. More than anything, he didn't want to hurt her by being his usual self.

"Say it again." He kept his voice calm, his expression neutral, but Katie smiled.

She folded her legs underneath her on the leather seat and leaned over the console. Cupping his face with her hands, she swayed closer until her lips were almost grazing his and he sucked in her breath each time he inhaled. It was sweeter than he'd ever imagined. Her eyes held his as she spoke against his mouth. "I choose us." She brushed her lips against his, gentle and almost tentative, as if she expected him to push her away.

That was the last thing on Noah's mind. He took hold of her waist and hauled her fully onto his lap, pressing her to his bare chest. His hands moved up and down her back as he deepened the kiss, sweeping his tongue into her mouth, groaning as she met his passion. Her nails dug into the muscles under his shoulder blades and he welcomed the sensation, which only heightened his own pleasure in the moment. This was what he'd wanted—for so much longer than he'd realized.

A loud wolf whistle split the air and someone banged hard on the hood of his truck. "Get a room," whoever it was called as the sound of laughter spilled into the truck.

Katie still clung to him, giggling against his throat. He tipped up her chin, her lips wet and swollen from his kisses. He wanted to take her, right here in the cab of his truck, in broad daylight. He felt like a teenager again, light and carefree, his only concern the fastest way to get her naked.

The thought made him grin. "I'm going to take you home now." His grin widened as she frowned. "I'm coming in with you. I'm going to stay with you, Katie. All night long."

"Oh." She breathed out the one syllable, then climbed back into the passenger seat. After fastening her seat belt, she slunk down low, her face cradled in her hands.

"What are you doing?" he asked as he drove out of the parking lot and onto the county highway toward town.

She lifted her head once they were on the open road.

"People saw us…you know…making out. What if they recognized me? Or you? Or the two of us together?"

"I don't care who knows it's you and me." He reached for her hand, tugged it away from her face and laced their fingers together. "I want everyone to know you're mine, Katie. Because you are now. I'll kiss you all over the damn town if that's what it takes. In fact, there are lots of things I can think of for us to try." Then, her hand in his, he proceeded to tell her all the wicked things he wanted to do to her and with her—in Crimson, in the forest, in every room of her house.

It was the longest hour of his life.

By the time Noah parked the truck crooked against the curb in front of her house, Katie felt dizzy with need. All the way home, he'd whispered the details of what he wanted to do to her as his thumb traced a light circle on the back of her hand, and it was driving her crazy.

They laughed as they raced up the front walk. She'd locked her door when she'd left this morning since there were so many nonlocals in town for the holiday, but her purse was still stuffed into a cubby on Matt's boat.

"My hide-a-key," she said on a gasp, bending to lift the rock from under the bushes where the key was hidden. Then gasping again as Noah whirled her around, his mouth crashing into hers. They stayed there for several minutes, kissing deep and long. He was making good on his promise of claiming her in front of the whole town, and Katie wondered if any of her elderly neighbors were watching this public display.

Noah picked her up as he climbed the steps, and she automatically wrapped her legs around his lean hips. One of his hands inched up her back. "Give me the key," he said against her mouth, and she pressed it into his palm.

She wasn't sure how he was going to manage to hold on to her and open the front door, but a moment later the lock turned.

"You have mad skills," she said on a laugh.

He drew back enough to look into her eyes, his grin wicked. "You have no idea."

As well as she knew him, he might be right. The first time with Noah had been amazing, but this felt completely new. He'd chosen her. They'd chosen each other, and it made all the difference. She'd tried to convince herself that what was between them was only physical, but now she didn't bother to guard her heart. It was pointless anyway. Noah had her heart, and he had from the first. No matter what happened down the road, this was her moment to revel in all she felt for him.

He kicked shut the door then moved toward her bedroom. Bending to rip away the quilt and sheets, he dropped her on the bed with so much force she bounced once and her breath, already uneven, whooshed out of her lungs. "Tell me you have protection," he whispered as he followed her onto the bed. His hands were on her stomach, inching up her swim top. He pressed his mouth to her belly button then skimmed his tongue along her rib cage.

"I… Yes…oh, yes…" she whispered.

"Oh, yes, in general?" he asked and she heard the smile in his voice. "Or, yes, you have protection?"

"In the nightstand."

"Good. Now lift your arms."

She raised them over her head and he pulled her bathing suit up and off, leaning over her to open the nightstand drawer.

He sat back again, gazing down at her. "Has anyone told you today how beautiful you are?"

Normally Katie would feel shy at being so exposed, but the intensity in his gaze gave her confidence. She tapped a finger to her chin, pretending to ponder the question. "One of Matt's friends told me I was the hottest muffin maker he'd ever met. Does that count?"

Noah growled low in his throat. "I'm going to kill that guy." He planted his hands on either side of her head and lowered himself over her. His chest hair tickled her bare skin, and heat pooled low in her body. "You are the most beautiful thing I've ever seen," he whispered. He slanted his lips over hers, but when she tried to deepen the kiss, he broke away, his mouth trailing to her jaw then down her throat and finally to her breast. "So beautiful," he said again, then took one nipple into his mouth.

She arched off the bed with a moan. He continued to lick and suck at her breasts, driving her wild, as he tugged the bathing-suit bottom over her hips. Her hands splayed across his lower back, kneading the muscles there. She wanted to feel all of him, to stay like this and never let reality back into their lives. Nothing had ever felt so good, she thought, but still she wanted more. Reaching between them, she unsnapped the waistband of his board shorts, pushing at them.

He released her for just a moment, stripped off the shorts and his T-shirt then tore open the foil wrapper. He settled himself between her legs, moving just enough that the pressure made her breath catch.

"Yes, Noah. Please." She didn't care if she was begging. She needed him so much. He kissed her deeply as he rocked against her but lifted his head as he thrust into her. Their gazes locked and it seemed to heighten the pleasure, to increase the intimacy until Katie felt a tear drop from the edge of her eye onto the pillow.

Noah pressed his lips to her skin and she twined her legs more tightly around him. A groan ripped from his throat that sent shivers through her. Pressure built inside her until it finally burst, a bright shower of golden light engulfing her, soothing all the parts inflamed by their passion. Noah shuddered, burying his face against her neck and crying out her name.

It was the most beautiful thing she'd ever heard.

They lay like that for several minutes, the heat of his body cocooning her in warmth. He smoothed the hair back from her face, threading his fingers through it as he spread it across the sheets. The kisses he gave her now were gentle, tiny touches of light on her skin. She didn't dare move, afraid to break the spell and have him leave her as he had the last time.

"All night," he said, as if reading her thoughts. He gently sucked her earlobe into his mouth and she squirmed underneath him. "Right now if you keep moving like that."

As she laughed, he rose from the bed, padded to the bathroom then returned a few minutes later. Katie still lay where she was, staring at the ceiling, although she'd pulled the sheets and quilt up over herself.

He lifted the covers and climbed in next to her, dropping a kiss to her mouth just as she stifled a yawn.

"Sorry," she said automatically. "I'm always tired lately."

"It's the time on the lake," he said, turning on his side and tucking her in tight against his chest. "Swimming is tiring enough, but the daredevil stunt from today would exhaust anyone."

She yawned again. "Natalie told me it was *epic*."

"All I know is it almost gave me an epic heart attack."

He pressed his mouth to her bare shoulder. “How’s your body holding up after that crazy ride?”

She shrugged. “My cheek hurts and my arms are sore. I have another bruise on my chin. It’ll hurt worse tomorrow, I know. But I’m okay.”

“Just okay?”

“Tired,” she added and he nipped at her neck. “And blissfully satisfied. And happy. Mainly happy.”

“Me too. Go to sleep now, Bug.”

“Are you—”

“I’ll be here when you wake up. I keep a change of clothes in the truck for when Jase and I go for a run or to the gym after work. I’m not going anywhere. Promise.”

She wasn’t sure whether it was the words that made her trust him or the conviction with which he said them. Perhaps it was the overwhelming exhaustion she felt. The constant fatigue, even with her busy schedule, was starting to concern her. She’d worked long hours for years, but the past few weeks had been difficult to handle. As she drifted off, she decided she’d make an appointment with her family doctor next week. She wouldn’t tell Noah, though. No need to give him something extra to worry about after what had just happened with his mom.

But right now a nap was exactly what she needed. She fell asleep, happy to be enveloped in Noah’s embrace.

Chapter Fifteen

Noah registered Katie's surprise as she walked into the kitchen hours later.

"You're still here." Her voice was scratchy with sleep and she wore a tattered floral robe that was so worn it was practically see-through.

"I promised," he told her, tamping down the annoyance that flared at the thought she hadn't believed he would stay.

"I'm glad," she said, walking forward to kiss him. All thoughts of annoyance fled as he buried his face in her hair. She smelled like sleep, vanilla and like him. A wave of primal satisfaction rolled through him and somewhere deep in his gut the word *mine* reverberated.

She was his.

"Why are you always sniffing me?" She pulled back, looping a long strand of hair between her fingers and pulling it to her nose. "Do I need a shower?"

"No. You smell fantastic. You always do. You smell like…"

Home.

His chest constricted at the word. It was true, even if he hadn't realized it before now. Katie had always felt like home to him.

"You smell like the bakery," he answered instead.

"Mixed with a healthy dose of lake water." She grimaced. "The bruise on my cheek is darkening."

"Matt is an idiot."

She smiled, reached around him for the glass of water he'd set down. "I would have said the same thing about you a few weeks ago," she answered, taking a drink.

"I'm a slow learner." He tugged on the tie looped around the front of the robe. "How is it possible that an article of clothing your grandma would have worn can be such a turn-on to me?"

"This was Gram's robe."

"I feel like a sick pervert." His fingers worked to loosen the tie.

She swatted at his hand. "Stop," she said with a giggle. "I'm not wearing anything underneath."

"Doubly perverted."

She pushed away from him. "Before you go too far, I'm starving. Let me make us something to eat."

"Done." He inched the fabric off her chest and kissed the swell of her breast.

She moaned a little, but glanced around her empty kitchen. "How?"

The doorbell rang. "Delivery," he said against her skin.

"No one delivers on the holiday. All the restaurants are too busy."

The doorbell rang again.

"I pulled some strings at the brewery."

Reluctantly he stepped away from her. "You should put on some clothes, or the food's going to be cold before we get to it."

"Sweet-potato fries?" she asked, rubbing her stomach.

"Of course. They're your favorite."

She grinned. "I owe you, then." She quickly pulled the robe apart to flash her breasts at him. "Later."

"Forget the food," Noah growled, lunging for her.

She jumped away, running for her bedroom. "Answer the door, Noah," she called over her shoulder.

He set out containers of food, glancing up as she returned. She'd traded the robe for a tank top and black sweatpants. Her hair tumbled down in waves around her shoulders. When she moved, he could see a purple lace bra strap peeking through. Had she always worn lacy lingerie? What a fool he'd been all these years. He had so much time to make up.

"I can't believe how hungry I am," she said, taking plates from the cabinet.

They sat down to eat the burgers and fries. Noah lit the candle that sat in the middle of the table then dimmed the kitchen lights.

"Romantic," Katie murmured, her voice a little breathless. He had to agree. As casual as it was, this was indeed the most romantic dinner he'd ever had.

"But this isn't a date," he told her firmly. "I'm going to take you out for a real date with reservations at the best restaurant in Aspen."

"I don't care about that," she said, shaking her head. "Tonight is perfect."

"Agreed, but you deserve the five-star treatment, and I want to be the guy to give it to you."

Katie went suddenly still.

"What's wrong?"

"Nothing. We're missing the big fireworks display. I hope you didn't have plans to take your mom and sister?"

He shook his head. "Mom has a date tonight." At her questioning gaze, he shrugged. "Her surgeon. Second time out with him this week. She really likes him."

"And you're okay with that?"

"I am," Noah said, releasing a breath. "Dad would want her to be happy, so I want the same thing."

She came around the table and plopped onto his lap, snagging one of his fries in the process. "You're a good man, Noah Crawford." She kissed him on the cheek then popped the bright orange fry into her mouth.

"Do you really believe that or are you just angling for my food?"

"Both."

He kissed her then glanced at his watch. "I've got a surprise for you."

She angled her head. "Is it a good surprise?"

"I hope so." He lifted her to her feet. "I'll get the dishes cleaned up while you put on a sweater. We have about ten minutes."

"Where are we going?" She smoothed a hand over her tank top. "Should I change clothes or at least brush my hair?"

"Neither. It's a private party tonight. Trust me."

He said the words lightly, but something tender unfurled in his chest when she nodded and disappeared toward her bedroom. It had been a long time since anyone he cared about really trusted him. Sure, his mom said she depended on him, but even after her illness she'd been almost as self-sufficient as usual.

He put the plates in the dishwasher and repacked the empty boxes in the paper sack. By the time Katie came out, he was pacing the front of the house, anxious in a way he hadn't been since he was a teenager.

"I'm ready," she said, having buttoned a thick sweater over her tank top and traded the sweats for a faded pair of jeans.

"Great," he said, embarrassed when his voice caught. "Great," he repeated, clearing his throat.

She came toward him. "Are you nervous?" She sounded amused.

"Of course not." He wiped his palms on his shorts then took her hand. "I just want you to like what I have planned."

Katie had never seen Noah like this, especially not with her. He was always confident and sure of himself. He took very little in life seriously, and never his relationships with women—not since Tori had broken his heart.

An image of Tori flashed through Katie's mind. What would Noah think if his ex-girlfriend made good on her threat to expose Katie's part in their breakup?

Maybe it wasn't a big deal. It had been so long ago and Katie hadn't been the one to cheat or to break his heart. Surely he'd understand that? In fact, she should just tell him herself so she could explain why she'd done it. She'd wanted to protect him. Tori might accuse Katie of wanting him for herself, but that wasn't true. She'd never believed Noah could belong to her.

Now he did.

He held her hand as he led her through the front door, squeezing gently on her fingers. She'd tell him tomorrow. A little voice inside her called her a coward, but she ignored it. She wasn't going to ruin this night.

"Where are we going?"

He led her around the side of the house and stopped. "Up," he answered with a boyish grin.

A ladder had been propped against the gutter where the roof of the front porch sloped up to meet the house's roofline.

"I checked and we have a view of the mountain from your roof. Fireworks start in five minutes."

"I'd never thought of that," she said softly.

"Start climbing, sweetheart."

She grabbed the sides of the ladder, her arms still sore from hanging on to the inner tube earlier. But she was using them only for balance, so she began to make her way slowly up the metal rungs.

"If you need a break, feel free to stop for a minute." Noah's voice drifted up to her. "I'm okay if we miss the fireworks since I've got a better view from down here."

She glanced down to where he was grinning up at her. Careful not to lose her balance, Katie wiggled her hips a bit and was rewarded by his rich laughter. She understood Noah's popularity with the ladies, but he made her feel as if she was the only woman in the world who mattered. It was as if every part of her was desirable and he couldn't get enough. She also knew his affections could change in an instant, especially if she started to take what was between them too seriously. Once again, she reminded herself to simply enjoy the moment.

She hitched herself onto the roof then waited for Noah to join her. Her neighborhood was dark and mainly quiet. From a few blocks away, she could hear the soft sounds of classic rock playing and smell hamburgers on the grill—someone must be having an outdoor barbecue.

To the east of her house was downtown Crimson, lights glowing from the Fourth of July party the town hosted. To the west was Crimson Mountain, its top just visible in the darkness, a ridge that split the sky. The night was clear and stars dotted the sky over the valley. She hugged her arms around her waist as Noah's head appeared over the side of the house.

"This is great," she told him as he planted a foot onto the roof.

"We're not there yet." He pointed toward the high edge of the roof. "Can you make it a little farther?"

The truth was she felt nervous being up this high. Her roofline wasn't steep and she had no problem getting traction on the tiles with her gym shoes. Still, Katie wasn't one to go scaling roofs. But with Noah studying her, his blue eyes almost indigo in the dark, she wanted to be. She felt safe with him and that gave her courage.

"Lead on," she told him. "It's my turn for the view."

He laughed and began to scramble up the center of the roof toward her chimney. She followed, keeping her palms on the shingles as she did. When she got to the top, she glanced up to see a blanket spread over the tip of the roof and a cooler attached to the chimney by a bungee cord wrapped around the bricks.

"When did you do all this?" she asked, easing onto the blanket and dusting off her hands.

"While you were napping. You've always slept like the dead, so I figured I wouldn't wake you." He took out a pint of ice cream from the cooler, peeled back the lid and handed her a spoon.

"How—"

"I paid the delivery guy extra to swing by the store for dessert. I hope raspberry chip is still your favorite flavor."

She took the ice cream and dug in her spoon. Ice cream was her go-to dessert because it didn't involve any work on her part or elicit comparisons to her own baking. "You've been paying more attention than I thought," she said around a mouthful.

He leaned in and kissed her, licking a bit of ice cream from the corner of her lips. "Glad you noticed." Reaching into his pocket, he took out his phone and typed in the passcode. "I bookmarked the website for the radio station that's broadcasting the music for the fireworks. It should be starting any second."

There was a hiss in the distance. Then the sky lit up in front of the mountain.

Katie let out a breath. "It's amazing from here."

A crack split the night, and golden lights sprinkled down from the sky, followed quickly by a whistle and another pop as a colorful spray of red, white and blue filled the air. Noah inched closer to her, tucking her into his side as they watched. The mountain was a majestic backdrop for the lights and sounds of the Fourth of July fireworks. He balanced the phone on his knee and she listened to the choreographed music swell then soften as the night continued to glow.

Katie kept her eyes on the display but felt Noah nuzzling her neck after a few minutes. Despite the coolness of the air, her body automatically heated. She squirmed as he sucked her earlobe into his mouth. "You aren't watching."

"You're too distracting," he whispered against her ear.

"If you don't stop that," she said, ducking her head, "I'm going to lose my balance and fall off the roof."

"I'll hold you." As if to prove his point, he drew her

closer against him. But with one more kiss to her temple, he turned and watched the rest of the display.

Katie couldn't remember ever being so happy. For many years, she'd worked the Life is Sweet booth at the town's annual July Fourth party. She'd watched couples stroll by, arm in arm, and always felt a tug of envy. Especially when her friends fell in love and she was surrounded by so much togetherness while she was always alone.

"I normally watch the fireworks as I'm packing up the booth," she said softly during a lull in the display. "I'm glad that a couple of the college kids working for me this summer wanted the extra money to run the event. You haven't been back to Crimson over the Fourth for several years."

"I'm usually on duty over the holiday," Noah told her. "Lots of extra help needed with so many campers in the forest this weekend."

She tipped her head to look at him. "Why not this year?"

"I had more important people to watch over."

Katie smiled, then kissed him just as the big finale began. They both turned toward the shimmering ribbons of light. She felt the boom and pop of hundreds of bursts of color reverberate through her, even from miles away. Or maybe it was just her heart beating as the walls that guarded it came crumbling down.

Chapter Sixteen

On Monday morning Katie stumbled out of a stall in the community center's bathroom, only to find Emily Whitaker waiting for her. She grabbed the wad of paper towels the other woman handed her, dabbing at her eyes before wiping her mouth.

Even with the problems Emily was dealing with from her divorce and her son's issues, she still looked every inch the society wife, from her demure striped skirt to the crisp button-down and strand of pearls she wore.

It made Katie feel all the more tired and rumpled, especially since Emily had just listened to her throwing up most of the bagel she'd had for breakfast.

"Don't get too close," she warned as she stepped to the sink to wash her hands and splash cold water on her face. She glanced at herself in the mirror and grimaced. Under the bathroom's fluorescent lights, her skin looked even pastier, the dark circles under her eyes more pronounced. "I thought I was just tired from being swamped at the bakery and the extra work for the festival. I guess I've caught some kind of a bug."

Emily balanced one thin hip on the corner of the sink. "You're pregnant."

Katie's hand stilled on the handle of the towel dispenser. She turned to Emily, water dripping off her face. "No, I'm not."

Emily rolled her pale blue eyes. "Are you sure? Noah was lecturing me on how I need to do more for the festival because you're exhausted." She handed another paper towel to Katie. "I've seen how much you eat during the committee meetings."

"I don't..." Katie broke off. She had been extra hungry lately, but she blamed it on needing fuel to keep up with all of her commitments.

"And..." Emily waved a hand toward Katie's blouse. "No offense, but I don't remember you being quite so... well-endowed."

Katie glanced down at her chest, her eyes widening at the cleavage on display. She quickly fastened another button on her chambray shirt. "Maybe it's a new bra."

"Is it a new bra?"

"I... That doesn't mean..." She inhaled, her lungs suddenly constricting. "No, it's not new. Why are you in here anyway? Can't a girl puke in peace?"

"I was using the restroom and wanted to make sure you're okay." She leaned forward. "Are you, Katie?"

Katie placed her hands on the cool porcelain of the white sink, ignoring the slight tremble of her arms. She did the math in her head and moaned. "This can't be happening. We used protection," she mumbled, her stomach rolling once again.

"Nothing is foolproof," Emily said. "Is it safe to assume the baby is Noah's?"

"Of course. If there is a baby." Katie glanced up at Emily in the mirror. "I need to take a pregnancy test. Nothing is certain until then."

"Noah's going to be a father." Emily tapped a finger on her chin, one corner of her mouth lifting. "At least I won't be the most messed-up person in the family anymore."

At this comment Katie straightened and turned to Emily. "Noah isn't messed up." She hugged her arms to her stomach. "And my baby…" She paused, let the implications of those two words sink in. *My baby.* "If there is a baby," she clarified, "that's not messed up, either. Noah will make a wonderful father." There was that stomach rolling again.

Emily arched one eyebrow.

"But don't say anything," Katie added quickly. "To anyone."

"You're not going to tell Noah?"

"There's nothing to tell until I take the test and talk to my doctor." She bit down on her lip. "I don't want… Things are so new between us, you know? I don't want to freak him out if this is just me getting regular sick. It's the first morning I've thrown up, so it could be nothing."

"He cares about you."

"But he's not… We're not…" She brushed away a tear from the corner of her eye. "I told him I wanted a family. What if he thinks this is a trap? I don't know if he's ready for this. How can he be?"

"Are you?" Emily's voice was gentle.

Katie breathed through the panic that constricted her lungs, and the next instant it was gone. She took a few more breaths, put her hand on her chest and found her heartbeat returning to its regular rhythm. "Yes." She nodded once, suddenly sure of this one thing. "Yes, I'm ready. If I'm pregnant, I'll love that baby with my whole heart. I'll give him or her the best life I know how to create."

Emily's normally cool expression warmed as pink colored her cheeks. She took two steps toward Katie and wrapped her in a hug. "Congratulations, then. Being a mom is the best and hardest job in the world."

Katie opened her mouth to tell Emily that nothing was certain yet, then stopped herself. Her fingers drifted to her belly and she *knew.* "I'm going to be a mom," she whispered and looked at Emily with a new understanding. "Watching your son struggle has to be the hardest part." She didn't ask a question, but stated the obvious fact.

"More than leaving my marriage and my life or crawling back to Crimson after I'd sworn never to return." Emily bit down on her lip. "To me, Davey is perfect, but no one in Boston saw him that way. If I could take away what he has to go through, the challenges that his life might hold, I'd do it in a millisecond. But I wouldn't change him. I love him for the boy he is, not who he might have been if things were different."

"He's lucky to have you."

"And my brother is lucky to have you, Katie. You might be the best thing that ever happened to him."

Both women turned when the door to the restroom slammed shut. Katie took three steps forward to peer around the entrance to the community center's main hallway. No one was there, but something had made the door move. She opened it and looked both ways down the hall, but it was empty.

As Emily came up behind her, both women stepped out of the restroom.

"Weird," Emily murmured.

"You don't think someone was eavesdropping?" Katie asked, her voice a nervous croak.

"I think the only people here this early are on the festival committee, and I'm sure any of those women would have announced themselves."

Katie glanced at her watch. "The meeting was scheduled to start ten minutes ago. I need to get in there."

"Do you want me to handle it?"

Katie glanced at Emily.

"Not the festival," she quickly clarified. "But today's meeting. If you give me your notes, I can go over things with everyone. Organizing volunteers is one of my few useful skills."

Katie hesitated. She didn't like to depend on other people. It made her feel as if she wasn't pulling her own weight, weak and useless, even though she understood that was just the leftover dysfunction from her childhood. "That would be great," she said after a moment. "Jase will be there, too, and he can answer any questions that come up from the subcommittee chairs."

"Of course." Emily's smile was wry. "Perfect Jase can handle anything."

"He's not—"

"Never mind," the other woman interrupted. "All hands on deck and whatnot."

"Thank you." Katie took the binder from her tote bag and handed it to Emily. "I'm heading to the pharmacy—"

"You might want to—"

Katie held up a hand. "To the pharmacy over in Aspen where no one will recognize me. Then to my doctor if the test is positive. You promise you won't tell Noah?"

"Promise."

With another quick hug, Katie walked out of the community center into the morning light. This day was going to change her life, of that much she was certain. She just hoped the change wouldn't cost her Noah.

Three days before the Founder's Day Festival, Noah turned his truck off the Forest Service access road and headed for town. He'd been up most of the night, investigating reports of teenagers partying near one of the campsites above a popular hiking trail. The local emergency dispatcher had received an anonymous call about possible vandalism and a bonfire. The vandalism was bad, but a fire could potentially be catastrophic to the area.

Noah had had plans with Katie last night, like he had almost every evening since July Fourth. They took turns at her place or she'd come to dinner at his mom's. With Katie at his side, he'd even managed through a family barbecue with John Moore, who was quickly becoming his mother's steady boyfriend.

It had been strange to see another man in his parents' kitchen, gamely helping his mom chop vegetables for a salad and making beer runs to the garage refrigerator. Logan and Olivia had been there now that she was feeling better, along with Jake and Millie. Jake and John had done some shoptalk about the hospital, but Noah had to admit the older doctor was comfortable with all of them. And his mother had radiated happiness.

Noah understood that feeling, barely able to keep the goofy grin off his face every time he looked at Katie. He loved her. Was madly *in* love with her. He hadn't told her yet, but he planned to later tonight. As promised, he'd made a reservation at a five-star restaurant in Aspen. His relationship with Katie had been casual for too long. He'd taken her for granted and was determined that she understood how much he'd changed.

Something was off with her, and he worried it had to do with not trusting his feelings for her. She was quieter, sometimes staring off into space as if she was a thousand miles away. When he asked her about it, she claimed she was tired but it felt…different. He'd walked in on Emily and her arguing in the kitchen of his mom's house, both women startling when he came into the room. They'd said it was simply a disagreement about the Founder's Day Festival, but he didn't believe them. That night Katie had clung to him as they made love, holding on as though she thought he might slip away at any moment.

She didn't trust that he wasn't going to leave her. He needed to tell her how he felt so she could relax. The idea of talking about his emotions made him prickly all over, but he was in love with Katie. He hadn't felt like this for so long—his whole life, maybe—and he was ready to risk opening himself up again.

He took a quick shower then picked up a bouquet of flowers on his way through downtown. He couldn't resist a visit to the bakery before heading to his office. One night away and he needed to see her face before he started his day. He laughed, wondering what his friends would think if they could see him now. He didn't care. He finally understood why some of his buddies looked so content as their women led them around on a string. Nothing mattered more than wrapping his arms around Katie.

The bakery was crowded with both locals and summer tourists, the two young women behind the counter hustling to fill orders. Katie wasn't part of the action, which surprised him. Normally she was front and center with customers during peak hours. He waved to a few people he knew, then walked to the edge of the display cabinet.

"She in back?" he asked Lelia.

"Um… I think so," the woman muttered, not meeting Noah's gaze as she bent to select a pastry from the cabinet. "But she's kind of busy this morning. Do you want me to tell her you stopped by?"

"I'll tell her myself," he said, holding up the bouquet. "No one is too busy for flowers, right?"

He opened the door to the bakery's kitchen quietly. If he could manage it, he wanted to sneak up on Katie, wrap his arms around her and hear her squeal of surprise before she melted into him.

But it was Noah who was in for the surprise, because Katie wasn't alone. She and Tori stood at the far counter, in front of the deep stainless-steel sink. Katie was shaking her head, clearly distraught, as Tori spoke. Noah started to move forward, anger gripping him that his ex-girlfriend wouldn't leave Katie alone. He froze in place when he heard her hiss the words *pregnant* and *liar.*

Katie's gaze slammed into his. So many emotions flashed through her brown eyes—love, guilt and regret. He shook his head as if denying it would ward off the truth of the scene unfolding in front of him.

Tori turned after a moment, her eyes widening at the sight of him. "This isn't exactly what I'd planned," she said, visibly swallowing. "But I guess the secret's out now. Or is about to be. How much did you hear, Noah?"

"Enough," he said through clenched teeth, keeping his eyes on Tori. He'd thought she was perfect when they were together, but now her expensive sun-kissed highlights and flawless makeup made her appear to be trying too hard. And like before, what she was trying to do was ruin his life.

She gave the barest nod, took a step toward him. "Then you know I wasn't the only one guilty of hurting you that night."

"You were having sex with one of my friends."

"It was stupid," she agreed. "A meaningless fling before you asked me to marry you. You were going to propose to me before graduation."

"But I didn't."

"Because of the anonymous note," she all but spit. "Now you know who wrote it. Your precious, oh-so-perfect Katie-bug. You think she cared about you, but she only wanted to break us up so she could have you all to herself."

He saw Katie close her eyes and shake her head.

"Now you're stuck with her," Tori continued. "But she still won't tell you the truth." She whirled on Katie. "Was this all part of some master twisted plan?"

"Of course not," Katie answered, her voice shaking. "I didn't mean… This isn't…" She seemed to shrink in on herself, crossing her arms over her stomach as she spoke. A baby was growing in her stomach. His baby. Noah's knees went weak at the thought.

"Get out of here, Tori." He pointed to the door. "This is none of your business anymore."

"I understand." Tori's voice turned to the whine he remembered so well. "But she isn't—"

"Get out," Noah yelled, flipping his arm wide, sending several baking sheets drying on the counter crashing to the floor as he did. Katie jumped at the noise and Tori suddenly looked unsure of herself. Noah wasn't known for his temper. Even when he'd discovered Tori cheating, he'd simply compartmentalized his feelings and walked away. But now, in this moment, he could barely contain the emotions that rattled through him. It felt as if a virus had infected his body and was eating away at his heart even as it still beat in his chest. The pain was almost unbearable.

"I just want you to know I'm not the only one who deceived you," Tori said then stalked through the door to the front of the shop.

Lelia poked her head in a moment later. "Everything okay?"

"We're fine," Katie said in a shaky voice at the same time Noah growled, "Get out."

When they were alone, Katie spoke in a whisper. "I'm sorry, Noah." He felt her step toward him but kept his eyes on the ground. "I never meant—"

"Don't." He held up one hand. He could not bear it if she touched him right now. All that need for her had warped, and turned ugly in the space of a few moments. He hardly trusted himself to speak, but if she touched him he'd be a goner for sure.

"Are you pregnant?" he choked out, the words heavy in his throat. Bile and panic rose up, warred in his chest.

"Yes."

"And the baby is mine?"

He heard her gasp before answering, "Yes."

He'd wanted to hurt her with the words, for her to experience a tiny bit of the pain he felt. But even though he knew he had, it didn't give him any relief from his own tumbling emotions. This was why he'd walled himself off for so long. This gut-wrenching pain, the same thing he'd felt when his parents had finally told him about his father's illness. When it had been too late.

"How far along?"

"About seven weeks." He heard her begin to clean up the fallen baking sheets. "It must have been the first time we were together."

"We used protection."

She gave a small laugh. "That's what I told your sister but it's not—"

He whirled and grabbed her arms, hauling her off the floor, the metal baking sheets clattering to the tile floor. "What do you mean when you told my sister?" He brought his face inches from hers. "Emily knows about the baby? You told my *sister* before you bothered to share the news with *me*? Who else knows?"

Her eyes widened. "No one knows. It wasn't like that, Noah. She heard me getting sick one morning and she guessed."

"When was this?" He gripped her harder, forced himself not to shake her.

"Last week. At the community center."

He released her as suddenly as he'd taken hold of her. His head pounding, he stalked to the edge of the kitchen then back toward her. "Why does Tori know?"

"She overheard Emily and me talking. I didn't realize until she came here today with her threats."

"And the note?" he asked, remembering the other piece of venom that had spewed from Tori's glossy lips.

She nodded, squeezed her eyes shut then opened them again. "I left it for you."

"Why not tell me?"

"I don't know. I was afraid you'd blame me. Kill the messenger and all that. It was stupid."

"And at no time in the past eight years did you think to mention it?" His voice was steady even as his body shook with rage.

"I should have said something. I wanted to." She dragged in a breath. "I just didn't trust…"

"Me." He spoke the word on an angry breath.

"I can only tell you I'm sorry. I regret it so much."

"Because it was wrong or because I found out?" When she opened her mouth, he shook his head. "It doesn't matter now. *That* doesn't matter." He glanced toward the counter, saw a sheet of muffin tins half filled with batter. That must have been what she was working on when Tori had interrupted her. He could see ripe blueberries floating in the yellow mixture and wondered if he'd ever be able to stomach another blueberry muffin. "You're *pregnant*." A thought struck him and he scrubbed one hand over his face. "God, Katie, you were pregnant when you fell off the inner tube. When we climbed to the top of your roof."

"I didn't *know*." Her expression was miserable, and earlier this morning he would have done anything to ease her pain. The longer he stood here now, the less he felt. She'd brought him back to life, but he should have known it wouldn't last.

"I should have been with you, Katie. When you took the test. At the doctor. I deserved to know."

"I was going to tell you," she said, her voice pleading with him to believe her. "Tonight at dinner. I wanted it to be special."

"As special as my sister knowing a week before I did?" He knew he was being unfair because he'd planned to tell her how he felt during that same dinner. To say the words *I love you* and really mean them. Now he was bitterly grateful he hadn't revealed his feelings earlier. He'd feel even more the fool that she hadn't trusted him. "This wasn't the plan, Katie. Hell, I don't know how to be a father."

Her face paled at his words, but she straightened her shoulders. "I want this baby, Noah. I know it wasn't part of the plan, but it's a blessing. I want to be a mother. I want *our* baby."

"I want the baby, too, Katie. Don't put words in my mouth like I'm suggesting anything else. But I need time to get used to the idea. Time you should have given me."

"I know—" she began, but he held up a hand to stop her.

"I can tell you one thing I know for damn sure." He was made of rock, no feeling left anywhere inside him. "I want this baby," he repeated, hating the hope that flared in her eyes at his words. Hating her for giving him hope that someone could finally believe in him. "But I *don't* want you."

Chapter Seventeen

Katie stumbled back as if Noah had struck her. But the physical pain would be nothing compared to the heartache that ripped through her at his words.

She deserved it. She never should have waited to tell him. Despite what he believed, her own fear had held her back. The fear he wouldn't want her or the baby. That he would feel obligated to stay with her.

This was worse.

"I love you, Noah," she whispered, unable to offer him anything else. "I never meant to hurt you."

"It's not enough," he answered, but what she heard was that *she* wasn't enough. Because Katie had never been enough, and she couldn't bake or volunteer or smooth over this hurt. She had nothing to give him right now but her love, and *she wasn't enough.*

"I can't..." He pushed his hand through his hair. He looked as broken as she felt. But still strong and so handsome in his uniform. She wanted to hold on to that strength but could feel the invisible wall between them. She knew what that meant. She'd seen the way his father's death and Tori's betrayal had ripped him apart. Watched as he'd shut himself off, pretended nothing was wrong and moved on.

He'd be moving on from her.

"I want to be involved." He said the words with emotion, but his eyes were ice-cold. "When is your next doctor's appointment?"

"Three weeks."

He narrowed his eyes as if he didn't believe her.

"He wants to do some early blood work. Everything is fine with the pregnancy, Noah. I don't see the doctor regularly until closer to the due date."

He gave a brief nod. "Text me the date and time. I'll be there."

He turned and stalked out of the kitchen. Katie's legs finally gave way and she sank to the floor. He wanted the baby but not her. She'd lost the love of her life *and* her best friend. She wasn't sure which was worse. Even as her feelings for Noah had ebbed and flowed over the years, he'd always been a constant in her life. Now she was alone, but also tethered to him by the life she carried inside her. How could she raise a child with a man who hated her?

A keening sound reverberated through the room and she realized it had come from her throat. She didn't look up as Lelia came into the kitchen, couldn't register the words the other woman spoke. The only thing that filled her mind was the hurt and anger on Noah's face.

Later, maybe minutes or maybe hours, an arm slid around her shoulders.

"Let's go, honey." Natalie helped her to her feet.

"I can't go out there," she said, hitching her head toward the front of the bakery.

"Olivia's parked in the alley out back."

"Nat, I messed up so badly." She bit back a sob, her legs beginning to crumple once more.

"Shhh," her friend crooned. "Let's get you to the car. One step at a time."

Katie, who was always so reluctant to lean on anyone, held tight to Natalie and let herself be led out into the bright sunlight of another Colorado summer morning.

Natalie opened the back door of the Subaru wagon and Katie dropped into the seat. Her arms wouldn't work, so Natalie strapped the seat belt across her. She met Olivia's sympathetic gaze from the driver's seat.

"Katie, what happened? Are you okay?"

She shook her head once then sucked back a sob.

"We're going to take her home," Natalie told Olivia as she climbed into the car and shut the door. "We'll get her something to drink—maybe whiskey—and sort this out."

"It's not even noon," Olivia whispered to Natalie. She looked at Katie in the rearview mirror as she pulled out of the alley. "How about a nice cup of tea?"

Natalie groaned. "She needs something strong for whatever this is."

"Can't." To Katie's own ears, her voice was a hoarse croak.

Natalie waved away her concern. "We won't tell."

"I'm pregnant."

Olivia hit the brakes suddenly and the car lurched forward, the seat belt cutting into Katie's chest. She wished it would slice all the way through so she could reach in and pull out her aching heart.

Neither of her friends spoke, but she saw them exchange a glance across the front seat.

"Tea, then," Olivia said gently. "Or orange juice. OJ was my go-to drink in my first trimester."

"I liked milk shakes." Natalie shifted in her seat to glance at Katie. "Want us to stop for ice cream? We can make whatever kind of milk shake you want."

The casual conversation seemed to lift Katie out of the fog threatening to engulf her. "I have vanilla ice cream at home. And strawberries."

"Strawberry milk shakes all around," Natalie answered with a smile.

She should have said something more, explained the circumstances. Although maybe it was obvious. Both women knew how babies were made, after all. Besides, she needed more time to pull herself together, to clean up the emotional wreckage around her heart.

She managed to get from the car to her door without assistance. She kept Natalie's words in her mind—*one step at a time.* Moving still proved difficult, and once she'd made it through the front door her strength waned again. She collapsed on the couch, tucking her knees to her chest to make a tight ball as Olivia covered her with a blanket.

As she closed her eyes she heard the soft sound of her two friends talking in the kitchen then the whir of the blender. A few minutes later she started as something cool brushed her forehead. She sat up straighter, took the glass from Natalie and sipped. She was so cold on the inside that the milk shake almost seemed warm in comparison. But it was soothing, both to her stomach and her emotions.

"Our babies will be friends," Olivia said as she gave Katie a gentle smile.

"I didn't mean for this to happen."

Natalie reached over to pat her arm then took a slurping drink of milk shake. "You don't need to explain to us."

"I want you to understand. It was an accident..." Katie glanced between the two of them. "But I want this baby. I *love* this baby already."

"Of course you do."

Natalie made a face. "And Noah?"

"It's no secret I love him, too." Katie circled a drop of condensation with her finger. "But he wants nothing to do with me."

"That can't be true." Natalie shook her head. "I saw how he acted on the Fourth of July. He loves you, honey."

"I've known for a week," Katie muttered. "I was afraid to tell him, but Emily heard me getting sick and guessed. His ex-girlfriend was listening as Emily and I talked. Tori came to the bakery today and threatened to reveal another secret I kept from him. That was bad enough but the pregnancy on top of it... He's never going to forgive me."

"He'll come around," Olivia said. "I mean, you were *going* to tell him soon."

"You don't understand. When Noah's dad got sick, he was the last one to know. He'd had a tough senior year and his parents were worried about how the news of the cancer would affect him. They told Emily right away. By the time Noah found out, his dad only had a few months to live."

"An unfortunate coincidence," Natalie agreed. "But not insurmountable."

"It is for Noah. And for me, too, in a different way. I spent most of my childhood feeling like an obligation to my parents. Having me held them back from how they wanted to live. I'm not going to be an unwanted burden for Noah. He made it clear that this wasn't his plan. If he wants to be part of the baby's life, I'll welcome that. I won't ask him for anything more."

"And if he decides he wants more?" Olivia asked, placing her glass on the coffee table. "Today was a shock. He'll recover from it and move forward. He cares about you. Those feelings aren't wiped away in an instant."

"He cared about me like a *friend*. Maybe it could have developed into something more if we'd had time. I don't know." She gave a strangled laugh. "I've loved him for over half my life. I tried to deny it, tried to turn off my feelings when I knew he didn't return them. I *want* to be loved like that in return. Not because I'm having a baby or I'm helpful or easy to be with. I want to be loved in an everything sort of way." She pointed to each of her friends. "What you have with Logan and Liam. A whole heart-and-soul kind of love. I deserve that."

"You do, Katie," Olivia said.

"Without a doubt," Natalie agreed.

She shrugged. "I'm not sure Noah understands how to love like that." She took a final drink of milk shake. "I thought he could, but if you'd seen how he looked at me today… There was nothing in his eyes. No emotion. He completely shut down, shut me out."

"We're here for you no matter what happens." Natalie patted Katie's knee.

She felt color rise to her cheeks. "Thank you for rescuing me from my meltdown. Sorry if I took you away from something important."

"Nothing is more important than friends," Olivia said.

"I can take Austin this weekend." Katie turned to Natalie. "To thank you, as payback. If you and Liam—"

Natalie immediately held up a hand. "Girl, you better shut your mouth before I lose my temper."

"About what?"

"You don't need to *pay me back* for being your friend."

"I just thought..." Katie began.

"You do far too much for other people..." Olivia added, "For this whole town. But you don't owe anyone."

"That's what Noah told me."

Natalie snorted. "He might be acting like an idiot now, but on that point I agree with him. You have a place here, Katie. It's wonderful how you help everyone, but that isn't why we care about you. We're your friends. We'll love you no matter what."

"No matter what," Katie repeated. It was what she'd wanted her whole life, never let herself believe she deserved. "I like the sound of that." She glanced at the clock on the mantel above the fireplace. "I need to get back to the bakery. There's so much going on and everyone must be wondering where I am."

"You don't have to—"

"I want to go back," Katie interrupted Natalie. "The bakery is also part of me, just like helping out in the community. I like contributing."

"Just so you know, you don't always have to be the one on the front lines," Natalie told her.

"I'm feeling better," Olivia added. "I can take back some of the Founder's Day Festival responsibilities. I feel horrible that we expected you to take over so I could deal with my pregnancy when you were having the same problems."

"I'm fine." When Natalie rolled her eyes, Katie slapped her gently on the arm. "I mean it. I've been to the doctor and everything looks normal." She pointed at Olivia. "You had a serious scare. It's different."

"The spotting has stopped." Olivia pursed her lips. "But Logan is still squawking about bed rest."

Katie smiled at the image of bad-boy Logan Travers squawking about anything. "Most of the work is done," she said. "The subcommittee chairs have things under control. I'll talk to Jase about extra help, but it's not going to be you."

"I can switch around some of my shifts at the nursing home to be available," Natalie offered. Katie thought it was funny that although Liam Donovan was one of the richest men in Colorado, Natalie continued working as a nurse at a local retirement center and nursing home. And that Liam respected her choice.

Having a baby would definitely affect the hours she put in at the bakery, and she wondered how she'd balance everything. The thought made the milk shake start to gurgle uncomfortably in her stomach, so she tried to push the worries away. *One step at a time.*

"Thank you both," she said again, standing and folding the blanket from her lap. "I'm not sure how I would have pulled cut of my meltdown without help."

"You're not alone," Olivia said gently.

"For the first time in a long while, you've made me believe that." She bent to give each of the women a hug.

"Give Noah some breathing room," Natalie advised, picking up the empty glasses from the coffee table. "The men around Crimson aren't quick on the uptake, but they eventually do the right thing. Noah cares about you, Katie."

She nodded, feeling the prick of tears behind her

eyes. She still didn't believe he loved her enough to make things right between them. And she couldn't take having him in her life simply because he felt obligated to do the "right thing." She finally realized that as much as she loved him, something so one-sided wasn't enough anymore.

"Let's clean up your kitchen," Olivia said. "Then I'll drive you back to the bakery if you're sure you're up for it."

Thirty minutes later, she walked into Life is Sweet with a small pit of embarrassment widening in her stomach. Luckily, the café portion of the store was almost empty and only two customers waited near the front counter. Of course, it had been busier when first Tori then Noah had stormed out, and she didn't relish the thought of being a hot gossip topic around town.

She stepped behind the counter, absently wiping a crumb from the glass top as she did. Lelia and another young woman, Suzanne, stopped what they were doing to turn to her.

"Everything okay?" Lelia asked.

Katie thought about lying, glossing over what had happened, but answered, "No. Not by a long shot. But it will be eventually. I don't know what you heard from the back earlier, but I'm sorry for the drama. You shouldn't have to deal with that at work."

"Are you kidding?" Suzanne, a petite dark-haired college student who was a Crimson native, answered. "I'd give up my share of the tips to watch Noah Crawford stalk through the bakery every day. He's kind of old but still hot as—"

She stopped speaking when Lelia elbowed her in the ribs. "All we could hear from the front was when the baking pans fell. None of the conversation. Not much, anyway. Promise."

Katie looked at Suzanne, who nodded in agreement then turned to take the order of a couple who'd just walked into the store.

A bit of tension released from her shoulders. She didn't want anyone knowing about the pregnancy until she was ready to share the news. That thought in mind, she asked Lelia to follow her into the back.

When she went through the large swinging doors, she stopped short. The entire kitchen was spotless and a batch of perfect muffins sat cooling on the stainless-steel counter.

"I know the kitchen is your domain," Lelia said quickly. "But we had a lull and I didn't want you to come back to a mess. I hope you don't mind."

Katie shook her head, emotion surging at the small gesture. Or was it pregnancy hormones? She'd learn a lot about herself over the next nine months. "I appreciate it," she told Lelia, "and that's part of why I want to speak to you." She stepped closer to the counter, running her fingers across the cool surface. "I'm pregnant."

Lelia drew in a shocked breath. Okay, maybe the argument earlier really hadn't been heard out front. "That's why Noah was so angry?"

Katie nodded.

"Because it's not his?" Lelia continued, her tone dejected and a little bitter.

"What?" Katie blinked several times. "No. The baby is Noah's. Who else? I haven't been with—"

She broke off, noticed the way Lelia relaxed and a smile split her face. "Congratulations, then," the other woman said. "You'll be a wonderful mom."

"Who did you think…? Matt?"

Lelia's gaze dropped to the ground.

"I've noticed that he's picked you up after work the past couple of days," Katie said carefully. "Does that mean—"

"I feel awful about it." Lelia covered her face with her hands. "Stealing my boss's boyfriend."

"He's not—"

"But I really like him. We have so much in common and..."

"I'm happy for you, Lelia. Matt is a great guy but not for me. If you like him, I support you, especially because you're a great addition to our town."

Lelia lowered her hands. "You mean it? You're not mad?"

"Not at all. In fact, the reason I told you my news is because with a baby to plan for, I'm going to need to make some changes at the bakery. Delegate responsibility. I was hoping you'd agree to become my first official manager?"

"Really?" Lelia practically bounced up and down. "You mean that?"

"I do. We'll increase your hours and you can start learning the business side of the bakery. I think we'll make a great team."

"That's amazing." Lelia reached forward to hug Katie. "I can't wait to share this with Matt. I was so worried you were going to fire me for not telling you about us right away."

Pain pinched Katie's heart as she thought of the price she'd paid for waiting to tell Noah her news. "I wouldn't do that. Give me a few weeks to come up with a new job description. I have to get through Founder's Day and we have two big orders of wedding cupcakes for that same weekend."

"Of course. I better get back out front." She began to leave then turned. "Is Noah not happy about the baby?" she asked softly.

"It's complicated" was the only answer Katie could give without emotions getting the best of her again.

Chapter Eighteen

"Remember the good old days when life wasn't so complicated?" Noah asked Jase as he helped load hay bales into the back of Jase's truck early on the first morning of the festival.

Jase hefted another hay bale then wiped his gloved hand across his forehead. "Life has always been complicated. You were just too checked out of it to notice."

"I wasn't exactly checked out," Noah argued but realized Jase was right. Before this summer, he'd been living life without ever getting too involved. He was good at his job, but when things got too complicated or bureaucratic, he'd slip away into the woods to recharge. Instead of stepping up when he finally learned about his father's cancer, he'd let his anger and hurt over being the last one to know spoil the last days he had with his dad. He'd avoided anything in life that made him uncomfortable, using the excuse that he wanted to keep things light and fun.

Even with Katie… No, she was different. Wasn't she? He'd tried with her, put himself out there—at least in his mind—and she'd let him down. The pain was a killer, a reminder of why it was better to stick to the superficial.

"So what happened?"

"Nothing," Noah muttered and threw a hay bale, harder than necessary, onto the flatbed.

"Right." Jase put his hands on his hips and gave Noah his best attorney stare. "Because a few days ago you were burping unicorns and now you look like you're ready to breathe fire on anyone who crosses you."

Noah stood for a moment, thought about how to answer and finally settled on the truth. "Katie is pregnant."

"Whoa." Jase took a step back then reached forward and slapped Noah on the back. "Congratulations, man. That's awesome."

"Are you kidding? This is the opposite of awesome."

"Why? You obviously love her. She's been crazy about you for as long as anyone can remember. The two of you and a baby—it's the perfect family."

There was so much wrong with Jase's words, Noah didn't know where to begin. "What do you mean 'for as long as anyonc can remember'? Katie and I only started seeing each other this summer."

Jase looked genuinely confused. "If 'seeing each other' is code for 'getting naked' then yeah. That part might be new but you've been friends for years."

"Friends. That's it."

"Because you're an idiot," Jase agreed. "You were busy bedding the wrong women while the right girl was waiting patiently the whole time."

"No." Noah's world started to spin again and he wondered if things would ever get back to normal. If he'd even recognize normal. "I was her friend."

Jase arched a brow and stared.

"Do you do that in the courtroom?" Noah asked, adjusting the collar of his T-shirt, which suddenly felt too tight. "Because it's annoying as hell."

"I'm not a trial lawyer," Jase said calmly. "Don't change the subject. If Katie is pregnant, why haven't I seen you two together? Why do you look miserable?"

"She didn't tell me."

"What does that mean?" Jase shook his head. "She's already had the baby and hidden it from you?"

"Don't be an ass," Noah mumbled. "It took her a week to tell me and that was only because I heard her arguing with Tori about it. Emily had found out and somehow Tori was eavesdropping when they discussed it." He moved his shoulders as if that should explain everything, but Jase continued to stare. "It was like my parents all over again. I can't deal with that. Not from Katie."

"Oh, boo-hoo," Jase mock cried. For a man known for his levelheadedness, he looked as angry as Noah had ever seen him. "You can't deal? What's the matter? Is your ego bruised?"

No, my heart, Noah wanted to answer but remained silent.

"Let me make sure I understand." Jase all but spit the words. "You can't deal, so you've deserted Katie to manage with the whole situation on her own."

Noah shook his head. "It's not like that. I told her I want to be there for the baby. I'll be at all the doctor appointments."

"How generous."

"What do you want from me?" Noah scrubbed a hand

over his jaw. He'd forgotten to shave for the past several days, felt lucky he'd remembered to brush his teeth.

"I want you to grow the hell up." Jake pointed a finger in Noah's face. "Did you ever think she was afraid to tell you because of how you'd react? Remember, this girl has been by your side every time things got serious. And no offense, man, but you don't handle serious so well."

"That's not true."

Jase held up a hand, ticking off points as he spoke. "What happened when you found out your dad had cancer? You barely spoke to him the last two months of his life. You missed your chance to say goodbye."

Noah clapped a hand to his chest, the painful memory threatening to suffocate him.

"Then your girlfriend cheated and that was awful but—"

"Katie was the one who sent the anonymous note."

"More power to her," Jase said. "You were better off without Tori. But how did you deal with that? You dated the longest string of flash-in-the-pan women you could find. All with Katie watching from the sidelines. As I remember it, you made her run interference more than once when things went sideways."

Noah winced. "She was willing to help."

"Because she *loves* you. She saw the worst of your behavior and loved you anyway. Believed you were better despite yourself. Of course she'd be afraid to tell you. You've given her no reason to trust you. Her parents were as selfish as people get, and still she turned out good and kind. But lacking in self-confidence, a fact that—no offense—you've used to your advantage all these years. Now that she needs you, you turn on her." Jase lifted his hands, palms up. "Before you start calling me an ass, take a long look in the mirror. I wouldn't be surprised if you started braying at your reflection."

Noah felt his mouth drop open and snapped it shut again. As he did it was as though the blinders he'd worn for all these years were stripped away. He'd been a fool. He was still a fool. And worse. He'd hurt the one person who mattered most to him, all because he was too scared to do anything else.

"Are you sure you're not a trial lawyer?" he asked Jase, shaking his head. "Because any jury who heard that closing argument would convict me without a second thought."

"It's not too late." Jase took a breath, spoke more softly. "Unlike in the courtroom, in life you get a second chance."

"If she'll give it to me." Noah's stomach rolled at the thought that he might have blown it for good. How would he survive without Katie and their baby as a part of his life? Without the chance to prove how much he loved her?

Jake flipped him the keys to the truck. "Only one way to find out."

If it was possible to be asleep while working nonstop, that was what Katie was doing the morning of the Founder's Day Festival. It was sunny and warm, already close to eighty degrees, which meant it would be downright hot by the time the events began at noon. She'd been at the county fairgrounds since sunup, managing the volunteers who assembled booths and directed vendors.

She'd thrown up twice behind the beer tent, but luckily it didn't seem as if anyone except Emily noticed her nausea. The other woman clearly wanted to talk to her, but Katie had managed to stay busy and unavailable. From the sympathetic looks Emily shot her across the food-judging tent, Katie guessed Noah had talked to her. She'd seen his mother earlier, as well. Now that she was feeling better, Meg was helping to judge the baking contests. She couldn't tell what Meg knew, but was avoiding her just in case.

She wasn't ready to talk to anyone about her pregnancy.

Other than Natalie and Olivia, none of her friends knew. Each day Katie fell more in love with the life growing inside her, but she was unsure of the future. She also wasn't ready to admit how bad Noah's rejection hurt. Eventually the pain would dull. She'd had enough experience with heartache over the years to believe that. At the same time, this was different because no matter how Noah felt, they were tied together forever.

"You look awful," a voice said at her shoulder.

Katie spun around to find Emily and Meg standing behind her.

"What she means," Meg tried to clarify, "is that you seem tired."

"I meant she looks like death warmed over," Emily said then dodged a maternal slap.

"Can we help you with something, sweetie?" Meg's voice was kind, her eyes a little hopeful. "You could go home for a few hours, put your feet up and have a snack."

Katie shook her head. "I'm fine and I promised to organize the food contests myself. Edna Sharpe and Karen Solanes are both vying for a blue ribbon in the fruit-pie category this year, and they've been fighting and accusing each other of cheating all week. I have to be here to mediate so things don't get out of hand."

Meg sniffed. "Edna's crust is always too crumbly. She doesn't have a chance against Karen's strawberry rhubarb."

"Even so..." Katie shook her head.

"We're worried about you," Meg said then leaned in to wrap her arms around Katie. "I'm also excited for you and Noah."

Katie stiffened for a moment then let herself relax into Meg's motherly embrace. Katie hadn't told her own parents yet but didn't expect them to be rejoicing at the news of becoming grandparents.

"He'll come around," Meg whispered. "It takes Noah a while to process things..." Emily barked out a laugh at that assessment and Meg leaned back to shoot her daughter a glare before returning her gaze to Katie. "But he cares about you and he'll do the right thing."

Katie forced herself to nod, too afraid to speak and break down completely. There was that phrase again. But she didn't want to only be "the right thing." "I have to get through this weekend," she said after a deep breath.

"We can help," Meg offered again.

"I need to be here."

"Why?" Emily asked, one eyebrow raised.

"Because..." Katie started, not sure how to explain her reasoning.

Because she didn't want people to think she was weak and incompetent, the way she'd felt most of her childhood. Because she needed them to remember this weekend and her good reputation when the news eventually leaked that she was single and pregnant.

"Because I can't stand to be alone right now." The words slipped out before she could stop them.

"I'm going to kill my son," Meg said, shaking her head.

"This isn't Noah's fault," Katie answered quickly. "Don't be angry with him. He needs you right now."

"*You* need him." Meg gave her another hug then stepped back. "And to rest. Promise you'll take a break later. I'll handle Edna and Karen if things get out of hand."

The walkie-talkie clipped to Katie's belt chirped. Jase had given it to her this morning so they could communicate from opposite ends of the fairgrounds. At the same time, an older woman called to Katie from the far side of the tent. Katie pressed her fingers to her temples. Busy was difficult enough, but she couldn't very well clone herself to be two places at one time.

"You take care of things in here," Emily told her. "I'll go see what Jase wants."

"Thank you."

"I'll go with you, Katie." Meg straightened her shoulders. "Just to keep those women in line."

Once again, Katie was reminded that she wasn't alone. That she was part of a community that would support and care for her, even if her own parents never had.

Although she had Meg and Emily's help, she was pulled in a half dozen different directions over the next couple of hours. Her other friends arrived to pitch in, as well, but still everyone seemed to clamor for her attention. Her stomach continued to feel queasy, so she skipped the doughnuts and apples set out for volunteers.

By the time they were ready to open the ticket gates, she felt almost dizzy with exhaustion. Come to think of it, she felt dizzy, period. She was standing near the table that displayed the pies for one of the first tasting events. Her eyes drifted closed for a moment then snapped open as she felt herself sway.

The last thing she saw before she went down was Noah stalking toward her.

* * *

The first thing Noah saw as he entered the food tent was Katie drop from sight. Pushing people out of his way and vaulting over the corner of the table, he sank to the ground next to her.

"Katie, sweetheart." He lifted her head off the ground then took a breath as she opened her eyes, blinking up at him.

"Sorry," she whispered.

"No apologies." He smoothed a strand of hair off her pale face. "Are you hurt?"

She shook her head. "Didn't have a chance to eat. I'm fine."

"Katie, what is going on?" Edna Sharpe elbowed several onlookers to stand over the two of them. "You need to get up now, girl. The judging is about to start."

He followed Katie's gaze to where people were streaming into the tent, filling up the rows of chairs lined across the center. But when she started to stand, he scooped her into his arms. "She's not judging anything, Edna." He glared at the older woman, who glared right back at him. "I'm taking her home."

"You can't." Edna's voice hit a note that would make a dog wince. "We need her for the judging. She's the expert baker. She always judges the finalists."

"Not this year," Noah growled. "She needs rest more than you need her."

"It's fine," Katie whispered. "You can let me go, Noah."

He looked into her eyes. "No way, Bug. I'm never letting you go again."

Her eyes went wide as he leaned down and pressed a gentle kiss to her mouth. God, it felt so damn good to hold her again. How had he ever thought he could live without her?

He turned back to Edna and the group of volunteers who'd crowded around them. "You all should be ashamed of yourselves. She's been working too long, too hard, and none of you care as long as you're getting what you need from her." He caught his mother's gaze and she gave him an encouraging nod. "We should all be ashamed. Katie doesn't owe you anything. She helps because she's an amazing person. The best."

This got a round of head nods, so he continued, "But she does too much for others and we know it. We take advantage of her goodness and her generous heart. But she's more than earned her place in this community, and it's time she stop trying so hard. Time we stop expecting more of her than we do ourselves."

He gazed down at her, tried to show her all the things he'd never been able to say out loud, hoping she would understand. But when he saw tears cloud her vision, he knew he had to give her more. She deserved more and he'd come here to find her and prove he was willing to give it.

"It's time I show you how much you mean to me." He swallowed, took a steadying breath. "How much I love you."

He heard a resounding chorus of *awwws* from the people gathered under the tent. A bead of sweat trickled between his shoulder blades as he searched Katie's face for a reaction. She bit down on her lip and looked away.

"You don't have to say that," she whispered.

He knew what she was thinking, that he was doing this for the baby. And it was because once he'd wrapped his mind around the idea of being a father, he'd wanted the baby almost as much as he wanted Katie.

"I *need* to," he told her. "I should have said it a long time ago. I should have been brave enough to see what was right in front of me all this time." He gathered her tighter in his arms, adjusted his hold so he could tip her chin up to look at him. "I love you, Katie. I'm in love with you. As Buddy the Elf would say, 'I think you're really beautiful and I feel really warm when I'm around you and my tongue swells up.'"

She laughed at his lame joke and hope glimmered to life inside him, bright like a July Fourth sparkler.

"I love you, too, Noah." She lifted her head, brushed her soft lips across his.

"You're the key to all of this, Katie. I want you. I want a family. I want to spend the rest of our lives making you happy. I will never let anyone take advantage of you again."

"I didn't mean to take advantage," Edna said quickly, wiping at her eyes, her voice a plaintive whine. "But she's always been the one to manage everything."

"And we appreciate it," Noah's mother said, stepping forward. "But as much as we rely on Katie, Noah's right. She needs to put herself first for once." She draped an arm around Edna. "We'll manage this year on our own. You take her out of here, Noah."

He could have kissed his mother but settled for a grateful smile.

She nodded and gave him a little push. "Go on, now. Text me later to check in."

"I'll make you some chicken noodle soup," Edna called as he turned away.

He glanced over his shoulder. "She hates chicken noodle soup."

Katie gasped and he felt her shake her head against his shirt.

"What?" Edna put her hands on her hips. "I've been making her chicken noodle soup for years."

"Well, she doesn't like it. Try tomato basil next time."

"I really don't—" Katie began, but he stopped her argument with another kiss.

"We're going home," he said again. After a moment she nodded and buried her face in his shoulder with a small sigh. The shudder that went through her body as she melted fully into him propelled him forward, through the crowd and toward the fairgrounds parking lot.

Tater jumped up from where she was lying in the shade of the canvas tent as he strode by.

"Noah…" Katie said his name but he shook his head.

"Don't talk until we're at your house. I need a few minutes to recover from the shock of you hitting the ground back there."

"I just need to eat something."

"We'll take care of that, too." He got them both settled in the car and lifted her fingers to his lips. "We'll take care of everything that comes our way, sweetheart. Together."

"I love you so much," she whispered. "I'm sorry I gave you a reason to doubt that."

He shook his head. "I'm the one who should apologize. I've made so many mistakes over the years, Katie, and you've been the one to help me pick up the pieces from most of them. But things are going to change. I'm going to change. I'm going to be the man you saw in me when no one else did. I love you, sweetheart, for everything you are and for who I am when I'm with you."

He shifted in his seat, reached down to the outside pocket of his cargo pants and pulled out a black box. "This isn't exactly how I'd planned it, but I can't wait."

Her eyes widened and he smiled, not bothering to hide the slight tremble in his fingers as he opened the velvet box to reveal a square-cut diamond ring. “I want to be the husband you deserve and a father to our baby. I want every piece of you, every moment and year. Marry me, Katie, and make me the happiest man in Crimson?”

“Yes,” she breathed, and he slid the ring onto her left hand. “I love you, Noah. For exactly the man you are. I want to share my life with you. You’re my best friend.”

He leaned forward and kissed her. “Let’s go home,” he whispered and they both laughed as Tater barked from the backseat. As they drove through town, Noah felt a sense of peace he hadn’t known since he was a boy. His life made sense with Katie by his side, and he was going to savor every second of it. Forever.

* * * * *

PASSIONATE AND DRAMATIC LOVE STORIES

A sneak peek at next month's titles...

In stores from 10th March 2016:

- **Take Me, Cowboy** – Maisey Yates *and* **His Baby Agenda** – Katherine Garbera
- **A Surprise for the Sheikh** – Sarah M. Anderson *and* **Reunited with the Rebel Billionaire** – Catherine Mann
- **A Bargain with the Boss** – Barbara Dunlop *and* **Secret Child, Royal Scandal** – Cat Schield

Available at WHSmith, Tesco, Asda, Eason, Amazon and Apple

Just can't wait?
Buy our books online a month before they hit the shops!
visit www.millsandboon.co.uk

These books are also available in eBook format!

0316/51

MILLS & BOON®

Helen Bianchin v Regency Collection!

40% off both collections!

Discover our Helen Bianchin v Regency Collection, a blend of sexy and regal romances. Don't miss this great offer - buy one collection to get a free book but buy both collections to receive 40% off! This fabulous 10 book collection features stories from some of our talented writers.

Visit **www.millsandboon.co.uk** to order yours!

316_MB520